About the

Amalie Berlin lives with her family and critters in Southern Ohio, and she writes quirky, independent characters for Mills & Boon Medical Romance. Her favourite stories buck expectations with unusual settings and situations, and the belief that humour can powerfully illuminate truth – especially when juxtaposed against intense emotions. And that love is stronger and more satisfying when your partner can make you laugh through the times you don't have the luxury of tears.

With a background of working in medical laboratories and a love of the romance genre it's no surprise that **Sue MacKay** writes medical romance stories. She wrote her first story at age eight and hasn't stopped since. She lives in New Zealand's Marlborough Sounds where she indulges her passions for cycling, walking and kayaking. When she isn't writing she also loves cooking and entertaining guests with sumptuous meals that include locally caught fish.

USA Today bestselling author **Julie Miller** writes breathtaking romantic suspense. She has sold millions of copies of her books worldwide, and has earned a National Readers Choice Award, two Daphne du Maurier prizes and an *RT Book Reviews* Career Achievement Award. For a complete list of her books and more, go to juliemiller.org

Romance On Duty

Romance On Duty:
Irresistible Sparks

AMALIE BERLIN

SUE MacKAY

JULIE MILLER

MILLS & BOON

First Published in Great Britain 2025
by Mills & Boon, an imprint of HarperCollins*Publishers* Ltd
1 London Bridge Street, London, SE1 9GF

www.harpercollins.co.uk

HarperCollins*Publishers*
Macken House, 39/40 Mayor Street Upper,
Dublin 1, D01 C9W8, Ireland

ISBN: 978-0-263-41720-3

RESCUED BY
HER RIVAL

AMALIE BERLIN

CHAPTER ONE

FIREFIGHTER AND SMOKEJUMPER trainee Lauren Autry jogged with the rest of the herd to the large field behind the main hall at the old twentieth-century 4-H camp the Forest Service had repurposed for spring training facilities.

Every year since the nineteen-fifties new recruits and veteran smokejumpers alike descended upon a handful of camps littering the Northwestern United States for the intense training required to prepare them for the coming wildfire season. The elite firefighting service only took the fittest, the most capable of conquering and surviving the remote, treacherous terrain where wildfires tended to explode—parachuting in with simple tools and supplies to fight and contain big, dangerous blazes, only to be rewarded with a long hike back to civilization after the job was done.

Only the best made it through, and if Lauren had been lacking two years ago, she'd made up for it since then, throwing herself into every kind of study and training she could conceive of—even things not required, at least when her job and family responsibilities hadn't gotten in the way. She'd trained harder, pushed herself beyond her already insane standards. If only she could've figured out how to grow a few more inches, everything would be perfect. And if she'd gotten to complete the civilian skydiving course she'd been counting on. That was something she should've better controlled. Better planned for. Not required, she'd get to learn it here, but still. Prepared. Making up for any deficiencies. That had been the plan.

If she made it to a crew—*when* she made it to a crew—no one would be able to question whether she was capable. Whether she was tall enough, or strong enough, or *good* enough. Never again. Not her brothers. Not her father. None of the hundreds of dead ancestors who'd been serving the same San Francisco fire station since its founding in the nineteenth century…not that she could hear *their* critiques, at least.

No more of those questions she'd been suffering the six years since she'd become a firefighter. No more of the insinuations her failure two years ago had amplified.

No more holding pattern of derailed life plans.

This year she'd made it through the selection process, even under the authority of Chief Treadwell, the same man who'd passed her over before and given the last spot to a no-neck marine.

None of that mattered. She was here *now*.

This was really happening!

The thought sent a jittery, tingling wave washing over her scalp again, every cell in her body seeming to light up at once. It had taken every ounce of willpower to sit still and pay attention through orientation, before she began the endurance test she'd been primed for two years to run. The simple act of moving again, letting her body do what it had been conditioned to do, was the kind of physical relief she'd like to also have mentally.

The crowd stopped in the grass, and so did she, but behind a sea of broad shoulders and crewcuts, she couldn't see what was going on.

Right. Identify the problem, find the solution.

Turning sideways, she slipped and ducked through the crowd to reach the front, and the unexciting view of three older men with clipboards quietly conversing while everyone else waited. More waiting. More need to move crawling over her knees. An itch to get started. Prove herself. Prove to Treadwell he'd made a mistake passing her over for what's-his-face.

Soon enough, they began calling names and sorting those assembled into three different groups. When that was done, one look around confirmed: her group was peopled with rookies—she could tell by their yellow badges. All new people. All new *dudes*. And her. Which was fine. Expected, even. It was the smallest group, which was also fine. She'd get more attention that way. The right kind of attention. Training attention. Proving-herself attention.

Her group split off, moving to the side of the large dirt track to hear the rules again.

Endurance test, first. Mile and a half in under eleven minutes. Easy-peasy. She barely needed to stretch for that, but did anyway.

"Ellison!" Treadwell barked the name just as she'd caught one ankle behind her to stretch her quads, causing her to pitch to the side then scramble to stay upright.

"You're late!"

Chief. Shouting.

Someone late the first day?

Ellison.

The name caught up with her and she jolted again.

Beck Ellison. Her nemesis! Who likely had no idea he was her nemesis… The Golden Boy she'd only quasi creeped on online because when a girl had a secret nemesis… Well, social media was far too easy to peek at. Not that she'd been hoping to see anything bad. In fact, she hadn't seen anything at all in terms of a profile for the man. She'd just seen posts *about* him doing this and that, articles in different newspapers used as PR for the service. Stuff she couldn't help but see and feel the knife twisting in her spleen every time he did something else wonderful. *Smoke Charmer nonsense.*

She could do her job without an ego-stoking nickname. *Smoke Charmer.*

Then again, if she had to lose out to someone, better he be astounding than abysmal. If she *had* to lose.

Positive thoughts. Positive thoughts. Maintain habit of sending good intentions out to the universe.

Maybe he was there to teach them all how to become one with the fire, *Smoke Charmer* style.

She turned slightly from her position at the starting line to catch sight of a tall, shaggy-haired man jogging onto the track to join the group. Curls. That was new. The man had shiny black curls, wafting on the breeze as he jogged to the track—the only trace she could see of his past life as a marine was his fitness. Also new? He had a neck now.

And he was coming to run. Not there to teach. There to run. With the rookies.

His badge was yellow.

Rookie yellow.

He was being placed with the rookies?

Not again. He'd made it two years ago. He didn't need to weasel into her group now and start showing off.

She took a breath and got back in position at the track. In through the nose, out through the mouth.

This wasn't a competition. Not one that he *knew* about, at least. She just sort of…wanted to do better than he did. Today. And every day for the next six weeks.

"Did we inconvenience your plans to sleep in?" Treadwell barked, but Ellison—or the beefy, bipedal sheep-dog now impersonating the formerly chisel-cut marine—didn't respond. He just dropped something black and plastic beside the track and got himself ready to run.

With. The. Rookies.

Let it go. Let it go and focus. She could tumble down some kind of rookie revirginization rabbit hole later, after she smoked him on the track. His legs might be longer, but hers would be *faster*.

The chief blew a whistle and she launched forward. All the anxious energy that had made her squirm in her seat through the arduous sixty-three-minute orientation finally freed.

She ran, everything falling into place as she pounded down the dirt track, her sneakers giving only the slightest slide on the hard-packed earth and gravel as she flew down the center lane. The heavy feeling of worry she'd been carrying with her for days suddenly lifted.

She'd always been a runner. The intense conditioning she'd put herself through was built on a lifetime of running, ever since she'd started T-ball and soccer, because her brothers had all played and they hadn't taken it easy on her, even at six.

Doing what she was meant to do, made her strong. With the track underfoot, she felt peace. She felt in control of her destiny. Able to overcome that small mistake she'd made on her application...

In a matter of seconds, the group she'd started with thinned. Sixteen started at her heels, and before her lungs even began to burn, she no longer heard feet pounding beside her. Or behind her. Even when listening hard.

Nope. No one. She was alone.

Which was when she remembered: *this wasn't a race.* She wasn't supposed to be outrunning anyone. Not even Ellison. She was supposed to be *outlasting* them. This was an endurance test. And speed ate up endurance. Endurance she'd need to make it through the day.

It took some effort to slow herself down, she felt it every clap of her heels against the packed earth, jarring her bones.

Six laps was the expected minimum. She'd go longer just to show she could. Not faster. Longer. Longer than them. Longer than Ellison.

She made it to the third lap before she gave in to temptation to look behind her. The closest to her, who seemed to be moving at a much steadier lope? Ellison. Of course, he was taller. Longer legs didn't need to run as hard for the same speed.

Never mind.

By the fourth lap her lungs were pretty warm.

By the sixth she legit wanted to stop. She could still finish first, but she wanted to finish *best*.

By the seventh lap, he'd caught up to her and when she gave in to the temptation to look up at him, she was met with one arched brow that said three things.

I know you.

I remember how competitive you were last time.

I still think you're an idiot.

For the briefest second, her vision swam with a lovely little brain movie of her throwing one leg to one side and sending his curly arrogance into the dirt. But then her vision cleared, and the sweeter side of her nature took over. She looked back to the track, and kept running.

Eight.

When was he going to stop? Were they actually racing now? Was this a thing that was happening?

Other people had already stopped.

Eight and a half… Treadwell whistled again, loud and shrill. A call to stop. She let inertia carry her forward a few more yards to slow and stop naturally.

Hands on her knees, she kept herself up and gulped air, sweat plastering her shirt to her back, and the grit she'd kicked up from the dirt track rubbing like sandpaper against her bare legs. Should've stopped after the seventh.

"Not a race, Autry." Ellison panted too, where he'd stopped a couple lanes away, the curls she hated to admire a little crisper from the light sweat he'd built.

Of course he'd have better hair too.

And not the point. Not a race, he'd said, but he'd still kept up with her ridiculous pace.

"Tell yourself."

She straightened, less inclined to bear the grudging respect she'd built for him since he'd turned out to actually be something special, someone she could feel better about herself for having lost to, and walked much more slowly to center field, where the chief gathered his group again.

Ignore Ellison. What was next?

Maybe water. Please, let there be water.

Beck followed Autry off the track, his breathing more rapid than his sluggish thoughts. He'd been in a haze all week, trying to decide what his life was supposed to be, and had quietly hoped that once he'd made his decision the fog would lift, and he'd know whether he still had it in him to be what he'd felt called to his whole life.

No such luck. The only thing clear was his broken life compass. And that he'd somehow annoyed the woman he'd briefly met two years prior.

She seemed fit. Maybe a little harder than she had been. Normally, he'd say harder was a good thing—harder emotions meant distance, control, better decision-making in dangerous situations. But annoyed was just another flavor of the same emotional unsteadiness he'd seen in her when she'd gone teary after not making the ranks.

She'd sworn to Treadwell she'd be back next year. Last year. Was that another fail? Surprising, but probably no more than it was for her to see him as a rookie this year too.

Didn't matter. Once training was complete, she'd be off to her own unit and her emotionalism wouldn't be his problem. He had his own issues to focus on.

Before joining the others, he stopped to retrieve the radio he'd dropped earlier and wedged one earbud in to get another update on the wildfire he'd been monitoring since yesterday. A dry winter and an even drier spring meant the fire season had come early. When rain and runoff existed, spring wildfires were easier to handle and didn't grow at the vicious speed this one was. The team would be called in today, for sure. If luck was with him, the call would come before he'd spent himself on the rookie field, while he still had enough energy to give Treadwell a reason to stop looking at him like he was the embodiment of all human disappointment.

The radio crackled and he stopped en route to the coolers, but no report followed. Maybe luck wouldn't be with him. It certainly hadn't been with him last season.

He grabbed a drink and joined the others, half listening to Treadwell go over the next exercise, the other tuned into the earpiece. It was the first day, and his attention was rightly divided. He didn't need to hear the physical requirements, he remembered them. Listening for the call was an act of team spirit, for his true team. Not these rookies. Besides, no one was a spirited teammate on day one. Team-building took more than a day.

He worked better alone anyway—fewer distractions. Fewer *people* to worry about. Something that hadn't been a problem until last season. One mistake had turned the chief's opinion of him upside down.

Turned him upside down too. Getting back out there today would help in a way that four months tending his forest territory had somehow failed to help.

If his chief didn't also take the rookies every year, he might not have even had the opportunity to try again, and he wasn't ready to picture a future where this wasn't his job. That meant he had to show up, do whatever Treadwell demanded for the next several weeks. Wear his rookie badge. Take his lumps.

Be like Autry.

She stood so straight and stiff she might as well have been in a muster, her attention narrowed on the chief with laser precision. Though none of what he said could've been news to her, the physical requirements were public information. Requirements that included the height minimum, so she'd certainly have read them.

As if feeling his gaze, she turned his direction, and met

his steady examination with folded arms and a churlish bent to her brows. Still annoyed.

Whatever. He looked back at the radio because of another round of crackling static, and the next he knew, she was at his side.

"They stuck you with the new recruits?"

Her breathing had already leveled out, the only evidence of her prior exertion the pinkness of her cheeks. She'd run as if chased by wolves, but looked none the worse for wear. He should probably ask what had happened to last year, but that would only encourage conversation. And questions in return.

"Looks like it," he muttered, and turned up the volume on the single earpiece as a quick buzz announced an incoming report.

"What are you listening to?"

"Reports."

"Reports on what?"

He narrowed his eyes at the middle distance, feigning concentration, and pressed the earpiece into his ear, glad for a reason to tune out.

Not glad there was such a monstrous fire so early in the season, but he wanted to get at it. He was still on the team. If Treadwell went, he'd go too. His yellow badge was penance.

She finally took his silence for the hint it was and stopped prodding him for answers. There were plenty of other people to pester, and she didn't know the report had long since ended and now he pretended to listen to dead air.

Treadwell began calling names again, dividing his group into three, and Beck found himself sorted to the bar, along with Autry, who was now busy introducing herself to the others in their team, making friends. Smiling. Showing her team spirit.

"Ellison's not new," he heard her say, calling his attention back to the newly formed subgroup. "He made it a couple years ago. But…uh… I guess he got stuck with us because he was late."

Wrong.

"This is Alvarez, Finnegan, and Wyler."

Still talking to him. No longer annoyed. She actually looked excited, a brightness in her eyes out of step with what was actually happening. Push-ups. Pull-ups. Sit-ups… Not exactly a party.

Treadwell called his name, saving him from making nice, and he stepped to the bar, pausing only long enough to deposit his radio on the ground and free his hands. The chief's gaze wordlessly followed him and Beck said two words before reaching for the bar to pull himself up. "It's bigger."

A frown and a nod were his only acknowledgments, and Treadwell began to count as Beck got on with it. As soon as he'd passed the minimum number of pull-ups, he dropped down for sit-ups, then rolled to push-ups, stopping each time he'd passed the required amount, leaving himself room to "improve" as camp continued.

Treadwell's arched brow? Beck shrugged a touch. "Conserving energy."

His muscles buzzing, he pulled himself off the ground, retrieved his radio, then went for another drink so he could sit on the grass to watch the others work their way through as he listened.

Still no new reports to free him.

Autry had been in the middle of the five, but as he watched, she talked herself to the rear of the group.

She'd learn soon enough how to survive these days: go early, get it over with, don't waste energy showing off. Take all opportunities to rest.

Or not. Maybe it was better for *him* if she kept doing whatever she was doing. If she finished too soon, she'd be there beside him, asking questions. Making a nuisance of herself with her newbie enthusiasm.

CHAPTER TWO

THE INSTANT THE call for more crews came over the radio, Beck sprang to his feet.

Finally. Time to get out of this. He headed for Treadwell, who stood with clipboard in hand, counting the reps of another rookie.

The chatter he'd expect from Autry had never come when she'd gotten done with her turn at the bar. Treadwell had stopped her from showing off by making her finish her reps when it became clear she had no idea what a reasonable number was. She'd been sitting on the grass, sulking, ever since, her formerly animated brow becoming a little ledge above her pretty green eyes.

Pretty?

He mentally shook himself. They were striking, an evergreen ring around a pale center. If anything, they were unusual and therefore compelling. Him fixating on eye color meant he needed to get out of there. Had spent too much time alone in the woods, lost in his own head.

Then again, no one lurked in the forest to constantly remind him of this nonsense about him undoing core tenets of his personality over a few short weeks. People went to years of therapy to change habits and outlooks acquired over a lifetime, and he had no interest in that either.

"Chief." He interrupted the rookie doing push-ups with

one word and a meaningful waggle of his radio, indicating the call had come.

Treadwell's gaze narrowed and he nodded, but held up one hand in Beck's direction and told the man on the ground he could stop.

He and Treadwell might not be on the same page on everything, but over the past two years the man had learned to interpret Beck's admittedly spartan method of communication. Beck liked him for that. Liked him in general, really.

During his first year, back when it'd seemed he could do no wrong, he'd still had to actively work to be something like what they expected off duty. They'd accepted his tendency to go off on his own when he got a whiff of something during a fire. Let him come around to telling them whatever he'd concluded when he was certain.

He didn't know where that sixth sense had gone, could only hope it had come back over the winter. Knowing how far he'd fallen in the chief's esteem chafed.

After marking the rookie's reps and still carrying his clipboard, Treadwell strode in Beck's direction. The stout man was in his fifties, and probably as fit as when he'd joined. "What's the call?"

"Us and two other units." Beck nodded down the field to where the other groups were breaking up. "About a forty-five-minute flight. Kolinski said he'd pack our gear and hold the plane."

Treadwell listened and nodded, but just when Beck thought he was going to turn around and give the grunts the afternoon off he said, "Not you."

"It's a big fire. You need me."

"Not like this I don't."

The urge to argue burned his throat, but he clamped his teeth together. Not that he didn't buck orders on occasion, but only when he had some measure of certainty he was right to do so. He wanted to argue that no one in the unit read fires like he did, but he simply wasn't sure that was the case any longer. That was last year's argument. Before his mistakes. Before he'd been trapped by the flames.

Treadwell handed him the clipboard. Accepting the transfer of the hard acrylic gave him a sensation somewhat like the first time he'd jumped from a plane. Plummeting. Ground that approached far too rapidly.

He stood straighter. Even without that one selling point, he was still as capable as anyone else. "You're sure? I'm still boots on the ground."

"Your boots are on whatever ground you see fit. This is the first day. Prove me wrong and we'll talk."

He wanted to, if he actually knew how to follow orders he knew were wrong. As annoying as the yellow badge might be, at least probation gave him more time to sort things out.

When Beck said nothing else, the chief turned to summon Autry with a wave.

She'd been watching—everyone in the group had been—and at the summons she popped out of her sulk and trotted right over.

"You two finish morning PT with the group," Treadwell said, adding, "There's a fire, and Ellison has already expended too much energy to give one hundred percent this morning, he doesn't need to throw himself into the blaze at less than full capacity."

Yes, he did. He needed that.

"I'm fine," he argued finally, the prospect of minding rookies worse than simply sitting out a fight.

Treadwell shot him a hard look, one that Beck could also interpret. Punishment or probation, it didn't matter, he was out of the game until this was done, and Treadwell was trying to save face on his behalf.

Beck would've gladly taken the ding to his pride if it would've gotten him back into the fray. Sitting around with a clipboard while his team jumped into danger didn't sit right.

Treadwell thumped him on the shoulder once and before Autry could ask any of the questions bouncing around in those strange green eyes he finalized his orders. "Handle the rest of the baselines. Classroom was going to be protocols, but since it looks like most of us will be in the field, Ellison's going to do a Q&A about service, lessons learned his first couple years. Then you can all amuse yourselves for the rest of the day, but be on the field at daybreak tomorrow before the siren blasts."

Autry still looked confused, but she nodded and had now shifted her attention to *him*, her expression saying things he didn't want to hear—like she got just how little he wanted to do this. "What do you want me to do?"

All of it.

Eager to get rid of the clipboard, he passed the cursed thing over and gestured for her to follow. The sooner they got on with it, the sooner he could get it over with.

"Three crews have been called to a blaze, Treadwell wants us to continue," he announced, straight to the point, then added, because it would help them to know the course when it became mandatory, "After that, lunch, and then a five-mile run around the woodland course."

Autry cleared her throat, and for a second he thought it was because she was going to correct him about the run, but instead she said, "Don't forget the classroom Q&A before the run."

One tiny twitch of an eyebrow challenged him to argue, but she didn't correct Treadwell's orders—probably because she was obsessive about exercise. Couldn't rightly fault her for it, except that she didn't let him get away with sidestepping the exercise in public speaking.

"Q&A after lunch. Five questions. Then run." He returned her look. In unison, her brows and shoulders popped up. She might as well have just said, *Whatever.*

Whatever. He got back to the task at hand, gesturing to

CHAPTER FOUR

HER WORDS MADE Beck laugh, even if it smacked of a slight rebuke to his grooming habits. "I'm the hairy one?"

He was touching her again. He couldn't seem to stop doing that. The carry had been outside his control, but was this the second time he'd touched her hand? Third? He wasn't inexperienced with women, but he'd long since given up on the concept of relationships. His celibacy was a choice, and not one that usually required conscious thought. He normally didn't have to think about the way touching a woman made his perception shift.

Celibacy was easier than this, generally. Not something he kept *thinking* about. Touching her when she was teasing him? Confusing.

"Tell me you shave regularly when you're going into the field. Can't imagine a respirator making a seal over that scruffy face. And the hair on *top* of your head? You've really let that grow wild since you left the Marines."

"My hair doesn't make me heavier." He wrapped his fingers more tightly around her hand and hauled her the rest of the way up, then let go. "Walk. It'll help."

"I think you're full of crappity-crap." She wobbled but still began to walk and he walked with her.

Three steps and her upper arm impacted his, and she stayed there, slightly leaning, taking the steadiness he had to offer.

She was sweating, and he could feel the bone-deep shaking transferring through the shoulder pressed against his upper arm, and all he wanted to do was sling his arm around her waist. Not just to help but to anchor her there against him. Close. Keep on walking until they were alone, and find out if he could distract her as well.

"If I fall, tell Treadwell you tripped me."

Not currently distracted, still joking.

He should follow her lead and get his mind out of the gutter, but her mention of Treadwell did that just as well. His eyes landed on the chief, and the warm, fond feelings he'd been experiencing turned due to the general colorless, almost sagging quality of the man. "He needs to sleep."

"He looks bad…"

There was a grayness to his face that had both of them heading closer, her steps straightening so that she no longer leaned, they no longer touched. It helped him focus, or maybe the alarm tightening his shoulders did that.

"Chief?"

Treadwell held up one hand to make him wait and Beck held his tongue as the last two teams staggered across the line. Treadwell marked his clipboard and immediately handed it to Beck, as he had done yesterday.

"Partner assignments."

"Partners?" Beck repeated.

"We're buddying up this year." Treadwell topped his answer with a look that added weight. "Everyone is safer in a team, son."

Oh, hell.

Beck wasn't prone to thinking the world revolved around him, in fact he knew the world overlooked him more often than not, but with the specific complaints Treadwell had about Beck's performance within a team? His lone-wolf tendencies and *this* change, *this* year?

He'd heard the *everyone's safer* speech at least ten times

now. They were buddying up because Treadwell wanted to teach *him*.

This was about him.

"If someone fails because they're physically incapable, that's one thing. If they fail due to a failure of partnership, then both get a strike. Then it's baseball rules."

"Three strikes?" Lauren asked beside him, sounding a little better.

"Yes." Treadwell then nodded toward the mess hall, where several kitchen workers in white with large trolleys loaded with brown sack breakfasts were plowing in their direction. "After breakfast, announce the partnerships. Partners and cabin-mates. Trainers Ying and Olivera are leading at the tower. Then the pack carry."

In one day? He held his tongue. "Are Ying and Olivera leading the pack carry?"

"You are."

Treadwell walked off toward the cabins before Beck could ask if *he* needed an arm to lean on.

As much as he sucked at teamwork, his failure tended to go in one direction: he could help others, but had never been able to accept help in return. He could help his chief, even wanted to, despite everything.

Treadwell's stride wasn't steady. He wobbled almost as badly as Lauren had.

The ever-powerful leader stooped, as if he didn't have the strength to hold himself to his usual shoulder-squaring attention.

Because of the warning in his head, he didn't look away until Treadwell had slogged up the wooden stairs to the cabins and disappeared.

Lauren's voice came softly from beside him. "Did he say how he was feeling?"

"Just that he needed to sleep."

"Last time I saw someone that color, it was heart-related."

"Me too," Beck muttered. "But I'm going to let him rest, see if that helps, before I start prodding."

Clearly, she wasn't onboard with letting the chief go while looking somewhat corpse-like. "Worried about his pride?"

"Respectful of him as a person." Beck looked at her then, and turned fully, what had nearly gone down earlier before she'd carried him coming back to his mind. "I owe you an apology."

He didn't get to the apology before she'd completely frozen, staring up at him, her breath quickening again.

"Why?"

"I didn't take you at your word when you said you could do it. Neither did Treadwell. But no one questioned anyone else carrying their partner." Beck drew a deep breath, pausing to make sure he selected the correct words since even simply acknowledging the mistake affected her. "To be clear, I questioned because of concern you'd get hurt because you felt the need to prove yourself. Like it or not, you *are* smaller than any of us. But you did it. I don't know that I won't make that mistake again, but I'm aware of it now. I'll try."

She nodded quickly, a small, shaking acknowledgment of his words, eyes glassier than they had been, and he knew how much it meant to her to hear it. Despite the emotional reaction, he was glad for having said it. He might be an active disappointment to the chief, but he could be a good guy sometimes.

She took a moment, and had to clear her throat before she asked in a voice that was a little froggy, "What are we doing?"

He finally looked at the clipboard. "Using the buddy system, apparently. Partnering up, on the field and off."

A list, in Treadwell's bold slashing script, of eight sets of names.

Ellison and Autry

Top of the list. Partnered. Sharing a cabin after all the reasons they shouldn't had become clear to him.

Still, the simple thought summoned myriad images of Lauren and beds, and every part of his body erupted with some kind of excited dread. There was no other way for him to qualify it. Excitement because there was no way around excitement at being alone with a woman he was attracted to, and dread because he didn't know what would spiral out of it. He already felt protective of her, wherever that came from. If it was about her gender, her stature, or who she was.

Dangerous. He didn't even need to wonder how she'd respond to his protective feelings. She'd be pissed. Probably kick him in the junk just to prove she could.

"We're together." He forced himself to stick to the topic, then waved a hand to her to follow him toward the group. "Breakfast now. Tower. Lunch after. Then the pack carry. Going to be a rough day."

"How's the fire?" someone called.

What was the man's name? She'd introduced them yesterday.

Alvarez.

"Bad."

"Are they going back out?"

"I don't think anyone but Treadwell came back today. And he'll probably go back later. I didn't ask," he said, and cast aside his own concerns about whether or not the chief *should* go back out. Respect his wishes, and be there to help if the chief was wrong about his limits. That's what Treadwell had done for *him* on that mountain last season. Right up until Beck had smacked face-first into his limits.

"Focus on what's before you. Tower training with Wang and Olivera. I'll explain the rules on the pack after lunch."

Lots of talking. Lots of talking he didn't want to do, but having seen the chief it was something small he could offer.

"Chow time. Eat hardy. Protein first. Drink a lot."

Lauren stayed at his side, though she looked as unsettled as he felt—strange in light of yesterday's invitation to share a cabin. Did it feel somehow like being fixed up to her too?

"Do you want me to announce the names?" she asked, the look she topped her words with clear enough for anyone to read. *I have your back.* Hearing them wouldn't have made the sentiment any clearer than what he could see there in her eyes. She understood and had his back. Not pushing him to change, not joking about his issues, just backing him up. It was a small matter, but made even clearer what his own words had meant to her.

"There are eight pairs. They can read," he said softly, then handed the clipboard off to the nearest warm body. "Check your assignments. Work out who will be moving tonight, but not before the pack carry. Don't spend the energy. You'll need it later."

All through breakfast, Lauren worked at putting the idea of the tower out of her mind because of Beck. She was still warm all over from his heartfelt apology. He was a man of few words, but when he started using them, he could even distract her from all the imminent tower-shaped doom looming before her.

If she'd known how freaking attractive he could become just by saying the right thing, in the right way, at the right time, she'd have put as much distance between the two of them as possible, no matter the things she might be able to learn from him to get better at her job simply through proximity.

Now, with her protein-dense breakfast burrito in her stomach, heading for the place where her accidental lie might be discovered, she was forced to consider the more imminent source of danger to her. If she failed or fumbled through this, they'd know, and she'd be out of there so fast she'd be glad she hadn't unpacked.

Provided she survived the tower without looking like an incompetent fool, she could look forward to dealing with her hormonal reaction to a handsome, skilled man treating her fairly later. Some way that made distance possible. Maybe by making a long list of things she didn't like about him instead of focusing on the things she did.

The morning's laughing meatheads underscored what she already knew: she had to be twice as good for all the men to take her seriously. And how important it was she not put a toe out of line, let alone her lips.

Hormones would have to bow to the wily ways of logic.

Workplace romances weren't smart, even when you weren't one of three women in a group of seventy-six. Having a boyfriend in her workplace meant yet another voice telling her to be careful, to not go to this job or that, not to overestimate herself. Blah-blah-blah.

At least Beck hadn't said anything like that yet. He'd said the opposite, which elevated her passing appreciation with his attractiveness to something that made her heart quicken enough to rival the tower of concrete and cables now suddenly before her.

Beck walked behind her, and she was momentarily sad to not have him there being beefy and distracting. Several stories tall, it had a sideways launch platform to mimic jumping from a plane, and lines running down at slow-floating angles to the ground, designed to simulate the start and stop of a jump, from launch to landing with little drift in between.

Tilting her head back to stare at the top, her inner gyroscope wobbled off center. With how hard her palms sweated, it was good she wouldn't need her hands to stay in the harness.

"You all right?" Beck's question came from right behind her and she stopped to look back at him.

However stupid she felt for having missed the window to correct her application before it got this far, she'd kept taking a pass on making the correction because it could've been used against her, and history had taught her that when it came to her job, people in authority weren't much inclined to give her a fair shake. She hated thinking that way, so she'd avoided dealing with it, banking on her own skills bailing her out. Back when her skills had just been something in her mind, not something that she had to actually pull off in the flesh.

"I didn't realize how empty the camp was until just now." She'd said the first thing that came to mind, and a look around confirmed that it was only the sixteen rookies and a couple of trainers. "We'd be doing this with all three groups if the others weren't on a jump, right?"

He nodded. "Classroom stuff is universal, reinforcing the basics and more advanced stuff if it's especially beneficial."

The two trainers called them to attention, and began discussing the equipment worn during a jump. She paid complete attention, even though this was all information she actually felt confident in. Hearing what she already knew helped her relax some. Focusing made her feel like she was doing what she was supposed to be doing.

Too soon, the trainers sorted the group, calling only three names. Ellison. Alvarez. *Autry*.

"You three are with me. Suit up and climb the tower. Everyone else is with Ying."

One look toward the other group and she saw Ying leading them all to the three-foot platforms that she recognized from all the instruction she *had* completed before her classes had been derailed by family.

Her stomach bottomed out. They'd put her into the advanced group. Beck had jumped before. She'd wager Alvarez had also, unless he'd *also* had great plans and had answered on behalf of his future self when filling out the application.

Olivera hustled them to the tower. "We're testing technique to see how rusty you are, and if you need to be bumped back. I'll watch from the ground. If you panic and don't jump, you get bumped back. If you swing too much when you jump, you get bumped back. If you don your gear wrong, you get bumped back. Don't be sloppy."

They stepped into the room at the base of the tower and were directed to get into the jumpsuits and the packs they'd have to strap into. She'd also done this before, or the civilian versions of it, and had trained enough to fumble through.

As she pulled the last strap tight, she caught Beck looking at her again.

"What?"

"You're white as smoke," he whispered.

Crap.

"Breakfast isn't sitting well."

Not why she was white, but still true. Lord, she hated all this lying, she just didn't know how to fix it.

She hurried back out to let Olivera check her equipment. He gave the straps a sharp jerk. "Okay, up the tower, don't jump until I signal."

Verdict: not sloppy. She'd passed *that*.

Two more tests.

She could do this. She might even be able to make the partner and roommate situation work for her by asking Beck for fire-specific jump pointers—talk work, not anything personal.

For all her worries, by the time she made it from pack inspection up miles of stairs to the elevated platform the pit in her stomach was gone and everything seemed much more doable.

She *had* done a lot of simulations.

She *did* have the gumption to jump out of a plane over a blazing inferno.

She knew how to jump and tuck her head and arms, how long to count before grabbing the chute to steer it in.

And she would go first. A female trainer she hadn't met before sat at the top of the tower, whose very presence bolstered Lauren's confidence further. It took no time to strap her into the harness and when the signal came, she took a deep breath and jumped.

A short fall of a couple of meters, then the harness jerked hard enough to rattle her teeth, but she followed through the steps perfectly. Less than a minute later she landed at the levee and was helped to unhitch so she could run back and do it again.

Today wouldn't be her only instruction before she got to the point of jumping to a fire. The service was known for safety and they'd work their way up, practice at the tower first, then move to a number of low-altitude jumps free from danger, getting skills polished before they worked their way up to jumping near fires. That's how it always went. They'd hold that, even with early burns.

Everything would be okay.

CHAPTER FIVE

EVEN WITH GENERALLY keeping his distance, Beck knew one thing about smokejumpers and soldiers—everyone's rookie training was the worst in history. Bragging about something bad was cool if it proved how tough you were.

Even with their embellishments, he'd never heard of a Day Two that had gone quite so hardcore as this year. His own first experience with *Hell Week* hadn't got this hard this quickly. And even today, *his* today, didn't compare to Lauren's. He'd never been asked to carry anyone so much larger and heavier than he was, and that was the start of a day already asking for one hundred and ten percent of everyone else.

With only three of them jumping from the tower, it was a two-hour cycle of physical punishment. Jumping, being released at the end, and running back across the long field to climb another twenty-some stories to the top to hurl themselves out again.

The jump and glide weren't even relaxing. As easy as they were by comparison to a real jump, it was still very hard on the body. That initial jerk of the harness hurt, and going through it over and over did its own kind of damage. He'd made seven jumps in two hours, and had felt it in his shoulders and back even before carrying that person-sized pack through the wooded trail and twice around the old dirt track.

Hard day.

Now, standing in line for chow in a mostly empty mess hall, he didn't see her anywhere. Everyone else was there except her.

Had she already been and gone?

Sometime between them joking around after she'd carried him this morning and the tower, she'd gone from chatty and cheerful, if struggling with the aftermath of a hard slog, so far to the other extreme he had to wonder if something else had happened that he'd missed. Another jerk getting mouthy? Something worse than the horror of being assigned his partner?

After Treadwell's little bombshell, they needed to talk about whatever that meant. What she expected, what he needed to work on. He'd spent the past two hours mentally composing ground rules to go over with her, but where the devil was she?

It was possible she'd finished far enough ahead of him to have already eaten and gone, especially considering how much she liked being first at everything. He'd just assumed he'd been behind, doing what he did: conserving energy.

But she'd definitely had less energy at the start of the pack carry to conserve than he'd had. If she'd pushed hard down the wooded track...

No, she wouldn't have made that. The body could only do so much.

His watch confirmed an hour left before dinner ended—time to look for her.

Decision made, he headed back out.

Cabin first, and if she wasn't there, the woods. Then figure out some argument to make on her behalf so she didn't get booted for failing the time requirements.

Just as he reached the door, it opened and a dirty, sweaty, red-faced Autry shuffled in. Her hair, which had been neatly braided at the start of the day, now stuck out all around her face like a disheveled lion's mane.

She met his gaze, then lifted one arm and flopped it in a kind of half circle through the air, the sloppiest, most exhausted rendition of a wave he'd ever seen.

"You look like death."

A statement like that *always* merited an eye-roll. She only managed the verbal equivalent—a dry, hollow, "Thanks."

Before she could get around him, he grabbed her shoulders and spun her around to shove her right back out of the mess hall.

"I'm hungry," she said, but didn't physically resist. Didn't look like she even had the energy to walk, let alone put up a struggle.

"I'll bring it," he grunted, though his own hunger was suddenly gone. He steered her far enough in the direction of the cabin to make the order clear, but a roll of his stomach made him ask, "Did you finish in ninety?"

"Eighty-nine," she breathed, then stopped long enough to look over her shoulder. "Food?"

"I'll bring two dinners. Go."

"You showered already?"

He'd turned to head back inside, but the pang of defeat in her voice stopped him.

Even conserving energy, he was used to hauling that pack around and it had taken him less time than it had two years ago. "Yeah."

The defeat in her eyes twisted into something else, something more bitter. Something more like what he'd been avoiding feeling about himself since last season. The transparency of her emotions didn't do anything to make him comfortable with her ability to hold it together when things got hairy, but how hard she pushed herself made him want to root for her.

She didn't say anything else, just resumed scuffing her feet across the field to the wooden stairs and the cabins above. Treadwell had moved with about the same amount of energy, but her exhausted, splotchy pink didn't worry him like Treadwell's pallor. Autry's ills could be helped with rest and a little TLC. Not that he'd be doing any of that, but he could bring dinner.

Maybe tomorrow he'd bring lunch to check on the chief too.

Fifteen minutes later, he stepped into the small, spartan cabin to find her asleep at the dinette, sitting in a chair but sprawled from the ribs up over the small, circular table-top, cheek pressed against the faux wood laminate. Possibly drooling.

Man, he wanted to let her just sleep, but if she was going to be able to do all this again tomorrow, she needed to refuel, give her body some protein to undo the damage they'd done today.

Wake her up, feed her, but all the ground rules he'd been planning to lay out suddenly felt like taking advantage of someone too tired to bear another ounce of pressure.

"Lauren?" He said her name gently, then waited.

No response.

He tried again, a little louder.

Still nothing. She was *out*.

When she failed to even flinch after a third volume in-crease, he gave up and barked, "Autry!"

She jerked up, eyes wild and bleary. It took her staring at him for several seconds for coherent thought to show up. Her gaze fell to the take-out containers in his hands, and she held out both hands.

"You sure you're up to chewing?"

Lauren had to smile at the man's tease, even when her fin-gers failed to close on the box he handed her, twice. He placed it on the table in front of her.

"Be prepared to Heimlich me." She was tired enough to put her face in the grilled chicken and veggies and just start chewing, it'd free her from the arduous task of lifting plastic cutlery, but she still had enough pride to attempt civilized eating.

She could only manage to fumble the lid off her container and to fist her fork like a toddler before dropping it anyway.

It bounced once on the table and would've hit the floor but for Beck snatching it out of the air and handing it back to her.

Today had been hard, but worth it. She'd done fine.

Everything would be fine. There was no one here to tell her otherwise, so any fear she indulged in was of her own making. And that meant she could control it.

"Eat, shower, bed?"

"Eat. Bed." She could barely contemplate not just lying down on the floor of the kitchenette, where she'd definitely fall asleep.

"Fresh sheets are only delivered once a week. They're not coming to change them in the morning," Beck said, watching her too closely as he ate.

"I know I stink, don't beat around the bush."

He inhaled slowly, then shook his head. "Not stink. You're sweaty, but it's not like the stench that was rolling off me."

"My sweat is less stenchy? Good to know."

He looked like he didn't know quite what to say, then muttered, "You smell...like honey and dirt."

The description made her grin. It could've been a compliment, except for the *dirt* part. "You should make perfumes."

"Don't need to. I make bath bombs."

She paused the train of veggies and meat to her mouth, the words taking too much concentration to parse to allow any reaction but the honest one. Disbelief.

"You do *not* make bath bombs."

"They're more like bath salts. Not formed up into some kind of hygiene hand grenade."

"Too bad. Hygiene hand grenade sounds good right now."

"Bath sounds better. It'll help with the soreness."

Bath that took pain away *did* sound better, but there was something she knew she needed help with.

"Do you think you could help me stretch out my shoulders?"

He looked confused, but said nothing.

"This muscle." She ran one finger along the top of her shoulder between cuff and neck. "Trapezius. It's not much, just help me lift my arms from behind to stretch that. Only take a minute."

He nodded, still looking confused, but continued eating.

"So, you didn't learn to stretch in the Marines. Did *they* teach you to make bath bombs?"

It took him a while to answer, and when he spoke, the softness in his voice told a story of heartache. "My mom taught me."

She didn't even need to ask to know his mother was no longer with him. She'd grown up with that tone, heard it in her father's voice any time he spoke of her own mother.

"I'm sorry," she said, not knowing quite what else to say to the sad direction she'd pushed the conversation.

He looked up swiftly, brows pinching as he visibly scanned the conversation in his mind. She could see him replaying the words. "How did you know she was gone?"

"My mom died when I was five. My father never remarried, still wears his wedding ring, still carries his grief. There's a way of speaking… It's hard to describe."

"Regret," he murmured. "What you're hearing is regret. What happened to her?"

"She developed breast cancer not long after I was born. I guess that happens sometimes with older mothers. She wasn't really old, but she was older than the usual birth mother age twenty-four years ago. Sick most of the time I knew her. I only have a handful of memories, really. My siblings and I stayed with our grandparents for long stretches when chemo knocked her immune system down and she couldn't afford four germ monsters around her, not and keep fighting."

"I'm sorry, echoed." He watched her with such compassion, she grew more certain his grief was fresher. Was that why he'd ended up back with the rookies?

She'd been looking for reasons he'd been grouped with them, and her speculations had ranged from teaching them, to some oddity of numbers, and through Treadwell's irritation with him to some kind of punishment. Beck participating in the pack carry today fit punishment. That was something only rookies had to do. Those who returned for refreshers had already proved they could carry a body for miles.

Something was wrong, and considering the grief she still saw in his eyes...

"So your dad is just very protective?" His question gave her an excuse not to ask, but she wanted to ask. Maybe she *should* even ask, since he was her partner now.

Instead, she ate and stuck to the subject, at least for now. "Because he couldn't protect her, I guess. And my brothers take their cue from him."

"So why are you all at the same station?"

"It's still my birthright. And as annoying as they are, they can't keep me from doing my job. Besides, I'd rather be there with them and at least have a shot at helping than at a different station and hear about some calamity after the fact."

"But you're here."

She nodded slowly. "Yeah..."

"In the off-season, you'll be with the park service. Not with them."

"I know," she said, but had truthfully done everything

she could to not dwell on that—she still wasn't too sure she'd be a great forest ranger. She liked being outside, but she wasn't overly informed about trees and wildlife. "I guess I got tired of swimming upstream. I just haven't reformatted my answer yet. Or thought much about it. Been trying not to think about how I'll feel if something happens and I'm not there."

He went quiet, but she didn't see judgment in his espresso-black eyes. That was sympathy. And shadow.

He hadn't offered more information about his mom, which should tell her enough about how much he wanted to talk about it, but she couldn't *not* ask. Not when there was so much up in the air about this man, her partner. Whatever had gotten him in trouble, she had to know.

"When did you lose your mom?"

It was rude to ask such a question and then keep chowing down, so she waited for his answer, long enough she began to doubt whether she had the energy to continue eating and bathe.

"I was ten."

At least fifteen years ago. A long time to not have developed some distance.

Or maybe she was an anomaly.

Her eldest brother had been older than Beck when their mother had passed, but he'd also developed greater distance than Beck had seemed to.

Her family's loving misogyny, if that was a thing, was definitely a manifestation of their loss. Fear of losing her too. Probably the only reason she'd put up with it so long.

But her mother had died a quiet, slow, terrible death. An expected death, finally.

"How did she die?"

Again, a long silence. Was it not wanting to talk about it or pain that kept his words from coming easily?

"Wildfire." The one-word answer effectively wiped everything else from her mind.

"Oh, God, Beck…"

"I don't want to talk about it," he cut in, as if she had anything else to say that could ever be sufficient.

He had been ten. She'd died in a wildfire. Did Lauren really need to know anything else about why the man had joined the smokejumpers? Why he'd gone into firefighting for the military?

Not when she felt the sudden truth of who he was down deep, where she stuffed all things that could hurt her. It didn't explain what had happened to get him back here after he'd been so lauded, but pressing him felt wrong, as did abandoning the topic entirely.

"How do you make bath bombs?"

If she'd had the fortitude to be silent as long as he could, maybe she could've come up with something more sensitive or compassionate to say. But this was related to his mom, and something he might be able to speak about. It felt like a way in. An acknowledgment, but safe.

Beck lifted his gaze from his meal again, but shifted to the mom-adjacent subject, and began to explain the process and ingredients used.

"I've got a batch made. All that's missing is the pine needles. I can get them out back if you want. They'll help the soreness."

"Thank you. That's…" She swallowed nothing, tried again, bypassing the usual denials she'd make to conceal any vulnerabilities. "I could use a little help right now, I think."

"In the future, you'll hear about *Hell Week* from everyone, and how theirs was the worst," Beck said, closing the container on his dinner. "Trust me, you're going to win those misery competitions."

"I did the same things you did today."

"I've never been asked to carry someone so far who outweighed me by so much. Out in the field, it's always going to be a two-person job, barring catastrophe. We have collapsible stretchers for it."

The subject moved on, and they both eased. And what she heard in his voice now? That was admiration. She felt her smile return, along with the strength to get through the rest of her meal.

Beck not only went after the pine needles, he tied them up in a handkerchief to keep them from poking her in the bath, and ran the hot water to mix it all up.

If this was how it was to have a partner who helped instead of held her back, she was in trouble.

It wasn't as if she'd just dated jerks, but any time she'd got involved with a firefighter—who were the men she most frequently encountered—he had invariably been tied to her station, which had left him subjected to her family's pressure. Troy had just been the one she'd most wanted to believe was on her side, and whose preference of her father had hurt the most.

Troy could also be sweet at times, when they'd been alone and only if work wasn't involved.

That was how this was different. That was how Beck was far more dangerous. He was helping her so she could be ready for tomorrow, not giving her reasons to bail.

And if he was doing all that, she could find the energy to get some clean clothes and get her honey-dirty self into the water.

By the time she dragged herself into her room and out, he was back at the table, sitting, staring off into space. "Water's ready. You want to do your shoulders before or after?"

"Before." She stopped in front of him and folded her arms back to press her fists together in the center of her back. "Just pull my elbows back until I cry *uncle*."

His large, strong hands cupped her elbows and slowly pulled back, stopping when she made an accidental, pained noise, so she had to convince him to go a little further.

Then repeated from the front, stretching out the muscles that had tightened this morning and never really relaxed.

"Thanks," she said, breathing a little hard because stretching unruly muscles could hurt, and made for the bathroom.

She didn't make it. He caught her by the back of the shirt, wordlessly wrapping one arm across her shoulders from the front to brace her so he could mash his palm against that same, suffering muscle and rotate. He repeated the motion through several rotations on each side of her spine, tracking halfway down her back as she let her head hang forward and used up every last ounce of strength to stay upright when her body just wanted to fold in on itself.

It wasn't long, minutes she'd have paid money and dignity to continue, and he released her. "Don't fall asleep in the water."

She wobbled, then stepped into the bathroom, intent on bathing as quickly as she could before the truth of his words sank in. There was no way she'd stay awake once she sank into that water. Not alone.

"I hate to ask you for another favor when you've been so kind, but I'm honestly afraid of falling asleep in there."

He'd already sat back down, but turned in his chair toward her. "Okay."

"Keep me company?"

Her words had him on his feet like he was actually *made* of energy.

"Lauren, that's not a good idea. You're very appealing, but bathing together... Bad idea. I didn't mean to give you that idea."

He babbled, speaking faster than she'd heard him say anything, and with so many pauses she suddenly understood she wasn't the only one experiencing the strange pull.

If she'd had any energy left, she'd be embarrassed he thought she was hitting on him, but she didn't. She also wished it didn't sound so appealing. Too tired to blush, she waved a hand. "Not asking you to have a bath with me. Just stay there, talk through the door so I don't drown in my sleep."

He shifted from foot to foot, the way she often did before running.

"And how about I forget anything else you might have said before that?" she added.

A slow nod and he sat back down.

Pride took energy. She had none to spare.

A few minutes later, with the bathroom door just ajar, she settled into the steaming, lavender-scented water and it became obvious how bone deep her soreness was and how nice it would've been to just go to sleep there.

"What do you want to talk about?" he asked outside the door.

Him. She wanted to talk about him. His mom. His life. What had happened to re-rookie him.

That was something she should ask.

"We're partners, and tied together. You're probably worried I'll weigh you down after today."

"I'm not."

That'd be a good reason for him to be so helpful, actually. She *must* be tired, not having realized that before.

"Still, I won't. I'm not going to fail this." *You.* She wanted to say fail *you*, because his help—regardless of motivation—felt like a gift. One she wanted to return.

"If anyone fails because of it, it's going to be me," Beck said after a moment. "Treadwell introduced partnerships this year because I'm bad at teamwork."

Bad at teamwork meant something had happened and it had been his fault.

"What happened?"

"Close call. A risk I shouldn't have taken, I guess."

Also not what he was known for. And not full of details.

"What risk?"

"Chased a dog into a fire, got trapped. Had to be rescued."

"Oh." That didn't sound so bad to her. "Did you save the dog?"

"Had to knock him out, but they were able to drop a safety line from a chopper. It was close, though. Fire... Heat rises, makes it hard to fly in near. Put others in danger."

"But everyone made it?"

"Not the point."

At that moment, she wished she could see his face, figure out what he was saying. What did that negative sound mean? Was it directed at himself? Was he angry at Treadwell for busting him down, or was he angry at people coming to rescue him?

"How are you bad at teamwork?"

"Just am."

"Don't ask permission before doing things? Don't ask for help? Don't...?"

"Don't ask for help."

She could understand that one. "You know, friends don't always need to be asked for help. You helped me tonight, you're helping me now..."

"This isn't dangerous."

She picked up the hankie tied up with pine needles inside and shook her head. The hell this wasn't dangerous. She was in very real danger of making a mistake with this man. This man who was clearly thinking things about her too, even if she was supposed to forget that.

Soaking in the water and talking to him? Maybe also not so good for her emotional balance around him.

New plan: wash fast, say goodnight, go to sleep.

She hurried through the rest, dried enough to get her PJs on, and stepped out of the bath to find him still sitting in the chair.

"You've been great tonight. Thank you." The words failed to live up to what she was feeling, but they were the best she had right now. "You don't like to ask for help, I get it. What about if you just order me to do something?"

"You'd hate that."

"I would, but if it's just code for something else? That's different." She hoped so, at least. "We're partners, and even if we weren't tied together, I'd want to help."

"Why?"

She started dragging herself toward the bedroom. "Because you're a good person."

True, but a little shallow compared to the draw to him she felt.

She still didn't know what had changed in him that had caused his mistake. Bad at teamwork and needing a rescue didn't seem like the kind of thing to be punished for as a one-off. If it wasn't, why had she seen over a year of praise for him?

When he said nothing else, she wobbled on to bed.

More questions would have to wait.

CHAPTER SIX

DAY THREE CAME and went in a blur of exhaustion so intense Lauren could only focus on what was before her.

Although it had lacked another pack carry, after Beck had carried her for morning PT, they'd hit the tower twice and those jump hours—while populated by more rookies who'd moved up—had been rough and bracketed by boot-camp-style calisthenics and lots of running.

The physical exhaustion of Day Three built on Day Two, making it easier to ignore the messy other stuff, even if she saw it there every time she looked at Beck.

His mother. A wildfire. And whatever had pushed him into making mistakes.

The only thing they'd discussed had been the way the fire up north continued to grow, and Treadwell's status after Beck had gone to check on him and been told to "mind his own damned business."

Outside work, it seemed they'd both come to the same conclusion: yesterday had been too intimate and they needed to step back. And that was okay. They'd worked well together, pushed each other even. After hours, he'd shown her how to use the bath salts and she'd soaked her own aches away without asking for anything else.

When Day Four brought something entirely new, both eagerly volunteered.

Just over two hours into the day, Lauren climbed out

of the bus that had carried them north to land between the large, raging fire and a subdivision that could be threatened if the winds turned. They couldn't see flames but smoke clogged the air, turning it hazy orange with the sun filtering through, making breathing an act of endurance before they even began the prep work for a controlled burn.

Treadwell was with them today, but looked worn out. At least with them they could keep an eye on him if he did something more physical besides bark orders and whistle too loudly.

In short order, they were all given shovels—the least glamorous part of the job—and set about digging trenches. Digging down, past the brush and other fuel sources, set limits so they could safely section the wide field and burn the tall dry grasses in controlled patches. They started at the road with the goal of reaching the tree line in the distance.

The hard-packed earth demanded every ounce of strength Lauren could muster after days of hard conditioning, and she was glad for the silence in which everyone else worked.

When they made it to the end of their row, Lauren went for water, and when she looked for Beck afterward she didn't see him. He hadn't gone for a drink. Wasn't resting. Hadn't even gotten started at their next location without her.

Suddenly, not having discussed how their partnership would work seemed like a mistake.

One she should remedy. As soon as she found him.

He wasn't on the bus. Behind the bus. In the truck…

Treadwell saw her looking and gestured far down the field toward the trees and she saw a teeny tiny figure with hands on hips, standing there.

Looking at Treadwell again would've been a mistake, he might've had *strike* written all over it from their bad partnering. She grabbed her shovel, another water, and hurried downfield.

She found him examining the tree line and stabbing the ground here and there with the blade of his shovel.

They were far enough away that the bus and trucks appeared to perhaps have been built for ladybugs.

Somewhere she could speak without being overheard.

"Beck?" She called his name on approach, water in hand for him as a way to smooth over her coming critique.

When he looked up, she joked, "We playing leapfrog, or just avoiding the stench of fourteen sweaty dudes digging?"

"I smell smoke. We need to start down here," he answered, not smiling at all to her joking. Also not taking the water she held out.

"Everyone smells smoke. The air quality is flagged red today for the area."

"It's stronger than it was."

"Okay, did you tell Treadwell or Kolinski?" As if she didn't know the answer to that.

"They saw me."

This was what Treadwell meant by bad at teamwork. "Beck, remember the partnership talk?"

"Your point?"

"Treadwell saw you, he told me where you were. Example of not working well with your team."

He didn't roll his eyes, just looked at her long seconds, then resumed stabbing the ground with his shovel to loosen the dirt.

"Autry, come with me to go sniff some trees," she said in her manliest, commanding tone. "See? Easy-peasy. Then we're still working as a pair, even if we're ignoring the rest of our team."

"Fine," he muttered, breezing over her silly impersonation to explain. "The fire will come this direction, rocket over that brush, and build too fast and hot to be controlled. Digging here will slow it down some. Controlled burns are great, but we should've started here."

She couldn't argue with the logic, even if she knew

they were only there *just in case.* They didn't actually expect the fire to blow toward the subdivision. It could, but it hadn't—there was time to take it methodically, not like if they'd been in the middle of a war.

Things he knew. But the man seemed to only have one setting when it came to the fire. Combat Zone. And maybe that's what it was to him...

"I'll let Treadwell know what we're doing, in case he wants to send other crews down. Drink." She threw the bottle at him, and he dropped his shovel to catch it, but did pause his digging long enough to drink it.

This pattern was repeated twice more over the day— them finishing one task only for Beck to wander off to do something else, leaving her to track him down. By the time the afternoon sun was high and baking them all, she wanted to strangle him, or smack him on the head with her shovel.

The fire never arrived, despite shifting winds blowing smoke their direction. Around three, they lit the first section of field and took turns with shovels and hoses, ready to extinguish any escaping cinders. One section cleared, they moved on to the next. Methodical. Even kind of relaxing, once the shoulder-torturing digging was done. She didn't even have to chase Ellison down once the fire started, it fixated everyone's attention.

Which was how Treadwell collapsed without anyone immediately noticing.

She was the first to see when she handed her shovel off to get another drink, and saw the man stretched out on the ground, matting down tall, brown grasses.

"Chief!"

Her call, no match for the roaring fire, still managed to find Beck's ear. She ran for the downed leader's side, grabbing one arm to check his pulse as she did so, and Beck was right behind her.

"It's beating," Treadwell rasped regarding his heart, but he'd gone a terrible gray, and between the irregular, rapid fluttering beat of his heart and the speed of his breathing, she knew two things: this wasn't because of the heat, and he needed some clean oxygen fast.

Beck made it there just behind her, and dug out his cell-phone to call 911.

"Don't make me give you mouth-to-mouth." Beck hadn't so much as smiled at her or anyone else all day, but he attempted levity with the chief.

"First year, maybe you would've. Not now," Treadwell gasped from the ground, his voice holding no fond humor in response, just rebuke. "Autry would still be chasing you down if we hadn't lit the field. You'd never know."

"Quiet. Conserve oxygen." She squeezed Treadwell's hand, then looked up at Beck. "He needs oxygen."

"He never listens anymore." Treadwell kept going, sounding more like a disappointed father than an angry chief. But his speech was so broken, she really wished he'd shut up. "Maybe if he hears it from a dying man."

She chanced a glance at Beck to find any spark of humor gone, and worry in his eyes that bordered on grief.

"You're not dying," Beck said, voice a little hoarse, and hung up on the call. He disappeared directly into the supply truck and came out a moment later with a stretcher and portable oxygen.

She grabbed a bag with tubing and ripped into it to hook the nasal cannula over his ears and direct the oxygen up his nose. "No face mask?"

Beck shook his head. "We weren't packed for work. It's a camp bus."

She held the cannula to Treadwell's nose to make sure it was all going where it should be. "Breathe slow and deep."

"Can't," he panted. "Truck parked on my chest..."

"We're far from the road, the lane's blocked by the bus and trucks," Beck said, kneeling to count Treadwell's pulse. "Too fast."

"Tachycardic," she whispered. "Maybe in some kind of fibrillation. Why don't we have more equipment?"

"I don't know," he muttered. "We're carrying him to the street to meet the crew."

An order. A request. Progress, even if he kind of *had* to ask for it.

She helped Beck transfer the chief to the stretcher along with his oxygen bottle, and inside sixty seconds they had him strapped in and were hurrying over uneven terrain for the main road.

Medical personnel usually made the worst patients, and Treadwell kept up the tradition. He wouldn't stop giving Beck hell the whole time they carried him. Even when he could barely get enough air to speak. Even when he gripped his own chest and stuttered with the pain of it.

Sirens sounded, and behind them the rest of the crew had resumed tending the fire under Kolinski's command—it couldn't be abandoned, even if the chief was mid–heart attack, which was what seemed to be happening.

The ambulance arrived about the same time they did, and took over, lifting their carried stretcher onto their wheeled one and strapping it in.

Lauren and Beck stood back, but if she thought the team would get into gear, they didn't. One of them seemed young. The other seemed frustrated, but he climbed into the ambulance for supplies.

"What the hell are you doing?" Beck barked out when the younger one fumbled with the chief's suit too tentatively to get it open. Without waiting for an answer, he stepped over and grabbed the zipper, jerking it down, then ripping through the T-shirt beneath to bare his chest. As soon as the seasoned EMT stepped over, Lauren grabbed the pack of electrodes and began applying them. She wasn't a trained paramedic, but she knew how to do that.

"What are you two doing?" Treadwell asked.

Lauren ignored him, reaching for the monitor to pull

leads, which Beck took over applying with the experienced EMT. To the younger, who stood there doing nothing, she ordered, "Get him a face mask, he needs a higher oxygen concentration. Are you the driver?"

He nodded.

"Then you," she ordered the elder, "get a line in him and we'll do this. With the four of us, it'll go faster."

"Three," Beck muttered.

Whatever, she was charitable enough to include Skippy the Baby Paramedic in the count if he brought a danged mask.

It wasn't long before they could only stand back and watch the squiggling line track across the monitor. Worry tracked across Beck's face.

"Do you want us to come with you, Chief?" Lauren asked, and when rebuffed got all the details from the EMT about which hospital they'd be going to, then let them work.

Beck, as grim as she'd ever seen him, simply stood to the side, waiting. Watching. She could almost see the chief's gasped and panted tirade getting through to the man she'd spent all day not getting through to.

Treadwell wanted the old Beck back. First-year Beck.

Whatever had happened, it had happened last season. People didn't fall apart because they needed to be rescued once. There was something else, and if they were going to survive as partners, or survive in general, he needed to face it. Whatever *it* was.

The burning was the quickest part of their day. Not long after carrying the chief to the road, it was done.

The local fire department sent a crew to keep an eye on the smoldering remains, and the exhausted rookies settled in for a long ride back to camp.

Although Lauren had avoided Beck on the ride up, for the ride back she climbed aboard the bus and headed straight to him.

He sat sideways, his back against the metal wall, legs on the seat, eyes closed.

With water in her hands, she hooked a foot behind his legs and shoved them off the padded green cushion to make room.

"What the…?" He started to swear, but when he saw her, the words stopped.

He didn't immediately turn to sit properly, and she could see him considering ways to make her move.

Shove her off. Toss her over the seatback in front of them.

Escalation was standard operating procedure in man conflict world, throwing punches were communication tactics. But he didn't do any of those things. He took his time, but eventually swiveled to face forward. "There *are* other seats."

"I know." She handed him the water she'd brought as a peace offering.

As much as she wanted to check on him in the wake of Treadwell's tirade, she'd also reached the point where she couldn't just wait for him to deal with *whatever* anymore. Like it or not, his problems were her problems.

She didn't immediately launch in, just enjoyed some water and waited until they were on the freeway, where open windows and six big tires rushing over asphalt created a sound barrier to keep their conversation private.

"Treadwell's been your chief since you started?" she asked, turning just slightly on the seat so she could watch him.

His nod confirmed it, as did the tilt of his head away from the window. His gaze bored into the top seam of the evergreen seatback in front of them. He wasn't talking, but he was listening.

And he wasn't okay. Upset, and not just because he was worried for the chief—still clearly thinking about the chief's words, a man who truly cared about him but didn't understand what was going on with him either.

Check on him first. Be kind. Make him talk.

"Have you noticed anything up with him before this week? Slowing down? Getting winded easily?"

"Haven't seen him much the past several months. Like I said, in the off-season I wear a different uniform. Clear trails. Remove brush from the forest. Perform small burns."

The forest ranger part of the job. "You like it?"

He nodded again, but his eyes took on a kind of unfocused quality that told her he was thinking about something specifically.

"What?"

"Maybe Treadwell did have something going on that day he called me in to give me the talk."

The talk. This wasn't birds-and-bees territory, even if Treadwell was starting to feel strangely like Beck's surrogate father. He meant the probation talk.

"Because you're not good at teamwork."

"Don't try gentle criticism, Autry," he grunted, using her last name again, but telling her his frustration was pointed inward. "I know I screwed up."

"Okay." She capped the remaining half of her water, focusing all her attention on the conversation. "So why do you do it?"

"I don't know."

"I don't believe you. You're too solitary a creature not to be introspective. Everyone has a reason for the decisions they make, even if the reason is stupid. Even if the reason is like…executive function issues."

"Executive function…?"

"My middle brother has ADHD, and they call it executive function disorder or something. He has trouble with impulsivity, which basically stems from not understanding why he does the things he does, or that he's being driven to make decisions by his emotions. Like why he shouldn't trade in a car he's had for three months and buy another..."

"He's a firefighter?"

"He's really good at things when he's super-interested in them, and he is at his job. He hears everything, notices everything. If you're with him in a burn, he'll know something bad is about to happen before you do. It's almost creepy, really. It's the rest of his life that he has trouble with." She paused, realizing she was going off at a tangent, defending someone Beck didn't even know. "Point is, I think you know why you do what you do. You have reasons. And if you don't know, you don't want to know."

Beck had a tendency to take his time with any words he parceled out, and he took his time again now.

He didn't have the profile of a man searching his soul. He looked like a man who hated what he already knew about himself.

She interrupted, trying to prompt speech. "How do you see fire, Beck?"

"That's a stupid question. I see it as fire."

"You see it as something more than just fire."

He rolled his eyes. "Fine, what do you see fire as?"

She hadn't really thought about how to describe the difference she saw in her own feelings about fire and his.

It took a moment to summon the imagery, and although it felt stupid to correlate fire with water, she said it anyway.

"I see it like the deep end of a swimming pool, and I'm a lifeguard who's relegated to the shallows. I can see people drowning, but every time I try to help, someone important side-eyes me, hands me water wings and tells me to mind the kiddie pool."

And as soon as she put it into words, the mental images kept coming.

"Or a dance I've been invited to, but only so I can serve the refreshments."

"I get it." He cut her off and turned back to the window in silence.

Was he thinking or shutting her out? Probably the latter, but if she was going to get any kind of answer, she had to give him at least a little time to think.

Outside the windows, other cars passed in a blur of color and faces against a backdrop of gray concrete. It wasn't anything to look at, but she let him look for a long time.

"My adversary," he said finally. "I see the fire like a cop chasing the serial killer that killed his family."

He spoke quietly, and what came out was much bigger than she knew how to deal with. Adversary wasn't even accurate. Too civilized-sounding by comparison. Even hearing him say those words made her chest burn like she'd been inhaling cinders for days.

It was a lot. But it wasn't everything, it couldn't be. His mother had died terribly when he was ten, and two years ago he'd been the star quarterback. Something had specifically changed last year.

She leaned in closer so she could speak softly, as that kind of question should be asked with reverence. "Did your brush with the fire bring all that back? With your mom?"

He looked pained, and then shook his head, repeating, "I don't know."

He didn't know because he wasn't ready to go there.

She couldn't force him to do it either.

"How can I help you on the job? I know the job is important to you. How can I help you?"

"I don't know." He said the words again.

"Does Treadwell know about her?"

He didn't repeat himself, just shrugged, making clear they hadn't spoken of it. There were services that would've been offered to help him if he'd ever asked for help.

"You have to figure this out, Beck. Don't expect me to let up either. I know it sucks to talk about it, to relive it or to have someone trying to make you look at what you lived from some other point of view, but there's something to this and you have to figure it out."

"What other point of view is there?" he bit out. Aggression. An emotional dodge from the man-speak playbook to redirect the conversation. He needed to focus.

"Like how terrible it would've been for your mom had you been the one to die and she to live."

She shouldn't have said that, she knew it the instant the words flew out of her mouth and the meager color he'd regained since Treadwell's collapse drained away.

He looked back out the window, once again returning to his usual broody silence. She wanted to touch him, and probably would have—even there on the packed bus, where anyone could've seen.

In fact, she actually did rise up a little to look around, and saw fourteen other sweaty men sleeping in their seats, and that one jerk who'd laughed at her smirking at them.

Copeland.

He had one brow up, arching in challenge, eyes full of judgment, and mouthed, "Are you going to make out now?"

Beck turned just then, and caught her staring back at the man, and picked up the sudden shift in tension even though he'd missed the silent gibe. Still, he placed his hands on the seat to rise and confront the man for her.

Having Beck defend her again would only embolden Copeland to continue, get worse. Escalation was the male confrontational hallmark. Besides, she couldn't have Beck taking on another emotional landmine while he was tiptoeing around his own.

Not going to happen.

She sprang up, reared back, and with the half-empty water bottle as her only weapon hurled it at Copeland's head with as much speed and force as she could put into a wobbling, off-center, water-filled plastic missile.

It tumbled end over end, and the heavier, water-filled base of the soft plastic bottle smashed into his cheek. Because she had three brothers, Lauren hit whatever she aimed at.

Instantly, his face went red and he surged to his feet.

She'd learned that look from her brothers too. Confrontation face. She couldn't back down now.

Taking one deep breath, she hopped onto the padded seat she'd just vacated and launched herself at the man, but Beck was faster. He slung one arm across her hips as she jumped and pulled her back into the seat as other, more sensible men near Copeland got in his way too.

"Are you seriously going to fight that ass?" Beck shouted at her, dropping her in the seat. "He's twice as big as you are."

"I don't need anyone fighting my battles, Ellison. And I'm through taking crap from him." She slid to the side, got back on her feet, but didn't launch back in again, just stood her ground.

"No one's fighting." Kolinski seemed to have awakened in the shouting and kerfuffle, and pushed back through to the middle of them. "Did I just see Ellison keep his partner from doing something stupid?"

"Not stupid," she argued, ignoring the small amount of praise slipped in there for Beck, who'd apparently finally exhibited some team spirit by stopping her from stomping on Copeland's dangly bits. "I'm not putting up with sexist crap from that jerk. He's always running his mouth. If you want to nail me for not working and playing nicely with my teammate, look to him as well."

Kolinski turned to look back at Copeland. "What sexist crap?"

Copeland mustered the decency to look chagrined, and went for the traditional sexist cop-out. "I was just kidding. Not my fault she can't take a joke."

When Kolinski looked back at her, she snorted but gave up on the nonsense. It was over. He had been caught out. He probably wouldn't make the same mistake again, and if she hadn't let Beck get in his grill about it last time, he wouldn't have done it this time. "The idea of making out with your partner is hilarious. I'm sure you'd have said it to any of the dudes here chatting with *their* partners."

Point made, Copeland sat and glared out the window, and everyone returned to their seats.

Beck's steely glare leveled at her brought the frustration out that she'd been trying to contain. "I'm just going to add this and then I'll let it go for now. Whether or not we were tied together, it would be wrong of me to let you plod forward like everything was fine without at least pointing out that you're letting your emotions get the better of you in fires. I'm not saying you're imagining danger, or that your actions are increasing the danger to yourself and your team, but, like it or not, if you get stuck, someone is going to come for you. The safety record the service holds is as much about making smart decisions as having the best people."

"This from the woman whose emotions just made her have a Chihuahua-bulldog confrontation?" His voice rose enough that she saw heads turning out of the corner of her eye, and knew that the conversation was done.

"There you go again, thinking I can't handle what I say I can handle. Sort it out, Beck. I like you, I really do, but if you think I'm going to let up, you haven't experienced how tenacious a Chihuahua can be."

She stepped around the next seat forward and sat again. Not with Beck. She wasn't mad at him, she was just tired, and the knowledge they hadn't come to any kind of understanding was the cherry on top of a long, emotion-laden day. All she wanted to do was shower, eat, sleep and survive tomorrow.

One more day of *Hell Week*.

CHAPTER SEVEN

AFTER THE FIELD, after Treadwell's ranting collapse, Beck spent the kind of night where he wasn't sure whether he'd slept or not. Even after hiking directly into the woods upon arriving back at camp, and staying immersed in night song and the cool dampness of the forest. Even in the wooded embrace of his favorite tan oak.

If he'd stayed back there in the woods, he might've been able to sleep. But he hadn't. He'd thought about Lauren's words, and those malachite green eyes that pressed into him, and he'd returned to the cabin to thrash around in his bed until morning. Even if they weren't technically speaking, being under the same roof felt necessary. Probably some residual notion of partnership he'd only just grasped because it was ingrained in the genetic makeup of humans. It certainly wasn't something he'd done out of inspiration.

He'd dragged through the day, exhausted in a way that snowballed, mentally and physically. There had been news about Treadwell, a mixed bag: he'd definitely had a heart attack and they'd performed an emergency procedure to open those vessels up, but no word had come on lasting damage to the heart. For all Beck knew, this was the end of Treadwell's career. Which would mean a new chief, and one who wouldn't have this positive memory of the things Beck was capable of if he could get his head straight.

And that's what was keeping him from sleep. That and

the lingering frustration he had with Lauren after a day of purposeful avoidance, because opening his mouth would prove she'd hit on a sore subject with him, and not talking now probably proved her point. He was too emotional and let it impair his judgment.

He rolled over again and the clock's glaring, judgmental red numbers launched him from the bed.

Just tell her. Tell her what had happened last year, and let *her* chew on it, not him. Get the words out of his own head so he could sleep.

In the dark, he stormed out of his own room and knocked once, hard, on her door before opening it.

She bolted upright, but in the dark he couldn't see her expression. That was good. Then he wouldn't have to read it, or hide from it.

"I'm tired and I just want to go to sleep, but I can't stop thinking. I don't want to think about it. I just want it to go away. I just want to be busy and not think about it and have it go away…"

"Okay," she said groggily, then fumbled with the bedside lamp.

He launched forward, grabbing her hand before she could close around the key to turn it on, and pushing it back to her lap.

"Beck?"

"I just want to say it and go to sleep. Okay?"

"Okay," she said again. In the dark, he could hear her confused, sleepy breathing, but she didn't sound scared. She would. This wasn't going to make things better.

"There was a local fireman last summer in Oregon when we were called in. He got separated from the group and no one would let me go in for him," Beck said, stepping back from the bed, wanting distance from that too. "They wouldn't let me go, and he died. And I can't… I can't leave anyone behind. I can't do it. It's not in me to do that. If there's a chance, and there's always a chance."

"What do you mean, they wouldn't let you go? You listened to orders?"

"No. I mean…three of them wrestled me into the back of a parked police cruiser and locked me in." He really hadn't had a choice then. There was no opening those doors from the inside.

"Oh." She lifted her hand, almost turned on the light, but then remembered and rubbed her face instead. "There's not always a chance."

"There is."

"Okay." She tried again. "There's always a chance for a while, but there comes a time when the chance is so small that it becomes a bad call."

"If someone's willing to risk it…"

"That's not your call."

"The smokejumpers who saved me? They bucked orders. They bucked orders and came in anyway."

"Treadwell didn't send them?"

Right. He hadn't told her that.

"Not then. When I was a kid. When the fire came, they bucked orders. There was a chopper, they came after us. That's why I survived. I survived *after* someone decided it was too dangerous to risk." He tried to explain, but it was hard to put feelings into words. "Last year, there was a place where the fire seemed thinner. And there was a clear pocket in the middle where the man was. I could've gone through the fire. Or maybe gone up in a chopper and dropped to him."

"The people who saved you risked themselves to save a *family*. They risked for a family. For a child…" she said softly, picking up the thread of conversation as slowly as she climbed from the bed, the creaking of the mattress and the rustle of sheets distracting. The sound of rustling cotton had never sounded so nice, so enticing. That's what he wanted, to be distracted. "But you can't think it's smart to exchange one life for another, if there was even a chance that your death could've saved him."

"There's always a chance," he repeated. Without thinking, he stepped closer, hands restless, body restless, mind restless. "They came for a family, and left with a child. They had to leave her. I had to leave her. Do you…? You can't expect that to be something someone can do again. And I couldn't get to him. And now I don't ask permission. I just do what I need to do."

He hadn't actually touched her yet, though he'd reached out and retreated several times during his blathering, but when she took the next step and reached for his shoulders, he backtracked across the room.

"Why couldn't they get to your mother?" She focused in on that.

"Fire moved too fast. It was too late. They couldn't find her, they said." The burnt, scarred trees flashed into his mind, the remains of their cottage, and a lingering bitterness with himself that he still didn't want to believe them. "I guess it makes sense, the fire got all the way to the river."

"You saw it?"

"A couple of years later." Long past the time when anything could've still been smoldering, but that was how he remembered it: with smoke rising from everything. Their little cottage by the river. The trees surrounding it, the forest beyond. Even the grass smoldered in his memory.

Anyone would've picked the river over the flames, but the prospect of her dying in the water didn't make it better.

He'd lied to himself for years about that day, because the images he played in his mind of his mother were of her having *survived* the water. Maybe with a head injury, something that made her forget. No body meant no true ending to her. That was the only thought that actually soothed.

The smokejumpers who'd rescued him couldn't have known their story, true or not, wouldn't be the kinder alternative. Which was its own kind of twisted and sick to think he'd be in a better place mentally, feel less guilty, if she'd died in the flames.

His mother had worn the malachite pendant and crystals had littered their home because she needed their help for something. Something had happened and she'd drawn away from the world, using money left to her by her father to buy land and build the cabin *away*, where it was safe. He didn't know what had made her retreat, had only ever gotten vague cautions from her about the world being dangerous, and had known her to meditate with the malachite when her emotions got out of control. When he couldn't talk her through another panic attack.

Which was why the idea of her drowning wasn't better. He *couldn't* have helped her survive the fire, but if he'd gone into the water with her... There was a chance. If he hadn't let them take him. If he hadn't left her behind. It was torturous to think of her burning alive with him helpless to stop it, but thinking of her drowning because he abandoned her put her death on his hands.

He'd told himself a lie of hope, and during the first years, it helped him get through. Maybe never having found her was kinder than knowing it was one or the other, it left room for the denial that had let him survive. A little boy's dream he could no longer believe, the reason he could never leave anyone behind again.

Lauren stopped following when he reached the doorway, and the next step would mean leaving. In that moment, he wanted to see her eyes. With one hand, he found the switch for the overhead and flipped it on so they were both squinting and blinking against the sudden brightness. When she opened her eyes fully again, there it was. The malachite green, pale in the center, and impossibly dark at the edge of the iris.

Malachite was for healing, he'd looked it up. Healing and bringing hidden pain to the surface. Probably why he was subconsciously drawn to her. Maybe even why he felt compelled to tell her things he didn't even like to admit to himself. Because not doing so felt somehow like lying to *family*.

"Are you angry with Treadwell for not letting you go in after the firefighter?"

"I don't know," he said, shaking his head again, and this time he really didn't have that answer, and he didn't want to think about that right now, open up new avenues to keep him from sleep. He'd said what he'd needed to say, the things that had been running around in his head, and now he just wanted to sleep.

"You need to talk to someone about this, Beck. Everything about it. I'm more than willing to listen if you want to tell me everything, talk through it…"

"That's it. I don't have anything else."

"That's not it," she said, and there was no slow, gentle approach this time, she just was suddenly right there, her hands holding his face, making him look at her. "If it's not me, then it needs to be someone. Yesterday, on the bus, you said the fire was your adversary. I see it as a thing that's being held out of my grasp, you see it as something living and sentient—a monster hiding behind corners, waiting to take people from you. And I get it. I don't think there's any reason you wouldn't feel that way, with what you've experienced. But you can't outsmart fire. It's not a chess match with a serial killer."

"I know that."

"Do you?" Her hands gave one sharp, small shake, just enough to jostle him and command his focus. "Treadwell was right not to send you in. It was down to deciding if he lost one firefighter or two. And even if the man survived and you died getting him out, that's still bad math. His life wasn't more valuable than yours. The dog you went after later on wasn't more valuable than you are, even if it would've been tragic for him to burn up in that fire."

She still held his cheeks, her touch a spark of temptation that made him want to stay. Climb into the bed with her, take the peace that flowed from her touch.

"I know they called you the Smoke Charmer, but you were wrong about that fire with the dog. You were wrong yesterday when you thought the fire was coming and we should reformulate the digging plan. It didn't show up while we worked. If all that's happened has thrown soot on your crystal ball, then you have to rely on the judgment of others until you get it cleared off. And you need to talk to someone about it."

He stepped fully back out of her bedroom then, and to her credit she didn't chase him, just let go and stood there in the doorway, looking at him with those big, worried eyes.

"Treadwell wants to understand."

"He's ill. I'm not dumping all this on him."

"He'll be back. And if he's not, he still deserves to know what he's been beating his head against. Not understanding what's shifted in you, someone he clearly values, is unfair to him. It's unfair to you."

Unfair to him? He shook his head, refusing to give that another thought. He'd had two days giving everything he had physically, and no sleep. He needed to sleep. If he couldn't sleep now, then he'd just gone through all that for nothing.

A siren blast rocketed through the camp about the same time as the troops were normally called to morning PT, and jerked Lauren awake from sleep.

Heart pounding, one thought came: *I'm late.*

Stumbling from the bed, she fumbled to the bureau, not even needing to turn the lights on to see what she was doing. It was early, but the sun had warmed the skies enough to send something brighter than twilight through her window. She could see shapes, grab knobs to the correct drawers.

Inside, she grabbed blindly and came out with shorts,

socks, underthings and a T-shirt, of some random color combination. Her breathing took the form of the kind of labored panting usually accompanying a hard run just from wrestling her uncooperative body into her clothes.

With no time to fix her hair, or anything else, she grabbed a hair band and her shoes, and made it into the main room about the same time as Beck.

He looked similarly wild and out of sorts.

"You overslept too?" She choked the words out while hopping toward the door, trying to cram her feet into her sneakers.

The question stopped him staggering around and he shook his head. "It's Saturday..."

"Saturday?" She fell off-balance, smashing one shoulder into the wall and landing on her bum on the floor as his meaning dawned on her. "We're not late?"

"No."

"They're just messing with us?"

He thought a second, then shook his head. "Doubt it."

"But we're supposed to go to the field..."

He grabbed his own shoes, looking more and more certain. "That's what that siren always means."

They were either being tested and put off-balance for a reason, or something was wrong.

She took the time while on the floor to get her other shoe on, and gathered her hair back as neatly as she could in a few seconds, wrapped it in the hair band and was ready to accept the hand up Beck offered as he got to the door.

"Something happened, didn't it?"

"I think so."

His black eyes had the puffy, sleepy-five-year-old softness of someone who'd slept very hard. At least his midnight confessional had done the trick.

She probably looked no better, and that would continue if this day was going to go the way it seemed about to go.

They ran for the field. Others she recognized from earlier in the week before their teams had been deployed to the hellfire up north arrived at the same time, along with the rookies.

Kolinski jogged onto the field shortly after they got there, and delivered orders. They needed more bodies, but only three rookies had been cleared to go: Beck, Alvarez and *Autry*.

It was still a good couple of miles behind the current side-wall, but wind was a crazy thing and with a storm coming in it was definitely going to change directions. The plan was the same as they'd done Thursday—controlled burns to consume the fuel, but somewhat closer, with a jump to reach it.

Her palms started to sweat, and she did her best to ignore them.

Not a jump *into* the fire, a jump to the *other* side of the fire.

The fire up north had ravaged the mountains all week and had already chewed through three subdivisions and countless thousands of acres of woodland. Where they'd be going was hard to reach, but might keep it from spreading back in the direction of civilization, and that was as good a reason as any to ignore that voice in her head questioning whether she could do this.

Not jumping *into* the fire. The whole mission was skydiving with the goal of digging a lot when she got where she was supposed to go.

That wasn't so bad.

She could do that, even if she hadn't technically ever done the first bit fully before.

She'd practiced with the tower all week. With the months of on and off and simulator training when she'd been unable to actually go up in the air.

Don't panic.

"You all right?" Beck's voice cut through her mental tap dancing to shore up her confidence.

She managed to look at him like he was nuts for asking, because outward confidence was something she'd learned to fake a long time ago with occasional blips. It was the inner monologue she really struggled with, and tried to never let anyone see, past glimpses that made her new partner suspicious.

"Of course I am. This is like…a *jump*! For real. I'm totally ready." Lie. Lie until it's true. "Excited!"

The look he gave her said he bought it about as much as she did.

When she got into the plane, everything would be fine. It was just the shock of wrapping her head around the new, surprising turn of events. And the realization that she couldn't unwind this without doing actual damage to her career. Plenty of motivation to muscle through.

Once she'd made this jump, she'd have that experience she still regretted not correcting on her application. This one jump would set things right, she could actually claim skydiving experience. So it was good. Better than good. She wouldn't have to keep looking over her shoulder, wondering when they were going to find out she had no experience.

Even better, if she went up today, she'd get to help stop the fire from plowing into the next inhabited zone. Protect the families there. Maybe stop from happening to some other kid what had happened to Beck.

The pressure she'd felt in her head suddenly lifted, and her mental pep talk stopped being something she had to convince herself of. She *felt* it and it comforted her. Mostly.

She could do this.

All she had to do was throw herself out of a plane into a great big fire.

No, *near* a big fire. Not in. Near the fire. Everything would be fine.

Then she'd know for sure everyone, including herself, had been wrong about her.

* * *

No matter what she'd learned in school, Lauren was now convinced time didn't flow at anything in the vicinity of a constant speed. She'd blinked and perhaps acquired the ability to teleport or bend time. She was suddenly on the plane, fully suited with people moving ahead of her at a steady pace to exit the small, low-flying cargo plane. Their static lines were clipped along the tethers that would see their chutes open when they exited. In the front were the most seasoned, with the rookies—Alvarez, her and Beck—at the end.

He was the caboose on this crazy train, moving behind her so she had to keep going. All she knew was a dwindling line of people that stood between her stupid, trembling body and the open air. And that she couldn't feel her face.

This wasn't a situation where people paused and then jumped when they were ready. It was programmed through all training that you leaped as soon as you got to the exit. So the pace? Her heart was the only thing moving faster.

Alvarez went, which meant it was her turn. She was there at the door, and in her mind she had one leg lifted and ready to spring into the nothing, but instead of tucking, her arms shot out instinctively and grabbed the sides of the port to stop herself.

From high above, even though they wouldn't be landing near the thick of it, she could see the bright glowing reds and orange of the fire and the extent of it.

Throwing herself into a big fire.

Something nudged her from behind, not hard, just a suggestion she go, but she pedaled backward instead, plowing Beck back with her until she was a good four feet from the door.

He shouted something, but she didn't hear it. All she knew was him suddenly moving around her, and hooking his line back in.

When he looked at her again, what she saw made her

heart fall further than she would have if she'd stepped out. That wasn't pity she saw in his dark eyes. It was judgment.

He didn't say anything, just shook his head and stepped right on out of the plane, which had her hurtling to the portal again and craning to see his chute open.

There was a certain amount of time in which to jump and stay with your crew. And now she had to go, didn't she? He'd gone. She was his partner. She was his partner and she was leaving him to go down there without someone specifically watching his back. That was definitely a strike.

Crap!

There was no backing out now. She'd signed up. She'd given her word. She'd said she could do the job. If she couldn't jump now, what good was she? She'd fail, not because someone else thought she wasn't up to the task but because *she wasn't up to the task.*

Her stomach lurched and the breakfast they'd all inhaled on the bus en route to the hangar rose up.

If she didn't jump, they were all right about her.

The plane tilted a little, starting to turn back. If she didn't jump now, it was all over.

Before she could let herself think further, before she could miss that window, she stepped out of the door.

Immediately her training kicked in. She tucked her traitorous arms and ducked her head so that brief free fall didn't result in injury or a chute malfunction when it snapped her back and unfurled to carry her aloft over the hellish landscape.

Breathing was harder than she'd expected, some combination of the wind rushing against her face and how hard her heart beat probably. She gripped the straps of the chute and held up, but kept her face turned into her upper arm for a wind buffer until she caught her breath.

Time still meant nothing. She could've drifted down for an hour or a few seconds, however long it took her to get the hang of breathing, then she let herself look around and appreciate the landscape. The fiery landscape.

And the distinct lack of any other parachutes in the sky with her.

Twisting as best she could in the harness, she tried to spot them behind her, but saw nothing. Recalling training advice, she tried to steer herself gently around to spot them, but they hadn't jumped from high up, and when she got the thing spun the direction she thought she'd wanted, the only thing she saw was fire. Rapidly approaching fire.

How long had she failed to jump? It hadn't seemed that long...

CHAPTER EIGHT

DISAPPOINTMENT HUNG AROUND him longer than Beck hung in the treetop he'd gotten tangled in landing. He'd really expected her to jump. She'd projected such an air of fear-lessness.

She'd still frozen. He should've seen it coming, the way she'd paled and babbled over the prospect of it earlier. Got too far in her own head. Psyched herself out.

He pulled a knife from his belt and hacked through the ropes holding him up.

The tree he'd hit was two trees past the clearing he'd aimed for, and a quick survey confirmed that the best way down was up one stretch of a branch and around to the back where he could find a better path down.

He probably shouldn't have jumped without her. Did that count as a partnership failure? Who even knew?

He went up and around, using the height to spot where to go to get his suit and supplies. That was when he saw another white chute drifting down, far off target from the zone.

He'd been the last to jump.

His heart stopped cold for a second, and then began to hammer and bang around in his suddenly cold, hollow chest.

It was her. It had to be her.

He'd barely made the jump window, and they'd been

flying *toward* the fire, that direction had provided the best with the current wind patterns. And she'd jumped late. She'd jumped far too late.

Damn it.

He was supposed to be climbing down, getting his gear, getting to work, and instead he gripped the branches, holding on, his eyes fixed on her descent to the fire.

She was trying to spin it out, he could see the angle of the chute change as she did her best to steer it, including her legs stretching and twisting helplessly. The wind had her.

She was going down in the fire.

"Ellison!"

A voice barked through his comm. He should answer, but it was one more thing to do when he was barely managing the two things most important for his survival: holding onto the branches and following her progress against the burning mountainside they'd jumped to.

Just when he thought he was going to watch her spiral into the fire, she turned her chute toward the blaze, and straightened out, catching a wind gust. It blew her harder and faster, and maybe farther? Maybe into a pocket?

God, he couldn't tell. All he knew was trees and fire as he saw the white canopy of her chute disappear over the burning edge of the hillside.

"Ellison! *Answer.*"

Hands shaking, he continued to grip one branch but managed to press his earpiece and call out his position. "In a tree. Coming down. Does anyone see where Autry landed?"

He couldn't see anything else from up there. The only thing to do was get down, get suited, and see if there was a path for him to reach her and get her out of the fire. He could pack a suit for her on his back—she was only in her jump suit, no protection against the flames.

He wasn't a praying man, but in that moment he longed for the comfort of such faith.

Why had he jumped without her? He shouldn't have jumped. They were supposed to be partners, and he'd just told her less than thirty-six hours ago that he wouldn't go off on his own.

"She jumped late," someone said over the comm. And then, "Spotter said she's down in a small clearing. Landed hard. Not moving. Not answering attempts to raise her on the comm."

No. No. No. *No.*

"Is she in the blaze?" he asked through the comm.

"Not yet. Unless she doesn't get up and start moving. She has an exit if she's conscious."

He swung down from the tree and scrambled up the downslope he'd landed on to the clearing that had been targeted for landing. His team was there, gathered around the crates dropped with gear and supplies.

If she was conscious, she could either hike out to the nearest road or to another team—maybe one working the edges of the blaze, not at the safer distance of him and the crew.

"Can I reach her?" he asked, hurrying toward the group as they gathered around the dropped supplies.

There was a pause. He reached the group, and Kolinski, owner of the disembodied voice he'd been conversing with, shook his head to his question.

The wave of terror and adrenaline that had gotten him out of the tree seemed to solidify and turn to lead in his body, slowing his movements, slowing his feet, grinding his thoughts to a complete stop.

She'd landed where she was bracketed in by the fire. Not moving. Not answering.

He didn't even need to ask her why she'd jumped. He knew. God help him. She'd jumped because she couldn't let herself fail, but she'd also jumped because of him. He'd gone off and she'd chased him.

If they'd stayed on the plane, there were things they could've done—aided the spotters to direct the ground crews about changes in directions of the beast. Gone back to base to pack supplies for extra runs. Mount rescues for those who needed help. She needed help.

"Ellison. Get it together." Kolinski whacked the back of his head, jarring his thoughts loose from the spiral they'd funneled into. "Did you hear what I said?"

"Get it together," Beck repeated dully, the sense of detachment from his body growing stronger with every passing second.

"I said she's up."

Beck clicked his comm and called her, twice, but got no answer. His breaths were sharp, like knives going through him sideways, and he had to work to shove words through a throat that felt almost closed. "She's up?"

"She landed hard. Looks like her comm is busted."

"Is she hurt?"

"Not sure, but she's up."

"Who are they sending after her?"

Kolinski looked at him a hard second, then shook his head. "She has a map and compass, emergency supplies in her pack. It's on her to hike out and she'll do that. It's SOP."

Not enough. He'd throw away his responsibilities to the crew and go after her at that second if he knew where she'd landed.

Kolinski seemed to see that on his face too, and thrust a saw into his hands. "You're cutting."

All he could do was nod and make his body start working again, stripping off his jumpsuit and making for the real gear. "I want every update. If she starts going the wrong direction, I'm going after her, even if it's the end of my job."

The lieutenant nodded once, then pointed to the treeline in the southeast. "We need a wide firebreak. Cut ruthlessly."

* * *

Don't panic.

First rule of survival in a bad situation: Don't. Panic.

Lauren worked herself free from the lines of her parachute, which had wrapped around her as she'd rolled.

It wasn't on fire. She wasn't on fire. Her hands shook, but her fingers still obeyed when she found the buckles on her chute and got them open.

How had she rolled through that without catching fire? They weren't flame retardant... Felt like a miracle.

Heat baked in from three sides, causing her to sweat badly enough for her feet to slide around in boots just a touch too big for her.

She needed to move. Her suit wasn't the kind of gear made for facing a fire. They had to jump as light as they could, carrying only meager survival packs, with the expectation they'd regroup at the dropped supplies. That's what she should be doing.

Instead, she was surrounded by fire, and had just noticed her right shoulder throbbed in a way she could only think meant damage. Her heart slammed so hard and fast it might wear out at any second. So hard she couldn't hear anything but her heart beating in her ears. Was her comm even working? Were they coming for her? Did she even want them to do that?

North looked open. She began scrambling up the only bare spot of slope she'd been able to reach with her bad drop zone. The peak wasn't far. Then she'd be able to see what she was up against. She didn't know how far the nonburning patch of earth continued. It could be that just over the rise she'd find another firewall.

What had she seen on the way down?

Fire.

Lots of freaking fire.

She'd been blinded to anything else—just the fire and her efforts to steer her chute away from it.

If she didn't get better at this job fast, she might as well quit when she got out. If she got out.

The earpiece in her ear squawked suddenly, cutting through the swishing, pounding awfulness in her ears, then nothing. No time to stop and check it, she kept going.

Gasping from some motivating cocktail of heat, effort, fear, and pain, she made it to a clear spot at the top and the downslope spread out before her, a large valley of green. Not leaping red, orange, and yellow. Not burning. The fire blanketed the south behind her, and stretched out east and west, but north was clear. For now. Who knew how fast the fire was moving?

Go north. Get out of the oven. She'd be okay.

Get to the bottom of the valley, then stop to get directions and to see if her comm could be repaired.

"You can do this. It's just a hike. A vigorous, terrifying hike. Downhill. See? That's perfect. Downhill is awesome. It'll be fast." Sometimes an internal pep talk wasn't enough. Sometimes the words needed to be said out loud to drown out that damned internal voice of criticism she was so prone to hearing. The words even made it over the pounding in her ears while the roar and crackling of fire and trees splitting she should be hearing didn't.

Probably some kind of delusion.

Halfway down the slope, when the ground became a gentler incline, she plucked the earpiece out, found the wires apparently intact, but tugged on them a little bit to test the connection anyway. Looked right. She put it back in, tugged at the base of the wires, then slapped the box a couple of times. Nothing happened. As if banging broken electronics ever fixed them.

Should she turn it off and turn it on? Pop the batteries? Lord, she didn't know how to fix things. Why didn't she know how to fix things?

More importantly, why had she jumped?

Just thinking of the leap summoned the sensation of

free fall, those seconds before her chute had jerked her up clung to her, and got worse when she started berating herself for this failure. Another failure.

Why had she even gone up? She should've told them. She should've just *told* them. Confessed her error. It was an error, not made with malicious intent. Just an error that fear had exacerbated.

If she'd told them, at least then she would've scratched out of training because of her stupid application miscalculation, but at least she'd be alive for her family to give her hell over it.

Beck made it back to camp with daylight still lighting the skies, but came into an empty cabin.

Lauren wasn't back yet.

She'd had to hike out by herself because of him, and he still didn't know if she'd been retrieved or if she was still in the woods.

He slammed into the cabin, then straight on to the shower. He'd ridden a spike of terror all day, and stank of it.

There was nothing to do but keep busy. Keep busy and do the things that needed doing. Clean up. Get dinner. Get *two* dinners, so if she got back after they closed up evening chow she could still eat something. Something besides an MRE, because, God knew, those were awful.

The thought of food ration packs conjured the chemical taste he always had to fight to ignore when choking them down. But standing in the shower, he let himself consider every aspect of that fake, preservative-laden bite. It was better than the thoughts that had been consuming him since he'd seen her parachute drifting toward the flames.

Lauren burning. Fire eating through the suit she'd jumped in, turning her golden, beautiful skin to char. Her long caramel hair gone. Skin cracking.

He'd never actually seen someone burn, and he'd avoided movies with those kinds of special effects, but he knew what fire did. He knew the sound of bacon popping on the griddle. He knew what a forest looked like after a wildfire had consumed it. Even wood blistered and cracked in that kind of heat. Skin was nothing by comparison. He could picture it. Had been picturing it in ever increasing detail since he was a child, when his mind had been without the knowledge required to summon nightmarish levels of detail. Like it could now.

MREs and their cocktail of chemical flavors were heaven to think of by comparison.

Fake butter flavor.

The metallic taste of tomato sauces when the chemical heat was applied.

He made it through the shower, dried, dressed, and went on to the next task. Always the next task. He checked in with the office for word, learned she'd been picked up, sore and slightly injured. Went to get dinners.

Picked pine needles and tied them up in a cloth, getting salts ready for the soaking bath she'd probably need if she'd landed hard enough to kill her comm.

Then he sat on the front stoop of the small cabin and waited. Waited and tried to listen to the frogs singing in the woods behind.

Stopping Lauren from going up this morning when he could see how it unnerved her would've really pissed her off, but it would've been for her own good. Making her take time off now that she was injured would also be for her own good. Was she hurt badly enough to bow out until next year? God help the man who suggested such a thing to her.

He didn't see her small frame slogging across the dark field until she was almost on him, and it took every ounce of willpower not to rush over and scoop her up, frisk her for injuries, shout at her, shake her…kiss her.

Lauren stopped in her tracks, looking at him like he was everything wrong in her life.

"Are you hurt?" he asked, trying to play it cool as he rose from the cabin steps.

In answer, she walked forward, then turned sideways to get past him and up the few steps into the cabin.

There was nothing to do but follow.

And, because he could feel big emotions weighting the air like a summer storm, he closed the door behind him.

"You didn't answer." He reached to take her shoulder to spin her and look for injuries, but at the first touch she ducked and turned, smacking his hands away. In the low light of the cabin her scowl was unmistakable.

And she was hurt, he realized dully. She was right-handed, and had smacked at him with her left hand, her right arm held close to her body.

"Let me see."

"Shut up. You left me on the plane. You jumped without me!"

"I know…" He didn't reach for her again. Not yet, but the desire still lit him and his hand hovered between them, as far from his body as it was close to hers. "Let me see your arm. How did you hurt it? Is it broken?"

"It's bruised," she grunted, and shoved at his hand again with her left hand. "You're an awful partner, you know that, right?"

"I do." He tugged his hair back from his face, trying to stretch his scalp and defuse the tension headache he'd been nursing.

"Why did you just jump like that? Why didn't you say something to me? Ask what was wrong? Maybe there was some reason I didn't jump."

Her equipment had been checked before they'd boarded the plane, that was something Kolinski had been adamant about—checking the rookies' equipment. He'd known there hadn't been anything wrong with her pack. It had been inside, and he'd seen it before they'd even gotten on the bus to go to the hangar.

"You panicked."

She flung that one good arm up and in the very next second her eyes were wet and every ounce of angry color lurking behind her dirty cheeks drained away. "I *know*!"

"It's okay. It happens…"

"No, it's not okay. It doesn't happen to people who've… been…who've…" She stopped and shook her head, then started jerking at the flight suit's zip, wrestling it down so clumsily that he felt compelled to step closer and help with that, but did it with slow, open-palmed motions that let her know he wasn't going to do anything bad, just help.

Maybe taking care of that physical stuff would let her mouth take care of whatever wanted to come out. "People who've jumped into wildfires?"

The zipper eased down with her not jerking on it. He watched the slow descent, opening to the strong, supple body he knew he'd find beneath. She was dressed in shorts and a top, nothing too revealing, but a surge of heat still hit his middle and he had to step away, especially as her scent hit him.

"People who have jumped from a plane before." She whispered the words, pulling his gaze back to hers.

Even whispered, the words jarred. "What?"

"I never jumped before," she said, a little more firmly.

"Low altitude?"

"No altitude!" Her voice started to rise again, panic coming out despite the fact that her feet were firmly on the ground now.

"Why did you say you had?"

She'd lied her way into the air?

If he'd known earlier… Holy, blessed nature, he'd have hog-tied her to keep her off the plane.

The look of unconcealed helplessness she gave him made him want to shake her again.

He hadn't known her long, not really, but he knew that

she faked confidence when she didn't feel it. She'd done that this morning. And every day this week.

Right now, she was upset, scared, and either too over-whelmed to hide it or just didn't care enough to hide it any-more. Neither sounded good.

He should've figured it out by now, after all the signs today. That hint of fear at being told about the tower had made her go white. So had word they were going up. Then her inability to jump, and the god-awful landing. Landings were hard at first, and landing in a small patch of earth surrounded by fire without smashing into trees? It was a miracle she wasn't dead.

"Why the hell didn't you say something?" he asked, curling his fingers into his palms so he didn't shake her as she was already injured.

"I panicked! I panicked because I'm in totally over my head. Everything Dad said was right. I didn't mean for this to happen. I just… Things happened and everything snow-balled and I didn't know how to get out of it. And now I'm done. They're going to come and ask what happened, and I'm going to have to tell them and they're going to boot me out for lying on my application. Before I get myself killed, or worse, get someone else killed. I should've been able to do it. I should be able to do it. It's in my freaking DNA! Unless it's carried on the Y chromosome, hah!" The short, barked laugh hit like a slap. "He was right. He was right and I'm… I should just go be a *baker* or something."

The long self-berating babble stopped his anger cold.

Her left hand flew all over, gesturing, ranting, but she kept that right one to her chest.

He wasn't sure where this was going but, knowing she dealt with sexism in regard to the job, felt the need to point out, "I don't think being a woman has anything to do with you screwing this up."

"Thank you for that!" she grunted, then went right back into her self-targeted tirade. "Actually, I guess I'm selling my aunts and grandmothers short. They weren't just people who minded the kitchen. They were reporters. People who talked about all the heroics the menfolk got up to. Scrapbooks. They all made scrapbooks with the newspaper clippings. You know half that stuff they have on the history of the department at the local history museum is from the Autry women. Those fine scrapbookers."

Scrapbookers. Yep, she'd gone well past the point where sense was going to make a dent in this.

"Are you hungry? I brought food…"

"Man, now I feel bad because it sounds like I hate scrapbooks. I don't hate scrapbooks. I love them. I loved looking at them and reading all of them. Even the ones I had to wear those weird white gloves to handle. I just didn't want to make them. I don't have that talent. Maybe I don't have this one either. I want to be doing the things, actually help people. Is it wrong to want to do the things?"

"Stop," he said softly, and to stop her prowling around stepped close enough to breathe her in again. The fire she'd come so close to had left a smoky hint to that honey and dirt he still smelled, and grounded him again in what had almost happened.

Her voice dropped as well, the fire going out of it. "Stop what?"

"Take a breath." They both needed to take a breath. "Tell me what happened."

"On my application I said I had experience because I was supposed to have gotten it by the time it became relevant. But that's not what happened. Between all the things with my family and work, I just had no extra time. I didn't get the experience I'd planned for."

"Skydiving experience isn't a requirement. They train from the beginning, you know that. You don't move like someone without training."

"Maybe it's not a requirement for you!" Her volume went back up, but it was more like despair than anger pitching

her words. "I didn't have it last time, and I didn't make it.
I wanted to cover my bases. Got a trainer three times a
week at the gym. Got skydiving classes and went as far as
I could with them. When the application deadline came,
I should've had time to make the jumps. I even had them
scheduled and paid for when I filled out the application. But
my schedule got blown up and time ran out and then they
sorted us into different training level groups and I didn't
know how to backpedal the situation without completely
wrecking everything."

Despair and disgust with herself, and those beautiful
eyes that searched his, as if he had any solutions. Beck
did the only other thing he could think of, wrapped his
arms around her and tugged enough to get her that last
step to him.

She froze, stiff as an oak in his arms, and possibly
stopped breathing except she whispered, "You're hugging
me…"

"Yeah…" He tilted his head to the side as she tilted hers
up, dirty, pink, exhausted, and in that second devoid of all
the awful emotions that had been written in capital letters
on her face. "You should be warned, I'm also kind of thinking of kissing you. But that would probably be a bad idea."

Bad, and not something he did anymore. He just preferred to live his life on his own, free of the mess that came
with relationships. His celibacy had even become easy at
this point. And yet, with this woman, he wanted to forget all the reasons it was a bad idea to get more involved.

She nodded in return, but not in the way of someone who
believed, or even knew what she was agreeing to.

"I'm going to be kicked out anyway when I tell them
the truth."

She lifted her ranting hand and brushed the tips of her
fingers down his cheek. She wanted the kiss. And if that
wasn't obvious, she stared now at his mouth like her gaze
could act like a rope to pull him in closer.

It worked. Beck felt his head lowering, and her beautiful green eyes swiveled to his once more, wide and watchful until the first brush of his lips. The hand that had been a light, tender touch at his cheek slid back, hooking around his neck to pull him closer. The boldness he'd come to expect from her before tonight was nowhere to be found. She didn't demand so much as plead for a firmer embrace, deeper kisses, in the way she melted into him, and the way her tiny wanting sounds tickled his lips.

CHAPTER NINE

LAUREN HAD HEARD the old adage that confession was good for the soul but had never actually believed it. Confession meant consequences. Worse, it meant you'd failed at something, and that something was your fault. She'd done both today—had failed, and it had been her fault.

But her confession had brought a reward, a bone-melting kiss that distracted her mind and knocked the charred edges off a terrible, terrifying day. If she was smart, she wouldn't get used to it. Telling that to anyone, even this man with lips like silk, was the first brick gone in the complete dismantling of her career.

He held her close, relief pouring through her—hers, his, and built-in permission to let herself not be strong for once, to lean on him and borrow some of his strength.

He'd been worried, felt guilty, desperate. He'd cared, and his kisses were tinted with it, a shot of bitter with the sweet.

He'd had to be locked in a police cruiser to keep him from going after the fireman. Had they had to restrain him today to keep him from coming for her? Had his own actions been the lesson he'd needed to be a better team member, to not run off and abandon his team?

Was she just grasping at straws because she desperately needed a win? Maybe. But held tight against his strong frame, she let herself indulge in the fantasy that everything was fine now, and surviving was the happy ending they both needed.

His arms tightened around her waist, and she had to ease her right arm out of the space between their chests to wrap over his shoulders, needing to be closer too.

Kissing him was like an opiate. She barely felt the pain in her shoulder and the various bruises she'd yet to take inventory of. She barely felt the fear and dread of what was coming next. It was just a slow descent into honeyed warmth and blissful *nothing*. Supporting her weight in his arms, her toes lightly traced back and forth as he swayed with her, rocking away the horrible.

"Someone's here," he suddenly said against her lips, and she realized a second later she'd heard a knock at the door too.

"Kolinski." She whispered his name.

His arms relaxed slowly and she found herself on the floor before him, unable to tear her eyes off his mouth.

His…sooty mouth.

"Go wash your mouth. He's here for me."

"He'll want to talk to me too."

She tried again, gesturing to her own mouth. "Nose to chin, you've got a sooty clown mouth thing going on."

He looked completely baffled at her and she almost grinned.

"Didn't you ever get a lipstick smear before?"

"I never wear lipstick," he said, expression too serious except for a slight lifting of the corner of his sooty mouth. Joking. He was joking.

She grinned and played along, the teasing making things better somehow. "You'd look really nice in a soft, beachy coral."

Kolinski pounded on the door again, and she stepped back, giving Beck a small shove toward the bathroom while she went to face the music.

Her right arm clamped right back to her body because

the pain surged as her senses returned, she opened the door. "Come in, Lieutenant."

Kolinski only stepped in far enough to close the door behind him, and looked past her to Beck, who was drying his face.

"Who wants to tell me what happened up there?"

Beck looked at her a second, and she lifted her good hand, ready to spill the beans, when he cut in.

"I screwed up," he announced, keeping his eyes on the lieutenant, not responding to her wide *what are you doing?* eyes. "In the past week I've become…attached to Autry. When it came to it today, I tried to get her not to jump because I hadn't ever seen her make an actual jump before and panicked about her going for the first time over a fire."

Lauren didn't have to look in a mirror or have anyone ask, she felt her mouth fall open at Beck's words.

He was taking the blame for her screwup.

He was *covering* for her. Making sure her stupid lie didn't come out. It was such a thing that could never happen, she wasn't even certain it *was* happening.

"What did you do to make her not jump?" Kolinski asked, then looked at her, which prompted her to try and close her mouth again because she didn't know what to say.

Beck clearly hadn't put any thought into this plan. He *umm*ed a couple times, then said, "Said some nasty things about her being…not ready."

"You said nasty things about her not being ready, then went ahead of her and told her not to jump?"

"Yeah."

It sounded like a lie. It was so obviously a lie. Kolinski crossed his arms and stared at Beck, then included her in his stare. It was a lot harder to lie with your mouth than with pen and paper and the shame of poor follow-through on your planning.

Beck's jaw had clamped shut. She could feel her own

stunned expression like a mask on her face. Neither of them looked normal. They looked like liars.

Liars Kolinski was playing along with. "So he jumped without you and you decided to go anyway?"

"He…" She didn't want to blame him, and she really didn't want to lie anymore. They'd accept it if she said she needed more of a refresher before going back up, or if she asked to be bumped back with the rest of the rookies.

Whatever she said, she couldn't let him lie for her.

"I panicked when I saw the fire below," Lauren admitted, then added, "Beck's trying to help me now because he's my partner. And maybe because he feels bad for having jumped when I was struggling. He went ahead, it's his job, then I started feeling like a total failure and made myself go. Didn't think so much time had passed. It was my fault. He's just trying to look out for his partner now."

She didn't know what to think about that grown-attached business, so she didn't say anything about that.

Kolinski shifted his gaze from one to the other for several long, heart-stopping seconds. "If you've got a romance going on and it's screwing everything up, you should both be re-partnered."

"We don't need to be re-partnered," Lauren said quickly, shaking her head. "He was just covering."

Beck backed her up then. "It was a glitch. We both screwed up and it won't happen again. I'm trying. She's helping me…"

Kolinski nodded. "She knows?"

Beck nodded once.

The lieutenant shifted his gaze to her then. "Did you have your arm looked at?"

"I did. It's bruised."

"Not broken? Not sprained?"

She shook her head.

"Okay, then this is a warning. Formal paperwork will be

in your boxes tomorrow. Get your act together. One more and you're both out."

Kolinski delivered his lovely parting words then left, and Lauren locked the door behind him.

Then she was back at Beck's side, completely unable to summon the words to ask why he'd done that, gone to bat for her, lumped his fate in with hers.

"It was my fault. Stupid. I shouldn't have jumped. I shouldn't have gone up there. I can't let you *lie* for me."

"I was trying to have your back. Share the blame." He sounded a little put out, but there was nothing to be done for it. "And it was my fault too. You were my partner and I abandoned you. We have to do better than this."

"Why was this strike two? What was strike one?" She hadn't gotten anything official in her box before.

His lips thinned again, and he grunted. "Probably the day we burned the field."

When she'd had to chase him all over. He'd earned them that strike, but they'd both earned today's.

She nodded, and when she found herself looking at his mouth again, stepped back toward the bathroom. "I need to soak this grime off. And…erm…we should…we should file that whole…kissing thing under the *Romance Leads to Re-partnering* column, and, you know, maybe don't do it. We can't afford to get distracted."

"Kolinski did look against the idea of something going on," Beck said, brow beetled in the kind of deep thinking that never led to good outcomes. "I'll get the pine needles."

She'd almost gotten the door closed when his palm suddenly touched down and pushed it back open a bit. "After I see that arm."

"Beck…"

He shook his head. "I'm not leaving until I know how bad it is."

It sounded a lot like the kinds of words that usually ticked her off, but considering his attempt to help her with

Kolinski… She sighed and unzipped the suit and eased it down to her waist, baring the simple tank top she wore beneath.

"See? Not broken."

She barely got the words out when he sucked in a sharp breath and began muttering under his breath.

"It's okay."

She didn't want to look at it, she'd seen enough of the eggplant-colored splotch earlier when the EMT had checked her over, and seeing his reaction was enough to confirm it wasn't any better.

His touch was gentle, but he didn't shy away from making her move her arm, testing her range of motion through her wincing, making sure that ball joint functioned the way it was supposed to. "It's not broken, it's bruised."

"You need a sling."

"I don't need a sling."

"You've been keeping it clamped to your chest to stabilize it because it hurts. You need a damned sling, Lauren." He scrubbed his hands over his face and paced away then back to her. "In the morning, I'll get you one from the infirmary."

It was on the tip of her tongue to deny needing a sling again, but maybe it would help things heal faster. It would certainly help his mood.

"Okay. I'll wear a sling for a couple of days until it feels better."

He turned back to her, surprise pitching his eyebrows to high, crazy angles.

"What? I can compromise."

"Okay." He nodded, hands on his hips. "Can you accept help too?"

"You just helped. I let you."

"With jumping."

She stopped, the subject shift throwing her. "What…? Which part?"

"How we can fix it." His tilted his head and the way his black eyes fixed on her said as much as his words. How *we* can fix it. Not how *you* can fix it. We.

One simple word and the weight that had been crushing her lifted, letting her stand straighter, letting her smile again.

This was it. This was what having a partner felt like. She had to look away from those deep, meaningful looks to hide the mistiness in her eyes.

"You have an idea?"

"You know you can make the jump, but you need to practice landing." He let go of the door and nodded to her shoulder. "Don't worry about it now. A man I served with has a plane, operates a small business out of the local airport. I'll see if he'll take us up in a couple of days."

Us. The sweet ping of pleasure in her chest at the word only grew warmer as she caught up to the rest of it. He was going to *help* her, even after she'd refused to let him take the fall for her. Even after everything.

He'd already started moving again, saying something about salts. Another way he was helping.

She had to find a way to help him too, she just didn't know how.

The weekend passed for Lauren in a blur. She slept so long on Saturday Beck had come into her room to wake her up and make her go to dinner. She'd been having a dream so over-sexed she was sure he'd known. No one moaned when being woken up. That was never the appropriate reaction.

Lauren?

Moan.

Not at all humiliating. And the goofy smile? Yep. Just added to it. She might as well have moaned his name. She might *have* moaned his name.

If she had, he'd been blessedly tight-lipped about it. Just insisted she wear the sling he'd gotten for her, and not use her arm to do anything, despite him dragging her to the mess hall directly after. She'd missed breakfast and lunch, and healing bodies need protein, and blah-blah-blah.

He'd provided her with another sachet of pine needles and his tub-o-salts to put together her own soak afterward and gone to sleep outside for a reason he'd never explained, and she didn't ask about. Maybe he'd needed fresh air. Maybe he'd just wanted some distance from her so he didn't tempt her to more kissing…

God, she probably *had* moaned his name.

Sunday she'd been the one to make an escape—first shopping to lay in some supplies, then the Laundromat with her soiled *everything*, and her arm in the darned sling.

By Monday, she was feeling better, and although they still required her to be on another day of light duty—no push-ups or the tree-climbing designated for classroom work that day—she talked her way into being allowed the use of both arms. And she ran. In the morning, in the afternoon, and all without any existential emotional flare-ups. Another small miracle. Or a sign of her growth. She'd like to think so, at least.

Tuesday her week started to turn around. Beck got in touch with his marine buddy and as it was no longer *Hell Week*, they had somewhat shorter days, which left time to go up with Gavin, the pilot, for three low-altitude jumps to practice jumping and landing.

Her shoulder had done fine.

Between jumps, Beck had given pointers on how to land without breaking anything.

Wednesday they did it again.

Now, suited up and sitting in Gavin's plane, flying two counties away to a forest that had burned last week, Lauren turned to her partner-cum-trainer. "Why are we going to jump over an old burn again?"

"All new smokejumpers should see the aftermath of a forest fire."

"I was in actively burning woods. What am I supposed to be learning from that?"

"Devastation." He hadn't had them fly out this far for no reason, but she understood fire. It took a little work to not be insulted by the insinuation that she was unfamiliar with the destruction left behind, reminding herself he took fires personally. He saw fires like monsters, not natural things. Maybe *he* was the one who needed to come to the fire. Or maybe he just needed to be convinced she understood it.

If that was it, that was fine. She could deal with that. He didn't have to help her with this, and if his conscience demanded he make sure she fully understood what she was getting into, that was okay too.

"Are we climbing higher?"

A look out the window confirmed the land was much farther away than their two previous days of jumps.

"Higher altitude means longer time steering the chute. We're going to circle the woods and land in the burned field beside them so you can learn to maneuver better. You're landing well, now you need better control in the air. You had trouble turning that first day."

"We're here, you two," Gavin called back, interrupting her complete lack of an argument.

Beck handed her a helmet. "Ear bud inside and mic embedded in the mouth area of the helmet. Use the comm. I'll instruct on the way down. Tell me when you have trouble."

A minute later, she was in the air, her chute popping as expected, with Beck somewhere behind her. He'd jumped after she had. That was now always the new rule of jumping: he always went second so he could see if she had trouble.

Beck's voice came over the headset soon after, reminding her what she was doing while simultaneously distracting her. If she'd known how intimate it would be to have his voice in her ear, or that she'd feel it in tingles down her neck, she might have argued against it. She was supposed to be focused on mastering a new skill, not tingling in fun ways.

In truth, in just a few short days her confidence in the air had reached what she'd hoped it would be before entering the training program. The next time she was called to a real jump, she'd be fine. That was because of him. Had nothing to do with the goose bumps that swept over her from a deep, sexy voice in her ear, or the way the tiny hairs on the back of her neck stood up and saluted when his breath hit the mic and her brain supplied the sensation that would've accompanied his breath were he getting steamy in her actual ear.

She had to remind herself to start circling, but as they got closer and the blackened patch of earth became bare, broken trees, her lusty feelings evaporated. Before she knew it, her feet touched down in the burned field and she skidded along with a gust of wind dragging her chute, then rolled to a proper stop when the wind died, and was glad for the helmet protecting her face.

She gathered up her spent chute and turned in time to see Beck landing across the field, then jogged to meet him. Together, they helped one another fold their spent parachutes and stuff them into the empty bags they'd always jumped with to make the walk out easier.

"Is Gavin coming to fetch us?" she asked, falling into step when Beck began leading at a good clip straight into the blackened woods.

One step into the trees and she knew why he'd insisted on coming here. No matter what she'd thought she'd known about burned forests, walking through a wood where the trees were crusted with black, blistered bark and no rustle of leaves and twigs underfoot made the back of her neck go cold.

Fire was natural. The reason it had become a problem

in modern living was because of human over-expansion into wooded areas. In centuries past, forest fires had been allowed to burn themselves out, now they needed to be managed to protect people and property. Fire was natural, but in a burned forest her senses were all assaulted by the wrongness of it. It smelled bad. It looked wrong. No brush underfoot. And none of the usual forest sounds she always took for granted. Birdsong. Insects clicking or buzzing away. Fire was natural, but being in the forest afterward felt *un*natural.

Suddenly, the image of twelve-year-old Beck going to the burned-out woods where he'd lived and his mother had died was something else she couldn't leave alone.

"Was this what it was like when you went back home after the fire?" she asked, hurrying to catch up so she didn't have to shout such a question.

Beck stopped walking. "Nature is resilient. Within two years, everything was green again."

"Not the house…" she said, even though she didn't know what the house had looked like before. It might have been fully consumed, half-consumed, or just charred outside, gutted within.

"The house half burned," he confirmed. "Inside the remains of the house and workshop, trees were growing. Grass. Weeds…"

House and workshop.

"You went inside?"

He started walking again, though this time at a slower speed. "Had to make sure she wasn't there."

Her hand flew over her mouth and she blinked away the sharp pierce of sudden tears heating her eyes as she realized that his mother's body had never been found. No words came.

Her new muteness earned a look, and he stopped walking again to pull her hand from her mouth. "You asked."

"Yeah… Just… You didn't find her, right?"

He shook his head and started walking again, still holding the hand he'd pulled from her mouth. "Why *did* you ask?"

His large, strong hand in hers made it harder to focus. Hands of a man who worked outside and manned a shovel, with calluses her own hands were starting to mirror. They fit together like puzzle pieces, square here, round there, textured. Hands that could hold a person no matter the conditions, wet or covered in soot and mud. Strength she saw inside him daily expressed in the strong grip of his hand. He didn't hold loosely, his fingers wrapped around hers tight enough to meld flesh, but not enough to hurt. Not treating her like she was delicate but like she was something worth holding on to.

God, she was going to cry again.

"You're doing all this for me, and I barely know you. Except that you're brave, and good, and you have a very sad story. I guess I just want to know."

He made some sound that let her know he'd heard, but didn't say anything until they'd reached a large, gnarly tan oak, leafless and charred, which he, strangely, patted on the way past. "What do you want to know?"

"I don't know. What was the workshop for?"

"Mom was a carpenter. Artist, actually. Sculptor. But making ornate furniture was more lucrative than sculptures. She custom-made modern replicas and new designs with old-fashioned techniques and beautiful carvings. Paid well."

His mother had been a carpenter. She'd never actually heard those words from someone before. Father? Sure. Mother? Never.

"That's amazing. Have you ever looked for any of her work?"

"To buy back?"

"Yeah. To have it. What was her name? Did she mark her pieces?"

"Her name was Molly, and she'd mark the pieces with a brand in hidden places. I've never looked for anything, but I do have a trunk she made. It survived the fire. It's at my cabin."

The walk through the woods was probably a couple of miles, and then another mile south along a winding state route, but it flew by. Beck had said once he didn't like to talk about his mother, but in the woods, with Lauren's hand in his, he talked. Quietly. Reverently. How it was to grow up in such a quiet, isolated way. Home-schooled. Taught to tend a garden and help in the workshop. The two of them building him a treehouse he used to sleep in when it was warm enough. A life that taught a love of nature, and books, and quiet evenings looking at the stars. It sounded so idyllic she didn't want to think about what his life became after, and he'd only spoken of that enough that she knew it had involved foster care.

Soon he let go of her hand and waved to a taxi speeding down the highway, which pulled onto the shoulder to wait for them.

Before they got in, she asked one final question. "Have you ever been to see what's become of the land now? If someone bought it, built new?"

A quick, slight tilt of his head showed his confusion. "Nothing's built there."

"You've been?"

"I still own it. There's a trust and it's paid the taxes."

He'd kept it, but he never went there.

He gestured toward the open door, and she did the only thing she could: climb in and scoot to make room.

Asking why he'd kept it but avoided going there for over a decade felt like a bridge too far, even for their new little relationship. Their friendship. Partnership. Whatever. She couldn't ask him that. Not yet.

And not for the whole ride to the nearest airstrip, where Gavin was waiting for them to fly back.

From the moment they climbed into the taxi, he was different. Quieter. She didn't need to ask the question burning through her. The words he'd pick to answer didn't really matter, the act itself was an answer. It would've been more financially smart to let the unused land go, or to build his own cabin there rather than buying new land, but he'd done neither. It was a place he couldn't let go of, but still didn't want to go to.

They went through the motions for the rest of the evening, grabbing dinner on the way back to camp, eating, talking about her and the Autry clan—exploits of her ancestors and immediate family rather than him. He'd earned an emotional rest after their walk through a burned-out, lifeless landscape. But the switch in subject hadn't eased him.

As the hour grew late, she went to knock on his bedroom door and found it open, and he was pulling on a pair of sweats over a fresh set of gym clothes and a hoodie.

"Cold?"

He turned and looked, shifting the clothes for comfort before he sat and reached for clean socks.

"I'm going to go up the wooded trail. There's a tan oak I like…"

"The one you were sitting in that evening on the first run?"

He nodded, his expression too closed to read.

"You're going to go sleep in the tree?"

"It's really fine."

"I'm not worried about you falling." She was more worried about his insides than his actual body.

"No need to worry at all. I'll be there for morning PT." He zipped into his hoodie and came toward the doorway where she stood, stiff, wary, blocking his escape route. "Bring me a coffee when you come down?"

He tilted to slide through the space between her body and the door, but she still moved out of the way.

As bad an idea as she knew it was, the urge to stick

beside him and get closer had grown beyond her control. Especially considering that today she understood his retreat wasn't just about maintaining distance with her, it was a reaction to something. The burned woods. Maybe her questions.

Tomorrow she might not be able to say the thing in her heart she needed to say to him.

"You know, if you ever wanted to visit your land, I would go with you."

He stopped on the way to the front door and half turned back, his expression sad but at war with something lighter. Something like hope.

It was only a second and he prowled right back to her. No more hesitation, he wrapped his arms around her waist and pulled her to him. The next instant, his warm, soft lips pressed to hers, one slow, long, tender kiss, so different from the frantic, need-filled devouring kiss he'd laid on her after her bad jump. It was just his mouth on hers, one slow, sweet press of flesh, gentle and tender, and somehow more substantial, not built on out-of-control emotions or a needed confirmation of life. Intimate. An acknowledgment of the closeness they'd forged this week.

When he lifted his head to look at her, there was no way to conceal the tears she felt stinging her eyes.

"I'm okay," he said softly, then released her and backed toward the door. "Don't forget my coffee. You know I'm useless without it in the morning."

Not true. Words meant to normalize what was so far from normal, but she still felt herself going along with it, nodding and watching as he slipped out the front and closed the door behind him.

CHAPTER TEN

ANYTIME BECK NEEDED to find peace, he went to the woods. It always worked, at least enough to still whatever had unsettled him or prompted extreme inner tension.

When he'd been able to fall asleep in the crook of the tree, he'd expected that the off-feeling he'd been having would be better in the morning. It wasn't. It still twisted at his insides.

His offer to help Laura gain the jump experience she'd needed hadn't been as altruistic as she'd thought. Sure, he'd wanted to help her, but he'd also expected that once satisfied she could handle herself. However, the fear that had set up house in his guts when she'd been stranded and had needed to hike out of a wildfire alone hadn't dissolved. It was still there.

The prospect of her going back up into the air and to another fire filled him with the kind of anxiety he'd have thought would be reserved for someone actively in danger, not just someone in possible future danger.

Lauren wasn't just someone. She was the only person he'd actually allowed to get close since Mom had died, and even the idea she could die the same way brought the most horrific visuals to his mind.

He'd tried to fake normal with her all day, through the long looks and the faint worry line that kept appearing between her brows. Hadn't pulled it off, but didn't know what to say about it.

The last run of afternoon PT finished and they were both still catching their breath when Treadwell surprised everyone by slowly walking onto the field.

"He looks better," Lauren said quietly, a safe subject, one he could talk about. "Still pale, but not that terrible gray."

Unlike the rest of the group, they hung back and let the mob gather to welcome the chief. He wasn't a man to suffer fawning, and the shrill whistle he loosed through tight lips both cut through the din and summoned Beck and Lauren at the same time.

"I'm not back," he announced first. "Call just came in for assistance from a local station with a big fire at an apartment complex. It's bordered by woods and they need help. Anyone up for it, go now."

He finished with directions by pointing toward the main building, then turned to slowly walk back in that direction.

Beck needed only a glance at Lauren to know she was going. Her gaze connected with his, and they turned in unison to jog for the main building. They were a team now, and he had no choice about letting her face any fires alone. In the future, when she was assigned to a team, that would change—something he didn't want to think about. Right now, he only knew that, no matter how skilled she might be, she'd be safer at his side than anyone else's.

Half an hour later, they were both in full gear at the site and being directed to the last building at the back, which was supposed to have been evacuated but had finally caught fire and needed a final sweep.

Others followed with hoses and began the attack.

"Upstairs down," she said. "Keep to the cement breezeways as much as possible. These buildings are built with metal skeletons. If the floor looks iffy, stick to the joists."

Over what was probably only ten or fifteen minutes,

they scouted the third floor of the building, found nothing, and moved down to the second.

She moved quickly, assessing everything and gesturing him off on different paths he might not have traveled without her. Contrary to how he always felt in a wildfire, really contrary to how he'd felt in the hours she'd outrun one alone, even contrary to knowing structure fires were statistically more dangerous, Beck didn't feel that spike of chained-up terror in his chest. Until the back of the second floor, when he suddenly did.

It took him a heart-squeezing to realize what his body had reacted to.

Screams. He'd heard a woman screaming.

And behind it a baby's cries.

One look at Lauren confirmed she'd heard it too, and had flipped up the visor on her helmet so she could hear more clearly, and it was there in the whiteness around her mouth.

Woman and child, trapped behind a burning doorway, and who knew what else.

"Is there another way?" he asked, praying she had an idea that hadn't come to him. All the apartments had balconies, but getting in through a balcony would require leaving, getting a ladder, climbing in—time they didn't have.

She flipped down the visor and gestured to the stairs and took them at a run, and he followed. In building fires, she was definitely the more experienced, and he'd take whatever wisdom that experience brought. A moment later, they were on the ground below a balcony, and she'd thrown down all the equipment except for her protective clothing.

"I'm going to climb, and you're going to lift me."

"Alone?"

"Do you have a better idea?"

He gaped for only a second, tempted to tell her to wait. To tell her if they didn't know she could go in safely, she shouldn't go—things she'd said to him before, but which he knew neither one of them believed at that moment. Woman. Baby. It was worth the risk.

Sweat that had been pouring off him below the gear ran like ice water down his spine, but he linked his fingers to offer her a step up. "Use the wall to steady yourself as I lift, and when you're high enough, grab the balustrade."

If she could reach it. If he could lift her high enough.

Climbing would require a sure grip, so she pulled the bulky gloves off and stashed them in the pockets of her jacket, then stepped into his hand.

A moment later, he'd heaved her up to the height of his shoulder. She tested the heat of the wrought-iron bars framing the balcony, then grabbed hold and began to lift herself, allowing them to share the burden as he extended his arms up over his head and she was high enough to reach one foot up to the balcony and climb.

In less than a minute she was over the bar, had her gloves on again and peeked into the sliding glass door. The locked door.

"Axe," she called down to him, then leaned over to catch it as he tossed it up.

That was the last word she said to him before he heard shattering glass, and then he was running, around to the front again to call for a ladder and crew. It couldn't have been longer than seconds, but time slowed, seemed like hours before his shouting was heard and he finally saw men with a ladder running for him, leaving him free to barrel back around to the balcony.

By the time they got back there, she'd returned and was leaning over the railing, a screaming toddler wrapped in her jacket, his face out in the air.

"He's okay. Needs oxygen. I need your help with the mother."

Beck stepped back for the men to place the ladder, then pushed through, climbing fast to reach for the child. He passed the terrified toddler off to the next pair of hands, then hammered up the ladder and over the rail while she buckled her jacket again.

One look back into the burning apartment explained why she'd had the baby inside her coat—the living room was a wall of flames. They were going to have to run through.

She flipped her visor down again, put her gloves back on, pointed, and repeated her earlier advice. "Stay on the joists."

It only took seconds for her to explain the distance between floor joists, then she was gone. He followed.

Once inside, even in a room on fire, the consuming fear he expected didn't come. The fire that surrounded them in that building wasn't a monster. It was a thing. It was her conquering the deep end of the pool, no one there to stop her. Not something plotting to hurt this family, just a sad, unfortunate event.

"Mrs. Rhodes," she called, visor up again, and moved around a recliner to the floor where the woman was sprawled.

The first sight of her almost took Beck's breath. The pink plaid pajamas she wore were singed on the top and almost entirely missing on the bottom, melted into her legs or consumed by the fire.

Her legs…

"We can't carry her out like that. She needs protection…"

"I have the fire blanket." Lauren was already shaking it out, but the bathroom was just right there…

Beck stepped in and yanked open the closet inside to fish out a couple of towels, which he tossed into the bathtub, and turned on the cold water.

"Beck?"

"One minute," he called, moving the towels under the fully open faucet until they were saturated, then carrying both out. "Here. Lay these over the burns to keep them from getting heated when we run through."

Lauren had already spread the fire blanket on the floor and eased Mrs. Rhodes onto it, but took one of the towels Beck offered and laid it over the leg that had taken the worst of it. The skin was gone in some places, and bubbled up to terrible blisters in others.

"I have flu," the woman sobbed, shaking her head. "I was asleep. I... The alarms..."

"It's okay. We're going to get you out."

"My son..."

"He's scared, but he's fine." Lauren spoke firmly, projecting confidence Beck didn't feel. Couldn't feel. Not while seeing those burns... "We're going to take you to him now, okay?"

Mrs. Rhodes nodded, and since they had her covered in the wet towels, Beck flipped his visor down then flipped Lauren's down as well before bending to wrap the poor woman in the blanket so they could pick her up and make a run for it.

In nothing less than a joist-to-joist sprint, they made it back through the fire and out onto the balcony, then down the ladder and on to the ambulances.

The fire alarms had woken the woman, and she'd run through fire to her son. She hadn't hesitated. No shoes, no protection, and she had gone for her son.

The story stuck to him, along with the way she'd sobbed her apologies to them, to the baby who didn't know what his mother had done to save him. The kind of love that allowed such sacrifice shouldn't hurt to witness, but even well outside the heat of the fire it burned straight through him.

Lauren handled all communication, getting new orders once their building was clear, and waved for him to follow. She'd already started moving to another building, setting a pace he'd fight to keep up with the rest of the evening.

They worked for hours, first making sweeps and then manning the hoses, and she'd never lost a drop of that energy. At the site or inside burning buildings, there was no hint of the hesitation he'd seen when they'd been digging or even at camp. She was confident and certain of herself, every bit the force of nature they fought, and he had to wonder if she'd joined the smokejumpers because she wanted to do the job or because she thought it would finally give her the validity in the eyes of her family.

This seemed to be what she was made for. If he was honest, he craved this *for her*. He needed this woman in his life, whatever way she'd take him, even after training ended. So he'd just have to accept her on the crew, battling wildfires, because he had no choice.

Unless she changed her mind.

"I know you're happy to have been able to help them, but I'm just not feeling celebratory," Beck said, driving them back from the fire in his faithful pickup, hands gripping the wheel and that scowl she saw so often on his face magnified by his surly profile.

Was that anger? "How *are* you feeling?"

The more they talked about things, the less she had to badger him into putting his thoughts into words. At that moment, she only had to ask and he admitted, "Can't stop thinking about what life's going to be like for them. There's no scenario here that has a happy ending."

"What do you mean? She could live, that's a happy ending."

"She could. I hope she does. But you saw the extent of her burns. They're not going to heal easily. If they heal at all, it means a lifetime of debilitating scars."

"Right, a *lifetime*. Are you saying it would be better if she'd died?"

"Of course not," he bit out, not taking his gaze from the road. It wasn't a long drive, and he'd managed to survive most of it with her blathering on in that verbal decompressing way she had of thinking through events with her mouth.

They pulled into the camp's lot and he exited the truck, leaving her to follow in his wake.

She held her tongue until they were back inside the cabin, where no one would overhear.

"Tell me what you mean, then. Because I have rolled your words around in my head at least twenty times since we parked, but it still sounds to me like you think her death would have been better."

"You're twisting what I said. That baby's too young to understand now, but once he grows up, even if she survives, he's going to think of what happened to her every time he looks at her. Every time he sees those scars, he's going to know she got them because of him. If she dies, he'll know it's because of him. There is no happy ending. There is only life or death."

"It won't matter to him knowing how much she loves him?" she said, recalling their conversation on the bus. It hadn't gotten through as much as she'd hoped it had.

He did look at her then, standing in the cabin, hands rolling at the wrist from the tension she could see biting through his peace. "What he'll know is if he hadn't been there, she could've run the other way."

It always came back to that. To this notion he'd caused his mother's death somehow.

"Is that what you think about your mom?" she asked, unable to keep her voice level. "You think if you hadn't been born, they would've saved her? Or if *she'd* gone first, something no good mother would ever do, she would've *ever* been the same if she'd lost you?"

"If I hadn't been born, there would've been time to save her, yes." He conveniently ignored her other question, because there was no way around it—or the concept just shut him down. It seemed to have done so on the bus.

Which was fine. He wasn't ready to deal so she'd fight him on the front he offered. "If I hadn't been born, my mother might not have died of breast cancer. Pregnancy hormones very likely triggered her cancer. Is it my fault she died?"

"That's health stuff. It's different."

"It's exactly the same. You're saying if you were never born, your mother could still be alive. If I was never born, my mother could still be alive. So, answer me. Is it my fault she's dead?"

"No," he said softly, then thumped onto the small, lumpy sofa, head in his hands. "Do we have to talk about this? We worked together well. We got the job done. You wanted to know what I was thinking. I told you. Why does it have to be a fight?"

"It's only a fight when you're thinking things that make no sense." But maybe he needed to hear these things said out loud to see that. He was talking to her now, and, as angry as his words made her, shutting them down wasn't going to help him. "Am I not supposed to try and talk you out of thinking this way? Just let you say these things that you know are wrong?"

"I don't know they're wrong. They're wrong in your head, you weren't there."

She couldn't contain the breath that rushed out of her, and she suddenly couldn't keep standing either. Two steps, and she sat beside him. "You're right, I wasn't there. So, tell me what you want me to do."

His laugh was mirthless, and he leaned back, laying his head on the back of the sofa so he could stare at the ceiling. "You don't want to know what I want you to do."

The words would've sounded depressed but for the undercurrent of bitter amusement.

She didn't want to know?

Suddenly, she knew she *did* want to know. And, was pretty sure she knew already.

He didn't want help working through this. He wanted help forgetting about it.

She stared at his profile—strong jaw, angular cheekbones, long eyelashes entirely wasted on a man—then let her gaze track down over his shoulders, chest, arms with enough definition the muscle always looked flexed one way or another.

He was a sight, one she enjoyed looking at.

Having an unreasonable voice on eternal loop in her head got exhausting, and hers had just broadcast the ways she wasn't good enough. His blamed him for the death of his mother. She couldn't shut hers up, and she didn't even have to wonder if he could his.

Tonight was too fresh a reminder of his loss, and even if she didn't think the memory was ever far from his mind, she wanted to push it out. Wanted him to forget, at least for a little while. With her.

"Tell me," she said softly.

He didn't answer, but his breathing picked up.

"Tell me," she said again, then reached over and brushed the backs of her fingers over his chiseled cheek.

He opened his eyes then and turned his head to look at her. "You're playing with fire, Autry."

Her skin heated just from the way he looked at her and she couldn't help teasing. "Am I? It's only a force of nature."

"So am I," he said, reaching for her. He picked her up for the second time today, this time pulling her onto him, not pushing her away. He guided her legs to either side of his hips so she straddled him, chest to chest.

She didn't wait for him to kiss her, just wrapped her arms around his neck to pull his mouth to hers. This mouth that could say such terrible things to himself was still heady and bewitching against hers.

Large hands slid up and down her body, seeking, squeezing, tugging, palming her butt to grind her against him, tight enough she could feel every inch of his firm flesh against her. But his mouth claimed more—demanding and thorough, he might as well have been kissing every inch of her body, she felt it sparking and sizzling everywhere. Pleasure-seeking exploration that only took a moment to rocket into something needier.

There was some roughly handled material, a bra that might never fasten again, and him rolling onto the couch with her, pinning her beneath his big body, then kissing his way down every inch he wrestled free of fabric. Sucking, licking, dragging his teeth along her slender curves.

She'd meant to touch and please, but he didn't hold still long enough for her to get her mouth anywhere near him. His curling black hair tickled the plane of her belly as he continued lower, not stopping until he had one of her legs over his shoulder and her staring, dazed, down at him.

"If you don't want this, say it now, please."

"Bed." One word, the only word she could muster, loath as she was to interrupt his intentions. The next she knew, he'd picked her up and whisked her to the bedroom, never pulling his eyes from her face.

Despite telling herself it would be foolish to get involved with him, she'd become involved. She wanted to become more involved.

Seeing him tonight, the fear in him for her, for the people who needed them, the dark emotions that swam over him that he pushed aside to do the best he could for everyone. She'd be lying if she tried to pretend she didn't want it to continue, to see what they could become together. She'd be lying if she tried to pretend she didn't care in a way she knew wouldn't ever diminish, even if she didn't want to put a word to it.

That feeling had only grown stronger, and had ruined her from that first, secret jump he'd arranged. She'd be lying if she didn't admit she'd known it would come to this since that following weekend, when, in a moment of

honesty while in town, she'd bought condoms despite her
declarations otherwise.

Beck laid her down on the bed, but didn't join her. There
was no seduction in the way he pulled and yanked at his
own clothes, but the way his dark eyes roamed over her
would stay with her forever. Appreciative, obsessed, soaked
with enough want to leave his movements a little mindless.
As soon as he'd stripped away anything that could separate them, he stretched out on the bed with her, and found
her mouth again.

She loved the heat and demand in his kisses. The way
he couldn't seem to get close enough to her, his hands constantly moving, his mouth always wandering, only to lunge
back to hers again, as if he couldn't go long without her
kisses. She loved that it wasn't practiced or smooth. Outside that room, in their lives, they were both so in control,
their bodies obeying when forced through the daily punishment that was their profession, but together, seeking only
to fit together, they were both clumsy and uncoordinated,
drunk on sensation and need.

With them finally skin to skin, every bit of physical
control left. She barely remembered the protection in her
bedside table, and it took three tries to babble some semblance of the words out. By the time she managed to get
the drawer open, she'd knocked the table around so hard
the lamp had fallen. Actually getting it on him required
complete cessation of all touching.

He stood and staggered several feet from the bed, gasping and trembling, desperate and tearing at the foil with his
teeth. It was only half rolled down when he was back on her
and thrusting the thick length deep, face hovering above
hers, eyes locked as he began to move. Under the ripples
and spasms of pleasure his body wrought on hers, there was
a connection that left her raw. Intense and overwhelming,
the unavoidable truth she saw in his eyes crashed over her.

Avoiding the word didn't change the feeling. She loved this man, every broken part of him, from the support he gave to the infuriating distance he threw up inexplicably; from the fierce heart that would risk everything to save someone, to the still-wounded little boy she caught in glimpses. Brave and a little crazy, but wasn't she too?

Beck so rarely indulged physical needs he'd either forgotten how it felt to be wrapped up in a woman, or had never been so thoroughly wrapped up before this woman. So wrapped up, nothing else mattered. The whole world could be turning to ash and soot, and he'd still want another hour with her, another minute. There was nothing else. Just her and him, no past to haunt them, no future holding bounty or punishment, nothing but right now, right here. The way she gripped him. The heat of her. His name sighed, whispered, pled. Her beautiful eyes, watching him, holding him, seeing him.

He was as shocked and gutted by the bonds he felt weaving around them both as by the pleasure of her touch, by his own urgency—moving too fast, too hard, too driven by primitive needs he could no more control than the weather.

He didn't know how long he'd been there, locked with her, moving in her, taking and giving, only that it wasn't long enough. Her strong, silken body had already tightened past the point of no return, and he saw it in her eyes. No shielding, no hiding, no bolstering of her confidence. Her kind, loving heart shone in her eyes, and she let him see everything, the depth of her feeling for him, and how much he could hurt her if he wasn't careful.

When her climax hit, her eyes took on an unfocused quality that wavered with every quaking pulse of her orgasm, taking him with her.

By the time the madness passed, his strength was gone.

He could do nothing but lie against her, his head on her breasts.

He was vaguely aware of her brushing his hair back from his face, and then nothing—the emptying he'd been after since that terrible day last season when it had all gone wrong.

All he knew was that he couldn't lose her.

CHAPTER ELEVEN

"WHAT ARE WE going to do when training is up?"

Beck hadn't fully opened his eyes yet, and she patted his shoulders and asked again.

"I don't know." Still too spent to do much more than slide off her and up the bed so he could pull her to him rather than smashing her into the mattress. "Somewhere. Can't make real plans when we don't know where you'll be stationed."

"Or if we'll make it through training without another strike." She settled her head on his chest, but there was enough tension in her shoulders to show the possibility of a third strike weighed on her.

He just didn't know if it should. She might be going all in on a life she wouldn't have even chosen if she'd been allowed to find peace and acceptance in her fire station.

It was still too early to start that conversation, but he had to say something. "Do you want to go to breakfast or sleep more?"

It was Saturday, they could lie in bed all day with the door closed and no one could say anything to them, though they might start a few rumors.

"Maybe one of us should go get breakfast so we have strength later."

"Later?"

She pulled from his arms and eased out of bed, moving somewhat stiffly. "For all the sex I'm planning to demand."

Even in the face of her moving like she was sore, he smiled. An easy smile, unfamiliar as that was. "Are you stiff because of all the sex *I* demanded, or the day before that?"

"Pretty sure the day before. Fire on top of all-day calisthenics." She dug clothes from the bureau. "I'll get breakfast. You'll get dinner."

"And lunch?"

"I'll get extra breakfast, because between the demanding sex, there will be more sleep and I'm not sure that leaves time for three cafeteria runs."

"We also need to make time to talk about something."

She froze, pants pulled half-up, eyes wide. "What is it?"

From playful to fearful just because he wanted to talk?

"Really?" He pushed onto his elbows. "After everything, after planning the day in bed, you think I want to have a *breakup* talk? Or a *this meant nothing to me* talk?"

She pulled her pants the rest of the way up, but now moved with less energy.

"Well?"

She shrugged in a helpless but disgusted-with-herself way. "Maybe. Before you said that."

He dragged himself up from the bed and didn't stop until he had her sweet face in his hands and shared a long, promise-filled kiss. "How about now?"

"Pretty much not now, but curious." Sparkling eyes, pressing closer, her voice slid to seduction.

Almost as eager to get back to bed as he was.

"I can do without breakfast."

"Well, I can't." She kissed the center of his chest, then pulled away to finish dressing. "I'll hurry, though."

Fifteen minutes later, she climbed back into bed with the food and a caddy of coffee, and kicked off her shoes. "Spill it."

"Don't want to eat first?"

"You said it wasn't bad."

"I said it wasn't a breakup talk, but you might still get mad."

A grunt answered him, and she shoved a breakfast sandwich at him. "Talk fast."

With last night's fire in his mind, and how she'd moved through it, he said, "I'm wondering if you really want to be a smokejumper."

Beck's words should've sounded like a question but rang in her head like a final statement. A statement built to make her hackles rise.

"Why else would I be doing this?"

He didn't answer for a very long time, no doubt formulating a follow-up statement-question.

Don't get mad yet. She had to mentally say the words to herself. Maybe he had some other reason for asking than criticism, but she'd heard no implication she couldn't do it. "I want to be here."

"I know you do," he agreed, speaking slowly—as he usually did. "But do you want the job afterward?"

"That's a weird thing to ask."

"Play along?" he asked, and were it not for the concern she saw in his eyes, she might have said no.

"I'm trying…"

He set his sandwich aside, and tugged the hem of her shirt up so she had to transfer the sandwich to get it off. "Let's say you've just had the best day at work ever."

"Okay."

"What happened?"

She shrugged. "A fire?"

There went her bra. He moved on to her shorts. "Close your eyes. Tell me where the fire was."

Being undressed while she was eating and being questioned by her lover about her career path meant at least thirty different sensations overloading her senses, not counting the knot of agitation that came from being questioned. The man spoke so infrequently she couldn't discount anything he said as flippant—he didn't do impulsive conversations, didn't think *as* the words came out. He thought, probably for a long time, before deciding to speak.

She closed her eyes.

"Picture your most exhilarating day on the job," he prompted again.

Not the easiest request. She laid the sandwich aside and concentrated.

He gave her a minute. "Tell me where you are."

Where was she?

The picture should be a wildfire. A mountain, like that one bad jump. Or even working as a spotter from one of the planes, but that wasn't what formed in her mind.

He didn't prompt again, just left her to it as she worked through her own thoughts.

"House."

Not usually a word that would make someone sad, but she felt the good feelings she'd been riding since last night float away.

"Are you saving someone?"

She nodded, then opened her eyes, trying to ignore the rotten hollow feeling in her belly.

"This doesn't mean anything." Even if she felt the weight of it squashing her insides. "I've been programmed to think like that since I was little. It's a remnant."

Suddenly, she didn't want to play along anymore. And she *really* didn't want to tell him she'd decided she had to come clean to Treadwell, despite having worked to get the experience she'd been lacking. At some point, probably after she finished training and they were more inclined to be forgiving. When it couldn't become her third strike.

"Do you want to know my best day?" The question came

softly, as if he knew he'd just set her internal compass spinning and felt guilty.

Hearing anything about him was a salve to the new cycle of self-criticism she teetered on the edge of. She nodded.

"During the fire season, my best day is doing what we did the day of Treadwell's heart attack."

"Helping someone you care about?"

"No." He shook his head. "Burning and digging. Figuring out how to beat the fire, how to control it. I don't enjoy going into the blazes. I hate it. It's part of the job, so I do it. But my best day? Carving that line in the earth. Protecting the land behind you, the homes, the families, the wilderness, the animals. Being the barrier between. That's my best day."

Not what she pictured at all when she thought of fighting fires. Digging felt like busywork, even if she knew it wasn't.

"You hated going into the fire last night," she said again, thinking out loud. "Even before we found them."

His actions hadn't been as sure as they normally were. He'd deferred to her there, but in the field always stormed ahead and left others to follow, or not. He didn't want anyone to suffer, not people, not animals, but he didn't get joy out of the rescue, because it meant someone had to suffer first, and suffer later.

"Yes," he admitted, and opened his mouth to say more, but that damned siren blasted again, like last Saturday all over again.

They reached the field ahead of the others, Beck's question still ringing in her head.

It was early enough that to the west the sky still faded into night. Lamps dotting the field provided enough light to see, not that she was paying much attention yet.

What if Beck was right? What if she'd only come here out of some juvenile rebellion?

She gave herself a mental shake.

Focus. Something was going on. No time to be self-absorbed. Siren meant emergency, the right mind-set was preparation.

And yet? She couldn't shake it. It was *only* her future. It was *only* what she'd been working toward for two years. Everything she'd thought she wanted, right up until he'd asked that stinking question.

Sure, she'd had some unease after bungling that first jump, but they'd worked on that. Knowing what to do next in the field wasn't instinct yet, and she definitely gave herself regular hell over even slight mistakes about anything, but she'd learn.

She'd always heard about her failures from her father, her self-criticism was worse than his. It drove her to fight for perfection. And she learned from that, just as she'd learn now.

"Kolinski," Beck said quietly at her side, jerking her from her thoughts. She turned in time to see the lieutenant jogging in from the admin buildings.

Seeing them, Kolinski snapped and pointed to the mess hall. "You two, we're taking more people out today."

"What's going on?"

"Lightning storm up north. Three separate fires started and not enough rain to put a damper on it. Biggest cut across the border to Nevada, and it's racing up the Donner trail toward Tahoe."

"The whole wagon train in the olden days where they ate each other?" Lauren asked, because for some reason that was the part that stuck out to her. That and the ruggedness of the terrain.

Kolinski and Beck looked at her strangely and her brain caught up.

"And, of course, the *lake*, where people vacation. Ringed by forests. Needing protection. Right. I'm with you."

"Because of the unseasonably warm spring, we have more people camping and exploring than usual."

"Families?" Beck interrupted, alarm in his voice—already convinced of the worst-case scenario. Not simply preparing for it, but sucked back to that dark place he'd been last night.

Kolinski seemed to pick up on it too, and nodded slowly. "Anything's possible. The storm was violent and sudden, and sparked separate locations. It's a big area."

Lauren tapped Beck's arm to get his attention, and jerked her head toward the main hall.

Kolinski left to inform others as they arrived.

"Does he mean more digging or jumping?" she asked, as much to pull his head back to the job as to know.

"Both," he answered.

Something in his voice made the hairs on the back of her neck stand up. Or maybe it was the lack of words. He'd become more talkative this week. And *Both* was back to one-word answers.

With how much she understood he hated fires, she didn't even wonder what it meant.

Twenty minutes later, Beck sat behind the wheel of his truck, driving them both to the airport. They'd eaten quickly, dressed in flight suits, and he'd somehow talked her into driving there with him instead of going on the bus. Not just because he needed to get her alone, but she'd need transportation back to camp if he could get her to agree to his request.

"You're quiet." She unfastened her seat belt and slid closer, then buckled back in.

"Preoccupied," he answered.

They were a good fifteen minutes ahead of the bus—corralling more people took longer, thankfully.

"Worried about the fire?" she asked, hesitation in her voice saying that no matter how close they'd gotten, she still felt the need to tread lightly after their interrupted conversation, even if she still wanted to be closer.

He'd intended on getting to the airport before picking another fight, but dodging wouldn't win him any points.

"Trying to figure out how to talk you out of going up."

She stiffened beside him, and even with his eyes on the road he could feel her stare.

"Bet you regret getting closer now."

"Bet you're right," she grumped, then unbuckled and slid her rear right back to her original seat. "All that talk was about making me quit? You said I'm ready, that I'm doing great. What's going on?"

"You *are* doing great." He turned down the access road to the airport.

"Then what? Did I do something at the scene last night to make you think I'm not capable?"

If only he'd had time to build an argument, but they'd only known about this less than half an hour, and most of that time he'd spent arguing with himself over whether or not he should even try to stop her today. "Let me get us there. The conversation deserves all my attention, not what I can spare while driving."

She didn't say anything else, but he could feel tension rolling off her.

Three quick turns, a couple thousand miles of access roads to the hangar, where he parked.

She didn't wait for him to get going, it was practically a miracle she'd waited as long as she had. "So?"

"When we were in the apartment last night, you were amazing." Beck turned in the seat to better see her. "You have a feel for structure fires I don't have. You know how it acts, the safest paths, and you were fearless. I was very proud of you."

"None of that adds up to *don't jump*." She unfastened her seat belt and turned slightly toward him, though her hand rested on the door handle. "You think I do a great job *and* shouldn't do it?"

Yes, it sounded stupid. He couldn't argue that. All he could do was try to explain.

"I wasn't afraid for you in the fire last night. That fire was dangerous, people were hurt, it was upsetting, but I wasn't afraid *for you* in that fire."

"But you are afraid for me with a fire that's out in the open?" she asked. "Not jumping or landing, you're afraid of me being at a fire on the land?"

"You asked me how I see fire. I thought I'd answered, but I was wrong. I don't see all fire the same. The monster waiting to take away the people I love? It's wildfire. I know it's irrational, structure fires are a thousand times more deadly, but they don't *feel* the same. They feel—"

"Like *things*?" she interrupted.

He nodded, then took a chance and reached for her hand. Although her fingers were stiff, tense, she didn't pull away. She splayed her fingers, let them slide together, and carefully flexed them to fit his. "You have to tell me the truth. Are you trying keep me from joining? Because that's not going to happen. Even if you don't want me here."

"I'm not thinking past today, but I think you might be in denial. Honestly. I'd feel better if you just joined another station instead of going back to be under your dad's thumb, but that's not what this is about. I only know that if we're both on the mountain today, I'll focus on you more than the fire, which does make me more dangerous to everyone else."

"Why?"

"Because something could happen! I know it's illogical. I'm admitting it's illogical. I know it's *stupid* to think you're worse off fighting a forest fire than in a building, but it's not something I can control. Maybe I *am* too emotional about this, but the idea... I've been seeing it in my mind over and over again. Of you being caught. Of you burning. It's… I can't have you there."

She drew a breath, a slow, stay-calm, deep breath, as if he didn't know how much his request would grate on her. To her credit, despite the frustration bubbling there, barely controlled in her voice, she still didn't pull her hand away.

"This is going to be my job. It took me two years to get here. And they *need* people today. You heard Kolinski say there may be people out there. They wouldn't be pulling in rookies if it wasn't going very badly, if they weren't fighting on too many fronts."

"I know."

"I'm not done," she said. "Just trying to be very deliberate with my word choices."

He nodded, giving her hand a squeeze, and stretched across that middle space where she'd briefly been sitting.

"If you're planning on going, then you're being unfair to me. They need bodies, but I'm not going to pull my body out of this if *you* don't also. You're my partner. I don't care if this is voluntary and not going to count against us if you go and I don't. If you bow out, I will too. That's the compromise I'm willing to make. If you stay, I stay. We can try to work on this thing that's hurting you together. But if you go, I'm going."

"And if I said I love you? If I said I love you and I'm… I'm desperate?"

She pulled her hand free. "If you say you love me to make me stay, I'm going to say you're treating me like my father and brothers do. I gave you a fair compromise. If you're not willing to take it, then it's not about you being afraid of the wildfire. It's about you not respecting that I can handle myself, and that's really not okay."

"I have to go…"

"You don't have to go. You're a rookie right now. You're volunteering."

"Not that. I mean… If I don't go…there won't be anyone

there to… If Kolinski or the other captains have to make that decision that it's not worth risking one life to save a life, I can make that decision for myself."

She jerked the door of the truck open and climbed out. "You either trust them or you don't."

"I trust them, but they have different responsibilities than I do." He climbed out too, and stopped her from storming into the hangar by grabbing her elbow. "I'm putting the keys in the back bumper. So you can drive back to camp if you—"

"That's why you wanted to drive? So I could drive back when I meekly accepted your demand to not go?" She jerked her elbow from his hand and launched forward, shoving him back. "And you're still talking like your life is expendable!"

The bus rolled into the area and Lauren stepped back, shaking her head and muttering to herself as she stalked inside.

CHAPTER TWELVE

IT HAPPENED MORE often than Lauren would like to admit, where she got this angry after being love-manipulated.

Her family did it.

Troy had done it.

And now Beck. Beck, the one who was supposed to be different. Beck, the one who had *helped* her overcome the major obstacle to her making the team.

Beck, who apparently still thought *he* was expendable.

She rounded the open doors and inside the hangar sat the plane and a ton of parachute packs, ready to be put on.

So do that. Give her hands something to do besides punch him, because, as violent as she generally wasn't, it crackled in the back of her head. One cranial lightning strike after another, composed of the words she wanted to shout at him.

She grabbed the first chute, and he stepped up beside her, scowling as he went about suiting up as well.

"You know, my family manipulates me that way. *'If you love me, Lauren, you'll find another job.'*"

"I'm not doing that."

"The hell you're not. This is brand-new, this is the first jump after..." She stopped, realizing her voice had risen and even if they were alone, she didn't want to be shouting about her sex life anywhere they could be overheard. "You love me? Tell me then, how would you feel if I was the one telling you that I was ready to run into an unsurvivable fire for any living creature. Tell me how I'm supposed to feel when you have this outlook."

"Are you saying you love me too?"

"Yeah, but you're a jerk and I'm not sure you deserve me loving you and worrying about you. Your worry isn't worth more than mine. The difference is that I'm willing to trust you. Which is kind of *stupid* considering I'm not the one who keeps saying that I'll take almost certain death on the tiny little chance that I could save a dog—even as someone who loves dogs, as I do. So, really, if anyone should stay on the ground, it's you."

"I know that."

"So stay. Stay and I'll stay, and we'll figure something out."

"There is no way out of this!" His voice went up then. "You think me going to talk to a counselor is going to magically make me okay with someone dying if I could save them?"

"You *can't* save everyone, Beck! You just *can't*. There are no-win situations. They're things that exist, and if you can't see that, you shouldn't be going out there."

The others began piling into the hangar, effectively shutting down their fight but doing nothing to shake the helpless feeling from her shoulders.

She checked the straps, making sure they were buckled right and tight enough, and grabbed another snack from nearby stashes so she'd have the energy needed for this, while Kolinski began checking gear before letting anyone onto the plane. Beck edged up to her and made a show of checking her buckles. "Tell me what I'm supposed to do."

"There are people around."

"So tell me quietly."

"Damn it, Ellison," she muttered. "You're supposed to hold yourself to the same standard you hold me to. It's not rocket science. But you hold yourself to the *I'm expendable* standard, and hold me to the *fragile flower* standard."

"I don't hold you to the *fragile flower* standard. And you know, if you were honest on your application, you wouldn't be jumping right now anyway."

That sounded...very much like a threat. Despite the heat roiling through her, a cold wave swept down her spine.

Escalating further would make this go exactly the wrong way for her.

"We'll talk about this later. The line's shortening."

She scooted that way, but he cut in front of her.

Probably so she could still back out. God, how did she keep getting these meatheads who thought so little of her capabilities?

He moved forward and upon reaching the lieutenant stopped and looked at her pointedly.

His body swayed lightly as the straps were checked, and when Kolinski cleared him, he didn't step onto the stairs up.

He kept looking at her. Not just looking, his gaze bored into her with so much anger it bordered on something darker.

"What are you waiting for?" Kolinski asked, and Beck faced their leader, jaw clenching, clenching, clenching, her stomach right with it.

He was going to tell Kolinski.

More cold. She'd planned to come clean before taking the job officially at the end, but not now. It was *her* call to make, her *confession* to make.

"Is there a problem with you two?" Kolinski asked. "I thought this was sorted out."

"It *is* sorted out," Lauren said, shaking her head, and when she looked Beck in the eye again, his held through several thundering heartbeats, then he wordlessly climbed aboard the plane.

"You sure everything is sorted out?" Kolinski asked as he got on with checking her straps.

The answer was a lot more final in her head than it had been this morning when they'd been wrapped up in each other.

"I'm sure."

Sure it was over. He hadn't actually ratted her out, but it had been on the tip of his tongue. And that was his *starting* position? It had nowhere to go but worse.

Kolinski took her word, even if it was obviously another lie on her conscience, and she climbed onto the plane to find her place in line.

Lauren's jump and landing were flawless. Other, more experienced jumpers landed in trees, but not her. Beck had jumped just after her so he could make sure she went where she was supposed to go, and had followed her with one spin to land lengthways across the bare spot she'd aimed for.

He'd be proud if he wasn't presently angry at pretty much everyone. Himself for being irrational. Her for not listening, not even once. The fire, for being a fire.

Twenty minutes later, he had a shovel and a saw on his back, and moved with a group of five others—including Lauren—to where they were supposed to dig and cut. With simultaneous fires breaking out all over a national forest where people camped and hiked, they were spread as thinly as possible while still making any headway. By the time this was over, Beck feared the forest would look like it had been clear-cut.

Lauren started by climbing and sawing branches to bring the tree down clean, while he stayed on the ground and dug. With her up a tree, it was easier to keep track of her, but he was still aware of her every moment, despite it being complicated by the density of the smoke in the air and monitoring the comm for calls.

Less than full capability.

While digging, something hard bounded off his helmet. Small. Woody. Something thrown.

He looked up and found Lauren gesturing through a clearing in the trees.

What? he mouthed at her, the saws too loud to shout over.

Dog, she mouthed back.

Dog. Another damned dog.

And she was sending him after it?

They were close enough to the fire to see it down the western slope and, sure enough, he saw black-and-white fur directly north.

It took only a moment to start moving. There was no way he wouldn't try to get the dog to come to him. He had rope. He'd tie it up, make it stay with them as they moved across the land.

He got halfway to it when the dog turned toward him and began to barrel in his direction at full speed.

Black-and-white. Kind of fluffy…

When it got to him, the breed became clear. Not a mutt. Purebred dog. Border collie. It barked and when he removed his glove and reached out to let it sniff, the dog snapped twice at his hand—biting, but not breaking the skin, just quick, near-frantic nips, then more barking. He ran back a short distance in the other direction.

"Beck!" Lauren's voice came through the din and he turned in time to see her running toward him, horror on her face. "It bit you!"

When she reached him, she grabbed his hand, looking for wounds.

"Not hard. He's agitated…"

She smoothed her fingers over the skin that was barely even pink, and looked over at the dog as he bound back.

Which was when he saw the tags and his stomach dropped through the earth.

Purebred with tags, alone in a national park, trying to get his attention.

"I think there's a family." He said the words as they came to him. "He's not here alone."

Beck knelt and the dog came running back. Before he got another bite in, Beck hooked his fingers under the collar so he could get a look at the tag.

"What's it say?"

"Henderson. Phone number."

"Crap."

"We knew there could be people out here."

"You think that's what this is? Lassie, Timmy's stuck in the well?"

He petted the dog, got nipped at again, and then let go so he could look at Lauren. "That's what I think."

"What do you want to do?"

"You know what I want to do."

She looked west, toward the fire, then the way the dog tried to lead them—northwest.

"There is another fire burning to the north. If the fire makes it past this break, we'll be stuck if we go that way," she said, and then reached for her comm to click it, and relayed the information, along with their decision to go.

Permission came unexpectedly fast. He wouldn't have even asked. And he didn't want to take her into an area where he wasn't already certain of their exit once they found the family, but he couldn't leave them there.

It was in him to apologize then, for what he'd almost done with Kolinski, but that would take time, and he didn't need to possibly make tensions even worse. No one needed to become more emotional in a deadly situation.

Later. Later he'd tell her he was sorry.

Lauren followed Beck and the dog at a near run up an incline steep enough she needed to use tree trunks to help haul herself up. There was no looking for a saner path up, not when they were following Lassie.

Never in her life would she have believed something

like this could happen. It was like those stories people told about dolphins fighting off a shark to save a swimmer. Something that happened so rarely it might as well be an urban legend. And yet there they were, her burning lungs and limbs convincing her it was happening. The dog might not lead anywhere good, but they followed.

Through the trees, as they climbed higher, she began seeing disturbing amounts of orange glow cutting across the terrain in every direction, and mentally replayed updates they'd been given before heading out. Separate fires. All should be moving the same direction, but what she saw... If her heart hadn't already been galloping, it would've rocketed up.

"Are you seeing four fires or three?" she asked, continuing to climb.

Beck couldn't stop and keep up with the dog, but he did look between the trees when he could, and opened the comm.

"This is Ellison. Want a fire check. Position. Size. Movement."

Did he usually call in? She knew from the day Treadwell had fallen and she'd spent so much time chasing Beck from one end of the field to the other that he didn't give updates.

Was he trying to change? She wished...

The suddenness of the change suggested otherwise, this was the kind of thing they'd been fighting about.

Report came in from the spotters quickly enough. Three fires, the one to the north large enough to wrap around the backside of a peak, appearing like a fourth, and the one they'd been tending had closed the gap behind them. Going back that way was no longer possible.

She stopped asking questions, he might think she was afraid.

She was, but letting him see that after the thing with Kolinski? Dumb. Once again, she was right back in that old pattern she'd had to operate in for years: hiding vulnerabilities from those she loved because they might use them against her.

There was nothing he could do to stop her from being on the mountain now, and he *had* included her in the decision to follow the dog, but she no longer trusted him. She might have won this time, but what would happen next time? This fire season was already one for the record books, and there would be a next time.

After she confessed, there would still probably be a lot more next times—the season was fierce and they needed the help. She might get a slap on the wrist for her application shenanigans, but if she confessed, that would help her case. If she could do the job, they'd keep her around. But Beck didn't want her doing it. He said *for now*, but she wasn't putting her life on hold to soothe him when he wouldn't get the help he needed to deal with his own problem.

Hell, at this point her application blunder was probably a lesser sin than her knowing Beck's issues and not reporting *him*. But *she* was loyal. Because despite knowing how this was going to go, and that it was over with them, she still wanted to see him whole. She didn't want anyone exposing her vulnerable spots, so how could she expose his?

They reached a rocky outcropping and the dog disappeared over it. Beck held out his hand to stop her going forward, and a moment later swung down himself.

"Sir?" His voice came from the other side, the one word the only confirmation Lauren needed to follow.

An unconscious man with a bloody leg lay on the ground, left femur protruding from his skin. The dog who'd led them there began a high, frantic whimper and lay down beside his human.

"Is he alive?" she asked, not able to see if the unconscious man's chest moved but noticing flies swarming the terrible wound, then the drag marks in the earth down the slope where he'd obviously scooted himself to reach the meager rock shelter.

Beck felt for a pulse, nodded to her. "Do you think he'll wake if I lift him? That break..."

"He's going to be in agony if you throw him over your shoulder," Lauren said, already pulling her pack off so she could fish out the collapsible stretcher that had been hers to carry.

"He might have to suffer it. If that direction isn't better..." he nodded down the other side from the one they'd traveled "...we can't carry him on a stretcher down the way we came up. It's too steep."

"Not if we go straight down, but we can cut across. Take it at a shallower angle."

"Fire's moving," he grunted, and then gestured for the stretcher, which she handed over for him to begin assembling.

"That bone is bad. I know it's already been exposed to the elements, and worse, but we should at least try to cover it," she said, getting the man's pulse and directing, "Call in. Tell them we found Henderson."

"Henderson?"

"The name on the tags," she explained, then let go of his wrist. "His heart is going too fast. And he feels hot. Do you have an unopened water bottle?"

She knew enough about first aid to know compound fractures became infected very easily, and he'd been there at least the night. The storm that sparked the fires hadn't dropped as much rain as it had lightning, but it had wet the ground so his dry clothes had become caked along the sides with mud when he'd slid under the ledge.

"Yeah, why?"

"I don't know. I just...feel like I should at least pour the water over the end and rinse the..." She wasn't going to say it. She didn't actually even want to think what bugs were in the wound.

"Sorry I don't have salt, seems like saline would be better for flushing any wounds."

"It would."

He laid the stretcher out, then pulled his pack off to dig out the water and first-aid supplies. "Here. Gauze and bandages. Wrap it, anything is better than nothing."

She took the supplies and began opening them while looking for some way to wrap the leg. He was out. They might be able to give his leg the kind of jerk that would pull the bone back into the skin, but that could make things worse. Drag infection directly into the body.

She laid the large gauze pad over the raw end of the bone, then lifted his leg enough to wrap the elastic bandage around and around, just to cover. Keep the bugs away...

"Should we rouse him?"

"Pain will be unbearable," Beck said, finally raising base on the comm.

Treadwell responded as Beck relayed the situation and their location, got directions where to go—down to the river. Follow it out. An ambulance would be waiting. And there they'd part. It might be possible for her to work with him out here, but continuing to do so for the rest of camp would be torturing herself for no reason.

"What about bracing his neck?"

Beck looked at the man, then shook his head. "He scooted himself up the mountain. His head seems well attached. Besides, I don't have a neck brace in there. And we need to move, the wind is kicking up. Everything's going to spread faster."

Right. Stay focused on what was before them. Injured man. Fast-moving fire. Treacherous mountainous terrain.

"Okay, I'll get his head until we clear the ledge, then we swap."

He looked at her strangely.

"Head's heavier, but the ledge wants someone short. Might as well use our advantages." They had a few of them, and even if a future together couldn't happen, they could use their advantages today.

Halfway down the mountain, Lauren could just make out something large and white on the riverbank. "Beck? I think there's a boat..."

"God, I hope so."

This trek was already worse than the pack carry, but at least it came with built-in reward. He might survive. And the dog...

As they hurried, and sometimes slid, Beck checked in for updates. All smokejumpers were rigged with GPS to make them easier to find if things got hairy, but he still did it. Small victory, but she'd take it.

CHAPTER THIRTEEN

A TWO-MILE TREK became a three-hour endurance test.

Beck had to fight every urge in him to put the unconscious man over his shoulder and abandon the stretcher, just so they could move faster. It wasn't that Lauren wasn't pulling her weight, but moving over taxing terrain was hard enough without carrying a stretcher and dodging a worried dog perpetually underfoot.

By the time they reached the water, it should've become easier, and would've been except for a stretch of narrow ledge they had to pass to reach the boat without climbing over another steep rise.

"What do you want to do?" She stopped and looked back at him, then pointedly over his shoulder to the burning hillside acres away behind them. She carried the handles of the stretcher at each hip so she could move forward instead of miles of dangerous backing. They didn't have time for anything that slowed them down.

"We don't have a choice." He nodded to the handles. "We might need to change the way we're carrying if you can't walk with your arms at the sides."

The sound of rushing water made the decision even more treacherous. It looked deep, and violent. Even if it were only deep enough to come to her ribs, it still moved with the kind of strength that would make it impossible to walk and carry the man—who'd yet to awaken.

"Cross that bridge when we come to it," she muttered, and then started walking. The warnings in his belly hit ear-splitting decibels, but there was nothing else. Nothing but the fire behind them and the water beside him. Nothing but remembering his mother's terrible decision. As they walked, it was right there at the front of his mind, taking the attention he should've been paying to his feet and the path. He'd slid twice and nearly dropped the man or knocked Lauren into the water by the time they reached the end.

"Give me a second, I have to wipe my hands…palms… sweating…" she panted, moving to a spot where she could bend to put her end down. Which was when she looked past him to the narrow strip of precarious land they'd just traveled. "Where's the dog?"

The dog?

He turned as well. The border collie that had led them to his injured owner was nowhere in sight.

"Damn," he muttered, and then held up one hand. "I'll go grab him, if I can."

A quick look back at the water offered no comfort to him. If the dog had fallen in, it would've probably been swept past before he'd known to look.

And the fire.

Running back toward the fire… He swallowed the bitter plug in his throat. It wasn't that far, not even half a football field. It was the bend in the ledge that made it impossible to see the other end.

"Be careful. Yell if you have trouble."

"If I have trouble, you grab the handles of that stretcher and drag it to the water," he said, pointing to another out-cropping with a far wider ledge. "The boat is just past that bend, if I remember right. You can make that with him if I don't come back."

Her eyes narrowed, and she folded her arms. Staying there to argue wouldn't serve any purpose. She'd move when the fire came, if he didn't come back. She wasn't suicidal.

Moving faster than the first time across, he'd reached the other end in minutes and found the dog pacing back and forth, whining as he looked at the ground then at the water.

"Come on, buddy. It's okay." He didn't feel like talking sweet, but flies and honey… If the dog ran now, he'd have to leave it behind. The very idea of that made his stomach lurch. He might have vomited on the spot if there had been anything inside him after a long day.

A little whistle, crouching, hand outstretched… When the fluffy black-and-white dog came to him, Beck snatched him up from the ground and turned to head back down the path.

Immediately, he knew he'd screwed up, holding the dog to face the water that scared him.

It took all his balance and strength to keep hold of the suddenly thrashing animal. About halfway there, the dog whipped his upper body hard to one side, knocking his head against Beck's temple. His head ringing, he became aware of gravity shifting below him. Tilting. Falling…

No hands to grab with. No land behind to step on. He heaved the loudly yelping dog toward the ground as he fell back.

There was cold, then pain, then nothing.

A terrible yelp sounded from up the path, and by the time Lauren straightened from the crouch where she'd been checking the unconscious man's pulse the dog came rocketing toward her, tail and hind end tucked down in fear.

Where was Beck?

"Beck!" She shouted his name, but caught sight of something orange bobbing in the water, and her heart slammed into overdrive.

Due to the nature of the water, he didn't rush in one direction but bounced like a pinball in the rocky, whirlpool-laden waters. As quickly as she could, Lauren scrambled onto the biggest, deepest rocky bend and held on with one hand while stretching as hard as she could over the water.

Two more hits, she couldn't even tell what part of him was hitting the rocks, just that he wasn't moving on his own. His head wasn't coming up but stayed in the water.

Any second, come on... He'd be there. She could grab him. Get him out somehow.

A sudden rush of the water nearly shot him right past her. Her fingers slid over the heavy heat-resistant material of his pants and jacket, only finding purchase at his collar.

"Beck!" She shouted his name again, jerking with all her might to try and get him out of the water, but the suit had filled, making him heavier.

She managed to lift his head out of the water and tugged him a little closer. "Come on, wake up. Wake up!"

He coughed, the first sign of life she'd heard, and she almost choked on tears springing to her eyes.

Alive. But not awake.

Bracing her foot on a closer, slippery boulder, she got enough leverage to drag his shoulders up the rock and did the only thing she could think of—let go with her other handhold long enough to slap him before the water jerked them both in.

On the second slap, he coughed again and began to flail. It took her screaming his name more times than she could count before he roused enough to find purchase on the rocks and help her pull him out.

Red water ran down the side of his face from his dark hair. His nose was also clearly never going to be the same. She almost regretted slapping him.

"Can you stand up?"

He coughed more, then looked in the direction they'd come from, and the even closer fire.

No direct answer, he just accepted her hands in assistance and staggered to his feet.

AMALIE BERLIN 165

The protective gear he wore weighed him down, and he began stripping out of it. "Go."

"Not without you."

"Drag him to the boat. I'll come. Don't come back. Go." He breathed hard and fast, and even with the water rushing she could hear wet sounds in his rasping breaths.

Disobedient as she was, she didn't start moving until she'd helped him out of the pants, leaving him in sodden shorts, T-shirt, and boots.

"Go," he said again, and since she couldn't help them both at once, Lauren did.

They weren't far from the boat, Beck had said, but she wasn't sure how far, only knew she had to get there.

As she dragged the stretcher, it began to come apart. Forty or fifty yards to a short stretch of pebbled shore where a motorboat had been pulled onto the shore. She dragged the now canvas sled and man there to find the dog waiting.

Wasting no time, she heaved the man into the boat, as careful as she could be of his leg, given the situation, coaxed the skittish dog in as well, then ran back for Beck.

She'd never felt fear like the thousand icy needles down her back. His head had to have hit hard to make it bleed like that, didn't it? Was he even still up and walking? Breathing? He'd breathed in water, and with those rocks he'd probably broken ribs.

She almost ran smack into him as she got around a bend, and ducked under his arm, spun, and slung an arm around his waist to give him something to lean on.

"I said…" he started. But when he looked into her eyes, and the tears she could do nothing to stop, whatever he'd been about to say died in his throat.

There was no time to explore it, no time to reflect. No time to let him rest, even if it felt cruel to make him continue. She could feel the heat from the fire now as it moved fast over dry brush. They needed to get to the boat, get the boat into the water, and figure out how to make it go—the one part of this she had no idea how to do, or even if he'd still be conscious by the time they got there.

"If you think I'm going to leave you here, you're too stupid to do this job." The hiccup that came from her at the end of her half-shouted words surprised them both.

Something like horror shrouded his dark eyes, an expression she knew she mirrored in the face of bright, red blood running more thickly now down his cheek.

"Shut up," she shouted, although he hadn't said anything, and sped up, making him walk faster than she knew he should be.

Every step pained him, she heard it in his breathing and the occasional gasp when she squeezed a little tighter to keep him upright—it seemed he was always about to fall over.

It felt like it took a year to make it to the boat, and there was a brief argument about him wanting to help push it into the water—as if he could—and she finally got them in.

"I don't know what to do."

"Motor," he said, then took a ragged breath. "Works like a lawnmower."

"Okay."

"Pull the cord." He gave the steps, with several pauses. Ending with, "Don't go fast."

Right. Because if she crashed them into something, the water would get them, not the fire.

The river became wider and more shallow dozens of yards downriver, and as it broadened out, it became less fast-moving.

"Your comm working?" Beck was still with it enough to keep her focused, prompting her to call in once the way got smoother.

Treadwell answered, and she asked for two ambulances and followed his instructions on where to take the boat.

Through the miracle of GPS, he'd been monitoring their progress and was ready for them.

It wasn't far or long. A couple of miles of awkward boating until they reached a bridge where two ambulances sat, lights on, doors open, EMT teams and police on the shore with stretchers, ready to pull them in.

Beck didn't put up a fight about being strapped onto the stretcher, and if she hadn't been worried before, she would've been then.

He'd gone quite pale, whiteness around his mouth speaking of the pain she knew he was in, and maybe reduced lung capacity—his breathing sounded so bad.

She and Treadwell climbed into the ambulance with him. The police took custody of the heroic border collie, and the other ambulance took the still-unconscious Henderson.

"What happened out there?" Treadwell asked *her*, and she wasn't entirely sure, but filled in what she knew. Beck had gone back for the dog, something had happened, he'd fallen. She'd fished him out.

The report didn't take long, and the only reason she knew Beck wasn't unconscious or asleep was the whiteness of his knuckles where he gripped the sheet.

Decisions that had been brewing in her mind came to a head all at once.

It wasn't because he hadn't wanted her to go today, or because she felt any confusion about where she belonged—whatever questions she'd had were answered. But she wanted to do this right, out in the open. Before she lost her nerve she said, "Chief, I need to tell you something."

Beck's eyes whipped open, skewering her over the short distance to where she perched at the foot of his stretcher. The chief opposite her watched her with equal attention. She turned her gaze back to the man in control of her career, focusing there.

"Before the first jump this season, I had never actually finished my skydiving training…"

CHAPTER FOURTEEN

DESPITE NOT KNOWING whether she'd be allowed at the camp come Monday, Lauren had the good fortune of being in for now and given the honor of a four a.m. ride the next morning by a local policeman Treadwell called in.

She'd been looked over immediately upon arriving, deemed perfectly fine aside from some dehydration, and released before nightfall. Beck hadn't been so lucky. His injuries required admittance in the hours in between. Treadwell had been kind enough to bring her updates about his condition after finding her loitering in the hallway outside his room, unable to go inside.

Concussion.

Fractured ribs.

Water in his lungs he hadn't been able to cough out and they were forcing him to now.

Prognosis: he'd live.

But he was out for the season.

Now, at five in the morning, she soaked in the tub, waiting for the sun to come up so she could call her father.

She'd made decisions over the long hours in the waiting room to learn Beck's condition, and even without knowing whether or not she'd be welcome at camp come Monday, she knew she wouldn't be returning to her family's station in San Francisco. She wanted to tell him that. Tell him everything, actually. Not to gloat, she didn't have that in her, even if she now knew beyond any doubt she was doing what she was meant to.

It was just time. Get her life in order. Make hard decisions. The only thing she could control was living her life without fear of what other people would say. Whatever Dad said didn't matter as long as she was satisfied with herself.

She couldn't pick her family. She loved them, and had to figure out how to deal with them and have a relationship.

But with Beck? They hadn't exactly talked about what they were going to do after camp, but she'd hoped there would be an after. Now all she could think was that she couldn't stay with a man who either held her back or had a death wish.

Death wish might not be fair. He *had* been trying to survive, walking to her through the pain that made him move at a slow stagger, the head injuries messing with his balance... He hadn't said so, would never say so, but he'd been *trying* to reach the boat.

Death wish wasn't a fair label. Martyr might be.

Someone who wanted his death to mean something?

Someone who wanted his *life* to mean something?

When the bath started growing cold, she climbed out, pulled on a robe, and went to get her phone.

Her father answered on the first ring, and in a tone so calm she even surprised herself, Lauren laid it all out for him. Her harrowing day. Her lie. Her possibly being fired before she was actually hired. The man they'd saved. That she wouldn't be returning home to work again.

"So, you're asking me to help you transfer to another house?"

"No, Dad. I'm not asking you for anything," she said, and then the thought occurred... "Actually, there is something you can do for me if you're willing."

"What?"

"My friend? His mom died and was swept away by the river near their house up here about fifteen years ago. Never found her that he knows of. If I can get you his DNA, do you think you can get one of your cop buddies to run it against any Jane Does they've found in the past fifteen years?"

"How are you going to get his DNA?"

"His toothbrush is here."

"Don't know if it'll fly, legally, but for another member of the service I'll ask. I know some people."

Of course he did. Chief Richard Autry knew everyone. "Thanks, Dad."

"You let me know where you land, sugar bean."

Her lower lip wobbled, but she managed to say, "I will. Love you."

She hung up before the tears really started to pour.

The smell of antiseptic was as far from a forest as possible, and made every second he was forced to spend in the hospital suck.

What made it worse was Lauren not being there. He couldn't believe he'd grown so hooked on her presence in such a short period of time. And he didn't want to believe what her absence probably meant.

Treadwell, currently sleeping in the recliner beside Beck's bed, had kept him awake for the first twenty-four hours by playing cards, making him do crosswords, play along with game shows when he found them on TV, narrated a fishing show in such a fashion that no one could sleep through it, and refused to listen when Beck told him for the thousandth time to go home.

"Here for vitals," a woman in scrubs announced when she came in, waking Treadwell.

Beck stuck out his arm.

"Is he getting out today?" the chief asked.

Beck grunted, "You're getting out today."

"Briefly, maybe."

"Have to wait for the doctor to come by, but probably

not. Want to make sure his lungs have recovered enough to be let loose in the wild," the nurse said, then gave him an encouraging smile that did nothing to encourage him. "You're one of the smokejumpers who brought in Mr. Henderson, right?"

"Yeah." Beck wanted to hear about Lauren, but Treadwell had refused to talk about her any of the times he'd asked. Hearing about Henderson was the next best thing. "How's he doing?"

Her smile widened and she wrote down Beck's vitals as she took them. "He's awake."

"Yeah?"

"Yeah. They're taking good care of him."

"Good news," Treadwell said softly from the recliner. "You and Autry made a good team."

Made.

Past tense.

Beck's stomach churned, but he held his tongue until the nurse was done prodding him. He wanted to contradict the chief, *make a good team*, but she might no longer be willing to put up with him.

When they were alone, he asked, "Are you talking about her now?"

"You're better."

Well enough to hear bad news. "Have you talked to her?"

"On all my trips out of your rooms until the wee hours."

"She's all right?"

"She's uninjured. Don't know about *all right*."

Of course she wasn't completely all right. He knew he'd scared her. He just hadn't really been able to consider how much until she'd come back for him, and pushed him along through her own tears. Lauren crying… Finally giving in to the tears she usually contained. The idea slammed him in the guts every time.

"Does she get to keep her job?" he asked, because he couldn't not ask.

Treadwell waited for him to look over and nodded. "She does. I let her know last night, but I'm busting her back to pure rookie status. No more jumps until training is over, and I'm making her lead a talk about what you two went through today."

"But you know she can do it, she doesn't need to go back a step."

"I know she can do it. Just like I knew you didn't need to go through the training to do your job. But it still helped you."

"I'm not so sure."

"Why not?"

Beck could tell him the truth. Tell him everything, the things he didn't talk about to anyone but Lauren. The things she'd said Treadwell deserved to know. But he might think the training had had a less positive impact on Beck than he'd thought.

"Are you glad she told you? We'd already remedied the situation."

"I need my people to trust I'll have their backs when the situation arises, that I'll make the right call for them and everyone else."

Treadwell couldn't have made a more loaded statement if he'd spent the whole night crafting and polishing the words.

Whether or not Treadwell knew that Beck still struggled with that, Beck knew.

She'd been brave. Her telling the chief the truth was a much bigger risk than him telling the chief now.

It wasn't so much that he wanted to hide these things, it was just hard to think about, to talk about. And there was something to be said for avoiding pity...

But he didn't want to be the mess he'd become. He wanted to be better. Be someone deserving of Lauren, not some pale shadow of her bravery.

Even if he'd already screwed up too badly to ever get her back, he could follow her example.

"Will you go home and get some sleep if I tell you what's been going on with me?" As the words came, Beck had already started shaking his head at himself. "I don't want you having another heart attack from the antiseptic stench and lousy food."

Lauren opened the door of the cabin after a long day, and stumbled over the single step up.

Beck sat on the sofa, calmly watching her.

Something gave her the power to grab the doorframe and stop herself going down at the last second and avoid eating floor.

"Hey…" she greeted him, as if it hadn't been nine days since she'd seen him.

"Hey," he said quietly in return, sitting forward slowly on the sofa. "I hope it's all right for me to come in while you're out. I realize it's not exactly my cabin anymore."

"It's fine. I mean, your stuff is still here." She swept her arm toward the bedroom he'd occupied, and saw it standing open with a stuffed duffel bag acting as a doorstop.

He probably shouldn't be carrying that. Broken ribs didn't heal overnight, and it only felt like forever since he'd been smashed along the river. "You should let me carry that for you."

"Yeah, maybe." He reached out and tapped a mason jar full of salts on the table before him. "Thought you could probably use another batch, and now I see you, I know you can. You look wiped out."

"I've been doing extra PT."

"Why?"

"To make sure I'm as strong as I can be," she lied. Funny how easy it was to fall back into patterns to cover those vulnerable spots. She'd sworn off them and proclaimed she was going to live in the open air, but with Beck... "Actually, I've been doing extra every day so that I sleep well."

"Why aren't you sleeping well?"

"I'm sleeping okay. I just want to be extra tired so I'll go right to sleep."

His gaze sharpened, and she noticed how dark he was beneath his eyes, a shadow deeper than simple sleepless nights.

"Are both of your eyes black?"

"Smashing into rocks with my head did it." He gestured to the place on the side where she remembered him bleeding. "Treadwell said it knocked some sense into me. I'm not sure it was the rocks."

"Did something else hit you?"

"Just you. Like a fire truck."

The imagery was so mixed she didn't know whether it was meant to be good or not. Hitting like a truck didn't sound good; knocking sense into him did...

"I'm pretty sure I didn't."

"You did," he said so softly she wouldn't have been sure she'd heard it if she hadn't been watching his mouth form the words. "Why do you want to go right to sleep? Don't want to lie there thinking about how badly I screwed up?"

Assigning blame to their catastrophe felt like a betrayal. He'd screwed up, she'd screwed up. They were both screwed up. "Don't want to dwell on what could've been. I guess."

Her throat tightened as she spoke, until the end when her voice cracked, unable to contain the emotion, even without looking at him and the sadness she knew she'd see.

It was enough to get her moving again, straight past the sofa into the little kitchenette where she'd stashed a cooler and drinks.

Her hands shook hard enough that the wet plastic bottle of electrolyte-imbued drink shot from her fingers, bounced between her feet, and ricocheted backward across the kitchen floor before she'd even touched the lid.

It rolled over the linoleum, then suddenly stopped.

When she turned around, Beck had picked up the bottle and now wiped down the wet exterior on the comfortable-looking gray T-shirt he wore, then opened it for her.

It looked like an overture, him holding the drink out to her in invitation, but all she could do was stare at it, and then past to the dark, worried eyes of the man she spent every minute thinking about.

"If you take the drink, you're not obligated to take me back, you know," he said softly, plucking the thoughts straight from her mind.

Not obligated to *take me back*.

Did that mean he wanted her back? God knew, she wanted him, but her self-esteem had become progressively stronger over the past week. Wanting something and being able to have it weren't the same thing. Wanting something didn't make it good for her.

Snarky responses were her emotional currency. She was good at them and other tactics that kept her apart from others. Kept her safe. But standing there, her mouth dry and her eyes damp, she couldn't think of anything to say.

Drinking the drink would at least keep her mouth busy, less pressure to say something.

She took the bottle and drank deeply until about a third of it was gone.

All under the weight of his sad gaze.

"I don't know what to say. If you want to say something, just—"

"I talked to Treadwell," he cut in, skipping over the relationship talk into something safer.

Something he'd know she wanted to hear, she'd been pressing him to do it. A safe subject.

"What did you tell him?"

"Everything," he said, not quite a whisper but the kind of soft talk that wanted closeness. To be closer than they were, standing across the tiny kitchenette from one another.

"What's everything?"

"What happened to my mom. Why I lost the thread of what I was doing last season. Why I'm still struggling to get my feet under me."

No ring of finality came with his words, they almost sounded like a question.

"What changed your mind?"

"He wouldn't leave." Beck chuckled a little. "Slept by my bed, couldn't get rid of him. Wore me down, I guess."

Ah. Nothing to do with their trip down the mountain. Or her.

"I'm glad he stayed. So he kept asking?"

"No. I asked him if he was going to let you stay." He watched her too closely, as if also afraid of putting a foot out of line. Was this him trying to salvage a friendship? A working relationship? Something more? "He said he'd already talked to you about it, and you were staying. He was glad you told him because he needs his people to know he'll have their backs."

"Oh." She could see how that would be motivating. Not something to feel disappointment over. "I do feel that way. I guess he just needed to absorb it a bit, and in the ambulance, it was kind of a lot to take in while your condition was obviously the biggest concern. I probably should've waited, but once I'd decided..."

"When did you decide?"

She shifted, the urge to conceal again proving to her how far she still had to go to live in the open air. Not so much because the answer would hurt her this time, but it might hurt him. It definitely was a much closer blow to the subject they weren't talking about.

"In the hangar," she said finally, then drew a deep breath to fortify herself. "Treadwell has said he would welcome me onto his team after camp. But I told him I needed to talk to you first. It's your team too..."

"I want you there," he said without hesitation. "I want

you there even if you won't take me back today. Not because I want to keep an eye on you but because I'm hoping that eventually I'll prove myself to you, that I'll be able to get myself out of the red."

"Beck…"

"Because I love you. I knew it that morning, before we left. I can't excuse what I came damned close to doing, but I need to explain to you how I actually got there and said I loved you the first time in that way. I know how dirty that was. I know you probably don't even believe it…"

"I believe it." She waved a hand. "Slow down. For a man who never talks, you're saying a lot of things. I think I may have gotten used to listening slower."

He grinned then, and before she knew it he stood before her and had her cheeks in his hands, his lips pressing softly to her forehead.

"That's not slower," she choked, eyes stinging and ears suddenly itching, because that's just how lucky she was— every time she cried, she wanted to sit on the floor and kick her ear like a dog.

"Sorry. Sorry…" He reached up to scratch his head, seemed to remember the wound, and pulled his hand away again. "I don't remember what I was saying."

"You were saying you were a jerk to say you loved me to manipulate me not to jump."

"Wasn't manipulation," he argued. "It was pleading. Here's…here's the thing. On your first jump, when I went without you and then got to the ground to see your chute in the air, heading for the fire, the possibility of all the things that could happen to you became some kind of gruesome certainty they *would*. The more I felt for you, the bigger those ideas became in my mind. I know it's not fair. I know it's not rational. I know… Actually, I have a standing appointment with the counselor to try and screw my head on straight. I'm talking to her, and all I really want to do is talk to *you*."

Getting help, that was something real. Telling Treadwell. Talking to her without her having to badger and push.

"Or touch you. Which… I'm going to put my hands in my pockets to avoid."

It was cute. The man who glowered his way through life actually looked like he was about ten years younger as he stood there, hands stretching the pockets of his jeans down from how far in he'd shoved them.

"You're not angry that I didn't come visit?"

"I know why you didn't come, honey. But I want you to know, it wasn't your absence that changed my mind about what I've been doing."

"The chief?"

"It was your tears," he said, his hands jerking the pockets again, controlling that urge to touch and connect. "Seeing the misery and fear on your face. Something you said back on the bus that day about what if my mom had been the one to survive. I saw it in your eyes when you came back for me."

Her breathing sped up and her vision began to wave like rising heat. She was going to cry again. If she opened her mouth to talk, what came out wouldn't be words.

"I never want you to have to live with what I've lived with."

She gave up trying to make words take shape in her head and just held her hand out to him. Both of his shot from his pockets at once and he pulled her close, grunting a little from how hard he'd tugged and she'd impacted.

That got through.

"Your ribs!" She registered that her voice had gone screeching into the stratosphere, but he didn't let go of her even when she made to pull back.

"I have a fresh batch of salts," he whispered into her hair, and she gave in and rested her forehead against the center of his chest, her hands on his hips because she still couldn't bring herself to squeeze back as the tears began to fall and her nose stopped working.

The last sniff she managed through her rapidly swelling sinuses confirmed he still had the smell of hospital on him.

"You do seem to need a bath," she teased, tilting her head back to look at him. "But I do too."

"Honey and dirt." He looked at her mouth long and hard. "I'm about to ask you to have a bath with me while still wondering if it's okay to kiss you… See how much I have to learn about relationships?"

She lifted her mouth, not warning him about how salty she probably was. Or that her nose might be about to run and he should kiss her quickly. When his lips pressed to hers, trembling met trembling, regret and relief, and a golden ray of hope, warming like morning's first sunshine. Bright. So full of promise as to be blinding.

When he lifted his head, his gaze traveled over her wet cheeks and he lifted his hands to brush the tears away. "You're still crying."

"I've been working myself to exhaustion to avoid it." She laughed a little. "But it's easing up. We could have a bath, and then the wetness won't be so obvious."

His smile was all cheek as he turned with her to walk to the table to fetch the salts to take with them. "You have good ideas."

"Sometimes," she said, feeling the first urge to smile in forever, and with an uncontrollable urge to tease him, to play. "I hope you don't think we're going to have sex in here. You're hurt. You don't need jostling."

"You planning to jostle me?"

"Nothing strenuous. Like that bag. You can't carry that bag right now. Were you going to take it to your truck?"

He stopped at the bathroom door, still holding her hand, still looking a little worried. "If you're not ready."

"Really?" she asked, rising on her toes to kiss him. "There you go again, thinking I can't handle what I say I can handle."

EPILOGUE

Two years and three months later...

LAUREN ELLISON STOOD at the kitchen window to the newly rebuilt wooded cottage she shared with her husband, staring out at the shiny new workshop he'd disappeared into. It had been almost two hours since they'd returned home from his mother's long-overdue memorial service.

California's records had provided no matches for Beck's DNA, but two months ago officials in southern Oregon had contacted them. Scant remains washed ashore years ago had finally been tested. They'd found her. Proof she'd drowned, not burned. A few weeks' bureaucratic wrangling and they'd finally obtained the permission required to bring Molly Ellison home.

He'd seemed all right after the quiet service, surrounded by his new family, people who'd never met his mother but who wanted to pay their respects to the woman who'd given the Autry clan its fourth son. It had been two hours, alone in the one place on their little homestead she'd promised not to go.

They'd reached that unbelievable place where anything could be said as long as it was said with love. At work. At home. Anywhere. Best friends. Partners. Lovers. And, someday soon, parents.

Actually, he was in the one place she'd promised not to

go *inside*. She could go to the door. Just to check on him. Make sure he knew she was there if he needed her.

She hurried out the back door and soon stood at the door of the man cave, and knocked. "Babe? You still in there?"

In seconds, he appeared there, still looking crisp in the white button-down he'd worn to the service. Not falling apart. Not bereft, although she still saw the sadness of the day lingering in his inky eyes.

"I'm not going anywhere."

He leaned down to steal a little kiss, and since it seemed final, she nodded and made to step back from the door.

"Just needed to make sure you were okay." She still wasn't sure he was, but the hand at her waist firmed and began to steer her around so she stood with her back to the door. "Um…if you want me to go…"

"I don't." He stayed with her outside the building, and when she looked over her shoulder at him, he smiled. "I have a surprise in the workshop. But I want you to close your eyes. It's not wrapped."

He wanted her to come inside his hideaway? She'd spent months wondering what he was making out here—chairs, tables, a fancy hutch for the metric boatload of papercraft supplies she'd accumulated after realizing last winter she had time to put together scrapbooks of their exploits for their future children.

"Is it furniture? People don't wrap furniture, do they?" He'd brought in wood and supplies the day the small building had been considered functional. The woodshop was his second favorite place to be, outside the woods. Or maybe third, if bed with her got counted as a prime location, and it did. "It's big, right?"

"Play along." He put one large, warm hand over her eyes, then wrapped his other arm around her waist to spin her slowly back toward the building, using his body to propel her forward. "Step."

She did, trusting him to steer her but still reaching out ahead of her with waving hands to keep from hitting anything.

Not ten paces in, he stopped them, pulling her back against his warmth and breathing in her ear. "You ready?"

"Uh…*yeah*! You know I'm not good at playing along or playing it cool." She wrapped her hands around the hand covering her eyes and gave a little tug.

His hand dropped and with the low lighting inside it took her eyes time to adjust.

Darkness began to fade and lines appeared, then shapes, and finally detail.

Arcs for feet, legs, wooden spindles, a mattress. And a teddy bear in the center. Cradle. Rocking cradle. For the children they didn't yet have and hadn't actually started to plan yet.

She felt herself moving forward again, and he let go so she could touch it. Running her fingers over the smooth, polished wood still didn't make it seem real. "This is what you've been making all this time?"

"Don't like it?" he asked. "I thought…make the cradle and then, when I was ready, I'd give it to you."

Ready? Did ready mean…?

"When did you get done?"

"This morning."

She couldn't stop touching the smooth, cool gray wood. "What kind of wood is this?"

"Tan oak." He answered all the questions except the one she hadn't asked. She never wanted to push when it came to children, but this… She had to ask.

"So, this morning you got finished and you're just really excited and want to show me?"

"This morning I got finished, and realized as soon as I placed the bear in it that I was ready."

"You're ready?" she repeated, and left the beautiful,

still-rocking cradle to return to her even more beautiful husband. "Are you trying to tell me you've gone and gotten yourself in the family way, Mr. Ellison?"

He smiled at her teasing and pulled his arms around her as she pressed close. "I'm willing to try. We can just have lots of unprotected sex and whoever gets pregnant first can do the heavy lifting on this one."

"That's good to know, because I have something to tell you." She tilted her head back to watch his face, to experience every drop of joy this life had to offer. "I win."

* * * * *

A SINGLE DAD TO
RESCUE HER

SUE MacKAY

PROLOGUE

KAYLA JOHNSON COUGHED out a mouthful of snow and forced her eyes open enough to blink into yet more snow. Her arms were jammed against her sides, preventing her from wiping her face clear. What the hell? This was weird. Frightening. She was immobilised, not sure where she was. Scary. What had happened?

Wake up, Kayla. It's a nightmare.

Except her arms didn't move. This was real.

'Help. I—I'm stuck,' she shouted, except it came out as a croak.

How long had she been out for the count? Was she really awake? Or was this truly a nightmare? Trying to move proved she was awake and this was real. Didn't it? Deep breath, pain in her lungs. 'H-help.'

'Hello? Anybody there?' A booming voice cut through the cracking sound of restless snow.

'H-here.' Waving might catch someone's attention, but she needed her arms free for that. The weight holding her immobile felt enormous and expansive. Her legs couldn't move, and from their direction a trickle of pain was making itself known. More damned snow. Her teeth chattered. She was so, so cold. If she ever got out of here she was moving to an island in the sun.

What the hell happened? Slowly it came to her, one

image at a time. She was skiing. Then a deep rumble like an approaching road train. Her feet going from beneath her. Hurtling down the slope, head over boots, head, boots, tossed about like a pebble on the side of the mountain. An avalanche maybe…? All she knew was that she was stuck.

'I'm over here,' she yelled, putting everything into it and managing a little better than the previous croak. Why couldn't she move? If she didn't get someone's attention soon she would be in big trouble. Panic rose. She was helpless, unable to do a thing. Except keep squawking. 'H-help.'

'Hey, I see you.' A dark shape reached her, covered her with a shadow as he blocked out the little sunlight left, chilling her further even as relief rose.

'Hello,' she croaked. *Get me out of here.*

'I'm Jamie.' He looked over his shoulder and waved. 'Over here, guys.' Thankfully he turned back to her. 'There're teams out looking for people caught in the avalanche. How many were with you?'

She thought about it. 'Two. Women from the club.' So it was an avalanche. With the confirmation came the horror of having been thrown about totally out of control and fearing for her life, swamping Kayla as she stared at the giant of a man kneeling beside her. She tried to hang onto his presence and the sense of reality he brought. She wasn't alone any more. Or was this still a nightmare she had yet to wake up from? Or worse. 'I am alive, right? I mean…' Her voice petered out as she began shaking harder. What was wrong? Why *was* she unable to move? She hadn't broken her back, had she? Panic rose. Her mouth dried, her heart banged erratically.

The man locked a strong gaze on her. 'Yes, you are

well and truly alive. What's your name?' He began scooping snow away with his gloved hands.

My name? Think.

She tried to clear her mind with a shake of her head, and a throb started up.

Think. Got it.

'Kayla Johnson. I'm a paramedic.' Like that was of any use right now. She needed a paramedic helping her, not to be one, because that pain was racing now, taking over, beating the cold aside. 'Something's wrong with my legs.' At least her mind had cleared.

'Easy now, Kayla.' A large gloved hand tapped her shoulder. 'First we've got to get you out of the snow and wrapped in a thermal blanket.'

'Don't move me until you've checked me over.' Once a medical brain, always a medical brain. She didn't think her spine was injured or surely she wouldn't be feeling this pain from her legs? But her rescuer had to be careful until she was certain. 'Who are you?' she asked. What had he said his name was? He looked a little familiar. That deep voice also struck a chord. 'Do we know each other?'

'I'm Jamie Gordon. The local fire chief. I do search and rescue in my spare time.' Other people were now working with him to shift the snow. Her saviour took off his gloves and reached for her first freed hand, wrapping it tightly in his strong, warm fingers. 'Are you visiting Queenstown?'

Was she? 'No. I've moved back permanently.' Of course. She had come home three weeks ago to kick-start her life, to put the debilitating sadness behind her and find some of her old zest for living that had died with her husband.

Doing a great job of that, Kayla. This is going to set you further back.

'Kayla? Are you with me?' A deep, tense sound was like sugar to her ears, warmth to her cold.

Opening her eyes, she stared up at a concerned face. 'I think so. My head's thumping and I feel like I'm coming and going.' She understood why he was making her talk; it would help keep her focused.

Jamie nodded. 'You're doing well. I'll check your vitals shortly but first we need to get you out of this snow and warming up. We're nearly done.' Another squeeze of her hand then he withdrew his touch, put his glove back on.

Leaving her feeling alone despite two other people working to free her.

Come back, Jamie. Hold me.

'There's a doctor waiting at the chairlift building for anyone we find. Also a helicopter on standby.' He hadn't gone anywhere.

Relief again filled her. It was great having a man at her side when she was feeling so out of control. She hadn't had that, or allowed that, since Dylan had died. Dylan? Why think about him now? He'd been gone three years, and she was still trying to get back on her feet and move on, but not like this. Was she going to be all right? 'I'm not joining Dylan, am I?' Was Jamie a figment of her imagination? She tensed, squeezing her muscles to see if she was alive. Pain ripped through her legs up into her abdomen, telling her, yes, she was very much alive. Her head swam. Her eyes seemed to roll backwards. Was she dying?

'Kayla. Stay with me.' A deep voice. Jamie What's-His-Name's voice. Nothing like Dylan's. She *was* alive.

Her eyelids were too heavy to lift.

'Kayla.' Sharp now. 'It's Jamie.' Her hand was being squeezed. 'Your rescuer.'

Her eyes refused to open. But she could hear the man, could hold onto his presence by digging in deep to stay with him.

'Come on, Kayla. You can do this. We've lifted you onto the stretcher and wrapped a thermal blanket around you and are carrying the stretcher to the building where there's shelter and a doctor. We're looking after you, Kayla. You're going to be all right.'

That voice was a lifeline giving her strength. Finally she was staring at him.

Thank you.

The words were tangled in the thumping in her head and the need to hold onto the sight of this amazing man stomping through the snow, holding her hand, sharing his warmth while urging her to stay with him as others carried the stretcher. When had they moved her? Had they been careful? How had she missed all that? Concussion, said her medical brain. She preferred not knowing, chose to keep staring at Jamie Whoever and go with his words, 'You're going to be all right.' Except it wasn't true. The pain in her legs was killing her. What did it mean? Fractures? Bad ones? So bad she—

Stop, Kayla. This isn't doing you any good.

True, but what if she had such serious injuries that there'd be no getting past them? Was this life's way of telling her she had no right to want to kick-start things and begin enjoying life again? Should she crawl back into the dark hole and wait for another year to go by?

'Here we are. Now you'll get warm.' Jamie interrupted her fears, slowed them down. 'Doc, this is Kayla Johnson. We had to dig her out of the snow.' He turned away to fill in the details.

She couldn't hear what he said. His quieter tone wasn't getting through the ringing in her ears that had started the moment she'd been brought inside to the warmth. Frustration took over, and she shoved her arm out of the blanket to bump his hip. 'Tell me what's wrong,' she snapped, cringing when it came out as a whimper.

The big man came into focus as he crouched down beside her. 'I'm not a medic of any kind, but you were feeling pain in your legs and they aren't as straight as they should be.' He pulled a glove off and wrapped those comforting fingers around her hand again. 'It's hardly surprising you might've broken a bone or two, Kayla. From a witness's account of the avalanche you copped the worst of the three women in your group and are very lucky to have survived it.' He squeezed gently.

'Keep talking to me.' He anchored her, helped her believe she was alive. 'Was anyone else caught in the avalanche?' She gabbled so he wouldn't leave her, gripping his hand tight, regaining a sense of reality, along with relief at having made it back from the brink of something too horrible to think about.

'Not that we know.' Jamie stood up, still holding her hand. 'But I have to go out for a final check in case there was someone else on the slope we don't know about.' His chest expanded and he looked hard at her. 'You take care and look after yourself, okay?'

Of course he had to leave her. She'd get through this. She had to, without hanging onto his words and deep voice that held her together. 'I'll do my best. Thank you very much for finding me. Thank the others who helped, too.'

'I will. Now, can I have my hand back?'

His smile struck her deep, made her soft inside, and lifted some hope out of the chill shaking her body. It was the first time she'd felt hope in years. Would there be some good to come out of this latest mess she'd got herself into? History said no, while hope said possibly. She'd hang onto that over the coming days, which she suspected weren't going to be too wonderful. The pain in her legs was excruciating and had nothing to do with cold.

'If you have to,' she gasped through clenched teeth. Slowly unbending her fingers, she let her saviour go. 'Bye, Jamie.'

See you around sometime?

CHAPTER ONE

PARKING OUTSIDE THE Queenstown hospital five days later, Jamie stared at the building as though he'd never seen it before. Which was ridiculous. He'd often been here to follow up on people he'd helped rescue from fires or found with the search and rescue team.

Both his boys had had their share of misadventures that'd brought them to hospital, appendicitis for Ryder and a sprained wrist for Callum, to name a couple. But this was the first time he'd come to see a woman who'd touched him in a way he'd only known once before—the day he'd met the mother of his boys.

Rescuing Kayla had been intense. The pain etched in her face. The fear of dying in her eyes. Her demand to make certain her spine wasn't injured before moving her. His need to make her feel safe. Nothing new for the situation.

But Kayla Johnson's fierce grip on his hand as though she'd needed him to be strong for her and had been afraid to let go in case she lost hold of who she was had reached through the darkness that was his broken heart. Her fear mixed with determination that she would be all right had darkened her gaze, and made him aware of something he'd forgotten. The need to be strong and true to himself, no matter what was thrown at him.

That had brought him to this spot today while his brain was saying he was an idiot. What was to be gained by calling in? He wasn't in the market for a woman to share his life after his heart-wrenching divorce. Leanne had been the love of his life and now that he'd finally got back on his feet he wasn't ever opening up to being hurt like that again.

Whoa. He wasn't attracted to Kayla. Not at all. He couldn't be. There'd been a connection on the mountain, sure, but it didn't mean anything deep and serious. She might've woken him up to himself but that's where it ended. He'd visit as he'd done others and get on with his life.

According to her close friend Mallory—the on-duty pilot who had flown Kayla from the mountain to Dunedin—Kayla had been transferred back from the hospital there to Queenstown yesterday to be nearer her home and family. She'd broken both legs, one of them in two places, and suffered a serious concussion. The head injury explained her floating in and out of consciousness, and some of the odd things she'd said, like, 'am I alive,' and something about Dylan and was she joining him. He hadn't asked about any of that, figuring Mallory would tell him to mind his own business.

Really, he shouldn't be needing to visit a woman he didn't know and couldn't forget. The pain in her eyes, her fear, plus the relief and gratitude that had appeared every time he'd taken her frozen hand in his had got to him. It might've been normal for someone in shock, but that instant connection he'd felt made him wonder who she was other than a skier in need of being saved from those freezing temperatures and the dangers caused by the avalanche.

Rushing to help people kept other worrying thoughts

at bay, like were the boys truly happy now. Except he was about to visit Kayla because he actually wanted to get to know her a little bit more. Hold her hand again? Not likely. That would be going too far. She'd likely kick his butt—if her legs were in good working order, which obviously they weren't. This annoying need blindsided him in the middle of the night when he wasn't sleeping. But there was no denying that he really didn't want to drive away now Kayla was just beyond those brick walls.

So get on with it.

Pushing out of the work truck before he overthought his reasons for being here even more, Jamie headed for the main entrance of the hospital.

There was a small gift shop just inside the door with buckets of colourful flowers arranged seductively at the entrance to tempt people to get their money out. 'I'm such a sucker,' Jamie muttered as he strode along to the general ward, a bunch of blue and yellow irises in one hand. What had taken over his usually straightforward mind? Since when did he take flowers when he visited someone he'd helped rescue? Never. But then no one had drawn him in with eyes like Kayla's beguiling ones. She had appeared a kindred spirit—tough, soft, fierce about what she believed in.

That brought about a flicker of longing for a future he'd long put behind him. Where had she returned to Queenstown from? Why? Was she getting away from something that hadn't been good for her? Dylan? Like he had, was she re-establishing herself after being dealt a bad hand?

Pausing when he saw 'Kayla Johnson' scrawled on a whiteboard attached to the wall, he shook his head. Crazy. He wasn't interested in women other than as colleagues. He'd had his woman, loved her to bits and married her for ever. Then she'd done a number on him by leaving and taking their sons with her. At first Leanne had refused to accept they'd share raising the boys, saying his dangerous work kept him too busy to be able to take good care of them.

Winning the battle that had given him shared custody of Ryder and Callum had come at a cost. He'd never trust a woman to be a part of his life again. Certainly not while his sons were young and vulnerable, and probably even after they'd grown up and left home—perhaps sometime after they turned thirty and could fend for themselves. So why was he standing outside Kayla's room? It wasn't too late to leave.

'Looks like you've got another visitor,' said a woman inside the room, giving him no option but to continue his visit.

Ducking through the doorway, he stopped abruptly. Pale with dark shadows staining her upper cheeks, Kayla looked frail, unlike the fighting woman he'd found on the side of the mountain. Sitting in an awkward position, with long, dull blonde hair lying over her shoulders, she looked so uncomfortable he wanted to pick her up and carry her out into the sun that was trying to banish last night's storm clouds.

'Hello, Kayla. I'm Jamie.' She might not remember him when she'd been suffering from shock and a head knock.

She stared at him. 'I remember that steady gaze. It gave me strength to stay on top of what was happening.' Her words were followed with a tight smile.

'Your concussion can't have been too bad, then.' He'd given her strength? Something moved inside his chest. She was giving him a warmth he hadn't known in years. *Knock it off.*

He couldn't afford to get all cosy warm. Kayla might've been beating around in his head for days, but that's where it ended. Apart from this visit, that was. And the flowers in his hand. Too late to leave them outside the door. 'These are for you,' he said stupidly. Who else would they be for? It wasn't as though he could walk out with them for someone else. He looked around for a vase and saw three bouquets lined up on the windowsill in glass jars.

She gasped. 'They're lovely. You've spoilt me.'

Lady, you've only gone and made me glad I did buy the flowers.

'Any time.' Huh? What was with these dumb comments? Kayla must've unhinged him more than he'd realised. It could be because there'd been a steady stream of call-outs over the last week and he was overtired.

'I'll take those and find something to put them in.' The other woman in the room reached out for the bunch he held, her blue scrubs a giveaway to her role.

'Jamie found me.' Kayla watched him as she explained, a tenseness he didn't understand filling her tired eyes. 'He heard my feeble attempts to yell out and came across to start digging away the snow with his hands.'

'Lucky for you.' The nurse nodded at her patient.

'Very.'

'It was a good result.' The only sort he accepted. The bad ones stayed with him too long, destroying sleep while making him go over and over what he'd done and what more he could have tried, even when there had been no chance whatsoever of saving someone from a horrific event. The worst ones also made him more protective of his boys, while at the same time had him teaching them to be strong and take on obstacles so they could become confident and capable. He had become strong and so would his sons. Strength hadn't stopped life's knocks but it had let him survive them.

'What brings you here?' Kayla slowly put aside the e-book she'd been gripping.

'Thought I'd see how you're coming along.' Like he did with others after a rescue. Wasn't that what he was doing? Not in his book, it wasn't. He didn't usually feel sparks in his blood when he looked at a woman's face, or want to persist in learning more about her. All parts of his body and mind were supposed to be on lockdown around women.

Her eyes widened, obviously not missing his discomfort. 'You were very good to me. I appreciate how you talked so I didn't lose focus too much. I must've blacked out towards the end, though.'

Jamie gave in to the need to get closer and pulled up a chair and sat. 'You did. It was probably for the best as it would've been very painful when we shifted you onto the stretcher once we knew you hadn't injured your back. Your toes kept twitching every time I touched them,' he explained hurriedly when doubt entered her expression. Being a paramedic, she'd know they shouldn't move her without first strapping her to a board if there was any doubt about her injuries. Only problem with that theory was that it wasn't always possible. Certainly not when someone was contorted in a snow hole.

'Surprising they moved at all considering the fractures I received.' She shivered.

'Mallory filled me in on your injuries the next day when we were on a search for two little boys.'

'She told me.' Kayla sounded as though that was the last thing she'd wanted.

'She shouldn't have?'

Kayla shrugged. 'Mallory's convinced me to join S

and R when I'm back on my feet. I did go out once before this happened. I'd like to do more, especially after all the help I received.' She was ignoring his question, then.

'We're always looking for people to sign up, especially anyone with medical knowledge. I heard you've started working on the ambulances.' There'd be no getting away from her. His hands tightened, loosened. Why did that not scare the living daylights out of him? He was used to turning away women who tried to get close but this was different. Kayla had sparked an interest in *him*, not the other way around. He shouldn't have come. Should've dug out last summer's fire prevention plans and studied them in depth, even when he already knew them almost word for word.

But there was no denying there had been something about Kayla's tenacity and that vulnerability on the mountainside that had snared his interest and wasn't letting up. She didn't seem like someone who'd change her mind once she'd committed to something—or someone. His hands tightened on his thighs. Neither had Leanne in the beginning.

Forget that at your peril.

When he'd met Leanne they'd clicked instantly. Both had known what it was like to grow up feeling unloved. Her father had been harsh and demanding, nothing she did was good enough, and her mother had never stood up for her because she hadn't been good enough either. His parents didn't have any time for him or his five siblings. He'd asked his mother why she'd had children if she didn't love them. 'I was careless,' she'd told him. Right then he'd determined never to be like his mother or father, and would find love and give so much back. Yet it had still blown up in his face.

Kayla was talking. 'I started at the ambulance base as

an advanced paramedic three weeks ago.' Despair briefly glittered in her gaze as she stared down the bed. 'The doctors say I'll be out of action for up to four months.' A tight smile crept onto her face. 'I intend to prove them wrong. I'm aiming for three. I mightn't be able to climb mountains or go on long searches by then, but I'll be behind the wheel of the ambulance and helping people in need.'

Like he'd thought—strong. Resilient. And at the moment not happy with him for some inexplicable reason. 'Go, you.' And he'd better go before he got too caught up in trying to figure out what her problem was with him. That message can't have got through to his brain, though, because he asked, 'So what brought you back to Queenstown?'

Her mouth went flat. 'It was time to come home.'

He'd gone and put his size elevens in it. 'You grew up here?' he asked, unable to shut up.

'Yep.' She stared at her hands then looked up at him. 'Mallory, Maisie and I have been best mates from our first term at primary school in town. You probably don't know Maisie. She lives in Tauranga but is thinking of coming home early next year if there's a nursing position in the new children's department when it opens. We've all been away, and now one by one we're returning.'

The resignation in her voice finally stopped him from asking any more. She was hurting. So much for cheering her up. A change of subject was required, but he wasn't turning the conversation onto him. Talking about his divorce was not up for grabs and nothing else came to mind so he stood up. 'I'd better get back to the station.' Yeah, needs must, and he needed to get away before he sank further into that troubled golden gaze. 'It's good you're back in town, if not at home yet. I'll drop by again.'

He would?

Shut up, or you'll come up with something utterly stupid, like you're interested in her.

'I'll keep in touch about S and R, and when you're more mobile we'll get you to a meeting.'

'Got a trailer?'

'You're not feeling sorry for yourself, by any chance?'

'Hell, yes,' she growled. 'I'm not used to being physically stuck like this. I suppose I could take up knitting.'

'Make some mittens to replace the gloves you lost in the avalanche?'

'Get out of here.' Kayla paused, then suddenly reached for his hand, squeezed his fingers gently, sending little wake-up prickles down his spine, reminding him of that connection he'd felt—of why he'd come here in the first place.

He shouldn't have come. Tell that to someone who'd believe him. He liked the little he knew of her, wanted more, which went against the lessons the past had taught him.

He'd been out of contact the day Ryder had been admitted to hospital with appendicitis, which had upset Leanne big time. Sure, he'd been gutted not to be there, but it had been two days of hell. As one of almost one hundred firefighters trying to halt a runaway inferno razing homes and bush like a stack of cards in the wind, he'd been focused and exhausted. They'd also lost one of their firemen in a fireball, which had taken some getting over.

Worse, Leanne had begun saying he wasn't guaranteed to always be there for the boys and they needed constancy in their lives. Within a fortnight she'd packed up and moved to a house she'd rented, leaving him with nothing but memories and pain. And anger.

He hadn't seen it coming, had thought they were still

strong despite the arguments they'd begun having over anything and everything. Showed how trusting he'd been. But wasn't love meant to be like that? You'd think he'd know better after his upbringing, but there was always a knot of hope inside him. Always had been. *Always would be?* He was here, wasn't he? Still unsure of everything.

Kayla said, 'Thanks for dropping by. I wondered if I'd dreamed you'd found me or if it was real.' She stared at their joined hands and colour filled her cheeks. Jerking free, she muttered, 'You do exist.'

So she'd thought about him too. Which, with everything else she'd had to contend with, tightened the connection. He'd ignore that. He was going solo. That wouldn't change because he liked Kayla. 'You were a bit woozy.'

You held onto my hand as though you never wanted to let go.

Tighter than she'd just done but equally disconcerting. Holding Kayla's hand, feeling her slim fingers against his palm, was why he hadn't been able to stop thinking about her. That link he'd felt on the mountain was back as though it refused to break. 'Your medical mind was working, making sure we didn't do any damage to your spine.'

'I wondered about that.'

'A right old nag you were.' He forced a laugh, fighting the need to lean in and kiss her cheek. Definitely time to go. A good talking to was required to remind himself why he no longer had anything to do with women intimately, or in any other way outside his work. 'See you again.' He headed for the door and freedom.

'Maybe when I'm fit and healthy, and not appearing so damned useless,' Kayla said in a low voice.

What? Her mood was about feeling vulnerable? He turned back into the room. 'The last thing you are is useless. There's nothing wrong with your mind or most of your body, and your legs will be catching up as soon as possible.' He didn't add that while she looked wan and tired, her face was lovely and her body, what little he could see of it, was attractive. See what one good gesture got him into? Trouble.

'You don't know me well enough to think that.' Annoyance filled Kayla as she watched Jamie return to sit back down beside her bed. She'd been relieved he was heading away. She'd felt awkward and helpless, which made her squirm. It was so unlike her. She was supposed to be done with feeling sorry for herself. To be scared of falling in love again in case it went horribly wrong was one thing, but she could still live with her head held high and get on with making the most of everything else.

Yet Jamie seeing her like this made her feel vulnerable and that was something she never showed, not even to Maisie or Mallory very often. Did this mean he was reaching her in ways no one had since Dylan? She'd smiled and laughed with all her visitors so far, then along comes Jamie and the cracks in that façade started appearing. She'd clung to him on the mountain and now he'd have the wrong impression of her.

Go away, Jamie. You're worrying me. I am not ready to take chances with any man.

Not taking chances? When had she begun thinking she was even interested in him? She hadn't. She was over-emotional at the moment. That was the problem. Not the warmth spiralling out of control in her gut.

Stretching those endless jeans-covered legs she just had to gawp at across the carpet, Jamie said, 'As we dug you out of that snow you weren't giving in to the cold or pain, or the fear gripping you. You're one tough lady.'

When he decided to speak his mind, it seemed there was no stopping him.

'You think?' He didn't have a clue.

Jamie's beaming smile might've once made her smile in return but not these days. Not since her husband had died after falling asleep at the wheel while driving home to be with her through her second miscarriage in five months. It was too much just to let go and relax with a man who tickled her bones. Being incapacitated with nothing to do except watch endless movies on her device or work her way through the stack of books people had brought in made her yearn to do something useful. So much for returning to her home town and picking up what had once been a carefree and happy existence where she'd get amongst it on the mountains or as a paramedic and hopefully—finally—put the past behind her. Instead she'd gone and added to the sense of uselessness that had been a constant companion since losing Dylan.

Toughen up, Kayla. Be the woman Jamie says you are.

'There is something you can do for me.'

His eyes widened, but he didn't look at all perturbed that there might be a difficult request coming.

Her mouth split into a—a smile? She doused it. Back to normal. Smiling at men she didn't know well suggested she was trying to get too friendly, and she wasn't, despite the feeling of wanting Jamie to stay around. 'Find me a new pair of legs so I can get off this blasted bed and do something useful, like drive the ambulance or go searching for some idiots who've ignored weather warnings to go for a short hike and ended up in the bush overnight.'

'So you're not an easy patient?' His smile widened. It suited him, and created a warmth in her that expanded to where there'd been nothing but a chill for years, which was shock enough.

'Not at all.'

Stop smiling at me.

Her plans for coming home did not include falling for a man. She'd lost her husband and baby on the same day. No way would she ever risk facing a loss like that again. Far safer to keep her heart locked down. 'Who does enjoy lying around because they *have* to?' Whenever she did manage to drag herself upright to do some laps of the room on crutches as part of her new exercise routine, the leg with the minor break hurt like stink and the other with all its bits of metal in the form of plates and bolts never played nice, instead impaling her with pain and making her stomach ill and her brow sweat.

'I can't imagine you lazing around for any reason. You're full of suppressed energy, itching to get moving. I bet you'll be running on your crutches by the end of the week.' Now he was laughing softly.

Damn him and his smile. 'Of course I will,' she snapped. This was getting ridiculous. Unfortunately she *did* like him. He kept getting under her skin when she knew she had to avoid that. He showed that even if she was laid up, she was still Kayla—who he didn't even know. She knew she was more than the Kayla she'd become over the last three years, if the way she was reacting to him meant anything.

That blasted smile wouldn't go away. Ignoring the way his mouth curved upwards and laughter filled his eyes wasn't working. Did he know he was winding her up? It was a smile, not a hot, sexy 'touch me let's have fun' hint. Was that the reason he got to her? Because he wanted nothing from her? She was always susceptible to a challenge. Damn it. How to tell him to go without sounding mean?

'Where were you living before returning to Queenstown?' His smile had backed off a little, but remained brilliant enough to light up the room.

Or was that her heart? Couldn't be. It wasn't available. Which was plain out of left field. 'Auckland.' She pressed her lips together at the memory of finally leaving behind the city and all the memories of Dylan that had been in the apartment they'd owned near the waterfront, in the local eateries and on the roads they'd run along side by side. If she told him, he'd leave her in peace. 'My husband died three years ago and I finally decided it was time to leave.'

'I'm sorry to hear that. Was that Dylan?'

Her brow creased. How did he know Dylan's name? 'Yes.'

Jamie nodded. 'You mentioned him on the mountain.'

Kayla closed her eyes as cold filled her. Cold from the snow, from the fear, from— 'I thought I was dying.' Her eyes flew open and she stared directly at Jamie. 'Didn't I?'

'Yes, you did for a moment.'

She'd held his hand and everything fell back into place. Another squirm. He'd been there for her and she'd taken it to heart. He was her rescuer, not a man to get wound up about. She started talking to shut down her disappointment. 'I used to be a competitive skier and looked forward to lots of time on the local ski fields.'

'Then one bit you on the backside.'

'It's been a few years since I've done any serious skiing so I probably shouldn't have gone off the main field.' She couldn't stop watching him, held there by a feeling of hope that came with that smile. Hope that she didn't want to acknowledge. 'When my companions suggested giving the more difficult slope a crack I couldn't resist. It never crossed my mind that there would be an avalanche.

But, then, when does nature send out a memo that it's about to disrupt things?'

Talking too much, Kayla.

'You're quite athletic when your legs aren't letting you down?'

Relax.

He was going with the easy option, not about to grill her about the past. 'I run a lot. Used to hike in the hills when I lived in Queenstown before. I hope to get back to that. I'm an outdoor girl through and through.' There were endless numbers of walking tracks in the district and she couldn't wait to put a pack on her back and get out there. 'You're into rescues so does that mean you like hiking in the hills?' Still talking too much. Dragging her eyes away from that strong face, she drew in oxygen and uncurled her fingers.

'When I get time. I like nothing better than a night in a hut in the middle of nowhere, just me and a cold beer, a steak on the fire, and the birds for company. And the mates I go with, of course.'

They had something in common. Her mood lightened a little. 'So you're not a two-minute-noodle hiker?' Many people took instant food packages to save weight in their packs and time cooking over a fire. She always took meat. 'Nothing like the smoky flavour of steak at the end of a hard grunt getting to the hut.'

'I agree. Sometimes I take my sons overnight to a hut that's easy to get to. They enjoy being out in the bush, until they start thinking about ghosts lurking behind the trees.' Jamie suddenly looked shocked and glanced at his watch before standing up. 'I'd better get going. My boys will be waiting at the school gate if I don't get a move on, and then I'll be in trouble.' For the first time there wasn't a smile to be seen.

He hadn't intended to mention he had children? Was he being dishonest by wanting to hide the fact he wasn't alone? Or was there more to his story? 'How old are your boys?'

'Six and seven.' His gaze was fixed on her. 'They keep me busy.'

No mention of a wife or the boys' mother. 'Are you a solo dad?' If she didn't ask she wouldn't know. Did she need to know? No. Did she want to? Yes. Why? Because he interested her, touched her, in ways she wasn't ready for. She shouldn't have asked, because nothing was happening between them. Especially if he already had a family.

'My ex-wife and I share raising them fortnight about, though that's not fixed in concrete with my hours and Leanne sometimes travelling for her work.' He turned towards the door.

There was more to this story. She felt it in the sudden flattening of his voice, the way he rubbed his thumb over the fingertips of his left hand. She understood his need to keep things to himself. Another thing they had in common. 'Jamie.' She hesitated, waiting for him to look back at her. 'Thanks for calling in. I do appreciate it.' When she was being honest with herself.

'I'll keep in touch and let you know when I'm up and about.' He'd probably only been doing his job as second in command at the rescue unit, but he'd broken the boring moments of her day and for that she was grateful. Though not so grateful for him waking her up in unexpected ways. Finding a man who lit her lights was not meant to happen.

'Take care and get back on those feet ASAP, okay?' His smile was back, not as large or enticing, but it was there.

And just as warming—if she allowed it. Why was it

getting harder to ignore this sense of finding something that had been missing for a long time? These feelings scared her. She knew too well how it could all go wrong in an instant. But it seemed she couldn't help herself. 'I'll do that.' She even managed a small smile of her own.

'Bye.' He was gone.

Leaving her with a sudden sense that he wouldn't be back to see her again. Leaving her feeling flat, let down, and very, very confused. She bashed her pillow with her fist. What a stuff-up.

CHAPTER TWO

'MALLORY, TAKE ME with you,' Kayla begged her friend. 'I'm going spare, doing nothing.' Two months of sitting around feeling useless had driven her insane.

'It's a training event in the hills. You're on crutches. It won't work for you or anyone else.'

'I can observe.' Sitting on her backside in the hills would be a great change from her couch. No doubt she'd be on her own most of the time but breathing fresh air and listening to the birds was way better than sitting in her lounge, which she was heartily sick of.

Mallory grinned. 'You always were stubborn. I'll check if it's okay with Zac.'

Zac was a cop and head of the local search and rescue teams. He'd visited her a couple of times since she'd returned home from hospital, always cheerful and telling her stories of rescues in an attempt to get her interested in joining. He needn't have tried so hard as she fully intended to, but she enjoyed his company so had let him tell his stories.

An hour later they pulled into the grass parking area where a group of search and rescue members were milling around something on the ground. Something or someone? 'Trouble already?' she mused, reaching for her crutches as Mallory braked.

'I'll go find out.'

'Not without me.' Kayla had her door open and the crutches under her arms to heave herself upright.

'Mallory, bring Kayla over here, will you?' Zac called out. 'Robyn's down.'

Swinging her crutches, Kayla made good time, ignoring the jabs of pain whenever she hit uneven ground. 'What happened?' She looked down at the young woman sprawled on her back.

Jamie looked up from where he crouched beside Robyn and stole the breath from her lungs. Those dark brown eyes had held her attention on the mountain, and then again in the hospital, demanding she stay with him. She'd never forgotten the depth of concern shining out at her. Today his eyes appeared to be smiling. 'Hello, you. Robyn was running over the ground, got her foot caught in a hole and tripped. Her left knee's painful and her leg's at an odd angle.'

Kayla smiled back. 'Hi, Jamie.' Then she looked at Robyn. 'Hello, I'm Kayla, a paramedic.' How was she going to get down to examine her? Face plant, then lie on the ground and push up on her elbows?

Robyn grimaced. 'I'm such an idiot. Wasn't looking where I was going.'

'We've all done that.' Kayla glanced at Jamie, and sucked air. How had she forgotten how he made her feel different? Real, alive, ready to take on anything. Except fall in love. That was too risky.

He was watching her, that unnerving smile knocking her hard. 'Tell me what to do from up there.'

Hold me? Take my hand? A fast tapping started up under her ribs. What was it about this guy? Whatever it was, now was not the time to be distracted so she focused on what was necessary, not desirable. 'First, Robyn, tell us where the pain is.'

'All around my knee.'

'Not your ankle?'

'A little, nothing like my knee though.'

'Jamie, can you take the lower part of that trouser leg off?' The trousers were designed to become shorts whenever the wearer wanted. 'Then roll the top half above the knee.'

'Sorry if I hurt you, Robyn.' Jamie carefully unzipped the lower half and then tug it down to her ankle. 'All right to remove her boot?' His eyes sought Kayla's.

'Since there's little pain, yes, but look for swelling. She might've sprained her ankle.' Kayla stood near Jamie. Watching those large, deft hands untie the laces and begin to slide the boot off, her skin felt as though light air was brushing across it, teasing her, drying her mouth. 'Don't tug or you'll pull the whole leg.'

One eyebrow rose as Jamie glanced up at her. 'Sure.' Then he nodded at Robyn's exposed knee. 'What do you think?'

'It's at an odd angle.' The patella wasn't straight. 'Robyn, Jamie's going to touch your knee and see if he can find anything out of order. Is that all right?'

'It's fine. Have you got any painkillers handy?'

Kayla looked around for her friend. 'Mallory, can you grab some tablets out of my bag?' There were plenty there for when her fractures got too much to cope with, and she knew they were all right to give to this woman.

'Sure.' Mallory was already heading to her car.

'Robyn, did you stand up after you fell?'

'I tried to but my knee gave way under me. It was excruciating.'

'Jamie, can you place your fingers on the kneecap,

like this.' She held her hand out, fingers wide. 'Gently try moving it to the left then the right.' She watched closely. 'It's moving.'

'Very little resistance,' he agreed. 'Dislocated?'

'I think so. Robyn, have you ever put your knee out before?'

'No. Is it serious?'

'You'll need some time on crutches and not overdo it with exercise, but dislocations come right fairly quickly. But it's something you'll have to be careful of for years to come. It's not uncommon in younger people, especially females for some reason.'

'What do we do now?' Jamie asked. 'There's a medical kit in Zac's ute.'

Kayla looked for Zac. 'Can we have the pack? I'm presuming there are crêpe bandages to wrap around the knee so when Robyn's being transferred to a vehicle for the ride back to town it won't swing and cause more pain.'

'Onto it. I'll bring the ute alongside.'

When he had the bandage in hand, Jamie asked Kayla, 'How tight? I'm thinking it has to be firm without causing too much pressure.'

'Exactly. You should be able to slide a finger—' though his were larger than most '—underneath when you've finished and feel it holding in place.'

He stared at his hand and smiled. 'Guess I've got some leeway, then.'

A jolt of pure lust hit Kayla. That hand, that smile. Did it to her every time. Unsettled her. Wobbled her carefully held-together equilibrium. Thank goodness for the crutches keeping her upright. Her head felt light, like it was floating. She'd felt the same on the mountain that day but then it had been caused by concussion. She hadn't taken a hit since then, but it felt like it.

Watching Jamie wind the bandage around Robyn's dislocated knee, she held her breath, absorbed in the confidence he showed, and the gentleness. He was a force to be reckoned with, if she let him. She wouldn't, though. Too risky. Anyway, what if he wanted more kids? Chances were she couldn't have any. Two miscarriages made her think that. Then again, he might think two children were enough and she'd love to have her own if at all possible.

He stood up and locked those eyes on her, reminding her why she was here. 'All done. We make a good team, even if I did do all the work.'

Lifting one crutch, she made to jab him in the backside. She stopped. He might get the wrong idea. His boot was more appropriate. 'You'll keep.' Now, there was a thought. Could she spend time getting to know the man who'd managed to stir her blood with a smile? Not likely. She'd lost too much in her life already and wasn't prepared to risk it happening again. Confusion clouded her thinking. Now what?

'I'll hitch a ride back to town in the ambulance. There's nothing much I can do out here, and I've had a break from my four walls.' Coward. Totally. Or another way of putting it, she was trying to save herself from more drama. Not that Jamie had made any advances, nor did she expect him to. But he gave her such a jolt of longing for all the things she'd persuaded herself weren't for her again that she had to get away.

'You could work alongside Zac, co-ordinating the practise rescue. You won't need to be walking for that. We've still got a man out there, waiting to be "found",' Jamie told her.

Glancing over at Zac, she could see how organised he was, and unlikely to need her hanging off every word. And when the rescue was over everyone would likely go to the pub for a beer, no doubt including Jamie. Looking at him, a longing for family and love again filled her. He had children. Did he want a loving partner too? Was she ready for all that? Would it be enough?

'Kayla?' It had been said like he had when trying to get her attention on the mountain. Wake up, it said. Focus. Concentrate.

'I'll go back with Robyn.' Running away from a jolt to her system? From a man who hadn't encouraged her about anything more personal than working together to help a woman who'd dislocated her knee? 'I'll catch up with everyone later in the pub and hear how the training went down. Hopefully better than it started out.'

'See you then.' Jamie strode away to join the team.

'Like him?' Mallory asked from behind her.

Kayla spun around, and gasped as her legs protested. 'How long were you standing there?'

'Long enough.' Her friend grinned. 'Don't go pointing the bone at me. I only want you to be happy.'

'Just because you're bursting with love for Josue.' Mallory deserved to be happy.

So do I.

But she'd take it slowly, make friends before anything else.

'You okay sitting here?' Kayla asked Robyn as they settled at a table in the pub where the S and R guys were relaxing after what had turned out to be a gruelling hike in the hills, looking for their 'lost' colleague.

'Perfect.' When Zac had turned up at the emergency department he'd offered to drop Kayla at the pub and take Robyn home, but Robyn had insisted on going with her after the doctor had dealt with her dislocated knee.

'I'm loaded with painkillers and can't feel a thing. Guess sparkling water is my drink today.'

'I'll get that,' Jamie said from the other side of the room. 'Kayla, what would you like?'

'A lager, thanks.'

And time sitting yacking with you.

It wouldn't happen, though, as everyone was pulling up chairs and cramming around the table, all talking at once. Kayla sank into the warm vibes coming off the hyped-up group. It was great being a part of the team, feeling she belonged despite not having spent much time with S and R yet.

'Here.' Jamie placed her beer on the table and handed Robyn her water before pulling up a chair between them. 'You stayed with Robyn at the hospital?'

She nodded. 'It was a way of filling in time till you all came out of the bush.' And her empty house had not been tempting. 'Her boyfriend's going to pick her up when he finishes work at six.' Why was her skin tightening? Because Jamie was so close? Because she'd been thinking about him a lot and he was here for real?

'How are you getting home?' He nodded at her crutches. 'You're not up to driving yet surely?'

'Not even I would drive like this.' How would she get home? Her eyes met Mallory's on the other side of the table. 'Mal?'

'Jamie can give you a lift.'

Thanks, friend.

They lived four houses apart. Jamie would see through that in a flash. 'My jersey's in your car.' Why was she protesting when there was a longing to have some one-on-one time with a person not mixed up in her life tripping through her?

Jamie cut that idea down. 'I'm not staying long. I have to pick up the boys from their mother's.'

Of course. His family. Drawing a breath, she turned to him with an attempt at a smile. 'That's fine. I'm not stuck for a ride.'

'Good.' He drained his stubbie and stood. 'I'd better get going.'

She got the message. He didn't want to spend time with her. Hadn't he sat beside her? Bought her a drink? 'You've got the boys for the next fortnight?'

'Yes.'

Okay, so he was making his point. Don't talk, don't get cosy. So why had he been friendly in the first place? 'See you around.' Two could play that game. It was a timely reminder she wasn't looking to hook up with anyone.

'Maybe at the next meeting?' he asked, then looked confused.

'I hope so.' She meant it, despite knowing she shouldn't. He did intrigue her with his no-nonsense attitude and obvious need to look out for his boys. She wasn't only thinking about his build and muscles and cheeky smile. They would make good friends. Didn't have to get seriously close. She could remain safe and steady—if only the fluttering didn't start up whenever he was near.

Jamie strode out to his truck, cursing under his breath that he couldn't stay.

Kayla had a way about her that set him wondering what she'd be like in bed, did she prefer steak or fish, was she moving on from her husband's death? He wanted her and he didn't. He could not have her. It would be too risky. He might fall in love and that must not happen.

Leanne had been his soul mate and she had still walked away, which told him not to trust another woman with his heart or his boys'. They'd grabbed the chance to be happy together yet it hadn't been enough. She couldn't say why she'd begun falling out of love with him, only that the day Ryder had gone to hospital and he'd been unavailable had been the last nail in the coffin.

She seemed very happy with David, something he accepted and wished her well about, but he wasn't ready to take the chance himself. Add in that the boys weren't as comfortable with David now he'd married their mother and he knew he couldn't bring someone else new into their lives.

David didn't get involved with the boys as he had in the early days, almost as if he'd been using them to win Leanne over and now he didn't need to. Callum and Ryder were upset with David's change in attitude towards them, and that made Jamie cross. Another thing to watch out for if he brought a woman into his home.

He'd be broken-hearted for them if that happened. Their insecurities hadn't gone away completely and he wasn't adding to them with anything he chose to do. So he'd got up from the table and walked out of the pub early when all he'd really wanted to do was sit there with Kayla and have a good time. A good move, if a disappointing one.

Kayla wriggled out of the small space in the squashed car, which she'd managed to squeeze her head and shoulders into with difficulty. Another six weeks had dragged past and now she was back at work—and happy. Except for the woman before her. 'We need the Jaws of Life fast. She's unconscious and bleeding.'

'On the way,' a voice she recognised called from the fire truck parked on the other side of the road. A voice that teased her, setting her pulse to 'fast' during nights when her legs were still giving her grief. Jamie Gordon added, 'I got them out just in case.'

Thank goodness for someone using their brain. 'Every second might count on this one,' she informed him and the rest of the fire crew now crowding around the mangled vehicle, which had been driven into a solid tree trunk. At speed, Kayla suspected, given there were no tyre marks on the tarmac and how the bonnet appeared to be hugging the tree.

'Fast and careful.' Jamie sussed out the wreck, indicating where they needed to use the cutting apparatus. 'Is there any other way?'

Kayla stood aside but as close as possible to her patient, and said to her ambulance partner, 'Becca, we need the defib, a collar and the stretcher all ready and waiting the moment she's free.'

'Very soon,' Jamie said over his shoulder without taking his focus off removing the driver's door. A man of few words when necessary.

She liked that. But, then, she liked Jamie, despite having seen very little of him since that moment in the pub when he'd upped and left in a hurry. They'd bumped into each other at the one search and rescue meeting she'd attended since but it had been crowded and busy and not a lot of talking to each other had occurred. She'd known he'd walked away from her with the intention of leaving it at that and he wouldn't be knocking on her door any time soon, and despite the way shock swiped at her when she did see him she'd respected his decision. Whatever his reason, which could even be as simple as he hadn't felt the same connection as she had, it was his to make. Damn it.

Becca placed the defibrillator on the roadside. 'The collar's on the stretcher, which a cop's bringing across.'

'Cool.' It was all hands to the fore, everyone help-ing where they could. 'The airbag didn't deploy and I'm worried about the woman's ribs as the steering wheel appears to have struck hard and deep. Pneumothorax is a real possibility.'

The sound of screeching metal as the jaws cut through made her shiver and raised goose-bumps on her skin. Stepping forward, she leaned in through the gap the re-moval of the door had created and held back an oath. 'She wasn't wearing a seat belt.'

'We need to cut the side panel and back door away so you can get her out without too much stress,' Jamie said as he lifted the jaws and began tackling the car again. 'Stand away, Kayla.'

Her teeth were grinding. He was right. If the door frame sprang free as it was cut she didn't want to be in the firing line, but the woman needed her. Fast. Especially if her lungs were punctured. From the little she could see, the woman's breathing was rapid and shallow, backing her suspicion of punctured lungs.

Come on, guys, this is urgent.

Ping. Bang. Screech.

The door frame and back door were cut through, and one of the firemen was hauling them away.

Kayla leapt forward. Pushing in, ignoring her jersey catching on sharp metal, she reached for the woman's arm, which had been flung sideways. The pulse was light but rapid. Too fast, like her breathing. 'Hello? Can you hear me?'

Nothing.

'I'm Kayla. A paramedic. We're going to get you out of here.'

Nothing.

A deep wound on the woman's left temple bled profusely. Kayla drew a breath, began to check the ribs. 'We need to remove the steering wheel, Jamie.'

'Ready when you give us the say-so.'

There was little Kayla could do. When the pressure came off the ribcage, bleeding would start and then she'd be busy. 'Becca, pads I can apply immediately.'

'Here.'

'We'll put on the neck collar before moving her.'

'I've got it ready.'

'Right, let's do this.'

In a short time the firemen had cut through the steering column and were carefully removing the wheel. Kayla hovered with the pads, applying them with pressure the moment there was space to work, all the time watching the woman's breathing, begging her to inhale every time her lungs let air out. 'Don't stop now.'

Becca crouched on the other side of their patient and applied the collar.

'Done. Now we need someone to take her shoulders, you, Becca, take that side. I'll be in here, getting her legs out. How close is the stretcher?'

'Right here,' Jamie answered. 'I'll take her head and shoulders.'

'We need to go fast but carefully. There's a lot of bleeding.' Too much. Kayla checked that the woman's legs were free of the tangled metal. 'On the count. One, two, three.' She strained to lift the woman's dead weight in her stretched arms, gritting her teeth and using all her strength as she helped the others, and the woman was soon out and being lowered onto the stretcher with care. 'Good work, everyone.'

Jamie's hand touched her shoulder, squeezed and lifted away again.

Kayla blinked. He understood how important it was

to her to save this woman. Because it was what she did, who she had been ever since she was a kid and had seen Zac save Maisie after a bee attack that had brought on a severe allergic reaction. That had stuck with her, made her aware how easily people got into trouble, and she always wanted to be the person helping them. Another point in Jamie's favour. They might start adding up to a high number if she wasn't careful.

Tearing the ripped T-shirt wide open, Kayla ran her fingers over the ribcage and tapped. She nodded. 'Hollow sound, indicating a punctured lung. Ribs moving as though fractured, and the gasping, shallow breathing all point to torn lungs. Regardless of other injuries, we need to get straight to the emergency department.'

'Right.' Becca had the heart monitor pads on their patient's chest. 'GCS is two. No reaction to touch, sound or lifting her eyelids.'

'Understandable. There's a lot of trauma. Still no response to sound, movement or the pain.' Kayla noted the odd angle of one arm and deep wounds on both legs, and a memory made her shiver. That pain would be intense. 'Load and go.' No time for anything else when the patient couldn't hold air in her lungs. That took priority over everything else.

A continuous sound emitted from the monitor. A flat line ran along the bottom of the screen. 'Cardiac arrest.' Just what the woman didn't need. Kayla immediately began compressions, not liking what she could feel under her clenched hands.

Becca grabbed the electric pads. 'Here.'

Slapping them in place, Kayla glanced around. 'Stand back, everyone.' She pressed the power knob. Please, please, please.

The woman's body convulsed. The monitor began beeping, the line lifting.

Relief flooded Kayla. 'Watch her head, Becca. Tip it back a little to make breathing easier.'

'Want a hand?' Jamie was beside her.

'We need her on board now. I'll do a full assessment on the way to hospital.'

I am not losing this woman.

Her mantra wasn't always successful, yet she always repeated it in serious situations.

'You need someone to go with you? I can't do much but read the monitor or note down facts as you find them. The guys don't need me here to finish up with the wreckage.' He took one end of the stretcher and moved towards the back of the ambulance with her on the other end and Becca holding the woman's head.

Having Jamie on the short but worrying trip would be a bonus. He always appeared calm. He didn't walk away when people needed him. She wouldn't think about that day at the pub because she hadn't *needed* his company then. But now she might. She didn't know how it was going to go with this patient so an extra pair of hands was a good idea. 'That'd be great,' she replied as she climbed into the ambulance and locked the stretcher wheels in place.

Becca stepped aside for Jamie, then pushed through to the front as someone closed them all in.

'Top speed, Becca,' Kayla instructed. 'Call ED, inform them we have a suspected pneumothorax and other serious injuries.' The medical staff would be geared up, ready to do everything required to save the woman's life.

With lights flashing and the siren shrieking, the ambulance pulled away.

Kayla checked her patient's breathing. 'Still rapid,

short intakes. Lips blue. BP please, Jamie.' She didn't look up as she began intubating her.

As he held a bandage to the woman's head he read the monitor screen. 'Heartbeat's sporadic.'

She glanced up. Swore. 'Bleeding out.' Other than the head wound, she hadn't found an excessive amount of external blood loss but combined with what might be happening in the lung cavity it would all be adding up. 'There could be other internal traumas. The steering wheel made a huge impact and was wide enough to reach her abdomen.' The liver or spleen might've been ruptured. Who knew? She didn't have time to find out. With a final push the tube slipped into place and she turned the oxygen on. 'Now for some fluid.'

'What do you need?' Jamie already had the medical pack at hand.

'Sodium chloride, needle and tube. Everything's in the top left pocket.'

The monitor beeping stopped, replaced by a monotone. Kayla yelled, 'Becca, pull over. We've lost her.' She placed the electric pads on the exposed chest in front of her, jerking sideways as the ambulance lurched off the road and braked.

Jamie grabbed Kayla's arm, held her for a moment while she got her balance. 'You right?' His concerned gaze was fixed on her.

She nodded, watching the monitor and holding her hand over the button that'd give a jolt of current to the woman's lifeless body. 'Stand clear.'

Don't you dare die on me.

Jolt.

Jerk.

The monotone continued. No, no, no.

Her heart in her throat, Kayla said again, 'Stand back.'

Jolt.

Jerk.

Beep, beep, beep.

Phew.

Air rushed across Kayla's lips as she removed the pads. 'Go, Becca.'

Immediately the ambulance was bouncing onto the road and picking up speed.

Lifting the woman's eyelids, Kayla found no response. They weren't out of the mud yet. 'Come on, lady, don't you dare let us down. Hang in there. What's your name?' Not knowing felt impersonal, considering the circumstances.

'The police are trying to find out. They say the registered owner of the car is a male, but they weren't having any luck getting in touch,' Jamie filled her in. 'There didn't appear to be a wallet and cards, or a phone.'

'Maybe she's a tourist.' This was the most popular tourist destination in the country. 'She looks to be in her twenties, though it isn't always easy to tell in these situations.'

'Here.' Jamie handed her the sodium chloride and needle.

Wiping the back of the woman's hand with sanitiser, she tapped the flat vein hard to make inserting the needle easier, slipped it in and attached the tube with the fluid and taped it in place.

'As easy as that.' Jamie smiled. 'You're good.'

A sense of pride filled her. 'I hope so. I've worked hard to be the best.'

'If I ever get into trouble I'd like you to be there to help me.'

As if someone like Jamie would need her, but then again no one knew what was waiting around the corner.

This woman hadn't known she was heading for a tree as she drove. 'Let's hope the need never arises.' She couldn't imagine a man with Jamie's build and strength being laid out, unaware of what was going on around him.

'Just saying.'

Say it as often as you like.

She cut away the woman's shorts to expose severe bruising on both thighs. 'Those'll be from where the bonnet pushed down on her.' Had her femurs been fractured in the impact? Pain nudged Kayla from her own legs. Shoving it away, she looked at the monitor. No change, which was on the side of good but not good enough. They couldn't get to the ED quickly enough.

The ambulance slowed and Becca began backing into the hospital's ambulance bay. 'After we unload I'll take the ambulance next door to the station to clean up and restock while you do what's necessary this end, Kayla.'

'Okay.'

'There's a crowd waiting for us.' The words were barely out of Becca's mouth when the back doors were being opened and helping hands were reaching for the stretcher.

Jamie took the top end to move the stretcher out and then with Becca and two nurses rushed the woman inside.

Kayla followed, filling in Sadie, the doctor on duty, with all the details, and what she thought were the major injuries. 'Her breathing's shallow and rapid, there's a soft area in the ribs on the right and a blue tinge on her lips and face. She's had two cardiac arrests and there's bleeding from wounds and a serious head wound.'

'You focused on her lungs and heart, I take it?'

'Yes.' The life-threatening problems, though who knew about the head injury? It wasn't something she could've dealt with anyway. That required a neurosurgeon, someone not on hand here in Queenstown, so she would have to be sent elsewhere.

'I've given the life flight helicopter lot the heads up that we'll probably need them before the night's out. It depends how quickly we can stabilise the lung problem,' Sadie told her.

Sadie had gone with the diagnosis she'd had Becca call through and believed their patient would be going to a larger hospital further away, which one depending on urgency and theatre requirements. Once again pride filled her. 'That sounds good. Oh, we don't know who she is. The police are onto it, and hopefully will have an answer before you send her off.'

'Great.' Sadie was already focused on their patient and that information seemed to barely register.

Kayla repeated it to a nurse, and then, knowing there was nothing else she could do, headed for the door out into the ambulance bay. She had done her damnedest for the woman and hoped it was enough. But she was in a very bad way and there was no knowing how it would turn out. Now she'd handed over, Kayla felt knackered and her hands were shaking, while her feet were beginning to drag as she walked down the ramp out onto the footpath. Drawing in a lungful of summer night air, she was glad to be alive. A normal feeling after a serious case, she sometimes wondered if she was being selfish or realistic.

'You all right?' A familiar deep voice came from the other side of the drive where Jamie stood, leaning against the hospital wall, his ankles crossed and his hands in his pockets.

'No.' Without hesitation, Kayla changed direction and crossed over, walking right up to him and into the arms suddenly reaching for her, wrapping around her waist to tuck her against his wide chest. She didn't question herself, only knew that she wanted to be close to someone who understood what she'd just gone through in trying to save that woman. Jamie did understand, would've been through many similar traumas as a fireman and a member of the search and rescue squad. 'It was awful.' Calm throughout a trauma situation, she always got wobbly as the adrenalin faded.

'That woman was lucky you were on duty.'

'She's not out of trouble by a long way.' Kayla was glad there were far more qualified people now working on the patient. Under her cheek the fabric of Jamie's shirt was like a comfort blanket; warm and soft. Relief at bringing the woman in still alive washed over her.

'You saved her life—twice. Be kind to yourself.'

'It's hard. I know from when Dylan died what it's like to get that knock on the front door from the police.' It was why she worked so hard to keep up to date on procedures.

Jamie's arms tightened around her. 'That's a bitch.'

Shoving aside her pain, she said quietly, 'I wish we'd had a name for her. It felt impersonal when what I was doing was very personal.' There were no restrictions when it came to saving a person's life but sometimes it still felt as though she was being intrusive.

'Know what you mean.' Jamie's hand was spread across her back, his palm and fingers recognisable, more warmth soaking into her.

She snuggled in closer and stood there, breathing in his scent, soaking up his heat, and just plain breathing. She needed this. She shouldn't be standing here in Jamie's arms, but she was, and liking the strength he lent her. It was as though she was allowed a history and did not have to explain it all in depth. He made her feel, briefly, like she belonged. Yet that had to be blatantly untrue. She put it down to being lonely in the hours she wasn't working.

Coming home hadn't worked out how she'd thought it would. Mallory had Josue, and Maisie still wasn't here. She and Jamie got along whenever they bumped into each other, but neither of them had sought out the other specifically to have time together. A sigh escaped. Just a couple more minutes and then she'd be on her way.

Jamie leaned back to look down at her. 'Kayla? You sure you're okay?'

She looked up into his eyes, which were as focused on her as they'd been on the patient a little while ago, deep and caring. 'Yes, I am.' But she didn't want to leave this safety, this comfort, this place. This man.

Big pools of brown goodness locked on her, coming ever closer, until his mouth was on her cheek, a light kiss on one, then the other.

Her feet were lifting her up closer to his warmth, his understanding. When Jamie's lips brushed her mouth she sighed. And brushed back, banishing more of that loneliness. Obliterating the feeling she'd had since the avalanche. It had taken over her determination to start again, made her feel that she was on the path to nowhere. It had slowed her down and dragged her back into the pool of sadness and worry clouding her future.

Standing this close to Jamie made her yearn for fun and happiness—with someone else, someone new. With him. Jamie. He made her long to kiss him and to be kissed. Her heels slammed down on the pavement. Her body tensed. This was all wrong. It could not happen.

Jamie's firm hands took her shoulders, held her away just enough to break the connection, keeping her upright while her head spun. 'We need to get back to our respective stations. We're on duty.' He stared at her as though boring a message into her.

'You're right.' She didn't get what the message was, other than she needed to move away, head back to work. But why, when she might've found what had been missing for so long? Why not grab Jamie's hand and run away to a place where no explanations were needed, where they could get to know each other, to explore this sudden longing pulsing through her? As much as he clearly didn't, she also didn't want that. Getting hurt again wasn't an option. Locking her eyes on his, she dug deep for air. Why wasn't she feeling relieved that there was a gap between them? A physical *and* a mental one.

'I am.' His smile was soft, gentle and gave her hope that he might've found something he'd also been missing.

'See you around?' She hadn't meant to ask.

The smile slipped off his lips. 'So far we've mostly only met at accident scenes.'

'We can change that.' Where had this sudden desire to spend time with him come from? Hadn't she started backing off from kissing him at the same moment he'd held her away? She wasn't getting into a relationship, be it a fling or a one-night stand, or the whole caboodle. Jamie did make her feel more like the old confident, happy Kayla when he was near. He drove away the sadness she'd carried for too long. She was beginning to think there might be a chance at a future of some sort. But it was too soon, if it happened at all.

'Kayla,' Jamie interrupted. 'I'm sorry. I can't follow up on more than as a colleague. Not saying you don't push my buttons. I'm saying I'm not in the market for a partner. I'm sorry. I shouldn't have held you like that.'

No, you shouldn't have. Then I'd be striding back to the station, totally focused on what's important.

Then his words sank in. He'd made a mistake, and was about to walk away. That hurt when it shouldn't. It had already been obvious he wanted no part of a relationship when he hadn't visited her again in hospital, or phoned through the months of her rehabilitation.

Whenever they did come across each other, she was jolted alive with one glance. Obviously the same didn't go for Jamie. Which made it easier to keep to her decision of not getting involved. Didn't it? She was tough so why not get to know him as a friend? 'You're rushing things. I don't want a relationship either. But we can have a drink together some time.'

He stared at her for a long moment then seemed to make up his mind. 'That sounds good. Now I need to get back to work. Let's hope we don't have any more call-outs tonight like the last one.' He was stepping away, turning towards the fire station a kilometre down the road.

Kayla watched him walking off, knowing he would not be rushing to phone and suggest meeting up somewhere. She should be glad. She wasn't getting caught up in a relationship again. She'd had her chance, the love of her life. It would be greedy to expect a second shot at a happily-ever-after marriage. As for a baby—forget it. Two miscarriages made her think she wasn't meant to be a mother. The thought of another miscarriage also made her feel ill. They took their toll, left her bereft and feeling useless.

But watching those long legs eat up the distance, there was no denying she wanted to spend more time with Jamie. Even as a friend.

Jamie strode away, feeling a heel for wanting to kiss Kayla when she was upset over her patient. He'd let her down. Hell, he'd let himself down. He should've been strong, ignored the need ripping into him as he'd watched her coming out of the emergency department, her shoulders slumped, her body oozing fatigue. It had been hard to keep his distance. She'd got to him more than he'd realised. There were the few memories of talking with her, holding her hand on the mountain, seeing her vulnerability in hospital, her medical confidence.

Tonight she'd been amazing. That woman owed Kayla her life. Those memories rubbed salt into the undeniable fact that he couldn't forget her, and it made him wonder if he was gutless for not taking a chance on a second relationship. Then he'd think of Callum and Ryder and know he was doing the right thing.

He'd kissed Kayla Johnson.

Holding her, breathing in her scent, feeling that soft body against his had turned him on. More difficult to ignore was the need she brought up in him for love. To have a special person in his life—someone to share the ups and downs, laughter and tears, someone to raise his kids with. A fierce need to run back and swing her up into his arms and kiss her senseless while carrying her away to some place where no one or anything could interrupt gripped him. No car accidents, no kids, nothing.

Passion had been missing in his life for so long he'd thought it was gone, but Kayla had woken him up. There was a bounce in his step that'd been missing. And it was all because of Kayla.

She was something else. From the moment he'd found her buried in the snow he'd felt a connection. Nothing large or all-consuming, more like an irritant, always scratching whenever he heard her voice or saw her with a patient. Not often. When their paths crossed he'd deliberately kept his fireman's hat or S and R cap on to remind her—and him—of their places because she got him wound up and starting to question his need to remain single while Dylan and Callum were still young. What the hat hadn't done was quieten the sense she brought with her of gaining something special.

He had to move on from temptation. The boys were finally settled into a smooth routine, having taken a long time to trust their parents to be there for them no matter what was going on between him and Leanne. How would he ever trust a woman to be there for ever? If Leanne could change her mind when they'd found in each other what they'd been searching for all their lives, why would another woman be any different? But Kayla set him alight with a need he couldn't deny. Need he wasn't going to fulfil. He wasn't thinking love stakes here. He had to stay strong and steady, and stick by his guns. He was single and staying that way. He mightn't like it, but that was how it was.

So there, Kayla.

So there, Jamie.

But he'd kissed her. What about a fling? He shook his head at that. A fling with Kayla would not be enough. He knew it in his bones. It went back to that connection the first time he'd held her hand, and knew it would be strong if he ever followed up on it. It might seem ridiculous, but he believed it.

'You need a change of clothes, man.' Ash stood in the doorway of the fire station.

His head shot up and he looked at his friend. 'Didn't know I was here already.'

'Yeah, you looked like you were doing a spot of thinking. What's got you in a twist?'

Nosy bugger. 'Life.'

'Profound.' Ash laughed. 'I'm picking it's either that

horrendous car accident I've heard about from the crew or the paramedic doing her utmost to save the woman's life.'

Like he'd thought, nosy bugger. 'Put the billy on, will you? Tea would be good about now. I'll get out of this gear.' Now that he was in the light he could see the blood smears on his jacket and trousers. 'It was a messy scene.'

'Apparently.' Ash was no longer laughing or even smiling. 'The cops called. The woman's from Germany. She had a fight with her Kiwi boyfriend and drove off in a rage.'

'That never works out well.' He'd seen too many accidents caused by upset drivers. It was why he was so skilled with the Jaws of Life and why it hadn't taken long to release the woman. Sometimes he wondered if he was a fireman or a vehicle dismantler.

He headed for a shower, the need to feel completely clean, to wash away the sights and debris from the accident taking over. There'd be no washing away the memory of Kayla in his arms, her back under his hand, her cheek against his chest, her hands on his waist.

No, it was going to take a whiteout to delete those images. But he had to try.

CHAPTER THREE

'YOU HAVEN'T SAID how your holiday in Rarotonga went,' Kayla said to Becca as they drove towards a dangerous fire where they were required on standby. Jamie had better not be there. Jamie and danger in one thought got her heart beating fast.

'It was great, swimming, eating and drinking. The perfect relaxation after a hectic year. I'd recommend Raro to anyone.'

Kayla laughed. 'I'm happy as a pig in muck, working. I missed this while I was out of action.'

'You need a life, girl.'

I know. The one she had was all right, though the excitement came at a cost. Jamie had been out of sight but not out of mind since that night a few weeks back when he'd held her in his arms while the tension from saving the German woman had slipped away. According to Mallory, he'd been spending more time with his kids over the school holidays. He attended call-outs from home when he was rostered on. It was great how the fire department made it work for him. She'd phoned twice since Christmas but he'd been busy so she'd stayed away, sensing she was somehow intruding on his family life.

'It's good being behind the wheel of this beast. What more do I need?' Kayla nodded at Becca.

'If I have to answer that then you've got a problem.'

'True.' After all those months laid up with broken legs, work made her feel useful and needed, and helped the loneliness. 'Thank you,' she called as a car in front pulled abruptly to the side of the road to let her past. The flashing lights had done their job. 'I hope nobody gets caught in this burning building we're headed for.' She had to voice her worry in the hope it stopped.

'It's an abandoned building beyond the airport, which used to be a hay and implement shed.'

'The smoke must be playing havoc with flights. It's blowing in the direction of the runway.' Billowing black clouds beyond Frankton were unmistakable, enticing nosey townies to drive in the same direction as Kayla, and as fast—legal for her, not so for them. 'Hope there's a police checkpoint before we get to the scene. This lot aren't welcome.'

'I heard the guys talking on the scanner while we were at base. Two squad cars should be there.'

'So the fire crew must want us because they're concerned one of their own might get hurt.' Kayla didn't mind that. It was better than sitting in the station far away, waiting for a call that might not come but if it did it meant one of their own was in trouble. Any of the firefighters getting injured did not bear thinking about.

Was Jamie on duty today? It would be great to see him. She just couldn't seem to get past him. Being held in his arms had made him so much harder to ignore. The way he understood her concerns, his gentleness when he was so big and tough. Lots of things about Jamie had her thinking about him way too often. 'I hope it's not a more dangerous scene than usual.'

Where had this negativity come from? Next she'd have all the fire crew in the back of the ambulance on the way to hospital just to get checked out for the hell of it. It was rare any of them got caught out at a fire. The safety precautions were intense, and from what she'd heard common sense was the first requisite for joining the service under Jamie's watch. No 'he man' antics allowed. Only men and women with his attitude need apply. Strong, focused on what they did, and calm in tense situations.

Yeah, Kayla sighed. Jamie was all of those and more. The times she'd spent with him had had nothing to do with fire—except for the heat he created in her. When he'd retrieved her in her half-buried state with severe injuries, he'd looked after her, made her feel safe, and had given his hand for her to cling to. He was something else. Something she was supposed to ignore, not waste time thinking about. Then they'd kissed when he'd held her, and forget trying to pretend he hadn't pressed her buttons. Impossible.

Becca diverted her with, 'How're your legs doing these days?'

'They're good.' Still hurt like stink at times, but that was to be expected, especially the right one with all the extra steel and nuts and bolts it now contained. 'I'm walking about six k a day, and should be fit enough to go on mountain rescues soon.' The day she'd gone on a rescue before the accident she'd loved being out with the other searchers, doing something exciting and useful. Attending the meeting last month had been a break in the routine of nights at home and catching up with the people she knew through work and from when she'd lived here previously. Especially Jamie. Every time she saw him her spirits lifted, despite the way he remained friendly yet distant.

'Gees, Kayla, don't take it too easy, will you?' Becca was shaking her head. 'We're glad you're back on board the ambulance. We don't need you having more time off due to overdoing the fitness regime.'

'I like to be good to go all the time.' Her head space also needed to be filled with work, medical problems, saving people, being busy. It dispelled some of the loneliness. Those months when she could hardly get around had driven her bonkers, the first weeks when she couldn't do anything and had spent too many hours thinking about the past had made her gloomy. Now she was finally crawling out of that hole of grief brought on by losing Dylan and the baby. At last she believed she'd done the right thing to come back to family and friends and a job she loved despite having been wiped out by an avalanche.

'You push yourself too hard.'

'You reckon?' Becca never hesitated over saying what she thought, and Kayla appreciated that after years of people tiptoeing around her after Dylan had died.

Their marriage had been wonderful. She'd felt loved and special and happy past measure. It had been beyond all her expectations and had tamed her rebellious streak while allowing room to be her own person at the same time. Life without Dylan had been empty. Now she was working at finding a balance. On her own. It was too risky to try for love. The thought of going through all that pain again terrified her.

Growing up, her mother had always expected her to be compliant while her brother, Dean, being a boy, had been allowed to do whatever he'd liked. Kayla had resented that and had gone out of her way to prove she was just as capable as he was, and nothing and nobody could stop her having fun. That attitude had got her into trouble at times but it had also made her strong and focused, which had helped to make her a champion skier.

Yet that strength had disappeared in an instant the night Dylan had died, replaced by despair.

Dylan had been busy with night shifts at the hospital and studying for exams, and she hadn't seen much of him for a few weeks. Then she had begun miscarrying for the second time and he'd dropped everything to rush home to be with her. Except he'd never made it, falling asleep driving on the motorway. His car had crossed two lanes and slammed into the barriers, spun around and been hit by a transporter. He'd never had a chance.

Stop it. Why turn all glum now?

Becca hadn't finished. 'Just go easy, all right?' Then she laughed. 'I'm wasting my breath so if you want a walking partner any time, give me a call. I like getting out of the house and taking in the fresh air. It's my thinking time.'

Kayla shrugged. 'Thinking's the last thing I need.' Do too much of that and Jamie slipped into her head space. Since she'd returned to work he should've been fading from her busy mind. Instead he was there more often.

Becca leaned closer to the windscreen. 'That's one hell of a fire.'

Kayla's heart pumped harder. 'Those firefighters had better not go in where it's too dangerous.' Except they'd do exactly that if they thought someone was inside. The whole idea of going close to an out-of-control fire, let alone inside a burning building, made her break out in a sweat. Each to their own, and fire wasn't hers.

Give her a head-on crash victim any day. They broke her heart and pushed her abilities to save a life, but they did not drag out fear of being devoured by heat and pain. It was one of those phobias that came without reason and had been with her since she was a kid. Her dad used to be very careful, sometimes to the point of paranoia, about their log burner, but that shouldn't have caused this aversion. Maisie reckoned she'd been burned in a previous life, which only made her laugh and had probably been the whole idea behind saying that.

The police had set up a barrier on the corner of the road they were headed for and were already waving her forward.

'Thanks, guys,' Kayla called through her open window, and received friendly smiles in return.

'That one's hot.' Becca twisted to look back the way they'd come. 'Haven't seen him around here before.'

'He's still in diapers.' Kayla laughed. If he was hot, she was so out of date she might as well be old. But it didn't matter, she wasn't looking. 'Here we are.' Backing onto the verge well out of the way, she stopped the engine and undid her safety belt. 'I guess opening up the back's not a good idea with all that smoke.' She leaned forward, forearms crossed on the steering wheel. 'Now we watch and wait.'

Firemen were spread out, their hoses pumping water onto the fire engulfing the massive shed. One member loomed above the rest, wide shoulders in heavy fire-proof yellow gear enhancing the picture. Jamie. His face was invisible behind breathing apparatus, but his defined movements spoke of control and power.

He'd dwarfed her hospital room, and out here where the spreading fire and billowing smoke made others appear smaller, he seemed taller, broader than ever. Must be the protective clothing. He was a big man but not huge. He'd been wearing jeans and a dark T-shirt under a thick jacket when he'd visited, clothes that had accentuated his virility.

She sucked air through her gritted teeth. Why remember that four months later? Like it was important?

It wasn't, never had been, and wouldn't be. Yet she was thinking of what he'd been wearing that day and how much space he'd taken up. She tapped her forehead. The doctors had never mentioned that her concussion could suddenly return to wreak havoc with her mind, but something was causing these images to fill her head. That near kiss.

Even weeks later, just remembering it sent heat throughout her body. Jamie hadn't phoned, despite saying he'd be in touch. She obviously hadn't affected him as he had her.

So she could forget noticing how solid he was and get on with why she was here—hopefully to wait out the fire and go back to town without any patients.

'What are they doing?' Becca asked.

'Are they going in?' Kayla's mouth dried. 'This doesn't look good.' She took a big gulp from her water bottle. 'Have they heard something? Surely it's a bit late for someone to be yelling out?' As if they'd hear anything above the roar of flames. She leaned further forward but the scene unfolding at the burning building didn't get any better. 'I'm counting three going in.' Including one large frame. 'That's Jamie on the left.' He shouldn't be putting himself in danger if he had kids to go home to. None of the crew should. Their families came first.

'I think the short one's Kate. No idea who the third person is.'

'They'd better be careful.' She knew Kate and her husband from when she'd lived here before. 'Sometimes it was easier living in Auckland. I hardly knew a soul.' Unable to watch any more, Kayla slipped out of her seat and squeezed through to the back to go over the equipment, even knowing everything was topped up and whatever she might need if they got a patient would be easy to lay hands on. 'Please, please, please, be safe, everyone,' she murmured. 'Jamie, that means you, too.' *Especially you.*

'Trouble. The overhead beams are falling outwards,' Becca called back to her.

So much for pleading for nothing to go wrong. A lot of yelling was happening. She shoved through to the front and stared at the horrific scene, her heart pounding. 'The framework's landed where Jamie and Kate were standing.'

Please, please, please, come out, Jamie, Kate and whoever.

'There, someone's at the edge of the fire.'

Unable to sit still, Kayla shoved her door open and dropped to the ground, grabbing the medical kit before running closer but not so close as to be in danger. She had to know if anyone was injured, had to be as near as possible without getting in the way in case her skills were required urgently. She had to know Jamie was safe.

Why Jamie and not the others? Of course she wanted to know if everyone else was safe. But she *needed* to know about Jamie. Kayla stumbled, righted herself, carried on, ignoring the questions popping up in her head. Jamie was one of the crew. No, he was more. He'd seen her weak and vulnerable. It was hard to forget that.

'Kayla.' Ash waved at her. She now realised he was the other firefighter who had gone in with Jamie and Kate. 'Over here. Jamie's taken a blow. Those beams came down as we were about to go around the other side. Got Jamie fair and square.'

She swerved in Ash's direction, shocked to see a firefighter on the ground at his feet, even when she'd half expected it. A big firefighter gasping for air, his face mask pushed aside, his chest rising and falling as he struggled to breathe. Smoke inhalation. Her knees weakened. Deep breath, straighten up, get on with the job; forget who this was other than a patient. A man she knew got no more help than anyone else because she gave her all, and then some, every time her skills were required. Turning, she yelled, 'Becca, bring the oxygen.'

'I'll help her with anything you need,' Kate, the other firefighter who'd been with Jamie, said.

'Thanks.' Dropping to her knees beside Jamie, ignoring the shaft of pain in her right leg, she said to Ash, 'Get on the other side and help me sit him up. He's got to breathe.' This was a role reversal, her turn to help Jamie, to do all she could for him and make him safe.

'The mask was knocked off when he hit the ground,' Ash told her.

'Jamie, it's Kayla. Did you inhale smoke?'

'A little,' he gasped.

A little was more than enough. 'We need to get your helmet off. I'll be careful but it might hurt. I don't know what we're going to find under there.'

'Do it.'

With Ash's help they eased the helmet away. When Jamie groaned, Kayla's stomach tightened. He must be in agony to make that sound. 'Sorry. I'll get you onto oxygen shortly. That'll help. Ash says you took a hit.' She began to feel his skull for indentations or soft spots.

Cough, gasp, cough.

Jamie nodded slowly.

'Back?'

Nod. Cough.

'Head?'

Cough, nod.

Jamie dropped back. If not for them holding him up, he'd have hit the back of his head on the ground.

'Careful. Here's the oxygen. I'm going to keep you

upright until we've got you attached, then we'll lay you down on your side so I can examine your back. Okay, Jamie?'

You'd better be.

'Yeah.' *Cough.*

'A nod does fine. Save your breath.' Her mouth lifted into a smile of its own accord. Then she saw blood running down the back of his neck from his head and she deflated. 'Becca, get the oxygen happening.'

With her latex-covered hands, Kayla continued checking his skull. 'You've got a cut behind your ear that's bleeding but I can't find any bone damage.' It was the best she could hope for without an MRI scanner on hand and it wasn't her place to order a scan.

Jamie flopped left, then right. The moment the gas was flowing into his throat, they lowered him full length on the grass. He tugged the mouthpiece aside. 'Why do I feel woozy?' *Cough.* 'Like I'm going to faint any minute?'

Placing her hand on the mouthpiece to press it back in place, she asked, 'Did the beam hit you on the head?'

'A glancing blow.'

Really? When something solid had hit him? 'You're possibly concussed. I'm going to examine your back.'

His chest was easing, the oxygen helping so that his breathing wasn't such hard work. Jamie tapped his left shoulder, tried to lift his arm and winced. 'Here.'

'Your shoulder copped it? Are you hurting anywhere else? Lift a finger if yes.'

'No,' he answered. Not very good at following instructions, then.

'Save your breath,' she growled lightly. 'I have to see if there're any obvious injuries elsewhere on your body.' Body. As in Jamie Gordon's body.

Hey, this is a patient. Not a man to get in a fix about.

She wasn't.

Tell that to someone who'll believe you.

'Then we're taking you to hospital.'

No nod this time. Instead he glared at her and took a deep suck of oxygen.

Kayla held up her hand. 'Don't talk.' She might've laughed if she wasn't worried about his condition.

He continued glaring.

'I get the message. You don't want to go, but I'm in charge here. That head wound needs stitches, and you need to be seen by a doctor.' There were some well-honed muscles under her hand as she examined his chest. She pulled away, growled to cover her embarrassment, 'Take a long slow breath.'

Jamie winced when he did as told.

'Pain in your chest?'

He nodded.

'Did you hurt your ribs when you fell?'

His eyes darkened as he gave that thought. 'Don't know.' Then his gaze closed over and his head dropped forward.

Kayla felt certain Jamie was concussed. The left shoulder was slightly out of line, suggesting possible dislocation. Her teeth ground together at the thought of having that put back in place. It wouldn't be a picnic, even for a tough man like Jamie. Heavy sedation would be required, and the sooner she got him to hospital where a doctor could perform the procedure the better. Too long a delay and he might need surgery. 'Becca, how's that pulse?'

'Strong.' The other woman nodded. 'Heart's good.'

No surprise there. Jamie was one tough guy, but having a beam hit him, even a glancing blow, was no easy thing. Reaching for his hand, she gave it a gentle squeeze. 'You're doing great, Jamie.' The relief was immense. She never wanted a patient to suffer, but this one... Even a scratch was too much.

'I'm doing great,' Jamie repeated under his erratic breath. 'Tell that to someone who believes you, Kayla. I've got a raging headache, pain in my shoulder like I've never known, and nothing looks very clear right now.' A freaking beam had wiped him out, and he was doing fine? Had to be something good in there, but he wasn't getting it. He felt like hell. Except for Kayla's hand wrapped around his. Being held like that softened his heart.

'Yeah, you are.' She'd leaned closer, like it was only the two of them in this conversation. 'Hang in there. I'll give you a shot to take the edge off the pain before we put you on the stretcher.'

'I hate admitting this, but bring it on.'

'I won't tell a soul.'

Her smile rolled through him, touching him softly, gentle and understanding. Right now he didn't care that he wasn't interested in getting close to a woman. It wouldn't hurt to bottle her smile so he could take it out during the night ahead and feel a little less uncomfortable and alone. He was surrounded by people intent on helping him, and he felt lonely—except for Kayla. Something was definitely not right, but he didn't have the energy to work through the idea, so he went with it.

'I'll get the stretcher,' Becca said, stepping away.

They weren't alone, despite Kayla making him feel like they were. He watched her dig into the kit and bring out a needle and bottle, saw her draw up a dose and waited for the prick as she injected him. 'You're good at this.' Anything to distract his banging head and maybe earn another smile. He must be in trouble if he was trying to win smiles from the paramedic.

'Had plenty of practice.' There. Another smile.

A man could get to like those. Except he wasn't supposed to be looking for them. Today he could be a bit lax. He was injured and hurting and therefore entitled to some tenderness as long as she didn't think he was a soft touch. 'I bet.' He glanced away from her endearing face, looked beyond to the destruction behind them for distraction. 'What about Kate and Ash? Did they get out without injury?' How selfish could he get? He'd been thinking only about himself. What sort of leader did that make him? Not a good one.

'Relax. They brought you out and, no, they didn't get hit by the beam. Neither did they inhale smoke.'

'They brought me out?' His head was in a bad way if he hadn't realised that. In fact, he couldn't remember being carried out at all. 'My memory's not flash,' he admitted grudgingly. Best to be honest with the medic even when it was Kayla. He didn't want anything worse happening all because he'd been reticent over letting her see he wasn't always strong. It was more important that he get home to the boys than to lie around in a hospital bed so the sooner they were through checking him over the better. 'Is that because of concussion?'

'Possibly.' Kayla nodded. 'But only the doctors can confirm it.'

'Your highly qualified medical opinion is?'

She took a moment to answer, then shrugged and smiled. 'That you've had a hard whack on the head and you're more than likely concussed. That'll mean time off until your mental faculties are up to scratch.'

'Bet that's not a medical phrase found in the textbooks.' How could he be talking like this when his memory was on the blink and he felt as though he was on another planet?

'I'm currently rewriting those.' There was a definite twinkle in the golden eyes watching him. Looking for his reactions to his injuries?

Bet she was. From what he'd seen, she never relaxed on a job. The smoke tasted gross as the air whooshed out of his tight lungs in a wave of relief. He was in good hands. And liking it. He gasped, coughed, then pain struck his chest and shoulder as his muscles tightened. So much for relaxing. It wasn't good for him.

'Careful, Jamie. Your lungs are super sensitive at the moment.'

He closed his eyes, blotting out the sight of a lovely, caring face. But her concern for him got past his eyelids and into his mind, settling in as though it intended to stay for as long as he needed her there. 'I don't need a woman at my side. Not now, not ever.'

'Only till we get you to the emergency department.'

Jamie groaned. He'd said that out loud? She'd think he was ungrateful and trying to shove her away. Wasn't he? Not now he wasn't. Fingers crossed, she'd blame it on the concussion and think he was hallucinating. More fingers crossed that he did have a concussion. Had to blame something for his random mutterings. What he'd said was true, but that didn't mean saying it out loud for everyone to hear. He wasn't that crazy. His head was getting foggy. Foggier. His body felt as though it was bobbing on water. 'Kayla? Where am I?' What was happening?

'It's all right. I'm here.' Her hand touched his. 'You're in shock, and about to be loaded into the ambulance and taken to hospital. I'll be watching you all the way.' She sounded so comforting. Her voice was soft and smooth, not worried something terrible might be happening to him.

He clung to that. Believed her. Trusted her not to tell lies, not to let him down.

He what? Trusted this woman? Something was wrong here. But then he'd had a beam bang his skull. Give it time and everything would be back to normal. Wouldn't it? Something else was nagging at the back of his mind. Something he needed to be doing. Like what? Putting out a fire was beyond him. 'Ash?' he croaked.

'He's gone back to the fire,' Kayla told him. 'Looks like he's taken charge.'

It's what he was trained for. 'Good.'

'Right, let's do this.'

'Do what?' Jamie tugged his eyes open and looked around, saw a trolley coming his way.

'Get you onto the trolley,' Kayla answered.

He shook his head, immediately regretted the movement. 'I can walk,' he muttered.

'You're light-headed, attached to oxygen and a heart monitor. You'll go by trolley.'

'Yes, ma'am.' Kayla was no pushover. He'd been put in his place and given in too easily. Be warned, he thought. This woman was one tough cookie. She was also knowledgeable. His head was pounding fit to bust, and he couldn't see himself carrying his helmet let alone even one piece of the equipment she'd mentioned. So much for being in charge on this job. It seemed he'd handed himself over to Kayla, and she was going against his wishes. Typical woman, and why he stayed clear of them these days. Except she wasn't that bad. Not from what he'd seen so far, but he barely knew her. Neither did he intend to other than working together occasionally in the future.

'Glad you understand,' she retorted.

If not for the slight uplift at the corner of her mouth he'd have believed she was being grumpy with him.

'Guys, help me up onto my feet,' he said to the two cops standing by.

Kayla spun around. 'You are not walking to the ambulance.'

'No, ma'am. But I am standing to sit on the stretcher trolley and save everyone's back trying to lift it from the ground with me on board.' It was the most he'd said since this mess had happened and he ran out of breath on the last words and had to gasp hard at the oxygen mouthpiece while ignoring the glint of 'told you so' in Kayla's eyes.

She was at his side, holding the oxygen tank, making sure he had the mouthpiece in place. 'Slowly, don't gulp or you'll start coughing.' She leaned closer and said quietly enough for no one else to hear, 'Don't ever call me ma'am again.'

Or what? There wasn't enough air in his lungs to talk. Damn it. Even feeling like he'd been run over by the fire truck instead of having ridden in it, there was a certain element of enjoyment tickling him on the inside at this silly game of words with Kayla. For a moment she made him forget the pain enough to think clearly, or clearer than he had been. Or that might be because of the jab she'd given him. For whatever reason, she was good at her job and he was grateful it was her who'd been called out. Speaking of which, 'How's the fire going?'

'It's looking more under control than it was twenty minutes ago,' a cop replied. 'Let's get you upright. Tobin and I will take an arm each and haul you up.'

'Won't be easy.' Tobin grinned. 'He's not exactly a nipper.'

Jamie held his breath, tried to ignore the stabbing pain, and gasped as the world spun. He was about to land exactly where he'd been dragged up from.

'Easy. Breathe slowly.' Kayla was right in front of

him, hand on his arm, eyes watching his every twitch and blink and breath. Calming him. 'That's it. Becca, trolley,' she said over her shoulder.

Slowly the world settled and he didn't feel as though he was about to go face first into the lovely woman before him. He'd flatten her. She might be tall, and strong, but he was taller and far more muscular. The guys manoeuvred him onto the trolley, and he focused on ignoring the pain. Impossible. He was better off looking at Kayla.

'Instead of pushing Jamie across to the ambulance, back the ambulance up to the trolley,' Kayla told Becca. 'That's rough ground to be getting the wheels over and I don't want to damage the trolley.'

Yeah, he knew he was heavy, especially with boots on and all the attached medical gear. 'You'll keep,' he sighed, closing his eyes as his sight blurred. He was getting more tired by the minute, unable to focus on any one thing. His eyes shot open. He looked straight at Kayla. 'Concussion makes you feel woozy, right?' A head injury was the last thing he needed. Then Leanne would be swooping to take the boys away for an untold time. No, she wouldn't. Everything regarding the boys and custody had been resolved.

Remember?

Remembering anything was difficult. Except Kayla and her smiles.

'It can. So can stress.'

Thanks for nothing. 'It has to be that.' Otherwise… Otherwise he mightn't be able to look after the boys for a while. That could never happen. He would not relinquish time with them. It had been a battle to win shared custody, but he and Leanne had finally come to an arrangement and everyone had calmed down to the point the boys could now plan time with their mates and know where they were living from week to week. If he had medical problems that might go down the creek temporarily and he couldn't bear to think of not having Callum and Ryder at home where he could look out for them. He knew Leanne didn't have lots of spare time these days as she was busy working for her new husband.

She always makes time for Ryder and Callum.

True.

Kayla gave him a long, hard look. 'The sooner we get you to hospital the sooner you might have the answers you're looking for.' Understanding underlined that look. She might not know what was bothering him, but she knew something was.

'Come on, mate.' Tobin was on the other side of the stretcher. 'You need help.'

He lay back and let everyone get on with their job of loading him into the ambulance. All he wanted was to fall asleep and wake up feeling normal. 'Fine,' he muttered, and held his breath until the stretcher stopped moving and was locked into place. 'Tell Ash to keep me posted, Tobin.'

'Will do.'

'Not today he won't,' Kayla said as she closed the back of the ambulance. 'I'm going to check your readings again.' She stood beside him, looking at the monitor behind his head. 'Your heart rate's fine.'

'I'd have thought it was going crazy with everything that's happened.' With her standing so close. And the way she thought she could tell him what to do. Any minute now she was going to tell him—

'Don't think so much.'

Exactly. He stared up at the lovely face above him. She'd be wonderful to wake up to every morning. 'Ahh!'

'Jamie? What happened?' Instant worry filled her eyes

and she began looking over his body, which stretched beyond the end of the stretcher.

'Nothing,' he snapped. Hadn't he learned anything over the past few years? A pretty face meant nothing when it came to knowing a person, to understanding what went on behind those enticing looks. Nothing at all.

'Jamie?' Her voice was lower, softer as she watched him and reached for his hand.

'I'm okay,' he answered less abruptly. 'Honest.'

Apart from letting my guard down.

How could he do that? There was more than his heart at stake when he started thinking a woman was lovely. The boys could get hurt again, and he'd sworn that was not happening. Ever. Yet he'd tried to convince Kayla he had no problems by saying, 'Honest'. Convince Kayla or himself? Another unanswerable question to deal with. Or ignore. Or deny.

'You're sure? It's important I know any little problem.'

Not this one you don't. I just had a moment of forgetfulness.

Now he knew how easily he could get sidetracked he'd be more vigilant. Tomorrow he'd be up and about, getting on with life as though nothing had happened. He had to be. The boys were with him this week and they weren't going back to their mother even for a few days because he'd taken a knock on the skull.

CHAPTER FOUR

BECCA DROVE SINCE Kayla was far more qualified to deal with Jamie's condition. Not that Kayla would move aside for someone else to look after Jamie until they reached the emergency department. She wanted to be there for him, to reassure him if he became bewildered or the pain increased or if he got upset at being in this situation. Like he'd been there for her after the avalanche, a lifeline to cling to while wondering if she was alive.

It still felt as though that connection ran between them, not to be severed until he was pronounced fit and healthy. Then he wouldn't need her and everything would return to normal for both of them.

Except she was still creating her new normal by working long hours and taking part in search and rescue. Her new life included wanting to spend time hanging out with a hot man who seemed to see right through her whenever she let her guard down.

The ambulance had never felt as claustrophobic, not even when she'd had two patients in there at one time. Studying the semi-conscious man on the stretcher, Kayla's heart fluttered. He was large, but so had been the guy she and Becca had taken to Invercargill by road on Monday, and she hadn't noticed anything different then. It was Jamie getting to her, making her look beyond where she thought she was with settling down, had her wondering if she should grab him with both hands to see where it led, or to remember Dylan and the ensuing pain when she'd lost him and the last chance of a family. The more she saw of Jamie the easier looking forward, not back, became.

Jamie groaned as he moved his shoulder.

'Try to stay still.'

He didn't open his eyes. Had he heard her?

Watching him made her feel slightly breathless, as though she'd fallen asleep and woken up in a different place with the same patient. It was like she wasn't back to full speed, as though her mind hadn't kept up with her legs on the road back to normal.

'Kayla?'

'Yes, Jamie?'

'I am in an ambulance, right?'

Long-forgotten words hit her. 'I am alive, right?' Jamie had been quick to reassure her then. Reaching for his wrist on the pretext of taking his pulse, she nodded. 'You sure are, only minutes from hospital.' Under her fingers his pulse was strong, and she automatically found herself counting while focusing on the timer to keep from diving into those deep brown eyes now watching her. Melted chocolate came to mind. Soft, creamy and delicious. Except she'd never seen anything creamy about Jamie Gordon. Delicious maybe. Snatching her hand away, she wrote the result in the notes. Normal despite the shock showing in his eyes and speech.

'I don't feel flash.'

Glancing at the heart monitor, Kayla smiled. Technically his heart was fine, but the knock he'd taken might've cracked some ribs, along with the damage to his shoulder and likely concussion. Throw in shock catching up and no wonder he felt bad. Glancing out the window, she saw the hospital coming into view. 'In case you're wanting better service, the emergency department's got way more gadgets to hook you up to, and doctors and nurses and proper beds.'

'In other words, stop moaning.' Jamie gave her a tired smile.

'No, in other words, you *are* doing well and shortly Josue will be giving you all the attention you need.'

'You've been doing that since I was hauled out of the blaze.' He stretched a hand out to tap her arm. 'Thanks.'

'You're welcome, but I'd prefer you didn't get into trouble again.' The strange thing about being an advanced paramedic was that while she loved the work, helping, saving people, she hated it that people had to get hurt for her to use her skills. She continued watching Jamie—how could she not?—looking for any signs of an injury she might not have picked up on, while knowing she had all the bases covered. Even strong men got knocked off their feet and took a bit to get back up and running.

The feeling of wanting to be there for him beyond the door to the emergency department had her looking over her shoulder to see where that had come from. That invisible cord between them tightening? All she saw was the familiar interior of the ambulance, no signs saying she might be getting off track. Good. Everything was normal. Back to watching Jamie. Enjoying the picture before her. Maybe not so normal.

When he closed his eyes he appeared relaxed, but that was probably the painkiller making him drowsy. What would it be like to run her fingers over his square chin covered with dark stubble? Tingling started in her fingertips. Thick black hair was plastered to his forehead. A working man with no frills. Who did he go home to at the end of the day? He'd never mentioned anyone, but why would he? 'Is there someone you want called and told about what's happened?' she asked quietly. They hadn't spoken properly in a while— Did he have a new partner? Her chest tightened.

His eyes snapped open. 'I'll sort it when I've seen Josue.'

Something not right at home? 'You'll probably have to spend a few hours in hospital while they monitor you.' Might as well give him the heads up so he could figure out if he needed to contact anyone. 'They may even want you to stay overnight.'

'Not happening.'

She wasn't getting into an argument. It wasn't her place. A stubborn tilt to his chin suggested he wouldn't take any notice of anything she said anyway. She still wanted to reassure him. 'Everyone will do their best for you. You know how the system works.' He'd also been part of enough rescues to know the people who worked at the small hospital. 'Wait and see what Josue says before getting wound up.'

'And you?'

'And me what?'

'Will you hang around to make sure I'm all right?'

She stared at him. What did he want from her? More than a paramedic? A friend? 'I'm still on duty for...' she glanced at her watch '...another three hours.'

'You might bring someone else into ED.'

He wanted her to look in on him? 'Then I'll come by and annoy you some.'

Becca was backing into the ambulance bay.

'We're here.' Kayla stood up to open the door, feeling a little shaky, not understanding what was behind his request.

Jamie reached for her hand. 'Thanks for everything.' Worry filled his face, and something else she couldn't read.

'What's up?' She could ask. He was more than a patient. Like her, he was part of the emergency services, and they all looked out for each other. They didn't all look at each other with such depth and confusion, though.

His eyes were fixed on her, dark chocolate this time. 'I'm not in control. I hate it.'

'Believe me, I see that all the time. You'll be back on your feet soon enough and everything will return to normal.' It hadn't worked like that for her. She'd spent months frustrated about having little control over her legs and therefore her mind because it wasn't getting distracted with work or other people's needs.

The door opened before she could think of anything encouraging to say. So much for being focused on her patient's needs. This particular one was tipping her sideways in ways none had before. Since when did any male upset her focus? She lived a solitary life, and her goals were simple. Be fit and healthy and help others. Enjoying herself came into that, but dating and having another relationship didn't. Losing Dylan had been too hard.

'Jamie, what have you done to yourself, *mon ami*?' Josue was striding towards them.

'I had a fight with a beam.'

'Came off second best by the looks. Kayla, fill me in.'

After running through the notes, she handed them over and crossed to Jamie, who'd been shifted onto a bed. 'I've got to go.' She didn't want to. 'Another call.' Which was good or she might've stayed to keep him company; the ambulance in the bay, the radio on hand. It wasn't unusual for the ambulance crews here to do that with a patient they knew with their base close by, but this need to hang around with Jamie was different. For someone she'd only ever seen as upright and positive, in command not only of his crews but himself, he looked so forlorn her heart melted. Was he all for show? Did loneliness lie underneath that tough exterior? Another thing they had in common?

'I'll catch up when we bring our next patient in. Okay?'

'Thanks.'

Jamie watched Kayla walk away, already focused on her next job. Her right leg dragged a little, making her limp more pronounced. A couple of times when kneeling beside him on the ground she'd winced like it still hurt. He shouldn't have encouraged her to check up on him later. They weren't becoming best buddies. Or anything else. He'd been trying to stay away from her as much as possible because of how she wound him up with longing. Yet he'd almost begged her to see him if she was in the ED.

At the last S and R meeting before Christmas he'd overheard her telling Zac it must've taken someone with an engineering degree to put together all the metal she was carrying now. The way she'd described it he'd pictured welding gear and metal cutters and had laughed. Which apparently had been her point, because Zac had laughed too. But today not once had she faltered or given in to the pain.

She'd been there for her patient, focused entirely on *him* and finding out what his injuries were, on helping him through *his* pain and getting him to hospital. Doing her job more than well. Putting her own problems aside. Holding his hand when he'd been losing focus. That soft, warm hand did wonders to his beleaguered mind.

She'd gone up a long way in his estimation, and she'd been fairly high up already for her competence with the German woman who was now on a long but steady path to recovery. Nor had he forgotten the quiet way Kayla had dealt with her injuries and fears when she'd been airlifted off the mountain after the avalanche. Yes, she was one strong woman.

It was hard to describe this wonder he felt around Kayla. It had started at the avalanche rescue and had stuck with him ever since. She brought sunshine into his world even when he wasn't aware of needing it. His life had been cruising along in a bit of a rut since Leanne had given him some space to get on with raising the boys, but the sense of having something to look forward to whenever Kayla was around wouldn't quieten.

As though he might be able to take another look at his world and chance a crack at a future he hadn't imagined in a long time. 'Might' being the word. It wasn't going to happen. His sons came first, first and only first. Never again were they going to be pulled in all directions as the adults in their lives fought their battles. Hence staying away from Kayla as often as possible. It hadn't been easy, but necessary. He didn't need the distraction of worrying about her getting between him and the boys if they fell out. But— But a lot of things.

'I'll check that head wound, then your shoulder and chest.' Josue stood above him, about to poke at his pain-racked body.

The drug Kayla had given him was wearing a little thin, but he'd been moved around a few times since she'd jabbed him so the pain level might've increased. Or he was a big wuss.

He was grateful Josue had cut through the meanderings of his brain and shoved Kayla aside. He wasn't meant to be thinking about a woman and his future in one sentence. 'Let's get it over with. I've got to collect my boys.'

'Slow down, *mon ami*. You won't be driving anywhere collecting anybody today.'

Everyone around here was beginning to learn a few words of French now that Josue was a permanent fixture in their midst, but Jamie hadn't learned the words for what he wanted to say so he went for something less expressive. 'You don't understand. I have to be home for Callum and Ryder.' All hell might break loose. It definitely would've once, maybe not now. Leanne had calmed down a lot and they were now getting on a lot better when it came to the boys, but he still held his breath whenever something out of the ordinary occurred. Old lessons weren't easy to forget.

'First things first,' Josue said, snapping on gloves.

Good idea. The sooner he got the all clear the sooner he'd be heading home. His neighbour and good friend, Christine, would pick the boys up from the summer school where they were learning outdoor skills, but he'd given his word he wouldn't be late tonight as she and Jack were going out for dinner for her birthday with their family. Damn, he'd forgotten to tell the boys where their gift for her was. He was slipping. Forgetfulness didn't used to be one of his problems. 'Is forgetfulness a known disorder? And, no, I haven't got dementia.'

'Concussion can make you forgetful for a while.'

He'd forgotten the present before he'd been hit over the head. Jamie gasped as Josue's finger found a tender spot on the back of his skull.

'Sorry, it might hurt as I assess your injuries. I'll try not to cause too much discomfort.'

'Do what you have to.' Jamie lay still, closed his eyes and tried to conjure up something a little more enjoyable than prodding fingers and damaged bones. Kayla slipped in behind his eyelids. That pert mouth when she'd been

cross was wearing a soft smile. A smile that he could recall in a flash. It lightened her face and put sparkles in
her eyes and sucked him in like a puppy to food.

Except he wasn't as soft and soppy as a puppy. He
wasn't anywhere near as trusting either. Just because
those glowing eyes snagged his attention more often than
he cared to admit, it didn't mean he was letting her in.
There was a steel grill over his heart that would take
more than a blow torch to cut through.

If he ever felt he was faltering because Kayla might
be moving past his shield then he only had to remember
Ryder clinging to his leg and crying that he didn't want
to leave and go with Mummy when he'd been promised a week with his dad. That day was etched in his
mind. Leanne stamping her feet and hustling the kids
into her top-of-the-range, brand-new wagon, yelling at
him that he had no right to promise the boys anything.
They were crying because they couldn't be there for their
dad's birthday.

It had been a horror of an afternoon, and he'd finally
backed off because the boys had started getting hysteri-
cal. The only way to calm them had been to explain he'd
see them in a few days and then they'd have a party, just
the three of them. It had been a turning point, though.
Since then he and Leanne had worked together for their
sons' sakes, and he had the boys two out of every four
weeks. It worked for him.

'A nurse will give you more painkillers shortly.'
Poke, prod. 'I'm sending you for X-rays. I don't think
your skull's fractured, but better to be certain. I suspect
some fractured ribs. Your shoulder's badly bruised and
might've pulled in the socket so won't move easily for a
few days but it's not dislocated.'

'Thanks, Josue. Nothing sounds too bad considering the size of that beam.'

'You might've got off lightly, but no holding fire hoses for a week. No driving until you get the all clear about the concussion.'

'In other words, get a bank teller's job.'

'Or sit at your desk, issuing orders to your staff.' Josue laughed. 'It won't hurt to take a few days off. When was your last break? In the time I've been in Queenstown I've only ever seen you in work attire, on rescues, or at S and R meetings.'

'I took time off over the school holidays.' No denying Josue had a point, though. He did put in a lot of hours at the fire department or with the S and R crowd, practising or doing real jobs when he could, banking time so that when the boys were with him he could step away and let someone else pick up his role temporarily. He hated handing over control but it wasn't as hard as not being with Ryder and Callum. Balance. That's what was missing in his life, and he probably wouldn't find it for a long time to come. Most likely when the kids were adults and able to fend for themselves, and even then he'd be keeping an eye on them.

They were little rascals; adorable and trouble, fun and heartaches. Like most children, from what his mates said about their kids. One day they had him wanting to pull his hair out, the next making him curl up all soft with love as they watched their favourite programme with him. Being a dad was the best thing to ever happen to him, and watch out anyone who got in the way of that, as Leanne had found out when she'd tried to gain full custody. It had taken a while, but he'd finally come to realise she'd had exactly the same fear of losing Callum and Ryder. After that it had all become easier to sort out the divorce details.

A yawn pushed up and out. His body ached with weariness and stabbed with pain. The drug Kayla had given him was definitely wearing off. Kayla. Once again she was in his head. Had she even left? After all this time living alone, why did this particular woman take over his thinking so easily? Why was he thinking about her at all?

She was a head turner. His head was always moving when she was near. He had to see her, get his fill of that open, friendly face, to see her beautiful eyes and those full lips. Hearing her talk in her southern lilt stirred him, as did her light laughter, which didn't come often enough. Though she had laughed on the way in here. Paramedic reassuring her patient, or had she been so relaxed with him that she'd been a friend as well?

'I'm giving you an injection before taking you to Radiology.'

Where had Damian come from? 'How long have I been here?' he asked the nurse.

'About thirty minutes. You haven't asked for anyone to be notified you're here. Can I get that sorted while you're having your X-rays?'

He shook his head and immediately regretted it. 'No.'

'You sure?'

Which bit of no didn't he understand? 'Yes.' His head was floating again. Was this normal for concussion? Where was Kayla? She'd know. She'd probably already told him but his memory failed him. As long as he got past this concussion sooner rather than later because he had to get out of here before six o'clock. 'What's the time?'

'Three thirty.'

He yielded to the drowsiness engulfing him. He still had plenty of time to get home to the boys.

Kayla stepped into the ED and looked around for Jamie. She should've gone straight home after finishing her shift but, hey, she was here now. Nothing to do with the fact that Jamie had been front of mind whenever she hadn't been with a patient.

When she and Becca had brought John Baxter in, Jamie had been having X-rays and Josue was busy, so she hadn't learned anything more about his condition. There was no way she could head home without seeing if there was anything Jamie needed, though she fully expected someone to be here for him by now. He did have a family, right? It wasn't her role, but there'd been that moment in the ambulance when he'd looked as though he'd been about to ask something of her, as if he didn't have anyone else to ask. She was probably making it all up because of some warped sense of wanting to get closer to him.

Best get out of here. Go home and unwind. Kayla turned for the exit.

'You here to see Jamie?' Josue asked from behind her.

Turning slowly, she looked at Mallory's fiancé, and kept her mouth shut.

'He's in cubicle three. On his own.' Josue's smile was gentle, as though he understood she didn't want to be here when there was little that could keep her away.

'How is he?'

'Very lucky there wasn't more damage. Go see him. I'll be along in a few minutes. There're some things I need to talk to him about and I'd like you there.' He headed away.

She called after him, 'Jamie might not be happy with

that.' What said she was? Josue seemed to expect her to hang around like she had a role in Jamie's life, which couldn't be further from the truth. But Josue knew that so what did he want to raise with Jamie in her presence? It didn't add up. So, was she leaving, then? Going home? She couldn't. Not until she'd seen Jamie. She just had to. No reason.

You sure about that, Kayla?

Most definitely.

A wave of sadness touched her. To have another relationship with a loving man would be wonderful, but highly unlikely. Some people didn't get one go at it. Why would she get a second chance? She was afraid to try again, remember? Even more now she'd met this sexy man. She wouldn't want to hurt him. Or herself.

Josue continued walking away.

Kayla rubbed her right thigh, easing the aches that had throbbed most of the afternoon. Physical pain she could handle, heartache she could not. She'd learned that lesson.

So go home.

She limped into cubicle three.

Jamie took up most of the bed, his eyes closed, his cheeks white, a bandage wound around his head, another around his shoulder, and large bruises coloured most of his exposed upper body where the sheet had been pushed aside. Jamie in his sleep? The concussion, drugs and shock were taking their toll but his underlying strength came through in his steady breathing and his relaxed hands. He'd do fine.

Kayla fought not to reach out and slip her hand into one of his. Her slim fingers would be warm against his, her palm smooth against his rougher skin, but it was the trust in his face, the gentleness on his lips, the strength in his jawline that were drawing her in. As though he had room in his world for someone else. Quite the opposite of the worry she'd witnessed in his face earlier when she'd asked if there was someone she could call for him. What would he say if she climbed onto the bed and stretched alongside him, draped her arm over his waist and held on?

She had to get away. This was all wrong.

Spinning around, she bumped the chair, making a racket loud enough to wake the dead.

'Kayla?' Jamie's voice was deeper than usual, filled with sleep, and well and truly alive.

She could still run. But she didn't do running. 'Hi. Thought I'd see how you're getting on, but you're not much fun, sleeping the afternoon away.'

'What time is it?' He licked his lips as though they were dry.

'It's just after six. Do you want a drink of water?'

'It's what?' He shoved upright, groaned and clutched his head.

'Careful.' Kayla reached for him, held him steady.

'I've got to get out of here. I have to get home for my boys.' He began shuffling his legs off the bed.

'Whoa. Josue's coming to talk to you first.'

'There isn't time.'

'Jamie.' She tapped him. 'Stop this. You've been in an accident. You can't just up and walk out of hospital. Is there someone else who can look after the boys?' She had to get away from the unusual sensations he created in her, but first she'd help him out of his predicament.

'No. Christine's going out.'

So there was another woman in his life. Gulp. 'Does she know you're in here?'

'Yes, but I told her I'd be back by six so she wouldn't miss any of her celebration.'

Christine was going out celebrating something when Jamie was in hospital? Okay, now she was confused.

A shadow fell over the bed. Josue had joined them. 'Lie down, Jamie. I overheard you telling Kayla you're going home. Sorry, but that's not happening when there's no one to keep an eye on you throughout the night.'

'To hell with keeping an eye on me. It's my boys who need looking after, and there's only one person doing that. Me.'

'You think it's all right for a six-year-old and a seven-year-old to take care of their *père* when he's not in good shape?' Josue asked.

'What else am I supposed to do?' Jamie demanded. 'You're saying I can't go home under any circumstances?'

Josue glanced at Kayla.

So did Jamie.

'After receiving a concussion it's important someone's on hand in case you black out or have a fall.' The words were out of her mouth without any thought of where this was headed.

'What are you doing tonight, Kayla?' Josue asked. 'Would you be prepared to spend the night at Jamie's house?'

'You can't ask her that. Take no notice of him, Kayla. I'll ring Ash or someone else from work.' His voice trailed off and he stared at her as though he hadn't meant a single word.

'You sure Christine—' whoever the heck she was '—can't change her plans for the night?'

'Not when she already gives up so much for Callum and Ryder. It's her birthday.'

Wasn't Jamie more important?

He was watching her. A big 'O' appeared on his

mouth. 'She and her husband are neighbours and take care of my lads whenever I can't be there.'

A knot loosened in her chest. Did she want to help Jamie out? Going back to his house and spending the night, keeping an eye on him and his sons, went against all the arguments she'd put up about staying away from involvement of any kind. She was already at odds with herself about Jamie, wanting to get a little closer and terrified of messing it up. Kayla looked from Josue to Jamie, then at her boots.

'Nothing you can't handle, Kayla,' Josue said.

Yes, there was, but she wasn't saying it out loud. 'What are Jamie's injuries?'

'Three cracked ribs, mild smoke inhalation, shoulder bruising, a large cut on his head and mild concussion. It's the last one that I want someone to oversee tonight and as Jamie needs to go home, you're a great option.'

Thanks.

What other options were there? Jamie wasn't rushing to say. What else did she have planned for the night? Not watching movies or serials, for sure. She'd had enough of them. After all Jamie had done for her when he'd rescued her, she didn't want him thinking she wouldn't do the same, despite the warning bells ringing in her head. She went back to appraising Jamie, who had a look of will-she-won't-she in that usually steady gaze. 'I'll take you home.' She stared at him. 'And spend the night at your house.'

The right corner of his mouth lifted in an ironic curve. 'You're sure?'

No. I'm stepping outside my comfort zone.

Being chaperoned by two young boys should mean not a minute alone with their father. Was that a good thing? Showed the mess she was in if she didn't know the answer to that. 'Absolutely. I'll just collect some gear from my locker at the station.' She turned for the exit, glad to be getting away for a few minutes. Fresh air might help settle her mind. 'Unless I get called out as an extra at a major incident,' she added less crisply over her shoulder. A six-car pile-up in the middle of town would certainly be a distraction. Guilt squeezed, taking the air out of her lungs. She'd never forgive herself if there was even a car versus rubbish bin with no injuries now.

Her comment was rewarded with a low, rough laugh, which didn't help her guilt.

Jamie shouldn't be laughing. He was lying on a hospital bed with his shoulder bound tight and a head filled with stitches and drugs to alleviate pain. Only since Josue had declared there were no other serious injuries had the worry begun to quieten in her chest. If Jamie had been hard to ignore before, now it was impossible.

CHAPTER FIVE

JAMIE WRIGGLED HIS BUTT, trying to get comfortable. It wasn't working. His head pounded and other parts of his body were having a grizzle. His bed would be far more comfortable but he'd insisted on the couch so he'd be around while the boys got used to Kayla.

'Ryder, Callum, over here,' he called. So far they hadn't said anything about the bandage around his head or the fact he was laid up. They'd just looked at him with their heads to one side and then at each other and had gone out to the family room, but he recognised the denial in their faces. They'd had to deal with so much in their short lives. They returned to stand staring at him, still not saying a word, which said it all. He longed to hug them, but they'd remain remote until they knew everything was going to be all right. 'Boys, this is Kayla. She's staying the night to keep an eye on me. I've banged my head and hurt my shoulder.'

'How?' Ryder asked.

'At work.' The less they knew the better. He didn't want them stressing every time he walked out the door to go on duty. Since that hideous fire, they'd often heard their mother complaining about how dangerous his job was. 'Nothing serious.'

'What were you doing?' Ryder always asked the questions. When Callum wanted to know something tricky he'd get Ryder to do the interrogation. And, man, could Ryder be persistent.

So could he. 'Listen up, both of you. Remember your manners. Say hello to Kayla.'

'Hi, guys.' Kayla was sitting on the armrest at the end of the couch, looking relaxed except for her fingers rubbing her thighs. There wasn't a wedding ring, but it could be on the gold chain that fell between her breasts, or she might've put it away for good. She was widowed, and there'd been no mention of a child. Didn't she like kids? Or was she just nervous? Kayla?

Try another one, Jamie.

'Hello, Kayla. I'm Ryder.'

'I'm Callum. Are you really looking after Dad?'

Jamie blinked. He looked at Kayla, but she wouldn't understand how unusual that was. Callum was shy around strangers. Seemed Kayla might be an exception. Was that good? His boys were vulnerable, wanted to be loved, then when David had withdrawn from spending time with them they'd become even more cautious. Kayla was only here for the night to keep an eye on him. For them to think she might become a long-term part of his life would be upsetting.

Kayla smiled. 'I work on the ambulance so I know how to look after your dad. When a person gets a bang on his head, it's best someone stays with them for a few hours. Is that all right with you both?'

'Yeah.'

Ryder's eyes lit up. 'Can we have takeaway for dinner?'

'What's your favourite?' Kayla asked before Jamie could.

'Chicken nuggets and chips,' Ryder was quick to reply.

'Hot dogs and chips.' Callum was right behind him.

'Then guess what you're having?' She turned to Jamie and winked. 'No, I'm not trying to score points. Not being the world's best cook, I'm thinking about their stomachs. Anyway, I'm too tired to go digging around your pantry.'

He was getting nervous about how well this was going. Ryder and Callum obviously liked Kayla. What did that mean for their future? 'You could heat up the casserole I prepared last night.' Though right this minute takeaways sounded a good idea even to him. He rarely bought them, and tonight, give him half an hour and he'd be beyond eating anything. All he wanted was to sleep and then wake up ready to get moving.

'No, I'm having chicken nuggets.' Ryder punched the air.

Callum copied the gesture. 'No, I'm having a hot dog.'

Kayla shrugged. 'We'd better keep Dad happy. He's the invalid here. What do you think, Jamie? How about a treat tonight?'

'What's an invalid?'

'Someone useless, lying on a couch while his kids get to choose what they want for dinner.' It took effort to wink at them. 'Go on. Order in something to keep them quiet,' he told Kayla. 'And something for yourself. I'll have a beef burger.' It would probably still be in its box tomorrow morning, but he'd try to get some sustenance on board before he crashed. 'My card's here.'

She leaned towards him, laughter in her voice. 'Behind that gruff exterior lies a softie.'

A warm softie at the moment. Despite the aches and pain forcing everything out of his head, he was comfortable having Kayla in his house and around his boys. They weren't bothered by her presence at all, which was unprecedented. They usually got wound up whenever anyone other than Christine or Jack came over. Progress? Or Kayla's genuine caring nature? 'Don't tell anyone.'

'I won't. What time do these guys go to bed?'

'Nine o'clock.' Callum this time.

Jamie locked one eye on him. 'Really?'

'Um, no.'

'Seven thirty,' he told Kayla, who was holding back a laugh.

'Just after you, then,' she murmured, and stood up. 'Right, boys, I'm phoning out for dinner. Definitely nuggets and hot dogs?'

'Yes,' they shouted, and followed her to the kitchen.

Jamie sank deeper into the couch, closing his eyes but not his ears. The boys were happy, not a hint of wariness around Kayla. That had to be good. Or not, since she wasn't becoming a part of their life. Why not? She was another person not connected to the past they could say hi to if they bumped into her in town. Someone new.

Who are you trying to convince here, Jamie? Why are you trying to persuade yourself Kayla could slot in with the boys when the only way they'd have anything to do with her is if you do?

Did he want that? She was the only woman since Leanne who'd made him feel there might be a reason to start looking forward. Careful. None of this meant he could take notice of how she had his blood heating and a fierce longing stirring where nothing had stirred for ages. At the end of the day he had to protect the kids from any harm whatsoever, and that meant putting them before his own needs. She could as easily upset them as not. Too early to know what she might do.

'Are you dad's girlfriend?' Ryder asked.

Jamie tried to leap up and stride into the kitchen to demand Kayla leave right now, but his body wouldn't play the game. He was stuck in a position that would take some leverage to get out of. Time for a new couch that didn't sag in the middle.

'Me?' Kayla squeaked. 'No.'

Did she have to make it sound as though that was the last thing she wanted? It was a small hit to his ego. Shouldn't have been, but was.

'Dad doesn't have a girlfriend,' Callum said.

Thanks, guys. You're supposed to be on my side here. Keep the family secrets in the family.

Not that there was anything secretive about not having a woman in his life. Everyone who knew anything in this town knew about his divorce.

'Don't you like Dad?' Ryder to the fore. 'He's cool.'

'Ryder,' Jamie bellowed. 'Stop it right now.'

Kayla carried on like he hadn't said a word. 'I've been on a rescue with your dad. He rescued me off a mountain once, so he's really cool. Now, Ryder, you grab the salt and pepper.'

So I'm cool?

Or else Kayla was taking the easy route through the grilling. Jamie's ears strained for more.

'Do you like him?' Persistent Ryder was not taking a jot of notice of him.

'Of course I do.'

'Where do you live?'

'Ryder.' Give that kid a bone and he'll make short work of it every time.

Kayla was handling the questions with ease. 'Up on the hill behind the school. I can see the mountains in the distance.'

'Can we visit some time?'

Kayla laughed. 'Are you always this inquisitive?'

'Yes,' Ryder answered. 'You didn't answer. Can we come to your house?'

'Only if your father agrees. Now, where's the sauce?'

You're not going to sidetrack them that easily. They're taking no notice of me so you might as well settle in for the long haul.

The little blighters seemed to like her. Good or bad? Of course it was good as long as they didn't get too connected. When they accepted someone they tended to leap in and not look sideways. It didn't happen often, so far only with Christine and Jack, and Zac who came round for a beer occasionally.

But those three people were open and friendly, honest and genuine, didn't knock their trust sideways, as David had. Obviously Ryder and Callum thought Kayla appeared reliable, but he knew from experience that people changed when things weren't going their way. He swore through the pounding in his head, now added to by the woman here to keep an eye on him. He needed more painkillers and something to make this exhaustion drag him under so he couldn't think any more. Then he *did* trust Kayla with his boys? Good question.

'I've got the sauce,' Ryder said. 'Do you have kids?'

'No, I haven't.'

'Why not?'

'Ryder, that's enough,' Jamie called out. Maybe he shouldn't trust the boys not to cause trouble. Who knew what the next question would be, and although he wanted to learn more about Kayla, he'd find out directly. He would? He coughed, tasted smoke. Or imagined he did. A bitter flavour filled his mouth. He would not get to know Kayla that well. He couldn't afford risking getting close and then having to deal with the ructions that'd follow if it went belly up. And what was to say it wouldn't?

What said it would? This was ridiculous. Kayla intrigued him when he wasn't looking for a relationship. Here he was wondering what might happen if knowing Kayla got out of control. He needed another bang on the head to clear his mind.

'Can we have a fizzy drink?'

'Do you usually have one before dinner?' Kayla replied.

'Dad says we have to have water at night.'

'Then water it is. Did you have fun at summer school today?'

'Yes.' The boys talked on top of each other, keen to tell her everything.

Well done, Kayla. Diversion in place.

Jamie relaxed further. Whether it was good the boys were totally comfortable with her or not, tonight it made everything simpler. He didn't have the energy to make them dinner, or oversee their showers before bed. That beam had done a number on his body and everything was catching up. He'd leave worrying about how Kayla was fitting in with his family too quickly, too well, till tomorrow.

Tomorrow. She'd be heading out the door to go to work. Out of their lives other than whenever they met through work or rescues. Wouldn't she? Or was she done for the week? Four days on, four off. Wasn't that how it went with the ambulance staff? The pounding in his head made it hard to recall details he knew as well as the scar on his hand from once pulling a dog out of a flaming laundry. Another fire, another memento. Another fib to the boys to hide the danger of his job.

A long yawn dragged in air and forced it out again. Dang but he was shattered.

* * *

'Here's your dinner.' Kayla spoke quietly in case Jamie had nodded off. Sleep was better for him than a burger.

His answer was deep, slow breathing. Good. She'd have to wake him soon so he'd go to his room and into bed. His body fully stretched out on a mattress would be easier on those bruises than having his legs hang over the end of the couch and his shoulder digging into a lumpy cushion. The drawn look marking his face had gone. She knew it would return when he woke, but for now his body was resting.

It was strange to be nursing Jamie, if that's what she could call this. Very used to giving urgent attention to people who'd had an accident or medical event, she wasn't used to caring for someone after the doctors had finished with them and didn't know much more than taking note of pain levels and watching for symptoms suggesting the concussion was worse than initially diagnosed. A nurse she was not. But Josue believed she was capable, and she was. Even stranger was how happy she felt. She wanted to make sure Jamie would be all right, that nothing untoward happened during the night. This wasn't about a patient, it was about Jamie, and how he'd held her hand, given her courage and strength when she'd been floundering.

She should be running for the hills, hiding until this new sense of wanting to be with a man disappeared. Dylan had been the love of her life, and he was gone. The emptiness that had followed had dragged her down, turned her life into dark solitude, a place that now she was out of she never wanted to return to.

'Dad, why aren't you eating your burger?' Ryder asked from the other room.

Kayla headed for the other room, her finger to her lips. 'Shh, Dad's sleeping and that's good.'

'Are you staying all night?'

'Yes, I am.'

'You'll have to sleep on the couch. There aren't any other beds.' Ryder was grinning like a cheeky monkey.

'That's okay. My legs aren't so long they'll hang over the end like your father's.' Not quite anyway. Kayla grinned back. She'd curl up on the couch, though those cushions didn't look very comfortable. Might be better to lay them on the floor and stretch out to soften the aches she got in her legs after a day at work. 'Do you have a shower at night?'

The boys looked at each other. 'No-o.'

'Guess what? You are tonight. Let's do it before Dad wakes up and then you can surprise him.'

And me, if you take any notice of what I say.

'Okay.' They headed in the direction of the bathroom, leaving Kayla shaking her head.

Were they really doing as she'd asked?

Squeals came from the bathroom, followed by shouts. Guess they were.

Kayla walked across to see if Jamie was still asleep.

'You have them wrapped around your little finger,' he said in a sleepy voice that made her feel as though a light scarf had caressed her skin and teased her with longing.

'They're probably outside the shower in their clothes, pretending to be washing.'

'Anything's possible with those two.' The love on Jamie's face told her all she needed to know about this dad. He'd do whatever it took to keep them happy and safe.

But he was also unbending when it came to rules. She'd seen him leading a search team with authority but not overdoing the I'm-in-charge part of his job. He led from the front.

'What woke you?'

'You insisting they have a shower.' His smile was slow and kept ramping up her need for him. 'You seem to understand kids. You told the boys you haven't got any.'

'No, I haven't.'

Come on, explain. It's part of getting to know each other.

'Dylan and I were trying. I had two miscarriages.' She nipped her bottom lip. 'The second one on the day Dylan crashed his car and died. He was on his way home to me.'

Jamie reached for her hands, clasped them, squeezed gently. 'Oh, Kayla.'

'Yeah,' she sighed. She liked the way he didn't try to say the right thing when there weren't any words to help. Time had diminished the pain, hugs from close friends had helped, but nothing she'd been told had gone towards her recovery. Sitting there, Jamie once more holding her hand, was enough. Then she went and spoiled it. 'I missed him so much, and it's taken for ever to start moving forward. I'll probably never have a family now.'

'You'd like children?'

'Yes. Absolutely. I was so excited both times I learned I was pregnant. Losing them was hard. I don't know if I could go through that again. Or if I can even carry a baby to full term.'

'Other women have multiple miscarriages and still go on to have their own children. It can happen for you.'

Her hand was being squeezed tighter. She held on, savouring the moment, glad she had told him. 'It's the heartbreak that's the hardest to deal with. And losing Dylan and a baby at the same time was agony. Another miscarriage would bring all that back and I don't think I could get through it again.'

'That I can understand. But you're a strong lady, Kayla. Don't ever forget that.'

Oh, wow. He said the most wonderful things. She'd just spilled her soul, and he was understanding. She doubted he'd forget this conversation by the time he woke up in the morning, concussion or not. Finally, after a few minutes, she straightened her back and asked, 'Are you hungry? Your burger will only be lukewarm, but I can get you something else if you'd like.'

Moving his head slowly from side to side, Jamie winced. 'I'll try the burger. I'm not ravenous but a couple of bites might shut my stomach up.'

'Thought I heard a noise.' She helped him sit up and went to get his meal. 'I take it I'm sleeping on the couch.'

Jamie's shoulders slumped. 'I didn't give that a thought. The boys can top and tail so you can have a bed.'

'No way. They need to sleep properly if they're going to summer school tomorrow. I'll be fine sprawled out in here.' Until the bones started complaining.

'Are you sure? It's hardly fair when you've gone out of your way to help me.'

She had, hadn't she? How cool was that? Helping people was her go-to place all the time. It was something she enjoyed and got a buzz from. Falling for a man wasn't like that. Jamie waking her up in ways she'd never believed possible again was very different, exciting and scary all in one, but she'd get through the night and go to work no worse off. She had to. 'Stop talking and eat. I'll cope.'

Jamie managed half the burger before putting it aside and clambering awkwardly to his feet. 'I'm going to bed.'

Kayla stood beside him. 'Your head spinning?'

'A little, but don't think you can catch me if I trip.'

'You reckon?' She laughed, feeling right at home with him. Same as it had been with Dylan right from the beginning. A sense of being with her other half, of becoming whole. She swore.

'Careful. There're kids within hearing.' He was serious.

'Sorry. I wasn't thinking.' She'd been out of line but it had been an instant reaction to that preposterous thought. Jamie was nothing like Dylan. In any way, shape or form. Other than his gentleness, love for his family, strength and determination. Nothing like Dylan at all. Nothing. Trying too hard to convince herself?

Not looking good, Kayla.

'What rocked your boat?' They'd reached his bedroom door.

'Nothing important.' Glancing at Jamie, she instantly knew he saw through her denial. 'Nothing I care to talk about,' she added to shut down ideas he might have of pushing for answers. There'd been enough talking tonight. 'I'll pull your bedcovers back and leave you to get undressed.' Heat filled her cheeks at the thought of helping Jamie out of his clothes. 'You won't need a hand, will you?'

Grow a backbone, Kayla. How many semi-naked patients have you worked with? Why would this man be any different?

Because he was Jamie, and like it or not he was winding her up something shocking. Shocking in that no man had done this to her for years, hadn't created any kind of reaction that had gone beyond friendship. These feelings were more than friendly. Unheard of, in her book.

He took a long, measured look at her, as though trying to read her, to see what made her tick. Or trying to fathom what she'd meant. What could be plainer than she wasn't interested in undressing him for bed? Then he gave an abrupt shake of his head and winced. 'I'll manage.'

Perfect answer. 'Good. Want a hot drink to down more painkillers?' Paramedic to the fore, not the blithering female who hadn't had anything do with a male in an intimate way in so long her body had probably forgotten the moves, let alone the emotions.

'Tea would be good.'

'How do you take it?' They were being distant. Probably the best way to go. Except she did like him, and wanted them to get along. She wasn't only thinking about how he made her blood race or her fingertips tingle. He was a great guy and she didn't intend walking out of here tomorrow and not have anything more to do with him outside work or S and R. She wanted to become friends. That was one word for these foreign emotions swirling through her. Friendship was safe. Didn't cause as much pain if it went wrong. But it could. Her heart was involved with Maisie and Mallory.

'White and one.' Jamie stood, hands on hips, waiting for her to disappear so he could get his gear off.

She'd laugh if it wasn't so damned ridiculous how her gut got in a twist over something so ordinary. Except nothing about a hot man taking his clothes off in front of her would be ordinary. It would be exciting and fun and—

Stop right there. If you can't be sensible, at least pretend to be.

'I'll see what the boys are up to.' Sensible enough? She sighed. More like boring. Not that Jamie's kids were boring. They were adorable, and Ryder was the spitting image of his dad. The same thick black hair and piercing brown eyes, and his mouth did that cheeky twist at the corners when he was being smart. Callum must have his mother's looks as he was blond with blue eyes, but that cheeky glint in his shy gaze instantly reminded her of Jamie. Not the shy, but the cheeky.

'Don't let them talk you into being allowed to stay up an extra half-hour. They'll try every trick in the book,' Jamie warned.

'Onto them.' She headed for the lounge where a programme was blaring on the TV screen. 'Okay, guys. Ten minutes before you have to be in bed.'

'The programme won't be finished,' Ryder muttered.

'Then you can record it.' Fingers crossed he was allowed to. 'Your dad wants to say goodnight. Don't bounce on the bed or jump on top of him. He's very sore.' She was sure these two would be exuberant if allowed to be.

'Is Dad going to be all right?' Callum asked, staring at the floor.

'Yes, he is.' Sitting on the couch armrest, she explained. 'He's got lots of bruises on his arms and shoulders, and his head. He needs time for them to get better and stop hurting. But don't worry, he's strong. He'll soon be playing games with you again.' There was a football and three bikes on the front porch, suggesting he got involved with these guys as much as possible.

'Will he take us out on the boat?'

'You'll have to ask him.' She wasn't getting caught up in saying things Jamie might not want to partake in. 'He knows his work schedule. I don't.' How did he manage the erratic hours of his work and the sudden, unexpected calls for S and R with these two to take care of? Christine obviously had a lot to do with them, but surely not every day of the week?

There was more to him than what she knew so far. At S and R he was always totally focused on the job at hand, and nothing else seemed to bother him, but who knew? He might be a master at covering up his worries. Or he might compartmentalise everything, dealing with the immediate problems and leaving everything else till later.

Ryder waved the remote in the direction of the TV and increased the volume.

Checking her watch, Kayla shook her head. 'Sorry, kiddo, it's time to turn that off.'

'But I want to watch it.' A pout shaped Ryder's mouth.

'Let's record it and go say goodnight.' Then she'd make the tea.

Moments later the only sound she could hear was giggling coming from Jamie's bedroom. A lovely sound that clenched her heart, reminding her of what she was missing out on.

CHAPTER SIX

'YOU'VE PASSED MUSTER with my boys,' Jamie said. Their reactions to Kayla were heart-warming, and surprising. He hadn't believed they'd be so trusting so fast after David. Maybe they weren't as jaded as their old man.

'They're easy to get along with.' Kayla stood with her mug in hand, appearing to be sussing him out.

Medically or otherwise? Surely she didn't think of him as just a patient? After talking about her longing for children? Would her emotions make his boys vulnerable? He didn't believe so but he still had to put them first in case he was completely wrong about Kayla. 'They usually ease into being friendly.' He'd only felt that way twice, with Leanne and now Kayla. It was still hard to believe that the strong and wonderful love he'd had with Leanne could go belly up so fast. He couldn't have loved her more. His heart had been completely invested in their love and marriage, so her leaving had crushed him. He hadn't known then how big a fright she'd got when she'd thought it was him who'd been killed in the fire he'd been attending, and if he had, she'd still have left because she was over him.

Caution was his go-to place now. Even if he could shrug aside the hurt of the past and find a woman he might—a very big might—fall in love with, he had to remember it wasn't on his agenda until Ryder and Cal-lum didn't need him for every step they took.

'Why are they cagey about strangers?' Kayla sat down on the end of the bed. 'I'd have thought Ryder was always outgoing. He's such a chatty little guy.'

Sometimes he just had to give up on holding out and move on as fast as possible. This was one of those mo-ments because he didn't want Kayla thinking he was being aloof. Not when she'd given up her night to be here for them. 'When their mother and I split, things got nasty for a while and sadly they were in the middle of the battle. Ever since then they've been wary around people they don't know. Except you.' Despite his worries he liked that she'd been accepted so readily. It felt as though he'd passed one hurdle on this new road he found himself on.

'It's been hard for you all.'

Her tone was non-judgemental but still he felt the need to defend himself. 'I fought hard to be in their lives, to have a solid footing in their day-to-day goings-on. I like being the father who takes his sons to the ski field or on a holiday or spoils them by occasionally buying the toys they ask for. I want to be there for the arguments over what I make for dinner, for the days they're unwell, and the football games and parent-teacher meetings.'

That's enough. If Kayla doesn't get the idea then she's never going to.

'A true dad.' A smile lifted her mouth, and sent warmth throughout his battered body.

That was the nicest thing he'd heard for a long time. She hadn't stopped to think about it either. He sipped his tea to hide the emotions rolling through him. Some-thing about Kayla made him open up a little. He'd never spoken about Leanne and their battle to anyone. If one of the men at work or S and R asked about being a solo father, he shrugged the questions aside with, 'I love my sons.' It was the reason he'd fought so hard for his right to be an involved parent. That, and taking his responsibility seriously. 'I do my best.'

His parents hadn't been a shining example of how a loving family worked. It had been every kid for themself and there'd been six of them in total. He and none of his brothers and sisters were close. As the youngest he'd tried hard to be loved by any of them, but it hadn't happened so he'd learned to hold himself tight and get on with things until he was old enough to get away and create a life of his own. One that had to include love and happiness. He'd found it with Leanne.

He'd also lost it with Leanne. But he had two sons he adored and would fight to the end of the world and back to be there for them. He lived how he wanted, not how he was raised—caring and supportive of others, and especially of his boys. 'Ryder and Callum are my world.' Just to emphasise the point.

'I can see that.' Her smile was soft and genuine.

A new ache started behind his ribs. One that any amount of painkiller tablets was unlikely to dull. Kayla was definitely getting to him, stirring a need for someone special to share his life with. Subject change required. 'Why did you choose to come back here? Family? Friends?'

Her smile dimmed as her gaze dropped from his face to the mug she held in both hands. 'After Dylan died I continued living in our apartment for nearly three years, believing my life was over. No man I loved, no children of my own. Then one day I realised if I didn't get out I'd be there till someone came looking for me and found a fossil sitting in the chair by the window.'

Sadness touched him. Obviously Kayla still hurt.

If only his body could move easily and he had more than boxers on, he'd be out of the bed and hugging that sadness away. Instead he gave her a heartfelt smile. 'Do you think you made the right move?'

She nodded. 'I grew up here, and rushed away as soon as I was old enough to support myself in the big city up north. It wasn't that I didn't like Queenstown, it was just that there seemed to be so much more to do out in the wider world that my parents didn't need to know about. They were quite possessive of me, growing up.'

'And was there?'

Kayla drained her mug, then nodded. 'Definitely. I found everything I was looking for. Fun, excitement, a career I put a lot into, and then there was Dylan. Yes, Auckland was good to me. And then it wasn't.' She stood up. 'How's your head? Still pounding like a bongo drum?'

End of conversation. He understood. 'More like a pair of them. When's my next dose of pain relief?'

Glancing at her watch, she smiled again. 'Not for a couple of hours but I can give you something lighter to be going on with.'

He watched her step out of the room. Confident without putting it out there too much. The type of woman he preferred. He sank back into the pillows, groaning as pain throbbed and his head filled with images of having fun with Kayla. The next groan was louder.

'Here, get these into you.' A slim hand appeared in his vision with two white tablets in her palm. The other hand held a glass of water.

Those pills weren't going to make the slightest bit of difference to what was ailing him. Kayla would not vanish as they dissolved in his gut. Her smile and soft voice would remain inside his head, teasing him, pestering him with her genuine concern and care. 'Thanks,' he muttered.

'Have you ever worried about the dangers of your job?'

He had to stare at her for a moment to make sure Leanne hadn't turned up. 'No,' he snapped. 'I have not.'

Those beautiful eyes filled with remorse. 'Steady. I didn't mean to upset you. Nor was I being critical of what you do.'

Then why ask? 'I'm probably less at risk than Joe Blogs driving to work on the main road. I trained to be prepared for when mistakes happen.' He paused.

Want to rethink that?

'Okay, things can and obviously do go wrong, but I don't spend my time worrying about it. I won't give up my work because of today.'

Kayla swallowed and said quietly, 'I've obviously hit a nerve. I wasn't looking for trouble or suggesting anything such as you shouldn't do your work because of the boys. Life's full of obstacles and there's no avoiding all of them.'

It was good to know she wasn't accusing him of not thinking about his boys when he went to a fire. But then why would she? 'I guess I'm the one who should apologise.' Old habits didn't die fast. 'Sorry.'

Her smile was brief. 'No problem.'

He'd hurt her with his reaction. Seemed he could still get annoyed over things Leanne had belted him with too often. 'There was a fire in the hills and along the lake edge. One of our firemen was caught in a fireball and died. That same day Ryder had appendicitis. Leanne tried to get hold of me but I was out of reach. When she heard about the death she thought the worst.'

Kayla nodded. 'Understandable.'

'It flicked something in her. She was afraid it could

happen to me and she didn't want the boys to suffer. That's when she packed up and left, taking Ryder and Callum to have a life where they weren't worrying about whether I came home or not.' His mouth tasted bitter.

'She told them what happened?'

'I'm not sure. The guy who died had kids at the same kindergarten so of course they heard. I didn't figure how much they'd understand. They were so young.'

'I can see why they were edgy when you came home with a bandage around your head.'

His sigh was full of despair. 'Me, too. But once you talked to them, they came right. Maybe honesty pays off, even about something like this.'

'No gory details.' Kayla smiled.

'Not a one.' He returned the smile around a yawn.

'Sleep time for you.'

She was right. If only he didn't have to be there alone.

Kayla stepped quietly into Jamie's room and paused, listening to deep breathing. He was either asleep or pretending to be. She'd leave him be. Groping around in the dim light from the hall for his wrist to check his BP wasn't going to achieve much except an annoyance factor.

'You all right?' Jamie grunted.

'I'm fine. I came in to check up on *you*.'

'You can't sleep?'

Tell him yes, save him worrying about something he had no answer for. 'No.'

There was movement in the bed. He was shoving to one side, leaving the other half empty. 'Get in. It's a damned sight more comfortable than the couch. I won't touch you, I promise.'

Did he have to sound so certain? Like she didn't ring

his bells even a tiny bit? 'I'll stick to the couch. You need your sleep.'

If you say I won't affect that then I'm going to curl up in a little ball and pretend I'm the most wanted woman in the country and deny the hurt you inflicted.

'You snore?' Was that a hint of laughter?

'Not that I've heard.'

'I'll be the judge. Get in. We can put pillows between us if that'll make you feel more comfortable. They're in the wardrobe.'

'Jamie, is your head throbbing? Your vision blurry?'

'Yes, to both. So I can't see you and I have no strength to do more than go back to sleep. Seriously, how do you think I feel knowing you can't sleep and that your legs are probably aching badly all because of me?'

'You have such a beguiling way with words.' That mattress was so tempting, no matter that Jamie was taking up two thirds of it.

'Take your trousers off. They won't be comfortable for sleeping.'

Another putdown. Take her trousers off for comfort, not because he wanted to see her shapely legs. She laughed. 'Charm isn't your thing, then.'

'Am I getting through to you?'

Yes, damn it. She went to turn off the hall light, returned to sit on the edge of the bed, her heart fluttering as if she might be making a mistake. Or was it because she felt happy, even excited? Why excited when Jamie was beyond doing anything more than sleep? Because he'd be close, if unattainable. The memory of being held in his arms was blinking like emergency lights. Appropriate considering she might be in trouble here. Except the cure was simple. Return to that uncomfortable couch, aching legs and all.

Shucking out of her trousers instantly cooled her over-heated skin. If only it cooled all her body. Grabbing a handful of sheet she lifted it, slid underneath and pulled it up to her chin.

Straight away her legs felt better, though still tense, as was the rest of her for fear she'd move and bump into Jamie, who, despite moving to make room for her, was sprawled in all directions.

'Goodnight, Kayla.' His voice was thick with sleep as his breathing deepened, slowed.

''Night, Jamie.' She waited and waited, and then heard a small snore and smiled. 'Go, you.' Oh, to fall asleep so easily. She should. The last few days had been busy with a spate of older people having falls, and there'd been the death of a paraglider after getting caught in a down-draught that had dropped him on rocks on the Shotover River. She'd longed for one of Jamie's hugs that day but hadn't had the guts to call and say what had happened and how she needed him.

Closing her eyes tight, she breathed deeply for calm. Close enough to Jamie that she only had to move her arm a few centimetres and she'd be touching his mus-cular body. Get out of here. Right now. Before she fell asleep and snuggled into him. She might hurt him. His bruising wouldn't take much of a knock to ache like hell.

Excuses, excuses. You're afraid of touching him in case you can't find it in you to move away again.

Kayla's eyes shot open. Really? She stared into the darkness above them. They hadn't even kissed. Not once. Near, but not near enough. She wanted to kiss him. Re-ally kiss him, long and deep, find the man behind the smile. But that didn't mean she cared more than a little about him. She might yearn to press her length against his hard body and absorb his warmth and strength and kindness, wipe away the sense of being too alone, but she could not give in. She mustn't.

Why did Jamie make her feel this way? Why not any of the other good-looking, friendly men she met as she went about her work? Tipping her head sideways, she tried to see him in the dark. Impossible, so she relied on memory, which showed how gorgeous he was and why she felt soft and gooey on the inside, hot and tight on the outside. Jamie did this to her. No other man. And here she was, lying right beside him in his bed. 'Why am I here?' she demanded of the darkness.

'Kayla? That you?' croaked Jamie.

'Yes.'

Glad I came tonight.

It felt like home, comfortable with this little family. Family. She tensed.

If only.

'You all right?'

'I'm fine, and looking after you, not the other way around.'

'We seem to have a knack of getting knocked over and the other one appearing to do something about it.' Jamie was starting to wake up properly. Not good when he needed to rest and sleep.

'We're quits. One accident each.'

A yawn filled the air.

'Go back to sleep, Jamie. It's the best cure for what ails you.'

'I don't think so.'

'Need more painkillers?'

'No.'

What was the problem then? 'Jamie?'

'Shh. You talk too much, woman,' he quipped.

She talked too much? Hadn't he said he couldn't sleep?

No, Kayla, he said he didn't think painkillers would help what was bothering him.

Oh. Had she got that right? Was having her in his bed disturbing him? She couldn't help smiling. She wasn't suffering on her own. Or she was because she'd got it all wrong. Wouldn't be the first time, and most likely not the last. Rolling over to face away from him, she muttered, 'Sleep tight,' and closed her eyes. She'd fake sleep until hopefully it happened. If it didn't then she'd be a grump all day tomorrow.

Jamie woke muscle by muscle, desperate to breathe slowly and not to over-activate the dull throbbing going on in his head and shoulder. It had been a long night, pain interspersed with sleep, tablets swallowed with water, and that tantalisingly warm body curled up beside him. Kayla did a number on him even as she slept.

Sometime during his last snooze she'd backed up against him. Whether she'd been aware or not, he hadn't moved away. Instead at some stage he must've draped his arm around her waist and tucked her even closer because there was a new warmth on his skin from his ankles to his neck where she touched him. Her hair was splayed on the pillow between them, and her chest was rising and falling softly.

Hopefully she wouldn't attack him when she woke, believing he'd done this on purpose. He should back away, withdraw while she slept. It would be safer. And impossible. Being so close to another person chipped away at the loneliness he'd carried since Leanne had left. It gave him hope. For someone to care about and who might do the same back. But what if it was thrown back in his face when the going got tough? That'd hurt too bloody much.

Was this why his parents had never been loving towards him and his siblings? They were afraid of losing their love? Of having it tossed aside like it didn't matter? Hadn't they realised how loved they were by all of their children anyway?

Kayla's background sounded loving. She spoke adoringly of her family, and there was only love in her face when she mentioned her late husband. Did she want to love again?

Jamie jerked, gasped. What was he thinking?

'Hello? What happened?' Kayla murmured beside him. Then she stilled. 'Jamie?' she whispered.

'Morning, sleepyhead.'

'How long have you been awake?' she asked, caution in her words and her body tensing.

'All night,' he teased, then realised he'd probably upped the tension. 'Ten minutes max.'

She began to roll away, and he retracted his arm instantly. 'We were like this when I woke, and I didn't want to disturb you.'

I was enjoying myself, making the most of having you close. It was magic.

Swinging her legs over the side of the bed, she sat up, scrubbed her face with her knuckles. 'How're you feeling?'

Hot. Tight. Needing you.

'Achy and ready to stretch the body.'

'I'll put the kettle on. What time do the boys get up?'

Jamie sat up fast, groaned as pain lanced his chest and shoulder. The boys. He'd forgotten them. What if they'd walked in here while Kayla had been lying in his bed, snuggled up to him? 'Seven, when I usually have to shake them awake.' What was the time? He tried to twist around to pick up his phone and more pain stabbed his shoulder.

Kayla was pulling her trousers on at the same time

as tapping her phone on the bedside table. 'Slow down, Jamie. It's just gone six. I'll go out to the kitchen and they'll be none the wiser.'

'I hope.'

Kayla's face dipped, and her mouth tightened. 'Right.'

She hadn't liked what he'd said. He couldn't blame her, but she didn't know how much he protected his boys from getting caught up in things that would upset them. 'They're smarter than you think.'

'Tea?'

He nodded. 'I didn't mean to insult you. They're still not happy their mum doesn't live with me and if they saw you in my bed they might get the wrong idea and think you're replacing her.'

She ran her fingers through her hair, tangling with the knots that had formed overnight. 'That's sad. For all of you.'

She was right. 'It's a work in progress. For me too,' he admitted. Kayla brought things out of him that he hadn't even admitted to himself, let alone anyone else. 'Be happy they accepted you so easily.' Hopefully it boded well for the future, and the day would come when he could have a woman—this woman—in his life, not necessarily in his house or family but there to have some fun with. 'I'm not in a hurry to get hooked up again. Too much to get my head around. And my trust levels barely touch the scale.'

Her eyes darkened. 'I understand how you feel. It's not been easy putting Dylan's death behind me. I'm not sure if I'm even meant to. Sometimes I wonder if people would think I'm selfish to want to be happy again when Dylan has no chance. It makes me cautious.'

'To hell with what other people think. Some will be like that, but most, especially your family and friends, wouldn't wish a life of unhappiness on you.' Yet here he was doing the same thing to himself. 'Stay for breakfast.'

Kayla stared at him for a long moment, then suddenly laughed. 'My first date in years and I wasn't even asked, just told to stay for breakfast. I like it. Except I have to get to work.'

That unexpected laugh dived right into him, lifting his spirits in a way he hadn't known for so long. 'That's a shame.' He slowly stood up.

Her eyes dropped to his chest, then lower to his boxers. The laughter died. 'I'll head to the kitchen.'

He hadn't thought when he'd stood up. That's how relaxed he was with her. 'I'll join you in a moment.'

'Go easy. It hasn't been twenty-four hours since you had a fight with that beam.'

'Yeah, but I won. It's probably ash by now, whereas I'm slower than normal but otherwise doing okay.'

Kayla shook her head at him. 'You're nuts.'

'I know.' He enjoyed this light-hearted banter. It was something else that had been missing for a long time. Maybe he did need to get out and start mixing and mingling with the opposite sex, then he'd be more relaxed, which had to be a good thing for them all.

Slow down. One night with Kayla in your bed not having the ultimate fun and you're thinking about getting amongst it?

'Why not?' It was the only answer he could come up with.

She popped back around the door. 'Who's driving the kids to school?'

'The neighbours,' he said, his breath stalling in his lungs. She was beautiful with her mussed-up hair and sleepy eyes. 'I'm glad you were here last night. I would've been worrying without someone to keep an eye on things. Thank you.'

Those golden eyes were fixed on him, her lips slightly apart. Her breasts were rising and falling too fast. 'Any time,' she whispered.

He stepped closer, brushed the back of his hand over her cheek. 'I might take you up on that.'

'I should go.' She didn't move an inch.

'I know.' Placing his hands on her shoulders, he gazed into her eyes, falling deeper into her hold over him. He didn't want her to leave. Not at all. But she had to. Suddenly he couldn't imagine her not being around to talk to or share a coffee with. 'Kayla?'

'Jamie?'

He had to kiss her. Had to. His lips touched hers, brushing across them to the corner, and returning to cover them completely. Her mouth opened under his in invitation and he was lost. Sunk in a softness that absorbed him, overwhelmed him, took charge of him. Wrapping his arms around her, he held her against his hungry body, felt her curves against his tight muscles as he tasted her mouth.

Kayla pulled back in his arms to lock her eyes with his. The tip of her tongue slid along her lip.

Hell, he wanted to kiss her some more. His whole body was responding to that tongue. But she'd lifted her mouth away from his. 'Kayla? I know I said I'm not leaping into anything, but I've been wanting to kiss you for so long.'

Her smile was slow and sexy. Then she was pressing hard against him, holding him tight around his waist, kissing him like she wanted to give herself. It couldn't get any better.

Bang. 'Callum, give me that book back.'

Jamie froze.

Kayla jerked out of his arms, stepped away, smoothing her hands down her clothes. Shock registering in her eyes, she murmured, 'Thought you said you had to shake them awake.'

'I usually do.' He puffed out the breath that had got caught in his throat.

"It's mine, Callum.'

The boys' bedroom door swung open and two little bodies hurtled down the hall towards them.

'I'll make that tea and leave you to it,' Kayla muttered.

'Hey, Dad, Callum's got my book.'

'Watch out,' Kayla warned from the doorway. 'Your dad's hurt, remember?'

Ryder slid to a stop before him. 'You still sore, Dad?'

'A bit. Why are you arguing?'

Ryder shrugged. 'Don't know.'

'Yes, you do,' Callum shouted. 'You took my book.'

'So what? Where's Kayla, Dad?' Ryder headed to the kitchen. 'Kayla, can you come to my birthday party at the weekend?'

Where the hell had that come from? This needed to be dealt with immediately. In the kitchen Kayla looked stunned. Would she say yes and make Ryder happy, or no and quieten his concerns? Or would she delay answering until she'd talked to him?

She glanced at Jamie, worry darkening her face. Looked at his son, waiting with something like resignation in his eyes, and smiled. 'Thanks for asking me. I'd love to come.'

'Cool.' Ryder's shout ricocheted around the room. 'You hear that, Dad?'

'I did.' He didn't know whether to be pleased or annoyed. This was raising the bar higher than ever,

'How old will you be?' Kayla asked.

'Eight.' Ryder was already racing back to his bedroom. 'The party's at the skating park. We're taking our skateboards. You can have a turn on mine, Kayla.'

'No, thanks. I've already broken my legs once. I don't plan on doing that again.'

'Chicken,' Jamie muttered, uncertain about this. He should be pleased she hadn't turned Ryder down.

Then be pleased.

'Thanks for not disappointing him.'

Finally she relaxed. 'That doesn't sound like me.'

'I agree. You don't let people down, do you?'

'Not if I can help it. But is it all right if I come? What about the boys' mother? Will she be there? I don't want to cause problems or give her the wrong idea.'

Jamie bit back a retort. Leanne would be there, but if she made any comments about Kayla she'd have him to deal with. She had a new husband so he doubted she'd react badly to him turning up with a woman, but he'd been wrong before. 'Leanne will be fine.' One way or another, he'd make certain of it.

'Then I'll look forward to the party.' Kayla stretched up on her toes and she brushed her lips over his. 'And to seeing you again.' Then her cheeks turned bright red and she stepped back. 'So much for being cautious.'

'Yeah.' One kiss and everything had changed. One damned kiss and he wanted more. Maybe not the whole deal, but more kisses and holding that sexy body, and getting to know her so much better.

Too soon, too fast.

This wasn't how the future was supposed to go. Not yet. But no denying he wanted more of Kayla. 'I'll see you Saturday.' He had to accept she'd be at Ryder's party, and that he was already looking forward to more time with her. As long as he could squash the idea she might let him down in the future and believe that his boys would be safe with her. So much for waiting a while before getting involved even a little. Right now he felt as though he was standing on a precipice and he could go either way.

CHAPTER SEVEN

'COME ON, KAYLA, you have to take a turn on my skate-board. It's my birthday.' Ryder stood in front of her, hands on his hips, wearing a cheeky smile that got her right in the chest—just where his father's smiles hit her.

The little ratbag. How did he know she didn't dodge challenges? Right now she was hyped up and ready to take one on, both for the hell of it and to quieten her nerves with Jamie's ex about to turn up. 'I'll give it a go.'

'You don't have to do this, Kayla.' Jamie joined them, worry reflecting out at him. 'Think about those fractures you sustained last year.'

Too right she was thinking about them. But she was a dab hand on skis and snowboards so balance was on her side. She squeezed his arm. 'I'll be fine.' Or sensible. Another challenge going on right there.

'Out of the way, guys. Kayla's having a turn and she might crash.' Ryder was running at his friends, shooing them back.

'I'm not that decrepit.' She laughed.

'Don't do it. You haven't had birthday cake yet.' Jamie sounded light-hearted but his hands were clenched.

'Watch this.'

Please, please, please, get it right.

She placed one foot on the board and pushed off

with the other, kept her balance as the board moved forward slowly.

'Too slow.' Ryder walked beside her. 'You've got to go faster or you'll crash.'

'Okay.' Same as snowboarding. Except landing on concrete would be inflexible. This wasn't her wisest move in a while but, hey, wise was highly overrated. Pushing harder, she was off, balancing better as she tucked her left foot behind the right one. Leaning to the side, the board began turning. Just like snowboarding.

'Cool.' Ryder was still with her. 'Do a jump.'

'Nope.' That was one challenge she wasn't ready for. She managed a sharp turn, wobbled, then pushed with her foot and headed back to where she'd started. Straightening the board by angling her body, she aimed for the grass strip and jumped off, holding her hand up to high five the air. 'How's that?'

Jamie shook his head. 'I'm impressed.'

'That easily?'

'I'm hoping the boys don't challenge you to anything else. You won't be able to turn them down. Weren't you worried about falling off?'

'Worry and it happens.' Something she'd learned on the ski slopes as a five-year-old. Strange how she couldn't react the same about a new relationship. Since leaving Jamie's house the other morning, she'd spent most of her time thinking about needing to get to know him even better. His kiss was something else, and waking up to find herself wrapped against his body beyond awesome. The sense of belonging had remained ever since. She'd dropped in to see how he was and had had a coffee with him the next day. It had felt right, and Jamie had been relaxed about her being there when the boys had come home. She was starting to let go of her worries over a new relationship.

'Hello, who are you?' A woman stood in front of her, dressed in classy trousers and a sleeveless top. 'I'm Leanne, Ryder and Callum's mother.'

Jamie stepped closer to Kayla. 'Hi, Leanne. This is a friend of mine, Kayla Johnson.'

'Hello, Leanne, nice to meet you.'

'I wasn't expecting you.' Leanne was sizing her up with a shrewd look in her eyes.

Glad she'd worn her new white three-quarter-length pants and snazzy red shirt, Kayla smiled.

'I invited her, Mum.' Ryder appeared between his parents, a frown on his brow.

'You didn't mention it to me,' Leanne snapped.

This could go either way, so Kayla intervened, 'Probably because I had to check my roster to see if I was working.' A little lie, and shouldn't have been said in front of Ryder, but he wasn't getting into trouble on her account.

Leanne studied her for a moment longer, then glanced at Jamie. 'I see.' Then she walked across to a group of mothers watching their kids skating.

See what? Kayla wondered. Jamie's ex didn't know he'd kissed her, made her warm and happy.

I'm not wearing a sign on my forehead.

But there was one in her chest, expanding even as they stood here. She liked this woman's ex-husband enough to want to become a part of his life. They'd connected instantly, and got on whenever they were together, which was never often enough. More than that, she felt as though she'd found her match in Jamie. Enough to want to have more. Nothing full time and permanent, but to be able to do things together would be wonderful.

'You want to try my board?' Callum asked quietly from behind her.

She wasn't letting either of these boys down. 'Sure. Shall I do the same loop or try something different?'

Don't suggest a jump or this time I might have to accept the challenge.

'What you did on Ryder's is okay.' A nervous smile appeared on Callum's face.

Kayla held out her hand for the board. 'Come on, then. Watch this.' She glanced at Jamie, and winked before mouthing, 'No jumps, promise.'

He grinned, surprising her. 'We'll see.' Then he called across to Leanne, 'How's David? I thought he'd be here.'

'He's coming shortly. He's got a problem to sort out with work first.'

'Good. Ryder was hoping he'd turn up.'

It was the weekend. Shouldn't David be here with his wife's kids instead of working? Kayla shrugged. Not her problem, though she knew where she'd be if she was in the same position. 'Okay, Callum, let's do this. Why don't you borrow another board and ride with me?'

Ten minutes later she rolled up to Jamie and stepped off the board. 'Your turn.'

'Concussion, remember? And a badly bruised shoulder.' He'd had the all-clear for his concussion but his shoulder was still stiff and sore.

She laughed. 'Wimp.'

'And proud of it.'

'Then I'd better do another lap.' It was fun zooming around.

'Thanks for letting Ryder off the hook.'

On the other side of the dome Leanne was watching them. 'I know I fibbed, but I didn't want him getting into trouble over me.'

'I think Ryder understands. Anyway, I'm fine about it. The last thing we need is him being scolded in front of his friends.' Jamie had his hands in his pockets as he stood watching the kids charging all over the skating dome. 'They're carefree and happy. It's all I want for them.'

'What about for you?' The question was out before she'd thought it through. 'Sorry, I take that back. None of my business.' Except it could be now that they were getting a little more involved. The other morning Jamie had kissed her like it mattered. She waited for his answer, but after a moment of tense silence she shook her head and made to move away. He wasn't sharing anything at this stage.

Jamie caught her elbow, pulled her against his side. 'There's a big gap between what I'd like and what I'm prepared to give up to get it.'

Still none the wiser, Kayla waited, making the most of her side pressed against his, the warmth between them, the strength she could feel that was inherently Jamie. This could be the beginning of a big let-down, but she was willing to give it a try. Ready to take the knocks on the chin and see if she was lucky enough to have a second chance at love. Falling for Jamie might happen, or it might not. Only one way to find out.

'Ryder and Callum come first,' he said.

'That shows in everything you do.'

His hand tightened on her waist. 'There was another woman about a year back who wanted a relationship with me. I liked her, but wasn't interested in more than friendship.' He paused. 'She overdid it, trying to get onside with the boys as a way to me.'

'They saw through her?'

Jamie nodded. 'They're not silly. Or they learned their lesson from how David treated them.'

Where was he going with this? She was here because Ryder invited her. Surely he understood that? 'What are you trying to say?'

'Want to come round for a meal one night next week?'

That'd been a long-winded way of inviting her. He was probably as nervous about a relationship as she was. 'I'd love to.'

'Great.' His arm slipped away and he wandered over to begin organising the barbecue to feed hungry kids and their parents, a smile lifting the corners of his mouth and a swing in his stride she hadn't seen before.

Christine joined her. 'I see you two are getting on like a house on fire. Though that's probably not appropriate, considering the work Jamie does.'

'You know what? I think we might be.' Kayla chuckled, glad someone was okay with it. 'But don't tell him I agreed.'

'How's that shoulder?' Kayla asked as Jamie handed her a glass of Merlot.

'Coming along well. I've been warned it'll take weeks to settle completely.' The bloody thing ached most nights and gave him grief whenever he lifted heavy objects like the rubbish bin. Not that he'd ask anyone to put it out for him. He sat down beside Kayla on the outdoor lounger and sipped his beer. 'Since Josue's given my concussion the all-clear I'm going on a small hike at summer school with the kids tomorrow. The instructors are all for parents tagging along and it's more time with Callum and Ryder for me.'

'Were your parents so hands on when you were growing up?'

'Nah.' Guess getting close to Kayla meant sharing some of who he was, and for once it didn't seem so bad.

'They didn't get involved in anything we did. I'm one of six and it was made clear we had to look out for ourselves.' It had been a harsh upbringing and one he was adamant his boys would never know. 'I grew up tough and independent, but every kid needs to know they're loved by their family.'

He stared at the beer bottle in his hand. Why did he feel so comfortable around her and not other people he spent time with? Could be her strength, or her easy acceptance of him. Or simply that he liked her heaps.

'Were you and your siblings close?'

He wouldn't look at her in case there was pity in her face, though her voice sounded devoid of it. 'Not really. It wasn't encouraged. I was the youngest and by the time I was getting around they'd all learned to stand alone. I swore I'd never be like that.' But it had taken Leanne to show him that love was real, even possible, and he'd grabbed it with everything he'd had.

Sometimes he'd wondered if he'd gone too hard and that's why they'd fallen apart, but she'd told him she'd just fallen out of love when she'd got in such a panic about what would happen if he didn't come home from work one day. He'd once had a lot of questions about that, but gradually he'd come to accept that if she didn't love him any more there was no point longing for what wasn't to be.

Kayla's hand was on his, squeezing lightly. 'You're very involved and loving with your boys. They're happy with you.'

A lump formed in his throat. 'Y-yeah.' Time to change the subject. He swallowed some beer. 'You always sound happy about your family.'

Another squeeze and her hand was gone. 'Our parents are great, though Dean—that's my brother—got away with a lot more than me because he was a boy.'

'That's why you accept challenges?'

Her laughter tinkled in the night air. 'Absolutely. I drove Mum crazy with some of the antics I got up to, proving I was clever as any boy.'

'I'd better keep you away from my two. Who knows what you'll teach them?'

'Come on. You don't want them to be wusses.'

'Not at all.' He laughed. He did a bit more of that whenever Kayla was around just because it seemed life was easier and more relaxed. Next weekend he'd be at the wedding where Kayla was bridesmaid. 'Josue's pumped about the wedding.'

'Best thing to happen to Mallory. She deserves someone special in her life.'

Don't we all?

Where had that come from?

Kayla's smile was lopsided, like it was exciting but also sad, no doubt a little unhappy for herself having lost her husband. 'It's going to be awesome.'

Jamie reached for her hand, held it, rubbing a finger back and forth over her palm. 'You're not skating down the aisle behind her by any chance?'

She grinned, sending shafts of heat through him. 'I couldn't find skates to match my dress.'

Putting his bottle aside, he removed the wine glass from her other hand. Tugging gently, he pulled her close and wound his arms around her. 'I've been wanting to do this from the moment you walked in the front door.' If not for two nosey little blighters he might have. Her mouth was soft under his, her lips opening with his. She tasted delicious. Behind his ribs his heart bumped along rapidly, caught up in the thrill that was Kayla. He couldn't help himself, he had to keep kissing her, deepening it so their tongues were entwined, and his body was reacting like there was no tomorrow.

But there was, so he'd only go so far. His boys were tucked up in bed, hopefully sound asleep. He still didn't know how far he wanted to take this. Kayla pressed a lot of buttons within him, but enough to be thinking there might be more than a bit of fun? Dangerous as hell. He wasn't ready for any risks.

She pulled back and gazed into his eyes. 'Jamie, I'd better get going.'

Disappointment warred with relief. When he was kissing her he didn't want to stop. But she was being sensible. 'Right.'

She brushed her lips over his. 'I want to take my time. I'm not sure I can be lucky a second time, and I don't want to hurt anyone while I find out.' Looking out for herself, by the sound of it.

Jamie nodded. 'I understand.' His arms fell away as she stood up. 'Kayla, I like you. A lot. I won't countenance the boys being hurt either, which in my book means staying away from a relationship for the next few years.'

She nodded. 'But?'

He rammed his fingers through his hair. 'But I also don't want to be alone for ever.' Damn it. 'Let's see where this goes.'

'I can go along with that.' Those soft, warm lips split into a wide smile, tightening his groin and making him want to throw caution to the wind.

But he wouldn't. There was too much at stake. For both of them.

Kayla was winning Jamie over, softening his stance on not getting romantically involved, though not far enough that he was prepared to dive right in. They were at Mallory and Josue's wedding. The formalities were over, and everyone was talking and drinking, and having a good time.

The band struck up a rousing tune and he scanned the guests, looking for Kayla. She wasn't hard to find, standing tall beside petite Maisie, that thick blonde hair piled on top of her head, her carefully made-up face so tantalising. She was gorgeous. All he wanted. Which was not good for his determination to remain single. Determination that was falling away the longer he knew Kayla. He'd admitted as much the other night as they'd sat on his deck after dinner.

Wandering past the guests standing with glasses of champagne as they watched the bride and groom take their first dance as a married couple, he was focused on the woman changing his life. He hadn't taken his eyes off her from the moment she and Maisie had begun walking up the aisle, leading their friend to Josue. The cream bridesmaid gown accentuated her curves and those seriously high heels made her long legs go on for ever. Her continuous smile set his stomach tripping like a community of butterflies lived in there.

Basically, he'd given in to the hope and expectation, the wonder and happiness Kayla caused. Emotions he'd thought he'd never know again. He'd held out for months but couldn't any longer. He wanted her in all ways. The other night when she'd come round to join the family dinner, it had been a normal, rowdy few hours with the boys constantly in their midst and she'd accepted it. For him, it had been the tipping point. He hadn't slept much that night, too busy thinking about how he wanted to hold Kayla and make love to her, wishing he hadn't agreed when she'd said they should take things slowly. She took his breath away. 'Would you like to dance?'

Her hand slipped into his. 'I'd love to.'

Tamping down the urge to sweep her into his arms and rush out to the garden to find a quiet corner where he could kiss her again and again, he led her onto the dance floor and began moving in time to the music.

Kayla clasped her hands at the back of his neck, pushing her breasts against his chest. Her hips swayed, cruising across his, sending thrills of hot lust zipping to every corner of his hungry body. 'This is how to dance,' she whispered.

There'd never be any other kind again. He breathed in roses, and adventure. When his hands slid around her waist heat came through the silky fabric of her dress, and excitement tingled in his fingers. Why had he held out on getting together with her? *How* had he?

'Hello?' She was watching him, that smile in her eyes luring him in, teasing, happy.

'Hi.' He leaned closer, his lips touching hers, his feet moving with the music, his body moving with Kayla's. Her breasts were tender against the hardness of his chest, her hands soft as they tapped a rhythm against his neck. 'Kayla.' Her name slid across his mouth into hers, long and low and filled with the need clawing through every cell of his body.

'We'd better slow down,' she murmured, that hot breath lifting the hairs on his arms. 'We're surrounded and unable to leave until after the bride and groom.'

'Damn it,' he muttered. 'I hate that you're right.' Keep this up and it could get awkward. More awkward. Reluctantly he removed his hands from her waist.

Kayla reached for his hands and began moving to the music again. 'We've got this.'

I don't think so.

But as they continued dancing, altering their moves to the different songs, he conceded she was right. They could dance and not get too carried away. Barely, but enough not to make a spectacle of themselves.

Maisie and Zac joined them, Zac dancing like he had nothing else on his mind except impressing Maisie, who was doing her damnedest to pretend she didn't notice and wasn't interested.

Josue and Mallory finally prepared to leave, doing the rounds of their friends and family, taking for ever. 'I thought they'd never go,' he muttered.

Kayla hugged Mallory, wiping her hand over her face and sniffing. 'I'm so happy for you both.'

Jamie's heart twisted and he stepped closer, reached for her hand and squeezed lightly. He held his other out to shake Josue's. 'Congratulations again.' He'd never seen a guy quite so happy as the Frenchman looked. A stab of something like envy caught him. He'd once had that, and he definitely wanted it again. He did. If he could make it work for himself and his kids. Other people in the same situation managed. Why not him? Had he turned into a wimp over the break-up of his marriage?

Mallory glanced at his hand holding Kayla's and then back at him. 'Glad you came.' She leaned in for a hug. 'Look after my friend.'

Or she'd kill him? He hugged her back. 'I'll do my best.'

'Then there's no problem.' Mallory stepped back and looked at Josue with love. 'Let's get out of here.'

'*Oui.* The sooner the better.'

Kayla laughed. 'Have a great honeymoon. I'll try not to spoil Shade while you're away.'

'Does that mean you'll take the dog on a search if

the need arises?' Jamie asked as they cheered Josue and Mallory off.

'Shade could show me a trick or two, being more used to searches than I am.' Kayla suppressed a yawn. 'What a day. Mallory deserves to be happy. And now I'm shattered.'

'I'll give you a lift home.' Kayla did look exhausted. Guess that meant what had started while they'd been dancing was over. He couldn't deny the disappointment filling him. He wanted her. No question. But if it wasn't happening then he'd get over it.

'You coming in?'

Please, please, please.

Kayla's heart was pounding in her throat. On the dance floor Jamie had been hot and coming on to her, and there was no way she could deny the need he'd created. What if he drove away? Left her on the front doorstep with a wave? She'd feel stupid. And sad.

'Yes.'

Yes? Yes.

'Then what are we sitting out here for?' She pushed the car door open, not waiting for him to come around. Nervous energy swept through her. She wanted to make love with Jamie. But it had been a long time and there'd been no one since Dylan. She might not be any good.

'Relax. I'm not rushing you.' He took her hand as he had the day of the avalanche. A strong, caring and supportive hold. 'We've got all night.' Then he laughed. 'That's if you don't turn me on as fast as you did on the dance floor.'

Was he nervous too? Not Jamie. He exuded confidence. Though there were moments when she'd see doubt in his gaze and wonder what caused it. How much had his marriage break-up altered who Jamie had been? She hadn't known him then, but it was hard to imagine him as anything other than the strong man before her. 'I'll put on some music.'

In the next moment she was being swung up into those arms that she'd seen haul fire hoses and operate the Jaws of Life as easily as carrying a loaf of bread, and Jamie's mouth was on hers. Kissing her like there was no tomorrow, and no time like the present. Kissing her so she forgot everything but the arms holding her and the expansive chest against her breasts. Jamie. One in a million. Had she got lucky a second time?

You're rushing ahead of things.

They were kissing, going to make love. Didn't mean they were in a relationship of any permanency. No, but she was going to grab everything and see where it led.

He tugged his mouth away. 'Key?'

'What?'

'I'm not making love to you on the doorstep.'

Shame…

Hussy.

Why not? She wanted this man. 'In the meter box.' Easier to get at than foraging in her bag, which was still in Jamie's car. She'd never shifted the key after Josue had discovered Mallory's hidden in the same spot by mistake and let himself into the wrong house. That debacle had led to today's wedding. Would hers lead to something equally exciting and wonderful?

Jamie crossed to the box, and still in his arms she retrieved the key and let them inside, nudging the door shut with her foot. 'Straight ahead.' Music would re-create that hot, sensational atmosphere between them with some moves. Not that they needed any help. First she leaned in and kissed him. Long, hard and breath-taking.

Without breaking the kiss, Jamie stood her up against him, tightened his arms around her, and spun her world out of control.

Walking backwards to the music system, her mouth still under his, she fingered the buttons and pressed the middle one. Anyone would think she'd planned this, she mused as soft, sensual music filled the air. But when she'd left home early that morning to join Mallory and Maisie to get their hair and make-up done, she hadn't imagined Jamie coming home with her tonight. 'Care to dance?' she whispered, slipping her hands behind his head.

Placing his hands on her hips, he drew her up to his length, and moved in time, taking them round the room, his steady gaze on her face, watching her every expression, seeing her smile. This was magic. The two of them close and getting closer. Sending quivers up and down her skin. Heating her blood. Turning her muscles into a molten blob of need. She found his mouth, and groaned as she tasted his wet heat.

Jamie's hands were in her hair, removing the clips, letting it free from the bob to swing across her back, his fingers combing it to the ends. Then he took her head between his hands and concentrated on returning her kiss, holding her at the perfect angle to get the best access. All the while, her hips moved in time to the music, up against him, against his manhood, turning it hard and long.

'Kayla,' he murmured in a deep, sexy whisper against her cheek. 'I want you. I need you.'

Her ribs were going to burst open under the thumping going on behind them. This wonderful man wanted her. Her, when she had felt so alone. Her, when there were other women less likely to hurt him out there. 'I want you, too.'

Their feet still moved in time with each other and the

music. Their bodies absorbed each other's heat. Their
mouths devoured each other, and Kayla's head was floating on the exotic sensations filling her. Hot, gentle, tough,
wonderful, demanding. Her knees buckled, tipped her
further up against him. He was her strength, her weak-
ness. Without Jamie she'd be a useless heap on the floor.
Her hands found his buckle and undid it, pulling his shirt
free and pushing under to touch the warm skin beneath.
To feel the muscles that tightened at her touch. His trousers slid down to his feet when she pushed at them.

He stepped out of them and kicked them aside. Reaching for her hips to draw her close.

She pulled back enough to look into his eyes. He was
so close, beautiful to touch, to gaze at. To want. 'Jamie.'
There was nothing more she could say. 'Jamie' summed
up her longing. She reached for his hand and held it tight,
as she had that day on the mountain. 'Please.' Please,
please.

'How can I resist?' Jamie's smile grew wider as his
hand tracked down her cheek, over her neck and reached
her cleavage.

Her eyes closed as she tipped her head back.

'How do we get you out of this dress?'

Blink. 'Easy.' The off-the-shoulder netting hid the
zip. Leaning forward, she scooped the netting up and
sighed with relief as Jamie's fingers unzipped her dress,
skimming over her feverish skin. Shaking her way out of
the soft fabric, she reached for him. Slid her hands over
those tight abs and down to the tightest, hardest part of
his body. She held him, felt his strong pulse against her
palm, and groaned with delight.

He swept her into his arms and walked to the couch.
'Don't stop,' he growled as he found her spot. Then, 'Yes,
you'd better stop. Now,' he growled. 'Oh, Kayla, seri-

ously. Stop. We're doing this together. No, I mean you first.' His finger was moving on her, fast, slow, fast.

Her hand was following his moves. Yes, they were together. She was so close.

'Whoa.' Jamie's head shot upwards. 'Stop. Protection.' He rummaged in his jacket pocket, removed a foil packet.

She could've laughed if she wasn't so near to exploding. He hadn't taken his jacket off. Shoving at it, she forced it off his shoulders, down his arms so he could shrug out of it without taking his intense eyes off her. They were smouldering with lust. And something else hovered. A depth of his feelings for her, for this moment. It gave her something to hold onto. 'Give me that.' Taking the condom, she began sliding it on, slowly, slowly, until he growled.

'Just do it, Kayla. I can't hold out much longer.'

Slowly, slowly, she teased with her hand.

He took over, placing his hand over hers and pushing down so he was encased before touching her again, hard and fast, and they were together, a rhythm of their own that became ever faster and then Jamie was inside her and she was shuddering and crying and falling into a deep hole of heat and stars. So magical she knew she'd never be the same again.

CHAPTER EIGHT

'KAYLA, IT'S ZAC. We've got a search going down and we need a medic. You available right now?'

'Absolutely. Fill me in.' Kayla headed for the laundry and her boots.

'Two people missing after a kayak was hit by a jet-ski on Lake Wakatipu. We're taking the police launch out.'

'I'll meet you at the jetty. You want Jamie too?'

'He's with you?' Zac didn't sound surprised.

Had they been that obvious last night at the wedding? Probably.

'What's going on?' Jamie asked, right behind her. 'We got a job?'

'Missing kayakers on Lake Wakatipu,' she answered, handing the phone over.

'Zac? I'm available.' As he listened he looked down at his clothes and grimaced. 'I'll change while you drive,' he said in an aside to her.

Great, now Zac would get the picture if he'd been in any doubt. 'Let's go.'

'Yes, bossy pants.'

'Nothing wrong with my pants.'

'I like what's in them best.' They raced out to his car, and he pinged the locks to grab a bag out of the boot before tossing her the keys.

She gunned the motor and headed away before he'd got his door shut. 'Zac didn't say how long these people have been missing.'

'Can't have been too long if the accident was reported immediately. Surely they won't be hard to find.' His trousers disappeared over the seat and those long legs were briefly visible, taking up all the space in the front.

Kayla grinned. Her legs had felt dainty lying between Jamie's when she'd woken that morning. 'Let's hope they've made shore.' Trying to ignore the undressing going on, or at least have some capacity for concentrating on what was important as she drove, she ran through a list of things to do when they found these people. Not *if*. That wasn't allowed to enter her thinking.

Zac had the motor idling as she and Jamie climbed aboard the boat. 'We've got everyone possible out looking for these people.'

'You wearing your police or your S and R cap?' Jamie asked Zac, already scanning the surface they were motoring through.

'Both. There are half a dozen boats out searching with locals, cops and Search and Rescue members on board, some on shore as well. I waited as we might need a medic. It seems whoever was riding the jet-ski has done a runner. There's no way he or she could've hit the kayak and not known.'

'I can't believe anyone would do that. What if someone's sustained serious injuries?' Bracing against the thumping of the aluminium boat, Kayla pulled the first aid pack out of the cupboard to check through the contents. Doing this kept her calm and ready for anything. When they were in position she'd join those on deck looking for any sign of life.

Reports came through intermittently on the radio. No

sightings so far, and the frustration was mounting in everyone involved in the search. Kayla stepped out into the chilly breeze and picked up a pair of binoculars to start studying the choppy water, the trick being to look for a movement or shape that was out of the ordinary, not to over-search everything in the viewfinder. It was a slow, methodical job, and kept them all busy until they reached the spot where the kayak had been found, and proceeded along the lake's edge.

Zac explained, 'If you have to go ashore, Kayla, Jamie will go with you.'

'When you take over as Chief of Operations you rub it in, don't you?' Jamie laughed, searching the water and the lake edge.

The radio crackled. 'We've got someone. On land. Male. Unconscious.'

'Co-ordinates?' Zac listened. 'We're almost on top of you.'

Kayla took the handpiece. 'Is he breathing?'

'Yes. Very shallow.'

'Have you laid him on his back?'

'Yes.'

'Tilt his head back to allow more air into his lungs. Keep a watch on his breathing—it can stop quickly.'

'He's not responding to stimulus.'

Not good. 'Try CPR for one minute. I'll be there ASAP.'

'What do you want me to do when we get there?' Jamie had already got the medical pack over his shoulder.

'I'll take over CPR if required. First I want to get water out of his lungs. I'm presuming he swallowed some or he'd be breathing properly.' She added, 'We'll need the rescue chopper, Zac.'

'Onto it.'

It felt like for ever, though it took only a couple of minutes to get to shore and clamber off the boat where one team member was waiting. 'Right here.' The woman indicated a large rock formation. 'I'd say he crawled away from the water before losing consciousness.'

Kayla dropped to her knees beside the lifeless-looking man and reached for his wrist, huffing in relief when she felt a light pulse. Better than nothing. 'You can stop the CPR, Simon, while I check for injuries.'

'Thank goodness. That CPR's no walk in the park.'

Jamie nodded. 'I agree. I can lift a power pole off a person in the heat of the moment but ask me to pump someone's chest for twenty minutes and I'm buggered at the end.'

'You wouldn't give up though,' Kayla said as she felt the man's chest, arms and then legs.

'True. We'll take over while you two get back to searching,' Jamie said to the others who'd been working with the man. He definitely had his second in command cap on.

'Roll our man towards you, Jamie. I need access to his back to listen to his lungs.'

As soon as Jamie had him on his side the guy coughed and water spewed out. 'How could he breathe with that in his lungs?'

'I never understand how lucky some people get. Not that he's out of trouble yet. But I can't find any other injuries, which is good. We need to keep him breathing and wait for the chopper.' Kayla reached for the man's wrist. 'Pulse still weak. Tilt his head back again, Jamie. I'll do some compressions and then we'll roll him on to his side again to see if there's more water in his lungs.'

Overhead the sound of rotors beating up the sky was getting louder, filling Kayla with relief. Never too soon for help to arrive. 'That was quick.' They must've been hovering in the air already, expecting urgency to be the main factor with anyone the rescuers found.

Becca was lowered to the ground and sent the hook back up for the stretcher. 'Hi, there. What've we got?'

Kayla filled her in on the scant details. 'Let's hope we find the second person in as good nick.' In other words, alive.

'You staying out here?' Becca asked.

'Yep, I might be needed when the second person's found.'

Jamie packed up the pack and slung it back over his shoulder.

'I saw that,' she growled.

'What?' he asked with false nonchalance.

'Stop being a bloke. That shoulder still hurts so I'll carry the pack.' She reached to take it off him, but Jamie stepped back. 'Or use the other one.'

'I'm fine. Anyway, I *am* a bloke. Or hadn't you noticed?' There was a cheeky gleam in his gaze.

'No comment.' She laughed. She'd noticed all right. More than once during the night. At the moment his height shrank hers while his shoulders blocked the wind coming from the lake, and his 'help anyone who needed it' attitude won her over every time.

Of course he put his kids before others, but he did the same for anyone needing help. Look how he'd had her back on the day the mountain had done its number on her. He'd held her hand and encouraged her to hang in there when she couldn't always focus on where she was. He'd made sure she was safe until the chopper had flown her off the mountain, and then he'd visited her in hospital. Yeah, this man had what it took.

A keeper.

Like Dylan. Gulp. Why did *he* have to pop into her head right after a night of over-the-top lovemaking that had caused her to feel as though she belonged with Jamie? Because she *was* more than comfortable with him. Could be she'd begun to let go of the past and by popping into her mind Dylan was reminding her of what had been? Their relationship had been wonderful, but it was gone. Though not entirely. She'd never forget Dylan and their special moments, no matter what came her way from now on.

Leaping onto the boat when Zac brought it alongside, Kayla reached for the binoculars, ready to focus again on what they'd come for from the moment they pulled away from the shore. She had to stop thinking about Dylan. It wasn't fair on herself or any man she became close to. And it would never be right to compare him and Jamie. But there were certain attributes she looked for in a man, and they both had them. Caring about other people was right up there.

'Take a pew.' Jamie gently pressed her down onto the steel seat at the back of the boat. 'Give those legs a rest.'

Now that she'd stopped working with her patient she was beginning to feel an ache niggling in her right leg, which might have something to do with last night's work-out. She grinned. Nothing to do with her injuries; they were months old and it was past time for them to get in the way of anything she did. 'Okay.'

'What? No argument?' One bushy eyebrow lifted in her direction.

'Saving it for something important.' He was too ob-servant. She put the binoculars to her eyes to keep Jamie from reading her mind and seeing how relaxed he made her feel, how hopeful for the future she was becoming. So much for never looking at another man or thinking she might not be able to get close to one again. He was knocking that idea down piece by piece. It was early days. He was special, but they were still getting to know each other. From her experience with Dylan, and watching Mallory fall for Josue, she knew true love was often an instant connection that only improved with time.

But she needed to get to know Jamie better before she threw in the idea of children and her worry about not being able to have any. She'd mentioned it to him before, but not in the context of their relationship.

'Zac, slow down,' Jamie called. 'Over there, just beyond those willow trees.'

'Where?' Kayla was up, looking across the expanse of water to the lake edge.

'See. Blue amongst the bushes.'

'Why don't people wear a colour that stands out?'

'He or she looks lost, dazed.' Jamie reached for the pack. 'Ready, medic?' His smile went straight to her gut.

'Absolutely.' She focused on the person they were getting closer to. 'There's profuse bleeding on the side of the head. It's a woman.' The figure dressed in a wet body-hugging sweatshirt and sports trousers was definitely female. 'Hello? Can you hear me?' she shouted over the idling motor.

No acknowledgement flared in the dull eyes looking around as though unsure why she was where she was.

Zac brought the boat close and Jamie grabbed a branch on the willow so the engine could be turned off.

Kayla slipped into the ankle-deep, freezing water and moved towards their second victim. 'Hello? I'm Kayla. A paramedic. This is Jamie, a rescuer.'

No response.

Reaching the woman, she went to take an arm and stopped. It hung at an odd angle. 'Broken below the elbow.'

Jamie took the other arm gently to lead the woman across to a fallen tree trunk a metre away. 'She flinched when she sat.'

'Could be severe bruising on her legs or buttocks.' Had she been hit by the jet-ski or the kayak as she'd been tossed out? The head wound suggested something had hit her hard. The woman had been walking so hopefully that meant her spine wasn't injured. 'I'm going to check her vitals, and then I think the best plan is get her on the boat so Zac can take us back to town.'

'You don't want another chopper?'

Kayla was looking at the head wound, and not liking what she saw. 'She needs a doctor urgently and by the time another helicopter gets to us we'll almost be back to town.' As they'd found the second person there was no reason to stay out here any longer. 'Unless there's one already in the air?'

Jamie shook his head. 'Not from what I heard.' He was holding the woman upright as she swayed on the log. 'We need the stretcher. She can't go into the water on her feet. Can you hold her while I get it?' He looked over to the boat. 'Forget that. Zac's bringing it.'

That's where a good team worked well. 'Pulse is rapid. Her breathing's erratic.'

Kayla talked to the woman while she examined what she could see. 'I've got you. Jamie and Zac will place you on a stretcher.' It was an old habit to talk to a patient even if they couldn't hear her. She liked to think either her words or the caring tone of her voice got through in some way. 'We'll get you in the boat and take you to hospital.'

'Zac, can you put the stretcher on the ground so Jamie and I can lift her onto it?'

'Sure can.'

'Jamie, on the count.'

Blink. The woman was staring at her as they lowered her.

'Hello. I'm Kayla, a paramedic.'

'Where am I?'

'By the lake,' she answered.

'What happened?'

As Kayla placed the woman's broken arm over her belly, she told her, 'You were kayaking and thrown into the lake by a passing jet-ski. Do you remember that?'

'No.'

'What's your name?'

'Lucy Moran.'

Good start. 'Right, Lucy. Is there pain in either of your legs?'

The woman's brows met. 'Not really.' She moved her feet. 'One foot doesn't move properly.'

'Wriggle your toes,' Kayla ordered. 'Tell me if you feel anything.' She couldn't see movement because of the woman's aqua shoes. Those would be removed once aboard the boat.

'Everything feels normal,' Lucy replied.

'What about your head? Any pain? Don't shake it,' Kayla cautioned.

'Big headache. That's all,' Lucy said, keeping very still.

Yet she didn't remember what had happened. 'Did you hear us talking when we arrived? Feel me touching your wrist? Before you opened your eyes?' Kayla added for clarity.

'I'm not sure. I don't think so.'

Then her eyes widened. 'Where's Avery? My boyfriend.' Tension began tightening Lucy's body. 'Is he all right?'

Under Kayla's fingers Lucy's pulse was increasing. 'That who you were kayaking with?'

Lucy was thinking, her brows knitted together again. 'What happened?'

'You tell me,' Kayla answered, needing to find out if there was a head injury at play. Lucy might've hit the water hard head-first. Apparently it was a sit-on kayak so the occupants hadn't been stuck underwater, trying to get free.

'I'm thinking. Yes, Avery and I hired a kayak yesterday to go camping on the other side of the lake.'

When she went quiet again, Kayla made up her mind. 'Let's go. I can't find any other injuries apart from that head wound and the fractured arm.' But the head wound worried her. Odd how Lucy had gone from dazed to aware so quickly, and was now rapidly fading again.

'Not good?' Jamie asked quietly.

She shook her head. 'I'm worried.'

The moment Lucy was loaded on board Zac had the motor running and Jamie untied the rope holding the boat in place. 'Let's go,' he said, then knelt down opposite Kayla. 'What can I do to help?'

'Try getting Lucy to talk while I deal with that head wound. I don't like her going under.' She called to Zac. 'Give the ambulance station a buzz, will you? Tell them Lucy's GCS is thirteen.' She began cleaning the wound, taking care not to cause pain.

'You feel anything where Kayla's touching your head, Lucy?' Jamie asked.

She blinked. 'What?'

Jamie frowned. 'I'm taking your shoes off, Lucy.'

Blink.

'Wriggle your toes, Lucy.'

'No problems there,' Kayla noted as Lucy responded.

Maybe it was shock causing her to wander in and out of full consciousness.

'See what you can find out about the accident,' Zac suggested.

Jamie nodded. 'What time did you set out this morning?'

Kayla found the cardboard splint in the medical pack and slid it under Lucy's arm, careful not to jar it.

'About seven.'

'So you do remember Avery being with you?'

'Did I forget?'

Jamie glanced up at Kayla, a question in his eyes.

'Keep questioning,' she mouthed. Whatever had inflicted the head wound might've hit hard and caused temporary brain impairment, though it was unusual that Lucy could remember most things other than this morning, and now that seemed to be returning. The sooner she was in hospital with the doctors the better.

Lucy's ankles felt normal. No swelling or bones out of place, no reaction to suggest pain. Her knees were the same. She could be wrapped in a thermal blanket without hurting her further.

'Are you a skilled kayaker?' Jamie asked.

'Only done it twice.'

'Do you remember how you got thrown out of the kayak?'

Lucy stared at Jamie. 'Where's Avery?'

He looked at Kayla.

She took over. 'If that was Avery we found lying beside the lake, then he's on his way to hospital, just as you are.'

She waited to be asked if he was all right, but the question didn't come. Lucy was staring over Jamie's shoulder at who knew what. Her pulse hadn't altered, nor had her breathing. 'Can you follow my finger with your eyes, Lucy?'

Lucy looked at her. Said nothing. Did nothing.

'Lucy.' Jamie spoke sharply. 'Can you see my finger?'

'Yes.'

'Follow it with your eyes.' Still a strict voice.

It worked.

Kayla nodded. 'Good.' Smiling, she noted down her observations for whoever met them with the ambulance at the wharf. Jamie was good. But, then, he'd spent years working in the fire service and would've worked with his share of injured people. She also liked how he read her well when she needed something done with a patient.

She liked Jamie. Full stop. Liked? More than liked. Cared about him, for him. Cared as in coming close to loving him. Yeah, life was heating up and there wasn't a fire anywhere in sight. Just the man beside her who flipped all her switches.

'I think we deserve brunch.' Jamie sighed as they stood on the wharf in town. 'Don't know about you but I'm starving.'

'The wedding dinner was a long time ago,' Kayla agreed with a cheeky smirk.

'We've been busy ever since.' He laughed. Hell, he felt good. A night like he hadn't known in years. Kayla was as sexy as sexy could get. They'd made love and settled into cuddling the night away, only to wind each other up to the point they had been exploding with need again. Oh, yeah, it had been a night and a half. Hopefully there'd be more on the horizon. Nah, closer than that. Tonight maybe. This afternoon? 'Come on. My shout.'

He took Kayla's hand and marched her along the narrow streets to a stone-walled pub hidden away from the tourists that served the best brunches in town. 'Are you catching up with Maisie today?' Just in case he was getting carried away with ideas on how to spend the day.

'No. She was on the first flight out this morning back to Tauranga via Wellington. She's on duty tonight.'

His heart soared.

Thanks, Maisie.

'When's she moving home?'

'In four weeks.' An elbow tapped his ribs. 'So we've got the rest of the day to ourselves.' There was a lot of teasing going on in those golden eyes.

Teasing he liked and would follow up on. Starting now. 'Champagne brunch? To keep the mood going.'

'Why not?' She grinned. 'Not that my mood's slipping. Not even those two people being thrown off their kayak and left to fend for themselves can dampen my spirits. My best friend married her soul mate yesterday and I had a night to remember.'

'We don't have to stop at one night.'

She squeezed his hand. 'I wasn't intending to.'

Her words didn't frighten him off. Life was looking up. Fast. Talk about suddenly rushing things, but he didn't want to stop, or slow down and think everything through—even if he could, which was doubtful. His body hummed tiredly with satisfaction and plain old happiness. If this was fast then he was up to running with it and seeing where it took them. 'Did I mention the boys are with their mother for two weeks?'

'About four times.'

'That all?'

'So this your way of filling in the hours till they get home?'

He knew a serious question when he heard one, even when it was hidden in smiles and laughter. 'I always miss the little blighters when they're away. I usually end up working extra hours at the fire station for the hell of it.'

'You need a life. Like I do. I'm all about work and avoiding the quiet times at home.' Now the smile was less intense.

But still knocking his socks off. Talking of which, 'Our boots are soaked from the lake.'

'We'll remove them at the door.' It seemed nothing could upset Kayla this morning.

Was he responsible for her happy mood? His chest expanded. That had to be positive. It meant they were in this together, having fun and enjoying each other's company. He felt valued, like Kayla wanted him for himself and not as a father or fireman. They'd turned a corner. 'Here we are.'

As they settled at a table with menus, Kayla asked, 'Are the boys okay with going backwards and forwards between you and Leanne?'

'They seem to be. At first they didn't trust it, thought we'd start fighting over who did what and where again, but they've come to accept we've reached an agreement and intend to stick to it. I was slower coming to terms with the arrangement.' Especially once David had married Leanne and stopped being so interested in Ryder and Callum, as if he'd used them to win over their mother.

'It must be hard—for all of you. I know how difficult it's been after losing Dylan, and there were no negotiations about anything to deal with, especially children.' She locked her gaze on him. There was no judgement in her voice, just understanding, pure and simple.

It was one of the things he liked best about Kayla. That, and her sexy body and cheeky smile. Right now there was a buzz in his body that made him eager to forget brunch and grab her hand to rush back to her house.

But he wouldn't, even though he had a shrewd feeling she'd be with him every step of the way. He wanted to get it right. Though exactly what that was, he couldn't be certain. He was interested in Kayla as a woman, as a friend, a lover, and was coming to care about her as someone special to look ahead with.

Interested? Turned on, hot, excited, more like. This morning the sky was more blue, the air clearer, his sense of purpose stronger. He had a life and suddenly he was enjoying it, and concerns about where this went with his boys had lessened. 'Come on. Let's get started on making the most of the rest of the day.'

Kayla laughed. 'Then we'll start on tomorrow.'

Tomorrow became two more days. Kayla hugged herself. Jamie was the *man*. They'd barely come up for air since the wedding, spending hours in bed here or at his house, watching movies snuggled up together on the couch, sharing meals and taking Shade for walks.

Last night reality had returned. Jamie had gone to work, and this morning she was at the ambulance station. She glanced around the room where the others on duty were quiet, eating breakfast or guzzling coffee, and on their phones, checking the internet, waiting for the first call-out while hoping it would be nothing too drastic. That's what she was thinking anyway. Something serious would bring her down to earth with a thud, and she so didn't want that.

Jamie was at home after knocking off at about six that morning. He'd called her a couple of times before she'd gone to bed last night just to talk some more. Like they hadn't said enough already. Every subject on the planet had been covered—except their burgeoning relationship. She hadn't wanted to raise it for fear of pouring cold water on her happiness.

What if Jamie suddenly decided he'd made a mistake and backed off? Or that he was only in it for the sex? What if he thought they were rushing things? Because they kind of were, and yet it seemed they'd been heading this way since they'd met on the mountainside months ago. And if that wasn't slow, what was?

Whenever the boys were mentioned, Jamie withdrew a little. What was that about? Didn't he think she'd fit in with them? He'd said they liked her and how good she was with them whenever they'd been together. He put them first, over everything, including his own happiness. She couldn't fault him for that, but surely he was allowed to have fun, and even another relationship? Surely he wasn't going to remain single because he was a father? That didn't make sense when he was such a loving man and had a lot to give.

'How was the wedding?' Becca asked from across the room.

'The best ever.' In more ways than one. 'Mallory and Josue cut a beautiful picture, and they're so happy.'

'Who's next?' Becca stuck her tongue in her cheek and winked at Kayla.

'Not me, for sure.' That was taking her newfound happiness too far. A relationship with Jamie, yes, but a wedding? *Why not?* She would never settle for less if she did fall in love again. A picture of a beautiful bouquet popped into her head. She'd swear Mallory had deliberately thrown it to her. She'd tried to give it back, but no such luck. It might be destiny waving at her.

Her phone lit up as a text came in.

Can't sleep. One half of bed's empty. Jamie xxx

Her heart softened.

You wouldn't be sleeping if it wasn't. xxx

Can't wait for the week to be over so we can get together.

She was working through to and on Saturday, and then, *Watch out, Jamie.*

Me too.

'We're on,' Becca called at the same time as the phone on Kayla's belt vibrated.

Reading the message, she grimaced. 'Eighty-five-year-old woman found on floor by bed, unconscious.' She shoved her own phone in her pocket. 'Let's go.' Being busy made the hours go past faster and brought Saturday and Jamie closer.

Jamie. She couldn't wait to hold him, have those arms around her. For the first time since returning to Queenstown the odd hours she worked were a pain. They didn't fit in with Jamie's shifts this week, and that was how it would always be. It was similar to being married to Dylan and her shifts not matching the long hours he'd put in. She was used to it, but that didn't mean she had to like it.

CHAPTER NINE

TWO WEEKS LATER it wasn't their shifts clashing that upset Kayla. It was because they'd finally got two days off at the same time, and Jamie was too busy to see her.

'I've got school enrolment to attend tomorrow, and then the boys have got a sports day to start the term off the day after. Sorry, there's not going to be much spare time at the moment.' Jamie sounded anything but sorry. More like this was how it would always be.

'I can come to watch them play sports,' she said.

'Maybe another time.'

She let it go. Arguing wouldn't win any points since he seemed determined about how this would play out. 'No problem.' But it was. There was a painful knocking in her chest. 'I'll see you later?'

'Why don't you join us for dinner tonight?'

Relief filled her, quietening the knocking. 'Love to. What shall I bring?'

'Yourself.'

'I like it. See you then.' Had she misread Jamie's reluctance about her going to the sports day with him? Could it be the boys' mother would be there and he didn't want any awkward questions? But if they were seeing each other, it wasn't to be a secret. She wouldn't stand for that. She couldn't imagine Jamie doing that either. Something else had to be worrying him. Not over her already? Her heart plummeted. Surely not.

Please, please, please.

Hang on, he'd said go round for dinner. She was over-thinking everything.

But when Jamie didn't kiss her when she got to his house, and made it clear she couldn't stay the night, it was hard not to wonder if she'd been right and he wasn't as keen as he'd appeared. 'Everything all right?' she asked when he returned to the kitchen after saying goodnight to Ryder and Callum.

'Why wouldn't it be?'

Leaning into him, she wound her arms around his waist, and rose up to kiss him. 'I've missed you.' So much she knew she loved him. He was a part of her now, always in her mind when she had decisions to make. It was Jamie who made waking up in the morning exciting and exhilarating.

His mouth covered hers and she fell into his kiss. Finally. It was as deep and full of passion as any kiss he'd given her. When they finally pulled apart, she was happy. 'That's better.'

'I've been wanting to do that since the moment you walked through the door,' Jamie admitted as he ran a finger over her cheek and started kissing her again. Suddenly he pulled back. 'Have to stop while I can.'

Her heart sank. 'You don't normally worry about stopping.'

Rubbing his chin, Jamie stepped back and sat on a stool, and reached for her hand. 'My boys aren't usually around when we get together.'

'So you don't want them barging in on us kissing, or more. I get that. But to be invisible isn't ideal. I am a part of your life now.'

Aren't I?

'I have to take this slowly, Kayla. If they get upset I'll call it quits and let you go.'

She stared at him for a long moment then pulled her hand free and sat down opposite him. Talk about blunt. Not what she'd hoped to hear. How well *did* she know him? 'Let's get this straight. I'm only a part of your life when the boys aren't around? When I get on well with them?'

His mouth flattened and his eyes dulled. 'You have to understand they come first.'

How could she not? It was plain as day. *And* he'd mentioned it often enough. 'I do, and wouldn't like you half as much if they didn't. I'm not going to hurt them, if that's what's worrying you.'

His sigh was sad. 'What if it doesn't work out between us? They've had more than enough to cope with in their short lives.'

'You're entitled to a life too.' She was all but begging. She wasn't walking away. She cared too much for him and wanted to share his life. Even some of it, if that's what it came to.

'Only when it doesn't affect my sons badly.'

'It doesn't have to. I get on with them and they don't seem to mind me being around. Not that we've done a lot together, but it's a start. You can have both them and me.'

'I want to, believe me.'

It hurt that he wasn't rushing to keep her with him and that wasn't only about being in his bed but everything they did.

Fight for him. Slowly, carefully, but don't give up already.

'Then we'll make it work. I don't expect to stay over when you have Callum and Ryder. Let them get used to me dropping in and out.' Was she getting ahead of herself? But the boys were always eager to see her and while Jamie hadn't said anything about her coming by often, his texts throughout the days when he wasn't being a dad at home told her he wanted more of her company. 'I don't want to lose what we've got, Jamie. You're special.'

He smiled.

At last. She relaxed. They would work this out.

'No one's said that to me for a long time.'

'Don't push it. I'm not going to repeat it just yet.'

'Damn.' He reached for her hand again, and tugged her off the stool to stand between his legs. 'You're pretty awesome yourself, Kayla Johnston.' Then he kissed her, slowly, mind-blowing with his sensitive touch.

It was hard not to leap onto his body and have her wicked way with him but they weren't alone.

Except four weeks later she was again struggling to understand where she stood with Jamie. For the two weeks Callum and Ryder were with Jamie, she hardly saw him. With her shifts not always lining up with Jamie's and what was going on in the boys' world, it was like doing a jigsaw wearing a blindfold. Jamie didn't seem to be making things easier. He always had something on when he wasn't working. Yet come the next two weeks when he was on his own, they were almost inseparable.

Now there was another fortnight to get through alone. At least Maisie was back in town, though it was hardly the same thing. After the amazing days and nights when she and Jamie had shared meals, bed, getting out on the lake in his runabout, to be suddenly alone at night and not have that sexy body to curl up against was doing her head—and heart—in. How could they go from full-on hot and sexy and sharing everything to quiet and withdrawn and no sex whatsoever and remain sane? She couldn't.

Worse, it hurt. Kayla was beginning to believe she was being used. Time to have it out. If he was going to break her heart then better to get it over with and she could go back to the busy, focused life she'd started on when she'd returned to Queenstown. Not that she'd got far with that idea what with the avalanche and Jamie interrupting her plans.

She drove to his house on a mission. Purposeful, ignoring the pendulum in her head asking, *What if he says go? What if he says sorry, please stay?* Only one way to find out and she was heading there to do exactly that. Not that she'd mentioned the L word. It was too soon to openly admit it, and she suspected it was not even on the horizon for Jamie. But what if he had no intention of ever settling into a permanent relationship that included the boys accepting her as part of the scene? That what they had was all about the sex and not much else? No. She refused to believe that. They connected so well.

'Where's Kayla? She likes sausages.' Ryder stabbed his plate with his fork.

'Yeah, when's Kayla going ride our skateboards again?' Callum added his two cents' worth.

Kayla, Kayla. Were the boys beginning to think she was letting them down? It was entirely his fault she wasn't here. Slowing things down until everyone was completely comfortable with her being in his life hadn't improved a thing and it had only made him more desperate to spend time with her.

Seems the boys are too.

So what was his problem? Afraid to take the next step?

Scared to get too involved and have his love thrown back in his face?

'Dad, where is she?'

'Working.'

'No, she's not. She's got tonight off. You're wrong.' Mr Know-It-All looked at him belligerently. 'I wrote it on the blackboard.'

'That's enough, Ryder. I've made a mistake, all right?' A big one involving a woman who had him in a state of amazement that he could even think of love again. A woman who had his kids writing down when next she'd be free to visit because they liked her so much. This was what he'd been hoping to avoid because he was afraid she might let them down.

More likely afraid to commit in case he was hurt again.

Starting over, trying to rebuild his confidence as well as the boys', trying to make them understand it wasn't anything to do with them or how they made their beds or brushed their teeth seemed too hard.

But what if it worked out for them all? Happy ever after? Did a relationship with Kayla have to go wrong? No avoiding how easily he'd fallen into loving being with her. They hit it off so well it was perfect. They liked similar food and being outdoors, shared a similar sense of humour. They had the same values about helping others and not hurting people. What could go amiss? Every damned thing. He'd loved Leanne, Leanne had loved him; they'd had a wonderful marriage. Where was all that now? He still didn't fully understand how Leanne had stopped loving him when little had changed in their lives, but she had. What if it happened again?

You'll never know if you don't take a chance.

'Kayla's here,' Dylan shouted, and jumped down from the table to race to open the front door. 'She's not working.'

'What? Are you sure?' Had she been reading his mind from afar, by any chance? Knew he was in a turmoil over her?

'Kayla, we're having sausages. Want one?'

'Best invitation I've had all day.'

Jamie sighed as her soft voice reached him, turning him to mush. How could he even be questioning himself about Kayla? He adored her. She did things to him he hadn't known for so long it was as though a drought had been overtaken by a flood of tenderness, excitement and hope. He wanted to believe in her, trust her with his heart, with his kids.

'It's your lucky day. I cooked too many.' He stood and hugged her. To hell with the boys. He kissed her on the lips, not fiercely, as he'd like, but just as longingly as he would if they were on their own.

She didn't reciprocate, remained impassive.

Warning bells started ringing. Something was wrong. Was she about to tell him they were over? Please, not that. He stepped back, pulled out a chair. 'Take a seat. Callum, get a plate and knife and fork for Kayla.'

She sucked a breath.

'You've already eaten?'

Easy, don't get uptight because you're fearful of what she might say. Wait and hear her out.

'No. I only dropped by to ask you something, and didn't think of the time. Sorry I've interrupted your dinner. I should've phoned.'

Since when did she have to do that? On the weeks he had the kids, that's when. 'Don't worry. It's great to see you. Really,' he added. It was. Whatever was putting that worried expression on her face, he was happy to see her, to have held and kissed her, however briefly. 'Like I said, there's plenty of food to spare. I got a bit carried away.' His mind had been on other things, mostly Kayla. She got to him in everything he did now.

'We got a new bottle of tomato sauce, Kayla,' Callum piped up. 'You can have plenty this time.'

She sat down. 'Sounds good to me. What's everyone been doing? How's school going this week?'

Jamie listened to the excited chatter from his boys, acknowledging how readily they'd accepted Kayla. They had right from the beginning, which cranked up his concern about being wary of her in their lives. She smiled as she listened to the boys talking over each other. A smile he looked for whenever he was with her, and hadn't received so far tonight. 'Here, get that into you.' He put the plate down and returned to his chair.

'Looks good.'

It was a basic meal, but the boys loved it, which saved a lot of arguments at the end of a busy day. Maybe not the greatest way to make sure they ate well, but anything that saved a lot of hassle was worth it. 'Careful or I'll cancel the food magazines I signed up for last week.'

'Trying to impress me, by any chance?'

'Absolutely.' Was it working? He wanted to rush the boys through dinner and into the shower so they'd go to bed and he could talk with Kayla, find out why she'd acted uncertain when she'd arrived. Instead he held onto his patience and enjoyed the moment. Like an ordinary family after a normal day at work or school. Normal. Family. Yeah, it felt good, despite Kayla's reticence. And his own.

'Can we have ice cream, Dad?' Callum asked, knowing full well it wasn't Friday night. 'Ple-ease.'

There wasn't a scrap of food left on either of the boys'

plates. He glanced at Kayla, saw amusement blinking back at him and caved. 'All right. Just this once,' he added, knowing they'd ask again tomorrow.

'You want some, Kayla? It's got jellybeans in it.'

'No thanks, guys.'

'What about me?' Jamie called after Callum as he headed out to the laundry and the freezer.

'You don't like it.'

'True.' He stood up to clear the table, reached for Kayla's plate. 'What've you been up to today?'

'Apart from dealing with a heart attack, a broken ankle and taking an elderly gentleman from the hospital back to the retirement home, not a lot.'

'A quiet day, in other words.' The heart attack victim would've made it or she'd be rattled. Unless that had been behind her quiet mood when she'd first arrived. 'You all right?'

'Fine.' Then Kayla looked directly at him. 'Can we talk when the boys are in bed?'

The alarm bells were back, tightening his gut, chilling his skin. Not fine at all, if that flattening of her sensual mouth meant anything, and he knew her well enough to accept it did. 'We'll have to wait a while. It's barely gone six.'

'No problem.'

Then why were her fingers digging into her thighs so hard? 'Kayla? What's up?'

'You've got more than me,' Ryder shouted.

'Boys, quieten down.' He crossed to the bench to sort out exact servings of ice cream, cursing under his breath. Holding out the plates, he told them, 'Take these to the other room and watch some TV quietly.'

'I didn't stop to think about what you'd be doing or

what time it was, sorry.' Kayla was rinsing dishes to place in the dishwasher.

His gut tightened some more. Kayla didn't do impulsive, unless there was a challenge involved. He shoved the ice cream into the freezer and banged the door shut.

A challenge?

'What's up?'

She inclined her head in the direction of the lounge. 'Later.'

Five minutes would be too long, let alone an hour that included showers, bedtime reading and lots of giggling. Plugging in the kettle, he made two cups of tea, all the time aware of Kayla watching him, winding him tighter than an elastic band stretched to its max. 'Come on. We'll sit on the deck.'

The sun was still strong, but the deck roof afforded some shade. Kayla sat on the top step leading down to the lawn that was long overdue a cut, and sipped her tea, staring at her feet. Looking vulnerable. Looking like all the fire had gone out of her. Like the Kayla he'd held after that traumatic accident where the woman's had heart stopped twice.

Suddenly Jamie's tension increased. Had he made her uncomfortable with his abruptness? He was only protecting himself, but he should've waited till she'd talked to him. If she was upset then he had to be patient and help her out. He wasn't used to standing back. If that didn't warn him how much he cared for her, then what would? He sat down beside her. 'Come on, spill.'

Her back straightened, her shoulders tightened as her head came up. 'You've told me Ryder and Callum must come first in anything you choose to do.'

He opened his mouth to reply.

Kayla shook her head. 'Let me finish.' She drew a

long breath, and as her lungs let go she continued, 'I understand, I really do. What I don't know is where I stand with you. I'm doing two weeks on, two off, my life revolving around the times you don't have the boys.' Her beautiful eyes were dark and serious. 'Am I being used?'

'No.' His heart banged hard. 'No,' he said, more quietly. 'Not at all.' He reached for her hand, trying to ignore the pounding under his ribs. She couldn't believe that. She mustn't.

She pulled away. 'You're sure? Because from where I'm sitting it looks like it. I can visit for a meal sometimes but don't get invited to sports days or to have a burger in town. Tonight's the first time you've even kissed me in front of the boys.'

What to say? She was right. He'd been deliberately keeping both sides of his life pretty much apart. Did he want to continue like that? Or was he ready to step up and meld it all together? 'I haven't been using you, Kayla. I admit to being cautious about getting too involved. Not only because of my kids but I'm afraid of being hurt again.'

'You think I'm not?' Those beautiful eyes locked onto his. 'I'm willing, ready, to take a chance with you, Jamie. I care for you, a lot.'

His heart expanded as love stole under his ribs.

'But if you don't feel the same about me then say so and I can get on with my life,' she added.

The warmth evaporated. She'd laid her feelings out for him to see, to decide what he wanted to do. He wanted her, all the time, in every way. Time to man up. Be honest. Lay his heart on the line. He opened his mouth, closed it again. This wasn't easy. It should be. Kayla wasn't going to make it any harder for him than he already did for himself. He adored her. He adored his boys.

Everyone had to be certain and feel safe. He had to try. But he had a feeling that trying wouldn't be enough. He had to commit or say goodbye.

'I see.' Kayla began to stand up.

Jumping to his feet, he took her hands in his. 'No, you don't. I want you in my life.' Hell, he hadn't said that to anyone since Leanne and it hurt because reality had shown him how wrong it could all go. This was like having a tooth pulled. He wanted Kayla to know how much he adored her, but saying it out loud? Hard to do. He squeezed her hands. Pulled her closer.

She tensed, leaned back. 'How much, Jamie? Fortnightly or all the time?'

There was no getting away with half-measures when Kayla was involved. Which was how it would've been with him too if not for his failed marriage. Did he want Kayla to walk away, never to come back? No. So was he ready to do this? He smiled, feeling good. She did that to him when she wasn't winding him up. 'How about all the time? See each other regularly every week and weekend and whenever?'

Her body sagged like all the air had evaporated out of her. 'Seriously?' A smile was finally starting, growing bigger by the second. 'Truly?'

'Yes, absolutely. We'll give it a go, see how everything works out.'

A flicker of doubt crossed her face. 'See how it works out? A trial run?'

'Sorry, that was blunt, but it's what I mean, yes.' Dropping her hands, he leaned back against the upright holding the roof above them. He had some say in what went on, and this was one time he wasn't backing down. He had to be certain their relationship would work well for the four of them before he committed one hundred percent. She must understand that. 'Makes sense to me. I'm not going through what I went through with Leanne ever again.'

'I am not Leanne. I'm Kayla.'

He held his breath. There was more to come. He saw it in her eyes, in the tightening of her body.

'I cannot "give it a go".' Her fingers flicked in the air between them to emphasis her words. 'For me it has to be all or nothing. Love's the whole deal, no part shares.'

'What if it turns out you can't handle being a stepmum or I don't like the way you care for Ryder and Callum?' His heart was breaking already.

'Then we'll work it out, talk about it. But it isn't all about them, Jamie. We're about us too. Our lives matter, our feelings for each other count more than anything otherwise we haven't got a chance. But a trial run? No thanks.'

The self-protective instincts began rising. 'You're not worried that your feelings of loss over Dylan won't taint our relationship? You won't be fearing you might hurt one of us if we get it wrong?' His fighting cap was firmly in place now. He wasn't giving up the idea of having Kayla in his life on a more permanent basis. But neither was he committing to for ever just yet.

'Of course the thought of anyone getting hurt worries me, but that's the nature of relationships. We all take risks. When I fell in love last time I never considered anything going wrong. Then life dealt a hideous blow, and I've carried the pain for a long time. Since I met you it's been ebbing away, leaving me happy and ready to start again. There are no guarantees, but I refuse to try out a relationship like taking home a dress to see if it is right for the occasion I have in mind.' Kayla leaned against the opposite post and regarded him. 'Jamie, I have fallen for you.'

Clang. That was his heart hitting his ribs. Kayla loved him? Was that what she was saying? Had he found what deep down he'd hoped would be his again one day? Bang, bang, went his heart. Yes, this could work out. It had to. He wanted this more than anything. Kayla was so special, he adored her with all his being. 'I care a lot for you too.' The L word was huge and stuck deep inside, not easily said, but he'd got close. 'I'm just asking for time. Time we can share as a couple and a family with the boys, taking it slowly.'

She nodded.

'Obviously there are a lot of things to talk through, such as which house to live in, though I'd prefer to stay in mine as the boys are settled.' Again he came back to his kids and what was right for them, ignoring what Kayla might like. Was he using the boys as an excuse because he was scared to commit? Was he really ready for a full-on relationship? Or did he want to continue living alone with no adult to discuss the day-to-day hassles with, to share a meal with, have fun with after all? The everyday things that couples shared and were more difficult when faced alone?

'Jamie?' Kayla was watching him with an intensity that warmed and worried him. 'You're not ready, are you?'

'Come on. I said we should give it a go and see if we are meant to be a couple. How more ready than that can I be?'

Her hair brushed her shoulders when she shook her head. 'I love you, Jamie, and for that I'd do anything to be with you. But I want the whole deal. Eventually marriage, maybe our own children—if possible.' Her voice wavered. Then she lifted her head higher. 'Definitely commitment. Not a "let's see how we go" approach, but a full-on, jumping-in, let's-do-it commitment. If you can't do that then it's best we call it quits now.'

The warmth chilled. Bumps rose on his skin, his heart was quiet and his mouth dry. He had no answer. He couldn't say, move in and marry me. It was far too soon. What if they argued all the time, or fell out over the kids, or she decided his job was too dangerous and asked him to quit, as Leanne had done? But she had mentioned more kids while knowing what his work involved. It was easy to feel they were good together when the pressures of everyday life weren't getting in the way. But he also knew how wrong even the best love could go, so he wasn't leaping in boots and all. 'I need more time.'

'I'm sorry, Jamie. I hoped we might've been on the same page, but guess I was wrong.' Stepping close, she stretched up and kissed him lightly on the mouth. 'Take care. I'll see you around.' Tears streaked her cheeks as she left, striding down the steps and along the path to the front of the house where her car was parked.

'Goodbye, Kayla,' he whispered around the lump blocking his throat. She loved him. No one had loved him for a long time. He wanted her back. Now. To share whatever life decided to throw at *them*. But his feet were stuck to the deck, unable to move. If he chased after her, he couldn't guarantee he'd give her what she wanted. And he wanted to be able to do that more than anything. If he weren't so scared.

CHAPTER TEN

'MAISIE, WHERE ARE YOU?' Kayla stared through the wind-screen at the crowds wandering through town. Couples walked hand in hand as they chatted and laughed, twisting her heart. Why hadn't she gone straight home from Jamie's? Because it was too damned lonely in her house, that's why.

'I'm heading home. Hang on. I'm pulling over,' Maisie said. 'Okay, what's up? You sound terrible.'

Nothing to what she felt. 'I just broke up with Jamie.' Was it a break-up when they hadn't really admitted to a relationship in the first place?

'Where are you?'

'In town.' She named the street she was parked on.

'Don't move. I'm coming in and we'll go for a drink. You can tell me everything.'

That's what good friends were all about. Kayla sighed and blew her nose. Damned tears wouldn't stop. She loved Jamie. And he didn't want her.

'That's not true,' Maisie said when Kayla told her every-thing as they sat in the bar with glasses of wine between them. 'You said he wanted to give it a go, that he cared about you. Sounds to me like he wants you.'

'You're saying I should go along with a trial run?'

Kayla stared at her friend. They were always honest with each other, sometimes too much, but tonight she'd have been happy with a hug and some agreement over taking a stand. 'That's not me, and you know it.'

'Hey, I'm merely pointing out Jamie obviously cares for you.'

'But not enough. I want to be a part of his life all the time but he doesn't seem to understand I'm serious and not intending to cause any problems, but apparently he's not a hundred percent certain we can make a go of a relationship.' Sipping her wine, Kayla remembered something else. 'I mentioned I'd like marriage and maybe kids one day. He never picked up on those.' She'd love kids of her own, and to have Jamie's would be amazing—if she could get pregnant and not miscarry.

Despite the grief Ryder and Callum had been through, it had never seriously crossed her mind that he mightn't want any more. Maybe it shouldn't surprise her, yet it did. He was a wonderful dad, and had a huge heart. Big enough for more children *and* her? She'd believed so enough to be prepared to take a chance on the hurt if she failed to become pregnant and see it through to holding their baby in her arms.

'It's not necessarily over. You've probably blindsided Jamie as much as he has you. Give him time to think everything through. He might come crawling up your drive to offer all you want and more.' Maisie looked sad, not hopeful, which didn't help. 'In the meantime, we'll get busy with shopping trips, and try to prise Mallory away from Josue's hip for a girls' weekend somewhere.'

'Something to distract me is definitely needed right now.' Or she'd go back to being a workaholic, filling in every hour to avoid thinking too much about what might've been. Maisie could say what she liked, but Jamie wouldn't come begging or try to put his case forward more forcefully. He was a man who made up his mind and stuck to it. So why couldn't he do that with them? Accept her love and let her into his heart? 'I need another wine.' She stood up. 'You?'

Maisie shook her head. 'Driving. We'll leave your car in town.'

Sinking back onto her stool, Kayla muttered, 'I'm being selfish. I'll drive home for the next wine. You want to join me? There's always a spare bed.' Two, in fact, since she had a three-bedroomed house all to herself. She'd invited Maisie to board with her when she returned to Queenstown, but Maisie was firmly ensconced in her brother's house. Damn it.

Feeling sorry for yourself?

Definitely. But she'd had her heart broken before, and this time didn't intend to fall into the doldrums quite so deeply.

'You really love him, don't you?' Maisie asked.

'It sneaked up on me. We've always had a connection, but it took a while to realise what I feel is love.' Silly, silly girl. She'd known there was every possibility of getting hurt and she'd taken the risk. 'When am I going to learn?' Long, lonely days loomed ahead. She could almost wish there was a search and rescue happening every day. Almost. But not even her hurting heart could really wish that on someone. At least Maisie was back in town, and Mallory did occasionally spend a day with them.

'Do we ever?' Maisie drained her glass. 'Come on.'

'Might as well.'

'Now you're being glum.'

Kayla followed, agreeing but unable to lift her spirits. 'Maybe I was too tough on Jamie. My way or no way.'

One well shaped black eyebrow rose as her friend nodded. 'There is that.'

'I was like that with Dylan sometimes.' He'd always taken it on the chin, sometimes giving in, sometimes not. A point in his favour. She'd never want a man to kowtow to her every wish. Today being an exception. Jamie in her life would be perfect. Couldn't he see how much she loved him and would do whatever it took to make it work for them? Except come second to all else. Was she wrong to be so adamant about what she wanted? Should she have given Jamie a chance? 'What have I done?'

'Stood up for yourself. Give yourself a break. I bet Jamie's going over everything too. Who knows what he might decide?'

I sure don't.

Kayla checked her phone. No messages. Not even a call-out from Search and Rescue to take her mind off everything.

The following four days off duty were long and slow. Her house had never been as clean and tidy as it was when she finally went back to work, and that was saying something. The windows gleamed, the oven looked as good as the day it had been installed. The lawns had been cut to within an inch of their lives, and not a weed showed in the gardens.

She rang Jamie once, only to be told he was on his way to a fire at Arrowtown and he'd call her later. He never did.

That told her where she stood. She didn't want to believe it. Pain flared harder than ever. She loved Jamie. They got on so well that none of this made sense. He'd said he wanted to spend more time with her, so why suddenly not talk to her? Was he struggling to deal with her determination to be together? She thought her call showed that the door was still open. But had he decided they were finished? Better to stop before they got in too deep and couldn't extricate themselves without hurting each other and the boys? Too late for her. She was aching head to toe with the love he'd pushed away.

On the second Saturday after their bust-up Kayla made up her mind to be proactive. Ryder was playing rugby at his school, so she'd go to the game. She missed the little guys almost as much as their dad. What if she had agreed to give it a try? They'd be sharing nights, having laughs and learning more about each other. But it would always be hanging in the back of her mind, what if Jamie decides to back off? Love was about commitment. Commitment got couples through the bad days, the hard decisions, the difficult moments. If they knew they could walk away from their relationship at any time, the chances of success were weakened.

When she'd fallen in love with Dylan there'd been no doubt about getting together. Neither of them could wait to share their lives. That's how it should be. But there hadn't been anyone else at risk. This time there was. Jamie always put Ryder and Callum first. She couldn't expect any different if he loved her. He hadn't mentioned love, though. Caring. Yes. A man of few words, it might take a bomb for him to utter the L word. He'd acted as though he loved her. Or had she been reading too much into his actions, his tenderness, his caring? Quite possibly, because she wanted it so badly.

Love had been missing for a long time. Her doubts of ever finding it again had overridden everything to the point she'd felt lonely, so when she'd admitted she loved

Jamie she'd expected the same in return. No hesitation, no worries, just acceptance.

She groaned. What an idiot. She'd been unfair. But he hadn't fought for her, hadn't said, 'Let's talk some more.' No, and neither had she. For someone who always fought for what she believed in she'd been hopelessly inadequate over her relationship with Jamie. What a shambles.

Parents lined the rugby field where two teams of young boys were running around, chasing the ball, with little idea of what they were supposed to do, Ryder in the midst of it all, a cheeky grin showing how much fun he was having.

Kayla watched for a while, happy to see him again. He was a character, pushed life to the full, and hated losing. A small version of his dad.

'Hi, Kayla. Why are you here?'

She looked down into Callum's upturned face and felt a knock in her chest. 'I thought I'd come and see how you guys are getting on.'

'Thought you didn't want us anymore.' He scowled.

Gulp. Is that what Jamie has told them? Please, not that.

'Of course I do. I miss you.'

'Might be best if you didn't say things like that,' came the deep voice she'd missed so much.

She spun around and stared at Jamie, her heart pounding hard. 'You don't like me being honest?'

'I don't want their hopes raised, then dashed.' Jamie stood tall and proud, but there were shadows in his eyes, like he hadn't slept much.

The intervening days since she'd walked away from him had made everything more difficult to understand. This need to defend herself wasn't how caring relationships worked. But, then, she wasn't in one, was she? 'You

didn't return my call.' Where was the determination to
see this family and hopefully clear the air a little that
had brought her to the school field? Since when had she
become so gutless? 'I remembered Ryder saying he had
a game every Saturday morning, starting this week, so
I thought I'd pop along and say hello.'

'I see.' But he didn't. It was obvious in the tightness
of his face, the unrelenting straightness of his back, how
his hands were jammed into the pockets of his jeans.

'I'm not using him as an excuse to see you. I miss
you all, okay?'

'Dad, did you see that? Ryder got a try.' Callum was
jumping up and down in front of them.

Jamie's head flipped sideways as he scanned the field
for Ryder, whose teammates were leaping around and
yelling happily. 'I missed it,' he growled.

'Dad!' Ryder was charging across towards his father.
'I got a try. I got a try.'

'Cool. Go, you. That's great.' Jamie high-fived his
son. 'You rock, son.'

The whistle went, getting all the players' attention,
and Ryder bounced back to join his team.

'First try ever.' Jamie watched him with love spilling
out of his eyes.

'And you didn't see it.' Regret hovered between Kayla
and Jamie. Because of her, Jamie had been distracted.
'I'm sorry.' It wasn't enough, but what else could she
say? 'I really am.' She turned to walk away, go home
and clean out the freezer or some such exciting activity.

A strong hand gripped her shoulder. 'Don't go, Kayla.'

Callum stood at his side, his worry staring up at them.

Hesitating, she waited. When Jamie said nothing more
she turned to study the face she adored. She loved this
man. She'd do anything to be with him. Anything except

let him procrastinate over their relationship. 'I'll stay and watch the rest of the game because I told Callum that's why I'm here.'

'Good.'

She had no idea what was good. The fact she was staying for the game, or that she'd walk away at the end of it. He wasn't explaining 'Good' and she wasn't asking. Standing beside him, arms and hips not touching, she watched the kids running around, trying to get the ball off each other and often not knowing what to do when they did. A bit like her at the moment. 'How's your week been?'

Bloody lonely. Sleepless. Full of despair. 'Busy with the boys and work.' Normal, except it couldn't have been further from how Jamie's life had become since letting Kayla in. The feeling of having found something so special he was afraid to break it reared up in his face to prove that's exactly what he'd done. He'd torn apart what they'd had going between them. All because of the fear of facing being hurt again. What was he? A man or a puppy? An idiot or a careful parent? Using his sons to protect himself rather than the other way around?

Kayla said nothing. Though she appeared focused on the game, he didn't believe Ryder was getting all her attention. Tension held her hands hard against her thighs.

'We've got an S and R training day next weekend on Mount Aspiring. You coming?' They were bringing in a guy from Mount Cook to take the teams out for a day on the lower slopes.

Her head dipped abruptly. 'I'm planning on it.'

'The ten-day forecast isn't looking great. Heavy rain's expected.' Jamie sighed. Who gave a toss? What he really wanted to talk about was them, and ask how she was getting on, and if she missed him. 'What are you doing after the game?' Hold on. Why ask? Because he couldn't help himself. He'd missed Kayla so much nothing felt right any more.

'Might visit Mallory since Josue's working.' Her voice lacked enthusiasm, which was unusual when it came to her friends.

He ached to pull her into his arms, hold her close and tight, kiss the top of her head and beg her to give him another chance. Ready to go all out, then?

'Run faster, Ryder.' Callum was jumping up and down.

Jamie looked over the field and saw Ryder racing towards the goal line with all the other boys chasing him, including those in his team. 'Go, Ryder, go.'

Ryder looked around as though he'd heard him, and tripped, sprawled across the grass, letting the ball fly out of his grasp.

Wanting to rush across and make sure he hadn't hurt himself, Jamie held back, holding his breath. The kid wouldn't thank him for turning up like a crazed parent.

Kayla's shoulder nudged his arm gently. 'He's fine. Look how he's getting up and giving his friends cheek at the same time. He's tough.'

Warmth seeped in, pushing away the chill that had been settling over his heart. Kayla understood him so well. How could he not live his life with her? Not dive in and take all the knocks on his chin? Because for every wonderful moment there'd be plenty more knocks. His arm slipped around her shoulders, tucking her closer. 'I know.'

Kayla smiled. The moment Jamie put his arm around her all the sadness and loneliness fell away. She'd come home. They belonged together. No doubt. But where did that leave her? In limbo? Because nothing had changed. There was a conversation that needed to be had or she'd have to walk away again.

'Are you and the boys doing anything this afternoon?' Her heart was banging, her hands clenching, opening, clenching.

'We're heading over to Leanne's. Her mother's visiting and I always got on well with her. Still do. And I want to catch up.'

So why did he ask what I was up to?

'That's got to be good for everyone.' Kayla straightened away from Jamie and stared out over the field, not seeing anything except her hopes disappearing.

'The boys are staying on. It's Leanne's turn to have them.'

Meaning?

'We could have coffee when I get back.'

Shoving her hands in her pockets, she turned to look directly at him. 'We could. But why do I get the feeling you're not sure you want to?'

'I've missed you. I know I've made a mistake, but…'

'But?'

'Dad, the game's finished. We've got to go.' Ryder was running towards them. 'I want to see Grandma.'

Jamie flinched.

When he opened his mouth, Kayla nearly put her hands over her ears. Excuses weren't going to make her happy. He'd made his choice and it didn't include her. He couldn't integrate his family with her. Shaking her head, she turned and walked away. Again. Only this time she would not be turning up to watch a rugby game or phoning Jamie. It *was* over. She'd been slow to grasp how far over, but now she got it in spades. That hug had undone her wariness so she'd just have to dig deeper to put it back in place.

A distraction was required. A seven-point-two earthquake might go some way towards one. Or a blizzard closing all the roads and stranding people in the hills that she could go out to rescue.

When her phone rang three hours later guilt sneaked in. Had she brought this on? 'Zac, what's up?'

'Where are you? I think I just passed you on the road in Sunshine Bay.'

The speeding police car. 'You did.' She braked, pulled over.

'Caff's Road. Three-year-old girl backed over by vehicle in driveway. Can you come?'

She was already pulling out. 'On my way.'

The first person Kayla saw was Jamie. Then the little broken body on the gravel drive.

'Excuse me.' She pushed past people, dropped to her knees, ignoring the sharp stones digging in and reaching to feel the toddler's pulse in her pale neck. Beat, pause, beat, beat. Weak but real. It was only the start. There was a long way to go if she was to save this child. Blood from a wound above her eyes had stuck black curls to the girl's forehead. Her body lay sprawled at an impossible angle. 'Ambulance?'

'It's been called, but there's a hold-up due to an accident in town,' Zac informed her. 'That's why I called you.'

'She's breathing,' Jamie said. 'Barely, but she is.'

Kayla nodded. 'There's a thready pulse. You keep watching her chest movement.'

'No one's moved her,' Zac told her. 'Her name's Sian.'

'Sian, I'm Kayla, I'm going to help you, okay?' Of

course she wouldn't be heard but it was how Kayla did things and she wasn't changing that just because this kid was so badly injured she was unconscious and unlikely to be otherwise for a long while.

A woman was screaming at someone in the driveway. The mother? The driver of the vehicle that had hit the child? Kayla shuddered, shut the noise out.

'Zac, can you put the hospital on standby and tell them this is a stat one emergency?' Then Kayla focused on what she could do, not what wasn't available. Blood was pooling below the child's groin area and underneath, spreading across the concrete. 'A torn artery. She'll bleed out if we don't stop this. I need a towel or clothing. Now.'

Jamie had his shirt off before she'd finished and was folding it into a wad. 'Here.'

Pressing the wad in place, Kayla looked at Jamie. 'Hold it down hard. Don't worry about hurting her. We've got to slow that bleeding.'

'Onto it.' He took over while she checked the little girl's chest.

How was Sian breathing at all with the trauma done to her ribcage? 'Is there a tow bar on the vehicle?'

Zac again. 'Yes. I think it knocked her down then the ute went over her. The driver panicked and drove forward when he heard shouts.'

'She's lucky she wasn't pulled along,' Kayla muttered. She couldn't believe the child was alive. 'Where's that ambulance?' Would the rescue chopper be faster? She didn't know how long the lungs were going to hold out after the impact from that tow bar. She continued assessing the injuries. 'Two broken femurs, left arm appears fractured in more than one place, and as for internal injuries, who knows?'

'Breathing's slowing,' Jamie warned.

To hell with protocols. This kid's life was in danger. Kayla leaned in and carefully exhaled air into the girl's lungs through her mouth. Worried about moving the girl's head in case of spinal damage, she had to wait for the lungs to deflate, then breathed for the child again. And again. Time stood still.

'I hear sirens,' someone called.

She didn't stop, kept breathing, pausing, breathing for the child. When a paramedic appeared beside her, she said, 'Carl, we need oxygen, neck collar, spinal board and splints.' For starters. 'And tape to strap that wad in place before Jamie can release pressure on the bleed.'

Carl nodded. 'Jessie, you hear that?'

Jessie handed Carl the medical pack and went to get everything else.

With speed and absolute care, the little girl was slowly attached to monitors, her head held in place with the neck brace, and Kayla inserted an oxygen tube so that Jamie could immediately begin pumping the attached bag to keep her breathing. Carl taped down the wad holding back the bleeding. Finally they slid the spinal board underneath and placed her on the stretcher.

'I'll come with you,' Kayla told Carl.

'Good.' He didn't waste time talking, climbing into the ambulance to take the stretcher as Jamie and Kayla pushed it forward.

Kayla felt a warm hand touch her arm and then Jamie was gone. The door closed and the ambulance was rolling down the road towards town. That touch melted her, told her she wasn't alone after all. The man she loved had been there throughout the trauma of dealing with this seriously injured child and had still had a moment for her.

'Sian, hang in there,' Kayla muttered as she read the monitor and cursed the low heart rate. Please, please,

please. 'I do not want to do compressions on those smashed ribs.'

Josue and Sadie were waiting when Jessie backed them into the hospital bay.

And so was Jamie when Kayla walked out into the fresh air after filling the doctors in on all the details. Leaning against the wall in the same spot he had been the night they'd brought the German woman in after her car accident.

Like that night he called, 'You all right?'

She crossed over to him, but not straight into his arms. She wanted to, more than a hot shower, clean clothes and a painkiller for the headache pounding behind her eyes. But if she did, they were back to square one. Weren't they? 'Sort of. I'm shattered.'

'That's normal for you.'

'It never feels anything like normal at the time. I'm always terrified I'm going to lose my patient.'

'You were fantastic. I doubt Sian would've made it this far if you hadn't been there.' He brushed her hair off her face, then gripped her shoulders and looked into her eyes so deeply she couldn't feel the ground underneath her shoes. 'I'd trust you with my boys any day of the week. For everything.'

She stared, trying to read him and afraid to acknowledge what she was seeing because she wasn't exactly great at reading men. Not the men she cared so much for, anyway. 'It's what I do,' she said defiantly.

'I know. I've always known, but I've been afraid to accept it. I don't want them getting hurt, but you won't do that. Not intentionally, and I doubt in any other way.'

One tiny step and she'd have those arms she longed for wound around her, holding her near, supporting her shaking body. One tiny step and would she have the future she yearned for. Holding back wasn't easy but necessary. He was still only talking about his boys. Not himself. 'I won't deliberately hurt you either, Jamie. If I didn't believe that I wouldn't be here.' She was so close to falling in a heap at his feet that any release of the pressure from his hands and it would happen.

'I know that, too.' He brushed a kiss over her cheek. Not like last time. 'Come on, I'll drive you home. We can collect your car later.' Taking her elbow firmly, still supporting her faded stamina, he led her to his truck and opened the door.

'How did you come to be at the scene?' she asked.

'Leanne lives two houses down. We heard screams and I went out to see what was going on. She kept the boys inside, away from seeing anything.'

'Right.' Too tired to think what that might mean, she laid her head back and closed her eyes.

At her house he followed her inside and went down to the bathroom to turn on the shower. 'Get in and soak away the exhaustion and grime, Kayla.' His smile was soft yet serious. Filled with care and concern. 'I'll go put the jug on for a coffee.'

His clothes were as filthy as hers after holding down on Sian's injury.

'You need to clean up, too.' Kayla pulled her shirt off, undid her jeans zip.

He skimmed her cheek with a finger. 'You sure?'

'Are you?'

'Yes, sweetheart, I am. Nothing matters but us.'

Stepping out of her jeans, Kayla hopped into the shower and shoved her head under the water. She needed to be clean, to wash away the horror of the accident, and then she'd be ready for Jamie.

Joining her, he took the shampoo bottle and squeezed

some onto his palm, then began rubbing it through her hair, soaping her head, her face and down her neck. Tipping her head back for the water to rinse her hair, she closed her eyes and went with those hands. Down her arms, back to her shoulders and over her breasts, stopping to circle her nipples to bring them to throbbing peaks. Then his palms were soothing her stomach, her hips, thighs and then between her legs.

Suddenly nothing was slow and gentle but pulsing and hot. Her hands gripped his shoulders as she was lifted to place her legs around his waist, felt his need for her at her centre.

He was sliding into her, slowly, bringing with him a need so great it overwhelmed her. 'Take me, Jamie. Now.' Please.

He retreated, returned to be inside her. 'Oh, Kayla, love, I adore you.'

'Now, Jamie.' She'd start screaming if he didn't bring her to a peak *now*.

Hot, gripping sensations rocked her, took over all thought as he plunged into her and roared as his need spilled, bringing her to a climax along with his.

Afterwards they dried each other with thick towels and slipped into clean clothes.

'You should carry something dressier than a pair of orange overalls in your truck.' Kayla laughed as she sipped coffee on her deck overlooking town. It was easy to laugh, even when she had no idea what the future held. It just had to involve Jamie. Was she giving up on holding out for everything? He had just shown a little was better than nothing, but could she do a little for ever?

'Nothing wrong with these.' Jamie grinned. 'You can see me for miles.' Then his smile faded. 'I mean it, Kayla.

I love you more than anything. I've missed you too much these past couple of weeks.'

He'd said love. He loved her. 'I hear you.' But she wasn't sure what he was offering with his love. She waited, her hands rolling the mug back and forth, back and forth.

'I'd like a relationship with you. No what-ifs. No asking if I'm sure. Just leaping in and believing in each other.'

Her heart spluttered, started pounding. Really? Had he just said that? 'Yes,' she whispered.

Jamie hauled her into his arms and took her mouth with a kiss like no other. Her head was light. The sun shone brighter. But best of all Jamie was holding her like a piece of precious crystal, as though he never intended to let her go again.

Kayla kissed her man back with all the love swelling in her heart. She'd do anything for him. Anything. He was her second love, and she was going to hold onto him so tight they'd always be a part of each other's lives. Pulling her mouth away just enough to say, 'I love you,' she smiled. A smile filled with all the wonder and love that was her life.

EPILOGUE

HANDS IN POCKETS, Jamie watched Kayla as she sat in the autumn sun with a book in her hand. Her legs stretched the length of the outdoor sofa. Her hair was tucked back in a loose tie. There were shadows under her eyes and one finger kept scratching at the page she was staring at. There'd been no page turning for five minutes.

His heart squeezed with love. Kayla had turned his life around, putting him back on track for a happy future. He and the boys had moved into her house two months ago as it was more comfortable for the four of them than being cramped in his boxy one.

But now something was worrying the love of his life. There'd sometimes been a haunted look in her eyes over the past week that had twisted his gut. He thought he knew what the problem was but had been giving her space to tell him in her own time. Except a week was too long and they had to talk. Now. Kayla needed him, and he was here for her. His hand tightened around the contents of his pocket.

'Jamie.' She was watching him as she shifted so her feet were on the deck. 'I've something to tell you.'

Damn but they were so in sync at times it was scary. He sat down beside her and reached for her hand. 'I thought so.'

'I'm pregnant.' A hopeful smile appeared and for the first time in days her eyes were filled with sunshine. 'We're having a baby.'

A bubble of warmth swelled inside, filling him so much it hurt and he couldn't talk. He was going to be a father again. With Kayla. Her hand was soft in his as he lifted it and kissed her palm. 'I thought so,' he repeated.

'You guessed? Because I stopped having a wine with dinner?' Her smile widened, hitting him in the heart.

He loved this woman so much sometimes he had to pinch himself. Swallowing hard, he answered, 'Because you keep touching your stomach when you think I'm not looking, because you haven't slept properly for the past week, because I love you and know you.'

And because you've been tipping out your wine when I'm not looking.

He kissed her forehead. 'I love you.' They were in this together. A baby. *Yee-ha.* As long as the pregnancy went full term… He didn't want Kayla being hurt again.

'I should've told you straight away but…' Her hand clenched in his. 'I was scared, Jamie.'

'Of course you were. Do you know how far along we are?'

Her mouth lifted at one corner. 'Eleven weeks. I only ever made it to eight weeks before so this time's looking good.' She gasped. 'If I don't hex it by saying that.'

He hugged her tight. 'You won't.'

She sighed. 'I'm trying not to get too excited, just in case.' Touching his lips with her forefinger, she shook her head at him. 'I didn't notice I was late for the first month, and then it was as though I refused to believe what was happening the next month. This morning I toughened up and had an HCG. The doc says everything's looking good and there's no reason why I won't go full term.'

So that's why she hadn't been at home when he'd got

back from work. 'This is the best news. I'm loving it. Seriously. We are pregnant. I'm going to be a dad again.' And he'd thought things couldn't get any better since they'd moved in together.

'Isn't it wonderful? Oh, Jamie, I'm so excited. Now I've told you it's like I've put the past behind me totally. We *will* have this baby.' Tears streamed down her cheeks. 'It's amazing.'

Leaning in, Jamie kissed her, gently. 'Kayla Johnson, I love you to bits. Will you do me the honour of becoming Mrs Gordon?'

Her eyes widened and her smile grew. 'Yes, Jamie— oh, yes, please.' The tears were flowing faster. 'I love you.'

Taking the small red velvet covered box from his pocket, he opened the lid and held it out to Kayla. 'I had this made last week. I hope you like it.'

She stared at the ring made of gold with a dark sapphire set between two smaller diamonds sitting on white satin. 'It's perfect.' She raised her stunned gaze to him. 'How did you know?'

'Your mother showed me the photo of your grandmother's ring.' Apparently Kayla had been promised the ring as a child but it had been lost when her grandmother had gone into a rest home.

'Mum knew you were going to propose? And Dad?'

'I had to make sure they agreed.' He grinned. 'It's been hard not saying anything while I waited for the ring to be made.' He lifted it from the box and reached for Kayla's hand. 'I love you, Kayla. We are going to have a wonderful life together.'

He believed it, heart and soul. She made him happy, and strong, and ready for anything. He'd found love.

* * * * *

DEAD MAN DISTRICT

JULIE MILLER

For the Grand Island Book Club, who so graciously took me to dinner and talked about my book! I was honoured, and I had fun. Lindsey, Micki, Jessica, Jodi, Mary, Jana, Kristen – you are all fabulous, intelligent, accomplished young women and terrific moms, and I thank you.

Chapter One

Smoke.

Kansas City firefighter Matt Taylor held the handles of the resistance weights in front of him, feeling the pull along his massive arms and broad chest. He turned his nose toward the doorway of the spare bedroom, where he worked out when he wasn't on duty at the fire station, and sniffed the air.

Definitely smoke.

Slowly, deliberately, he eased the cables back through the pulley system and let the weight drop down to the stack. He grabbed the towel off the floor beside him and wiped the sweat from his face and neck, then swiped it over the top of his dark, military-short hair before rising from the machine's bench. He was a lieutenant at Firehouse 13 now, and his years of training and natural low-key demeanor kept him from panicking as he stalked through his apartment and checked the usual suspect spots. Kitchen clean and clear. Furnace running efficiently despite it being two degrees and snowing outside. Even though he emptied it out faithfully, he opened the closet where the washer and dryer were stacked and checked to make sure there was no lint in the dryer vent.

No fire here.

But his nose never lied.

And then his ears tuned in to the distinctly high-pitched, repetitive beep of a smoke detector, muted by walls and distance.

The fire wasn't here.

Pulling the towel from around the neck of his gray KCFD T-shirt, he tossed it over the back of a kitchen chair and reached beneath the sink to pull out the small fire extinguisher he stored there. Sweats and running shoes were hardly standard gear to battle a fire, but he knew it was the man, not the equipment, that was his best weapon to locate and put out a blaze. Ready to do battle, he jogged to the door of his apartment and flung it open.

A woman screamed.

Corie McGuire, the single mom who lived across the hall, pressed a hand to the neckline of her navy cardigan sweater, her small chest heaving in and out as she huddled back against the door to her apartment. "Good grief, Mr. Taylor. Don't startle me like that."

"Where's the fire?" He was sharply aware of the panic rounding her mossy-green eyes that were tilted up at him, the fact she was keeping as much distance between them as the door at her back allowed, and the charred iron skillet she clutched with an oven mitt down at her side. The sticky residue in the bottom of the skillet was still smoking. Matt quickly kicked the welcome mat from in front of his door across the wood-planked floor. "Put it down."

She hesitated a few seconds before nodding. He'd spoken in a tone that people usually obeyed, and she did, kneeling to set the hot pan on the mat. "It will leave a mark on your— Oh. Okay." He sprayed foam on the skillet, pulled the mitt from her startled hand, and lifted the pan to spray the bottom and sides as well, ensuring whatever substance had burned inside it couldn't catch fire again. "Thank you. I was going to take it downstairs and set it in the snow beside the dumpster out back. Pitch it out in the morning before school. This works, too."

With the charcoal goop in the pan extinguished to his satisfaction, Matt stood the same time she did. And swallowed hard. Somehow, he had drifted closer to his neighbor, or she had moved closer to him, and her ponytail had brushed against the *So Others May Live* firefighting emblem tattooed beneath the sleeve on his upper arm. Objectively, he'd always known Corie McGuire was a pretty woman, probably about his same age, late twenties, early thirties. But he'd never been this close to her before.

He'd never felt this gut punch of awareness about her, either.

Beneath the scent of her shampoo, he detected something salty and sweet, like pancakes and syrup with a side of crispy bacon. Maybe not the sexiest scent to most men, but he found himself craving it. It was certainly a more enticing scent than the smoky haze seeping into the hallway from beneath her closed door.

"You have smoke in your apartment," he pointed out, switching off the man to stay in firefighter mode. "I can help."

"That's all right. I've opened some windows to air things out. Sorry if it bothered you." When she knelt to retrieve the skillet, Matt stuck out a warning hand, which she instantly straightened away from. "Leave it."

"Leave it?" She shook her head. "Mr. Stinson will hardly appreciate finding a burned mess in the middle of the floor."

Matt didn't care what the building super thought—he had a more immediate problem that needed to be dealt with. But he knew he wasn't handling tonight's encounter well. From the time he'd reached his full height of six feet five inches and started bulking up after high school, his adoptive mother and grandmother had gently warned him that people who didn't know him might find him intimidating. And though the women in his family knew he was more gentle giant than scary ogre, others, like Corie McGuire here, might misread his blunt demeanor and quiet ways and be afraid of him.

Not that he blamed her for giving him a wide berth. He was a big, scary dude. When he wasn't lifting weights, he was running, partly because the physical demands of his job meant he needed to stay in shape, and partly because he had little else to do, especially in the wintertime. Other than a Sunday dinner with his grandmother and some assortment of parents, brothers, uncles and their families once or twice a month, or an occasional trip to the bar after shift with his Lucky 13 firehouse buddies, he didn't really have a social calendar.

The top of Corie McGuire's blond head barely reached his shoulder, and the woman was built on the slender side of things. They'd exchanged little more than a nod in the elevator after she and her son had moved in across the hall. Even then, she kept her boy hugged close to her and shifted to wherever the opposite side of the elevator was from him. He'd helped carry her groceries up one time, and even then, she'd stopped at her door and had taken the bags without letting him into their apartment. Since he wasn't the most outgoing of people, he hadn't immediately noticed that she was right there with him, keeping neighbors at a polite distance and never having friends over. Now that he thought about it, the woman and her son kept to themselves pretty much. He should give her the space she seemed to want from him.

But there was a haze of smoke drifting into the hallway and a beeping alarm telling him something wasn't right.

And one thing that Matt Taylor never shied away from was his job as a firefighter.

"This is what I do for a living. Would you mind if I came in and checked to make sure there are no secondary hot spots trying to ignite?"

If possible, Corie's eyes widened further. "There could be another fire?"

"You said you opened a window?"

To his surprise, she reached behind her to twist the doorknob, inviting him in. "My son is in here. Please."

The moment the door opened, the shrill beep of the smoke detector pierced Matt's eardrums. Closing the door behind them, he followed her into the kitchen. Corie braced her hands over her ears as they walked beneath the archway where the smoke detector was blaring its warning. The smoke was thicker here, with a dirty-gray plume billowing out of the open oven. Matt wasted no time closing the oven door and moving past her to close the kitchen window. Then he reached up to pry the cover off the smoke detector and pulled out the battery. The sudden silence didn't immediately stop the ringing in his ears.

But Corie lowered her hands. "Thank you." She'd already turned the oven off, but he squatted in front of the appliance, peering through the rectangle of glass, looking for any stray sparks or glowing elements. "Is something still burning?"

"You want to keep the oven door shut and all the windows closed until you're certain the fire is out. A lot of fires reignite the moment you add fresh air to the mix." He watched for a full minute before he set the fire extinguisher he'd carried in with him on the counter. "I think we're good." She had leaned in beside him to study the oven, too. But he didn't realize how close she was, and he bumped into her when he stood. His instinct was to reach for her to keep her from falling, but she grabbed the edge of the countertop to steady herself and scuttled away to the kitchen archway to keep him from touching her. Matt let his hand drop back down to his side. "Sorry."

She growled and huffed a breath that stirred the wheat-colored bangs on her forehead, and he wondered if that was her version of a curse. "No. I'm the one who's sorry. You've never been anything but polite, and now you're trying to help us, and that was rude. I've already screamed at you once tonight."

"Self-preservation isn't rude. I startled you. You do what you need to do to feel safe."

"I…" Her lips parted to argue, but they snapped shut again. Her posture relaxed and she hugged her arms around her middle. And smiled. A real smile. The tension around her eyes relaxed, and her soft pink mouth curved into a grin. "Thank you for understanding."

He could point out that with his superior strength and longer legs, he could have reached out and grabbed her without any effort at all if that had been his intent. But why would anyone want to make that beautiful smile disappear? Especially when that smile was directed at him. It made him want to smile, too.

Um, what are you doing, Taylor? Sniffing your neighbor? Smiling at her? Stop it or you'll really scare her.

Turning away, Matt checked the oven one more time, assuring himself the fire was out and whatever had burned had been starved of the oxygen it needed. Instead of moving toward Corie and the archway, he crossed back to the kitchen window and opened it. Then he turned on the hood fan above the stove and waited to see if she would move out of his path.

"Is it safe to open windows now?" she asked, maybe

just to break the awkward silence of him waiting for her to move.

Matt nodded. But when he heard the furnace kick on, he took a step toward her and the smile vanished. He quickly halted. She didn't need a firefighter anymore. She needed a respectful neighbor who would finish his business here as quickly as possible and go back to his own apartment. "Where's your thermostat?" She hugged one edge of her sweater over the other, shivering at the cold night air filling the kitchen. "You might want to grab an extra sweater," he advised. "It'll take twenty, thirty minutes to get the smoke out of here."

She nodded. "Mother Nature hasn't exactly graced us with warm weather and sunshine. I loved having all this snow for Christmas. But it wouldn't hurt my feelings any if it warmed up and melted away and spring came early."

"Spring won't happen in January. Not in Missouri."

"You're right, of course." She grabbed her wool coat off the back of a chair and shrugged into it as she led him through the apartment. "This way."

Although the layout of her apartment was a mirror image of his own across the hall, and he could have found the thermostat on his own, his training as a KCFD firefighter had taught him that a woman alone at the scene of a fire of any size probably wouldn't appreciate a man barging through her personal space—unless the whole place was fully engulfed and him storming in meant the difference between life and death. So he politely followed her out of the kitchen, through the living room and down the hall.

Corie wore her ponytail high on the back of her head, and it bounced against her collar like a shaft of golden wheat swaying in the wind. There was a sway to her hips, too. He'd noticed how her jeans had curved with a womanly flare, but even with her heavy coat, her natural slenderness blossomed in all the right places.

Matt didn't realize his gaze was still plastered to her backside until she stopped at the hallway wall between the two bedrooms and a little boy with a longish mop of brown hair stepped out of the second bedroom. "What do you want?" He stepped in front of Corie and held up a beastly-looking blob built out of hard plastic blocks—a dragon, he'd guess, based on the plastic swirls of flame attached to the creature's snout and the triangular bits that were either short wings or Godzilla-like spines on its back. From behind the colorful creation, which he held up like a shield, the boy peeked up at Matt with green eyes that matched his mother's. "The fire will get you if you come too close."

"Evan!" Corie slipped her arm around her son's shoulders. "You remember Mr. Taylor from across the hall. He's our neighbor. Now be polite."

Matt had a little nephew who had mastered that put-upon eye roll. He also recognized the stance of a young man—even this slight little boy—protecting someone he cared about. He respected that reaction as much as he worried about being the cause of it. Evan McGuire tucked his homemade dragon beneath his arm. "Sorry, sir. Hi."

Matt was equally brief. "Hi." He adjusted the thermostat to a much lower temperature, waiting for the furnace to shut off.

If Corie McGuire barely reached his shoulder, her son, Evan, barely reached his waist. They must be built on the slim side of things in the McGuire family. Matt scarcely remembered his birth parents, but they had been tall and broad shouldered like him and his younger brother, Mark, who was also a firefighter with the Lucky 13 crew.

The boy's diminutive size didn't stop Evan from stepping forward, tipping his head back and sizing up their visitor. "You're big up close."

"I'm big far away, too." He parroted the phrase his petite grandmother had often teased him with.

Corie snickered at the joke. She snorted a laugh through her nose, then quickly slapped her hand over her mouth. She looked more embarrassed than he was by her noisy amusement. Whether it was for his sake or hers, she quickly hustled her son toward the hall tree by the front door. "Evan, get your coat on. It's going to get cold in here."

Matt recalled one elevator ride together where Evan had announced it was his eighth birthday before his mother had shushed him and ended any conversation before it got started. Like any self-respecting young man, he groaned at being told what to do, even as he tromped through the living room and pulled on an insulated jacket that had sleeves that were too short for his arms and that clung to his small frame as he zipped it up.

But his demeanor changed when he looked into the hallway and saw the ruined skillet on Matt's door mat. "I'm sorry, Mom. I didn't mean to make a mess. I tried to put the fire out."

"It's not your fault." Corie ruffled his hair and kissed the top of his head, ushering him back inside. "I should have ended my phone call with Professor Nelms and fixed you a snack myself so you didn't have to turn on that old oven."

"But I made the frozen pizza just the way you showed me."

"Then maybe there's something wrong with the oven. I'm just glad you weren't hurt."

He nodded. Then tipped his chin up to Matt. "I'm sorry we bothered you, Mr. Taylor." Evan glanced over at his mom. "Isn't that right?"

Matt glimpsed the sadness and regret that tightened her features before she forced a smile onto her lips that wasn't quite as pretty as the natural smile she'd shared in the kitchen. What made a child apologize for a simple, albeit potentially dangerous, mistake, and a mother regret that he felt he needed to apologize?

Matt had never been a parent, but he'd been raised by the two finest people he'd ever known. He remembered how his adoptive father, Gideon Taylor, had coaxed him out of his silence and fear as a traumatized orphan. He'd given Matt jobs to do, small responsibilities that he could succeed at and grow his self-confidence. Gideon Taylor had worked side by side with each of his sons, showing them what it took to be a good man, how to be part of a family, how to live in the world with a sense of purpose and not be afraid of doing the wrong thing. Again.

Emulating the lesson of his own dad, Matt unhooked the multidialed utility watch from his wrist and held it out to Evan. "Can you tell time?"

Evan scoffed a little snort through his nose, reminding Matt of the adorable sound his mother had made a few minutes earlier. "Of course I can. We learned that in first grade. I'm a second grader now."

"Good man. Take this." Evan's eyes widened as he looked at all the numbers for time, temperature and barometric pressure readings. His mouth dropped open before he took it from Matt's outstretched hand. "When thirty minutes have passed, I want you to turn this thermostat back up to seventy degrees and remind your mom to close the kitchen window. Can you do that?"

Evan danced with excitement. "Is that okay, Mom?"

"You'll have to give Mr. Taylor his watch back," she reminded him.

"Not for thirty minutes," Evan protested.

"It's not a gift."

"Please?"

Matt wasn't sure he'd be able to withstand the enthu-siastic energy pouring off the boy. Corie smiled the good smile again. "All right. Homework done?"

"Yes, ma'am."

"Good. Then you can use that same half hour to play your game before bedtime."

Corie combed her fingers through his hair and cupped his cheek. When she started to kiss him again, he glanced up at Matt and pulled away, perhaps embarrassed by the PDA, perhaps trying to be more like the man he believed being trusted with Matt's watch made him. "Did I tell you I earned a ronin to fight with my dwarf? Now I can shoot arrows at the bad guys."

"That's great." She smiled again at her son's delight over the video game Matt was familiar with. "Do you even know what a ronin is?"

But Evan was already dashing down the hallway past Matt into his room. "'Bye, Mr. Taylor. See you in thirty... twenty-nine minutes."

The furnace clicked off with a noisy jerk. Matt hadn't had this much conversation outside of work for a long time, and the urge to stay a little longer and keep talking with this tiny family felt odd. Didn't stop him, though. "Sounds like something my younger cousins have played. I've played it with my brothers, too, a few times. If I re-member correctly, a shapeshifter and sorcerer are next to join the team."

"You play *Bomba's Quest*?"

Matt wondered if his cheeks were heating with a blush or if he was succumbing to some weird kind of hypother-mia. "My uncle Brett wanted to know if it was appropriate for his kids to play. My brothers and I volunteered to test it."

"I wondered if it was appropriate for an eight-year-old, too. He likes figuring out the puzzles and solving the riddles. But the characters are all cartoons, and no one dies when they go to battle. Not like real violence where people get hurt." She stopped abruptly, as though she was surprised to hear herself say those words out loud. "I'm sorry. I'm rambling. I'll be sure to get your watch back to you. That was a nice gesture."

Matt was as curious about the shadow that crossed her features as he'd been about the things he'd said that had made her smile.

Get back to being a firefighter and get out of here.

"You make pizza in a skillet?" he asked, picking up on something her son had said.

"The cast iron heats up and works like a pizza stone. The handles should have made it easier for Evan to manage." When she headed back to the kitchen, Matt followed. "Usually, his go-to snack is popcorn in the microwave, but for some reason, my microwave isn't working tonight." She pushed a couple of buttons beside the handle, but nothing lit up. "I don't know if it's the microwave or the socket it's plugged into."

If her apartment was wired like his, there should be a circuit breaker on the microwave outlet. Possibly, it had tripped and neither Corie nor her son knew to push the button back in to reconnect the circuit. But an oven fire *and* a faulty microwave in one evening? That seemed to be an unusual amount of bad luck for anyone, especially a woman who seemed as competent and careful as Corie. Matt pushed the circuit breaker button, but nothing re-engaged.

"I tried that already."

Good. So, she knew that safety measure. Either the microwave itself was broken or there was a problem with the wiring. Matt unplugged the appliance and moved it to the opposite counter where there was another plug.

"You don't have to do that. I'll call Mr. Stinson tomorrow to look at it. I'm sure you were busy doing something important."

The moment he plugged it in to the new socket, all the lights came on. "It's not the microwave. Looks like a wiring issue." He glanced over his shoulder to see Corie frowning at the now-empty socket. "Is something wrong?"

"I'm not sure."

On a hunch, he asked her for a flashlight and then knelt in front of the oven again. After testing to make sure it wasn't hot to the touch, he rubbed his fingers along the heating elements at the top and bottom of the oven. A sticky, charred residue like what he'd seen in the skillet came off in his hands. He'd fought enough fires to know there was something unnatural about this one.

He tried not to jerk when he felt Corie's hand on his shoulder, balancing herself as she knelt beside him. "What's that?"

"I'm not sure." He could easily understand food overflowing its pan and spilling onto the heating element at the bottom of the oven. But something needed to be spraying oil or grease—and a lot of it—for it to coat the top heating element like this. And nothing about pizza sprayed when it baked. "Did you squirt anything on the fire to put it out?"

"Evan threw some flour on it."

"Flour burns."

"I know that. He knows that, too, now." She pulled her hand away and stood, opening the cupboard above the stove. "I keep a can of baking soda mixed with salt in here to put out small fires."

An old-school solution that worked as well as a chemical extinguisher. "It snuffs out the oxygen."

She nodded. "I showed Evan where I keep it and taught him how to use it. I was in my bedroom, on the phone with my professor about a project for my college class. I didn't realize there was a fire until the smoke detector went off. I ran out here, saw the flames, grabbed the can..." She opened the lid and handed him the can. There was only a dusting of powder at the bottom. "It's empty. That's why he went for the flour instead. The only time we've used the baking soda mixture was when I was teaching him how to put out a fire. I lit a match in a pan and had him put it out so he could practice. This should still be full. I don't know how..." A dimple formed between her eyebrows as she frowned. "I don't remember emptying it. I don't know why I would."

Maybe she hadn't.

Curious. And a little disturbing to think that all the safeguards she'd had in place to protect her son from a fire had failed.

Matt needed some time to ponder on that. Evan seemed to be a precocious little boy. And God knew Matt understood a child's fascination in playing with fire. But would an eight-year-old know how to sabotage an electrical outlet to make his story about using the oven plausible? Or was there something else going on here? For now, Matt simply wanted to complete his due diligence as a firefighter, and as a good neighbor. If there was anything he could do to help Corie feel safer in her own apartment—even if that meant him leaving—he would do it.

"My microwave works," he offered. "I'm at home on Tuesday nights. If he wants a snack, and you're busy with schoolwork, he could come over."

"Usually, he can safely occupy himself when I'm studying. And he knows he can interrupt me if he needs something." She placed the empty can back in its cupboard. Then she pasted a tight smile on her face and headed to the front door. Did she suspect her son of setting the fire, too? "I'll show you out."

This time, he didn't follow. "You want me to move the microwave back, or leave it here?"

"Leave it. You've done enough."

He was beginning to think he hadn't done nearly enough. "Talk to the super. He needs to replace that stove and the microwave outlet before you use either one again."

"I will." She was waiting by the front door.

"Do you have a safe place to cook your meals in the meantime?"

"Afraid we're going to start another fire?"

He didn't joke about stuff like that. And judging by the frown dimple that had reappeared on her forehead, she wasn't trying to be funny, either.

What was going on here? Just a series of unfortunate coincidences that had taken their toll on a tired, hardworking single mom? Or did she share any of the same suspicion he did that something was deliberately off in this apartment tonight?

Finally, he forced his feet to move to the door. "I'll leave the fire extinguisher here until you get your baking soda solution restocked. I have another one in my truck." When he moved past her into the hallway, he picked up the torched pan and handed her the oven mitt. "I'll take this down to the dumpster for you."

Her fingers brushed against his as she tried to take the skillet from him. "You don't have to do that."

No way could she muscle the ruined pan away from him, but another unexpected touch like that, sending ribbons of unfamiliar heat skittering beneath the skin she'd made contact with, and she could probably ask him for anything she wanted. What kind of sorry, solitary soul was he to be so attuned to a woman he hadn't said ten words to before tonight? He pointed back toward the kitchen. "When I'm done, I'll come back to reset the smoke alarm. Evan's thirty minutes should be up by then."

"Okay." She hugged the door frame, her shoulders lifting with a sigh that made him think she was either too tired to argue with him, or just agreeing to whatever he said that would make him leave. "I'll lock the door behind you. Knock when you get back."

Matt carried the pan to the first floor and braved the cold air without a coat to set it on the dumpster behind their building. He spared a few minutes to pull his pocketknife from his sweats and scrape some of the residue from the bottom and handle of the pan. Although there were definitely bits of cheese and hamburger that had turned to ash, there was also more of that same sticky substance he'd found on the oven's heating element. He cut a swath of plastic from a trash bag inside the dumpster and wrapped the sample inside before stuffing both the knife and the sample into his pocket. This hadn't been a big enough fire, nor an official KCFD investigation, to warrant sending the substance to the state fire lab, but he could ask his firehouse captain and some of the other more experienced firefighters at the station house if they'd run across anything like it before. A bracing wind whipped through the alley, chilling him from his speculation.

On the way back inside, he paused in front of Wally Stinson's door and thought about asking the super if he'd worked on any of Corie's appliances or electrical outlets recently, or if she'd filed a complaint about any of them needing repairs. He'd like to ask if there had been any other small fires in the apartment, too—anything that might indicate a boy playing with matches or other flammable materials. But there was no sound coming from within the apartment, and there was no light shining from beneath the super's door, so the man had either gone to bed or was out for the evening. He'd make a point to stop by the next morning on his way to work.

Matt walked past the elevator and took the stairs, needing time to think. One strange thing in Corie's apartment he could dismiss as an accident. Two made him curious. But three missteps, all leading to a potentially dangerous fire and no way to fight it, told him something was wrong. Now whether Corie was really good at hiding irresponsible behavior, or something more sinister was happening behind the walls across the hallway, he couldn't say. In the meantime, Matt would do whatever he could tonight to ensure that Corie and Evan McGuire had nothing more to worry about and could get a good night's sleep.

By the time he'd reached the seventh floor, Corie was waiting outside her door, holding his watch and a small plate wrapped in plastic. "I went ahead and put the battery back in the smoke alarm myself. All I had to do was pull out a chair to reach it."

"You tested it?"

She nodded. "It beeped." In other words, *stop butting in, already*. She handed him the watch. "Evan says thank-you. I appreciate the way you eased his concern and made him feel useful. Although I didn't know what half the bells and whistles on this watch are for. And trust me, he asked about every one of them." After he'd strapped the watch back onto his wrist, she handed him the plate. "And here. It's not much. But thank you."

Matt didn't need a thank-you, and he certainly hadn't expected a gift. He lifted the plate to inspect the thick slice of cherry pie. He hadn't grown to 250 pounds of muscle by turning his nose up at a free dessert. But he felt awkward taking anything from this woman who wore a coat with a frayed collar, and whose son clearly needed some bigger clothes—and possibly some counseling on the dangers of playing with fire.

Misreading his hesitancy, Corie quickly apologized. "Don't worry. I didn't bake it in that rattrap of an oven. I work at Pearl's Diner evenings after school. Except on nights like this when I have class. Sometimes I bake, but mostly I wait tables."

He knew Pearl's. Classic diner food that filled your belly and made you feel at home. He'd eaten there with his family many times over the years. He knew the original owner, Pearl Jenkins, had retired and sold the restaurant to Melissa Kincaid, the wife of one of the detectives his older brothers, Alex and Pike, worked with at KCPD. But other than adding some lighter fare to the menu, he hadn't noticed any changes in the quality of the food. And the pie from Pearl's was legendary. "My boss lets me bring home any extra since we bake it fresh every day."

"You made this?"

Corie nodded.

He finally remembered his manners. "Thank you. Cherry's my favorite."

"I'm glad." She opened her door. "Well, thank you again. Good night, Mr. Taylor."

"Good night, Mrs. McGuire. Ms.? Miss?"

There was a drawn look to her features that spoke of fatigue. "I'm divorced from Evan's father. Corie will do just fine."

"Matt will do, too. For me. I'm Matt. Not married. Never have been. Never baked a pie."

She smiled in that way that made him feel like he hadn't just stuck his foot in his mouth and made an awkward conversation downright uncomfortable. "Good to know. Good night, Matt."

He waited in the hallway, hearing the dead bolt, a chain and the doorknob engage. He liked that she was cautious about her safety. Even though the City Market district was being reclaimed by Millennials and real estate investors, the transformation hadn't taken hold everywhere. The McGuires were still a lone woman and a little boy alone in the city.

And Matt was the scary dude across the hall who'd come out of his solitary refuge just long enough to save the day…and scare her back behind her tightly locked door.

Dragging his door mat back across the hall, he stepped inside his apartment and locked the door behind him. He'd return to his weights later. For now, he turned the TV on the late news, leaned back on the couch and stretched his feet out onto the table beside the takeout wrappers from tonight's dinner. He unwrapped the pie and inhaled its heady scent. Sweet and delectable, just like Corie.

Matt didn't even bother getting up to get a fork. He picked the wedge up in his hand and took a bite. His grandmother was one hell of a cook, and this pie reminded him of that perfect blend of talent and experience. The second bite made him forget the niggling thought at the back of his mind that told him something was very wrong in that small apartment across the hall.

There was also something very right about that little family.

Corie McGuire had pretty hair, a pretty butt and a pretty smile.

Matt inhaled the last of the sweet, flaky crust and tart filling.

And damn, the woman could cook.

He might just be in love.

Chapter Two

"Okay, now you're just showin' off."

Ignoring the teasing voice, Matt pushed up off the snow-dusted pavement after checking to make sure there was no fuel leak and pried open the hood of the burning car with his long-handled ax. He wedged it upward, bracing the ax between the frame and the hood to keep it open. He turned away from the billowing smoke that poured out over the fenders to frown at his younger brother, Mark, who'd brought a second ax from the engine parked several yards away in the parking lot.

"Huh?" Matt lifted the hose he'd dragged to the burning car off his shoulder and pointed it toward the flames before opening the valve and spraying the engine block. The steam of water meeting fire forced them both to take a step back. They wore their turnout gear like the rest of the Lucky 13 crew, who had responded to the call to a car fire behind an office building just north of the downtown area. But since this wasn't a structure fire they had to walk into where oxygen would be scarce, there'd been no call to wear face masks and a breathing apparatus. His cold cheeks stung with the spray of steamy moisture on and around his goggles, forcing Matt to redirect the water. "Are you complaining because I'm doing my job?"

"I'm complaining because you're doing everybody's

job." Mark moved in beside him, waving his arm through the smoke and steam, clearing it away to get a visual on the origin of the fire to ensure that it was completely out. "Hell, I could have stayed at the firehouse where it's warm and finished my lunch instead of getting in the truck and riding here to watch you do all the work."

"I let you turn on the water and pressurize the hose, didn't I?" Matt covered the engine with one more spray of water before shutting off the valve and giving a high sign to Ray Jackson, another firefighter, who was waiting beside the hydrant to turn it off.

"Big whoop. I know this is small in the grand scheme of fires, but we are trained to work together as a unit. You're making me look bad in front of our adoring audience." Mark turned his blue eyes to the group of curious bystanders huddling together for warmth on the far side of the parking lot. "Unless you're trying to impress one of those ladies over there?"

Matt glanced across the way. Although he'd been aware of the small group of people, making sure they'd remained at a safe distance while he put out the fire, he hadn't really noticed that there were three women in the group. He didn't seem to notice any women since last night's visit to Corie McGuire's apartment. Honey-blond ponytails and big green eyes must be his thing. The two brunettes and a bright, unnaturally platinum blonde were attractive enough, he supposed, but not one of them had been compelling enough to divert his attention. "No."

"Of course not. Big bad Matt Taylor's just doing his job. Like always." Mark's groan echoed Matt's as Ray Jackson turned over shutting down the hydrant to another teammate and jogged across the parking lot to chat up the three ladies. "Can't say the same for Jackson."

"Maybe he knows one of them," Matt suggested, giving his teammate the benefit of the doubt.

"Would it matter if he did or didn't?" Mark swung his ax onto his shoulder and shook his head. "How am I ever going to find you a date to Amy's and my wedding if you got to compete with that?"

Matt shrugged as Ray took off his helmet and the three women eagerly shook hands with him. Matt had never possessed the gift of gab or the movie-star looks of their buddy Ray. He'd been a natural to represent Firehouse 13 on the KCFD fund-raiser calendar last year. Matt probably should be jealous. Instead, he was glad he'd never been called on to do any PR for the KCFD. Although he'd fought more dangerous fires than today's car fire side by side with Ray Jackson and was happy to let Ray or Mark do the friendly conversations with the witnesses and victims they interacted with, he was a little embarrassed to see Ray focusing squarely on the women in the group, barely acknowledging the two men standing with them.

"If we had a sister," Matt announced, "I'd never introduce them."

"Agreed." Mark clapped him on the shoulder, pulling his focus away from Ray and the onlookers and back to cleaning up after the fire. "Come on. I'll help you drain the hose and roll it back up. Water's freezing fast. Careful of that ice. I think we just turned this place into a skating rink."

They worked in silence for a few minutes while their firehouse captain, Kyle Redding, stood farther down the sidewalk talking with a uniformed police officer and the older couple walking their dog who had called in the burning car. Apparently, there was some issue in finding the owner of the vehicle. He'd like to think that Ray was following up on the investigation by chatting with the onlookers, but it didn't seem as though anyone who worked around here recognized the car or knew where the owner worked.

Matt pulled the hose out straight and began the laborious task of clearing the line before something Mark had said in jest—he hoped—sank in. "Don't set me up on any dates. Not even for the wedding."

Mark stopped abruptly and straightened, grinning from ear to ear. "Why? You seeing somebody I don't know about?"

Matt replayed the images of Corie walking away from him and the sweet smile that had softened her pretty mouth when he'd made her laugh. He wasn't sure exactly what he thought might happen with his neighbor. Probably nothing more than just that—being neighbors. But he wanted to savor last night's encounter with the small family across the hall awhile longer before he tried to work up interest in any matchmaking his brother and future sister-in-law might have in mind for him. "No. But I'm not interested in meeting anyone new."

Mark's blue eyes narrowed suspiciously. "So, you *have* met someone," he prodded, fishing for information.

Matt's answer was to pull off his goggles and toss them at Mark. "If you're so anxious to do some work, stop talking and get to it."

But Mark never gave up that easily. "Do I know her? Has anyone in the family met her? Did you find her on one of those dating sites?"

Matt gave the hose a strong tug, pulling it right out of Mark's hands. "I outrank you, Taylor," he teased, knowing with his brother, it was a useless threat. "I said get to work."

"Yes, sir, Lieutenant, sir." Although that cheesy grin

never wavered, Mark had the good sense to let the matter drop so they could get the hose prepped for the truck.

Of Matt's three adoptive brothers, his younger brother, Mark, was the only one who was his brother by birth. Unlike their older brothers, Alex and Pike, who were cops, Mark had followed Matt into firefighting, making for a friendly family rivalry in interdepartmental softball games, blood drives and fund-raisers. Sometimes the cops won; sometimes the firefighters came out on top. But nothing could ever break the bond they shared. All four brothers had lived in the same foster home and had been adopted by Gideon and Meghan Taylor—the firefighters who had saved them in more ways than one, and who had inspired Matt to follow in their footsteps. The six of them had become the family that, as a child, Matt hadn't believed he'd ever find—or even deserved.

If Alex, the oldest, was their leader, and Pike, the second oldest, was the intellectual, then Matt was the quiet one. And that made Mark the obnoxious one. There was something about being the youngest—and something about being ridiculously in love and planning a summer wedding—that made Mark particularly ornery lately. Although he'd nearly lost his fiancée, Amy, to a serial killer who'd hidden his crimes in a series of arson fires, and had nearly lost his own life saving her, Mark was now as happy as Matt had ever seen him. Amy was good for Mark. She'd brought him out of his grief and guilt after the traumatic loss of their grandfather had hit Mark particularly hard— and she thought his goofy sense of humor was actually funny. No accounting for taste, he guessed.

Mark elbowed Matt's arm, drawing his focus back to the work at hand. "What's up with you today? I just caught you smiling. There *is* a woman."

"Nah. Not me." For now, Corie McGuire and her cherry

pie were simply a good feeling Matt wanted to keep to himself. The musical trill of a woman laughing carried across the parking lot, and both Taylors paused to see Ray Jackson leaning in and saying something that delighted his captive audience. Knowing Ray, he'd have all their phone numbers before the conversation was over.

Mark snorted a laugh. "Maybe you and I ought to kick back and let Ray finish cleanup duty."

Matt shook his head, preferring to stay busy and keep moving in the cold weather. He hefted his section of hose and carried it several feet closer to the fire engine. "What would you do if Ray flirted with your Amy like that?"

Mark followed with the next length of hose. "I love the guy. But I'd lay him out flat." Mark chuckled as he dropped the hose alongside the lines two other members of their team were winding onto the truck. "Unless Amy laid him out first."

Matt laughed with him, suspecting Mark's fiancée wouldn't put up with anyone or anything she didn't want to. Matt liked that directness about Amy Hall. Not only did it make it easy for him to have a conversation with his future sister-in-law, but her honesty left him with no doubt just how much she was in love with Mark. While Matt was a little envious that his three brothers had found their soul mates, and the two older ones had even started families, he was also happy that Alex, Pike and Mark had each found the right woman. One day, he hoped for the same.

He silently wondered if anything would come of this unexpected attraction to Corie, and if he could handle the ready-made family that came with her. Not for the first time since last night, Matt debated his suspicions about the oven fire in the McGuire apartment. He'd shown the residue he'd collected to Captain Redding this morning before they'd been called out, and the captain—who had almost twenty years of experience on Matt and agreed the substance was suspicious—promised to run it by some of his old cohorts in the department. Something was off about the whole story of baking a pizza gone wrong. Something more than the sooty remains of a fire had coated the heating elements in the oven. And Corie had seemed so certain that she'd had a fire-suppressant mixture stored in her cabinet for just such an emergency that he had a feeling there was something deliberate about that fire.

Somebody had wanted it to burn.

Matt had set more than one fire himself when he'd been barely more than a toddler. He'd been curious, yes, but he understood now that he'd been acting out against his birth parents' neglect, and later against being stuck in foster care and the guilt he felt at putting him and Mark there. Was there something going on in Evan McGuire's life that was making the eight-year-old experiment with fire? It would require Matt drawing on some painful memories, but maybe it was worth prodding Corie a little to see if she suspected her son might have picked up a dangerous hobby, and if he could get the boy some of the same type of counseling that had helped him as a child.

"Yo, Matt." Mark's summons pulled Matt from his thoughts. "Take a look at this." Mark was standing in front of the sedan's charred engine block. Now that the fire was out and the smoke and steam had dissipated, they could make a clearer assessment of what might have caused the fire, despite the ice frozen around the parts Matt had hosed with water. "You're the fix-it guy. Those wires don't belong there, do they?"

Matt frowned at the blackened metal wires crisscrossing above the radiator and battery. If they'd been part of the car's makeup, they should have been coated in rubberlike polymers or plastic to prevent sparks or accidental electrocution to the unwary handler. Even with the intense heat of the fire, some trace of the insulation should have remained. Reaching under his turnout coat, Matt pulled out his pocketknife and chipped away at the ice. "Looks like some kind of homemade repair job." He peered down between the frame and engine parts. "It doesn't look like they're holding anything together, though. Just a sec."

Without regard for the snow or ice, Matt dropped down to the ground and slid as much of his bulk as he could beneath the car. Between his flashlight and the pocketknife, Matt quickly found what the wires were attached to—the melted remains of a cell phone and a wad of charred, waxy cord that fed into a hole in the oil pan.

Talk about wanting something to burn.

This fire was no accident.

"Hey, if it isn't the wonder twins." At the sound of approaching footsteps and a man's familiar voice, Matt slid from beneath the car.

"Uncle Cole." Mark was already trading a handshake and friendly back-slapping hug with the dark-haired older man by the time Matt was on his feet.

"Mark. Matt." Other than the lack of silvering sideburns, Cole Taylor was a dead ringer for their father, Gideon.

"Uncle Cole." Matt reached out to shake hands with the family member, too. His gaze dropped to the KCPD badge and gun peeking out from beneath his leather jacket before sliding back up to slightly lined blue eyes. That meant he was on duty. It didn't explain why he was here at the scene of a small fire, though. "Good to see you."

He pointed to the man with the dark sideburns and stocking cap standing beside him. "This is Agent Amos Rand, my new partner. I'm showing him the ropes while

my regular partner is on maternity leave. He's on temporary assignment from NCIS."

"A Navy man?" Matt extended his hand in greeting.

"Marines." Agent Rand could give Matt a run for the
money in the stoicism department. But his grip was solid
and friendly enough.

"Like Grandpa." Mark shook hands with Cole's new
partner. "He served during the Korean conflict, and in
the reserves for several years after that. He died earlier
this year."

Matt reached over and squeezed his brother's shoulder. They all missed the family patriarch, who'd suffered
a fatal heart attack while helping Mark rescue the victims
of a car accident. But Mark seemed to take it personally
that he hadn't been able to save their grandfather, as well.

Agent Rand buried his hands in the pockets of his coat
and nodded. "I would have liked your grandpa."

"You would have loved Dad," Cole agreed, erasing the
wistful grief that had momentarily darkened his expression. "He'd have been telling you stories for hours. A few
of them might even have been true."

Amos chuckled. "Sounds like a good man."

"He was the best," Cole and Mark echoed together.

Matt nodded his agreement. "What brings you two to
our parking lot on this cold day? You're not working arson
now, are you?"

Cole shook his head. "We're still major cases, organized crime division."

Amos pulled out his cell phone and nodded toward the
sedan. "You all catch up." Matt watched the NCIS agent
type in the license plate and send it off in a text before he
circled around the car, sizing up the blackened engine block
and peering into the windows. "This was an arson fire?"

"Looks like it," Matt confirmed.

Cole shoved his hands deep into the pockets of his coat, his breath gusting out in a cloud of warm air. "We're supposed to meet a CI on a case we're investigating."

"CI?" Mark asked.

"Confidential informant." Cole Taylor scanned the people around the parking lot before tilting his gaze to the windows above them on either side. "Don't suppose you've seen a skinny, hyperactive guy with dark hair? Possibly wearing coveralls. He works at a garage over on South McGee."

"We cleared the immediate area." Matt pointed to the gathering across the parking lot where one of the brunettes was typing on Ray Jackson's phone. "Except for that group over there, it's too cold to have a lot of onlookers. Is one of those men your guy?"

"In a suit? I don't think so." Cole glanced back as Captain Redding dismissed the couple with their dog. "The guy talking to your captain is too old to be our man. Our CI requested we meet on neutral ground where the chances of anyone recognizing him would be next to nil. He'd stand out like a sore thumb here in the business district. Unless he was dropping off somebody's car he was working on."

Amos returned from inspecting the car. "It's Maldonado's car," he confirmed. "Plates and VIN number are in his name."

"Ah, hell." Cole looked up at Matt, his expression grim. "Please tell me you didn't find a body in it?"

"Hadn't looked beyond the front and back seats."

"Can you open the trunk?" When Matt hesitated, Cole pulled back the front of his coat to expose his badge where anyone passing by the scene could see it. "We have probable cause that our man could be in danger. I'll take full responsibility."

"Not a problem." His firefighter's training included

a vow to save people before property. Since Matt's ax was currently wedged between the hood and frame, Mark picked up his ax and followed them to the back end of the car. He wedged the blade into the locking mechanism and forced it open. Suspecting it was useless to warn the two officers to stay back, Matt raised the trunk. Although some of the smoke from the engine has made its way through the car's interior and drifted out to dissipate in the wintry air, it was easy to see that there was nothing inside but the spare tire and a toolbox. "The car looks abandoned." He reached inside to open the toolbox. "He's got the means here to rig that fire. But then, it wouldn't take any special tools to set that up. Just a cell phone and the know-how."

Cole and Agent Rand went into investigator mode, snapping pictures of the vehicle with their phones and sending the information on to a third party—a fellow investigator or someone in the crime lab, he guessed.

"This fire was no accident." Matt led his uncle to the front of the car to point out the ignition device beneath the hood. Amos took a picture of the cell phone itself and then dropped it into an evidence bag from another pocket of his coat. "I figured it was some kind of insurance scam. Abandoned car. Remote ignition. Whoever set it only had to call the number on the cell. Like striking a match in the oil pan. A spark, oxygen and fuel to burn. Ignition 101."

Agent Rand stood on the other side of Cole and tucked his phone away. "You think Meade's people are sending him a message—keep your mouth shut or you'll be in the car next time it burns?"

"Meade?" Mark frowned at the name from Kansas City's storied criminal history. "I recognize that name. You mean Jericho Meade and his mob connections? I thought he was dead."

"Alleged mob connections. And he is." Cole shook his head. "Tori and I took care of them."

Matt had heard the story of the undercover op several years earlier where Uncle Cole had met his wife, then–FBI agent Victoria Westin. They'd both infiltrated the crime family and had been forced to become allies to protect each other's cover and complete their respective missions. Pretending to be a couple had become the real thing. They'd both left undercover work once they'd gotten married and had their twin girls. And though Cole had remained a detective with KCPD, Tori had retired from the FBI to manage a small art gallery and focus on their girls.

Cole reached up with a gloved hand to smack Matt's shoulder, including both him and Mark in the point he was making. "But, just like the next generation of Taylor clan brothers are fighting to keep Kansas City safe, we believe the next generation of Meade's crime family is fighting to regain their influence. Jericho's nephew Chad Meade was released from prison after seventeen years a few months back. He's trying to take up where his uncle left off. Our CI was going to confirm that Meade has been stealing cars and sending them to a chop shop. Auto theft may be old-school, but we suspect he's using those profits to finance his efforts to bring illegal arms into the city. And using some legit businesses to launder money for suspected terrorists." He nodded toward Agent Rand. "That's the connection that brought NCIS into our investigation."

Mark frowned at what Matt suspected was a glossed-over version of Meade's criminal enterprise. "All that's going on in KC? In *this* neighborhood? There's a lot of money here. I thought this was where the Millennials and old-school yuppies worked and tore down old buildings to put up condos."

"They do." Cole pointed to the office building where the

curious crowd had come from. "This isn't gang turf, but there are a couple of import/export and agricultural distribution companies headquartered in that building that we're monitoring. With KCI Airport and the Missouri River carrying so much traffic, Kansas City is considered a port city. That's why we've got all the embassies and customs offices here."

Agent Rand nodded. "Making it a hub for supply lines and money changing hands if the right man establishes a foothold here."

Mark snorted at the enormity of what Chad Meade was trying to accomplish after his stint in prison. "You mean the wrong man." He looked around the parking lot, tall buildings and crowd of suits and dresses that was dissipating now that the excitement of the fire was over and Ray Jackson had rejoined the team stowing gear on the trucks. "Although this would be a great neighborhood to find some nice cars to steal."

"Exactly. Not where our mechanic would be hanging out. We thought it'd be a good location to meet our CI." Cole studied the burned-out car again. "Apparently, someone else didn't agree."

Organized crime in their neighborhood? Were there really terrorist connections in the Firehouse 13 district? Matt thought of Corie and Evan McGuire, slight of build, super cautious and all alone in the world. Their building was about nine blocks from here—a bit of a long walk, but certainly doable. And Pearl's Diner, where Corie worked, was just around the corner, less than two blocks away. Several of the people working in these office buildings had probably eaten their lunch there. Maybe he should be worried about how safe any of them were.

"And you think this fire could have been set as a de-

terrent to your informant speaking out against Meade?"
Matt asked.

Cole shrugged. "No proof one way or the other yet. Your
first instinct could be right, and this is an insurance scam.
If Maldonado had a change of heart, he could be looking
for some quick cash from an insurance payout, or he could
have torched the car to throw Meade's men—and us—off
his trail. He'd have the know-how to rig a car like that."

Amos Rand shifted on his feet, looking anxious to
leave. "I'd sure like to get eyes on him. Find out if he's
had a change of heart, or if Meade's people got to him.
Make sure he's still in one piece somewhere."

Two mysterious fires in two days. Not that Corie Mc-
Guire would have any connection to a police informant
and organized crime. Matt suspected her son, left to his
own devices for entertainment last night, had been playing with setting a fire. This burned-out car couldn't have
anything to do with that.

It had to be a coincidence.

Not that he liked coincidences. But Matt was paid to
put out fires and save lives, not solve cases for his uncle
or anyone else in the police department.

"You okay, big guy?" Cole asked, pulling Matt from
his thoughts. "You seem distracted."

Mark grinned like the annoying little brother he was.
"That's what I said. I think there's a woman involved."

Matt slid him a warning glance. "Shut up."

That big grin must be a family trait. Cole matched
Mark's amused expression. "Definitely a woman judging
by that reaction."

Matt wasn't ready to admit to any emotion he wasn't
sure he understood yet. "Can't a man get any privacy in
this family?"

But Mark wouldn't let it go. "Hey, you're the only Taylor

bachelor left until our cousins graduate from high school and college. After being the baby brother for so many years, it's only fair that I get to pick on you for a change."

"Some things never change," Cole agreed. "Mitch, Brett, Mac, Gideon and Josh used to give me grief about finding a woman and settling down. Even Jess found a husband before I met your aunt Tori." He squeezed Matt's arm, offering some hard-won advice. "It'll happen when it happens. And it'll be worth the wait. But if there is some-body special, you know we'd all like to meet her. When-ever you're ready."

"Taylors!" Captain Redding shouted. He answered the dispatch summons on his radio before heading over to the first fire truck. "We got another call!"

Mark swore. "This whole neighborhood is turning into a dead man district."

"What does that mean?" Agent Rand frowned.

Matt explained the terminology. "A dead man zone is the spot where we suspect a fire will shift and spread to, given wind conditions, structural composition and so on. It's the place you *don't* want to be because the fire is com-ing your way."

Amos nodded with grim understanding. "You're saying this whole neighborhood is a danger zone."

"Yes."

Cole stepped back, reaching out to shake Matt's and Mark's hands again before sending them on their way. "Go do your job. We'll work the crime scene here and copy you on anything we find out. You boys be safe."

Mark traded a quick hug before he and Matt jogged on past him. "Say hi to Aunt Tori and the girls."

"Will do. Hey, are we getting an invitation to your wed-ding?"

Mark turned, backing toward the engines. "They should

go out next month. Amy's designing and making them herself. She's not just an artist, she's a perfectionist."

"She and Tori should have a lot to talk about at the next family get-together."

"Taylors!" Redding shouted from the captain's seat in the truck.

Matt tugged on Mark's coat. "Gotta go."

He doffed a salute to Cole and Amos before climbing up to his seat behind the steering wheel of the fire engine and starting it up. "What's up?" Matt asked.

The captain was still on his radio across the cab of the truck. "Class B fire at the recycling plant on North Front Street." Class B meant flammable liquids—several steps up in danger from an engine fire one man could put out. The recycling plant would definitely be a dead man zone if they didn't get there quickly enough.

All thoughts of Corie, Evan and mysterious fires he couldn't yet explain had to be put on hold.

"Let's go." Matt shifted the engine into gear and turned on the lights and siren. "Lucky 13 rolling."

Chapter Three

"Mom, if we had a watch like Mr. Taylor's, you could set the timer on it, and you wouldn't have to keep checking your watch every minute to see if we get home by my bedtime." Evan hopped from one foot to the next, following Corie down the aisle and off the bus. "Or we could use it to check the temperature to see if I need to wear my mittens and hat."

The bus door opened, and the damp, wintry night air slapped her in the face. Corie pulled her scarf snug around her neck and flipped up the collar of her coat before turning to her son and tugging his knit stocking cap down around his ears. "I don't need a fancy watch to know you have to wear your mittens and hat."

She looked over his head to Mr. Lee, the bus driver, who grinned from ear to ear at her son's persistent, supremely logical argument on the merits of buying a fancy watch for his next birthday, which was nearly a year away. "Good luck with that one," he said before bidding her good-night. "He'll keep you on your toes."

"That he will." She felt lucky and a little sad that the affable older gentleman who drove them home from the diner nearly every night was one of the most familiar faces she knew in Kansas City. Other than her coworkers at the diner and Evan's school, where she worked as a para-educator until she finished her teaching degree, she hadn't made any effort to form friendships since moving across the state. Not since her last new *friend* in St. Louis had turned out to have a connection to her ex-husband, and she discovered Denise had been feeding Kenny Norwell information about her work and school schedule, and she ended up getting an unwanted and unfriendly surprise visit from Kenny at the sports bar where she'd waited tables one night. It was one of the few times she'd been glad Evan was spending the night at her mother and stepfather's. That visit from Kenny and the subsequent lecture from her mother about blowing her chance at a reunion with the man whose money and connections she liked more than his treatment of her only daughter had been reason enough to transfer her college credits and move to Kansas City. "Good night, Carl."

Corie stepped off the bus, wishing she had on jeans or slacks instead of her waitress uniform. At least her sturdy support shoes allowed her to move quickly so that she didn't have to spend any longer than necessary out in the cold air. She reached for Evan's hand and, as soon as the bus pulled away from their stop, they hurried across the street and down the two blocks that would take them to their building.

Evan danced along beside her, full of energy after spending four hours obediently sitting at a corner table in the diner, completing his homework, eating dinner and playing a game on her phone. "Honestly, if it's any help, I don't mind staying up past nine o'clock."

"I appreciate the offer," she teased. "But I know how impossible it is to get you up for school in the morning if you're up too late the night before."

"Or I could get a new watch," he countered. "My birthday's coming up in November."

"How about we just hustle for now, little man." She

tightened her grip around Evan's hand and matched his eager pace.

If she could afford a Swiss Army Knife–like watch like Matt Taylor's, she'd be spending the money on a new, warmer coat that fit her son better, making a down payment on a cheap car so they wouldn't have to wait at a bus stop or walk these last two blocks in the open air, or, what the heck, maybe pay a bill or something. Making it completely on her own in the world was proving to be more rewarding than she'd imagined, even though it was sometimes a challenge to make ends meet. Even though a single phone call back to St. Louis would instantly fill her bank account, the help came with too many strings attached. Strings she had no intention of ever reconnecting.

Her life was here now, in Kansas City with her son. It might be a small life. But it was a good one. They were safe. Evan was growing stronger and more confident every day. And she believed—she hoped, at least—that one day they could have a normal life and be happy.

Corie's sigh formed a white cloud of air, and Evan slowed down to play at making clouds with his warm breath. Even though she played along to see how big they could make a cloud before it chilled and dissipated, she kept Evan moving beside her, worrying as much about his exposure to the cold air as their safety.

Fortunately, there was a bus stop on the same block as Pearl's Diner, and bus passes were cheap. But she worried about the January night air on Evan's young lungs and every alley or parking garage they had to walk past before they got safely inside the locked lobby of their building. She wasn't above scoping out the driver of every vehicle that passed, either, checking to make sure her ex-husband hadn't made tracking her down to their new apartment in a new city his top priority since his release from prison in Jefferson City eleven months earlier. He'd contacted her through her attorney in St. Louis demanding visitation rights with Evan, but a firm no and a reminder of all the custody papers and restraining orders she had in place had been her only reply. Being told no wouldn't have made Kenny happy, but Evan's panicked reaction to the possibility of seeing his father—even under the parameters of a supervised visit—had made her decision quick and easy. Corie's job was to protect her son from the man he only remembered as a monster. She hadn't even given her estranged mother her new name or address, and she hadn't listed her new phone number. Their life in St. Louis felt like a lifetime ago, but the wariness of her surroundings and the potential threat of that past catching up to them was as fresh as the diner's cheesy burritos for tomorrow morning's breakfast she carried in her backpack.

Since the lobby of the building was locked 24-7, she had her key card ready to swipe as soon as they climbed the granite steps and reached the outer glass doors. It was noticeably warmer the moment the door closed behind them, blocking the wind. Corie's stress level went down, as well, as soon as she heard the lock clicking into place. Once she and Evan got through the interior door, she inhaled a deep, calming breath, unbuttoned the top of her coat and loosened her scarf.

She considered stopping at Mr. Stinson's apartment while they were here on the first floor, but Evan had already run ahead to press the call button on the elevator. Nodding in silent agreement that her son had a better plan than knocking on the super's door, Corie followed Evan to the elevator, catching his mittens and cap as he shed them and stuffing them into the pockets of his backpack. Not that his energy level was showing any signs of ebbing, but she'd stayed late at the diner to fix their to-go breakfast and had missed their regular bus. Getting Evan to calm down and fall asleep by his nine o'clock bedtime was a challenge, even without the late start to his nightly routine. Mothering first. She'd run back down to see about the state of the oven and electrical outlet once she got her son in his pajamas.

Corie grabbed Evan by the shoulder when the elevator doors opened, checking the interior before following him inside the empty car. When the doors opened onto the seventh floor, Evan skipped down the hallway, leaving Corie to hurry after him. "Can I open it, Mom?"

Evan's fascination with gadgets, even one so simple as a key in a lock, gave her a moment to glance over her shoulder to the door across the hall. She idly wondered if Matt Taylor was home this evening. He'd said he usually had Tuesdays off, but what about Wednesdays? And just what did he do behind that door? Watch sports on TV? Work out? Maybe he was a gourmet cook or a fix-it guy with some carpentry or painting project going on. Was he into fast cars or monster trucks? Maybe he read books.

Evan pushed the door open and tossed her the keys, running inside to shed his coat and dump his backpack on the couch. Corie shook her head and followed him inside.

It didn't matter what Matt Taylor did behind closed doors. She had plenty to deal with right here inside *this* apartment. "Hey, little man." She turned the dead bolt behind her and nodded to the coatrack beside the door. "Hang up your coat and take your backpack to your room. You know we don't leave a mess in the living room."

"Yes, ma'am."

Corie was dragging with the length of her day after working two jobs, knowing she still had to get on her laptop to do more research for the paper she was writing for next week's class. But Evan happily bopped from one spot to the next, hanging up his coat and dashing down the hall to his bedroom before she even got her coat unbuttoned. "Get your pajamas on. Do you need a snack before you brush your teeth?"

"Can I have chocolate milk?" he shouted from his bedroom. From the sound of things, he'd opened a drawer in his toy chest and was riffling through his collection of tiny plastic building bricks to add to the ever-expanding fantasy fortress he was building on the table that had once been his desk. While she worried about the significance of her son building defensive fortresses and attack dragons, the school counselor insisted they were healthy outlets for the fears he'd carried with him since he'd been a toddler. "Cookies, too?"

"One or the other," she hollered back. "Pj's before playtime, okay?"

She smiled at his answering multipitched groan, picked up her own backpack and carried it to the kitchen. She flipped on the light switch and stopped in her tracks. "What the…?"

Her oven was missing. Not blackened up the front edge. Not under repairs. Gone.

"What…? Where…?"

Before she picked up the phone to call Mr. Stinson and ask how she was supposed to cook breakfast in the morning, Corie forced herself to inhale a steadying breath. What she noticed then wasn't much better.

She sniffed the air again. Something smelled off. Different. Extra.

Then she spotted the sticky note clinging to her microwave oven. She set her bag on the counter beside it and tore it off. She read it quickly, read it twice before breathing a little easier.

Mrs. McGuire—
    Got the plug fixed. Don't know how, but the wires
had disconnected. The microwave works.
Your oven will take me a little longer.
We need to talk.
Wally S.

"You're darned right we need to talk."
She crumpled the note in her fist and punched a couple of buttons on the microwave, just to reassure herself
that she could heat up breakfast. Then she pushed up the
sleeves of her cardigan sweater and got busy putting away
the takeout box and cleaning up the mess of rearranged
items and a grease smudge Mr. Stinson had left behind.
She wiped down the countertops and found a space underneath the sink where she could move the pots and pans
he'd taken from the bottom drawer of the oven and strewn
across the counter. Then she pulled the sweeper from the
pantry closet and swept out the dust bunnies that had collected under and behind the stove. She knew she should
be feeling grateful for Mr. Stinson's help instead of this
nagging sense of violation. But how could she explain to
the kindly older gentleman the sense of intrusion she felt
knowing that someone had been in her apartment while
she'd been away?
    He didn't know her history. No one in Kansas City did.
Not all of it. He thought he was being helpful, doing his job.
Wally Stinson *was* being helpful. She was the one whose
sense of *friendly* and *helpful* and *normal* had been skewed
by her ex-husband's violence and control, and her mother's
opinion that everything Kenny had done to her was just
part of being married. Even when he'd been arrested for
multiple counts of arson and witness intimidation and had
taken a plea deal that guaranteed his guilt in exchange for

less prison time, Corie's mother had begged her not to divorce him. Kenny had money and connections and a veneer of status her mother accused her of throwing away.

Corie had dropped the charges of domestic battery and attempted kidnapping, just to make sure Kenny went away and she got full custody of Evan.

But any sense of security was fragile and hard-won. Yes, she'd broken all ties with Kenny and her mother. She'd moved away, changed her and Evan's names and lived as invisible a life as possible. But that didn't mean she still didn't jump at shadows, worry when Evan was out of her sight, and fear the idea of someone watching her, touching her things without her knowing, trespassing on her life.

She'd called Mr. Stinson this morning, and he'd promised to stop by. The man had keys to get into every apartment in the building. She'd *known* he would be here today. A normal person wouldn't be upset by that. Oh, how she desperately wished for the day she could feel normal again. Her therapist in St. Louis had advised her to visualize what she wanted her life to look like in the future, and eventually she'd be able to let go of the past and she'd get there. During her counseling sessions, she'd also learned to think before reacting. Her feelings of fear and distrust were to be expected, given all she'd been through. But that didn't mean she had to act on them.

Take a deep breath.

Think. Observe. Assess.

Then react to what was really here.

Corie did just that, taking the time to put away the sweeper and calm her fears. The building had been locked. Their apartment was locked. She and Evan were safe.

Mr. Stinson's presence accounted for the whisper of an unfamiliar scent that lingered in the air. She squeezed her eyes shut and tried to pinpoint the fading smell of something woodsy combined with citrus. She opened her eyes and ran the water in the sink to rinse her dish rag. When she squirted the lemony hand soap to clean her hands, she thought she'd solved the mystery. Mr. Stinson had probably washed his hands here when he was done working. Moving the oven would have required a dolly and maybe some extra help from the part-time super who lived in the apartment below hers and helped with bigger projects like replacing a damaged oven.

But to completely dismiss her suspicions, Corie needed to do a little more investigating. Did the super wear cologne? Did his assistant? She wanted to verify that the extra scent in her kitchen belonged to one of them and her paranoia was simply an overreaction. It was yet another reason to get Evan into his pajamas and hurry downstairs to speak to the building super before he turned in for the night.

As she picked up a towel to dry her hands, her gaze landed on the dessert plate sitting in the drainer beside the sink. Matt Taylor had returned it early that morning, washed and dried, before heading to his shift at Firehouse 13. Since she and Evan had been in their usual mad dash to get ready for school and up to the bus stop, she'd thanked him again, thanked him for comparing her pie to his grandmother's and then, realizing the silliness of their rushed morning conversation, had told him goodbye and set the plate in the drainer before running back to her room to throw on some mascara, blush and lip gloss, grab their coats and backpacks, and get them up to the bus stop.

But that silly conversation at her door meant that Matt had been at her apartment twice now in the past twenty-four hours. Maybe that's what felt off about the apartment tonight. Other than the movers and Mr. Stinson, who was old enough to be her father, she hadn't had any man in here.

Did Matt have a scent that lingered in the air? Somehow, she had the impression that he wasn't a cologne kind of guy. But that didn't mean he didn't put off natural phero-mones that spoke to something purely feminine inside her. Was she just projecting her thoughts, imagining something had changed in her apartment because an attractive man had been here?

Corie put the plate away and leaned against the edge of the sink, staring at her reflection in the window there. She looked a little older and a lot more tired since the last time she'd thought of any man as attractive. She hadn't thought about a man that way in years. Not since Kenny and their ugly divorce. Not since remaking her life to keep her and Evan safe.

She was human enough to objectively appreciate a good-looking man, even to be a little bit in awe of the utter masculinity of size and strength embodied by her neighbor, especially in that sharply pressed, shoulder-hugging black firefighter's uniform he'd been wearing this morning. The day she and Evan had moved in, and they'd first met Matt Taylor, she had to admit, she'd been afraid of him. Her ex-husband, Kenny Norwell, was of average height and build, and he'd been scary enough when he'd used his words and his fists and his threats against her. Sharing the close quarters of an elevator ride with Matt had made her feel practically helpless. She appreciated him respecting her need to keep her distance. She'd never heard him swear or raise his voice in anger. Over the months they'd shared the same apartment building, she'd deduced that he wasn't a seething powder keg about to blow, that he was truly a quiet, gentle-natured person, despite his size.

Still, she'd been feeling like something was off in her apartment for a couple of days now, even before Matt's suspicions about the oven fire had reinforced her own and made her anxious to get him out of her space, no matter how kind and helpful he was being. The cherry pie had been as much an apology for her sudden haste in getting rid of him last night as it had been a thank-you for allaying her fears about the fire. And for impressing Evan with the watch and timekeeping responsibility. Being estranged from her mother and stepfather meant there was no strong adult male influence in Evan's life, other than a couple of wonderful teachers. And she certainly wasn't going to get involved with another man just to give her son a father figure. She'd learned the hard way that marrying a man didn't make him a good father—or husband.

Corie reached across the sink to pull the curtains shut and cancel out both her perpetually wary expression and the cold night beyond. Maybe she could ease up a little on her isolationist rules that had become second nature to her and strike up a friendship with Matt. Just so Evan could have him as a friend, too.

Only, she had a feeling that Matt might be interested in more than friendship. And she couldn't give him that. At least, she thought she'd felt those vibes of attraction, felt the heat of a wandering gaze plastered to her backside. And her mouth.

She couldn't even remember the last time she'd been kissed. The last time she'd wanted a man to kiss her.

Then again, she was so out of practice with relationships that she could be reading Matt Taylor all wrong. Matt was a quiet man who kept mostly to himself. As far as she could tell, there was no woman in his life. He was all about his work. And clearly, he worked out. Muscles like his didn't just happen. She'd seen him coming home in his black KCFD uniform or wearing a KCFD T-shirt like the one that had stretched across his broad chest last night often enough to know he was a firefighter, even before he'd announced it in the hallway last night. He was polite, a little awkward when it came to conversation, completely unaware of, or maybe embarrassed by, his dry sense of humor. But was he shy? Or was he reclusive for other reasons like she was?

Corie hung up the towel and headed out of the kitchen toward the bedrooms to make sure Evan was getting ready for bed. Certainly, she counted a few men among her friends—coworkers, classmates at Williams University. But they were more acquaintances than anyone she'd feel comfortable hanging out with in her own home. And nothing with them had ever fluttered with interest, much less real desire. Abuse, blackmail and living in fear of her and Evan's lives had made trusting a man impossible—and being attracted to one too big a risk to take.

She barely recognized the womanly impulses inside her anymore, but last night, something had definitely fluttered. Matt had sensed she was in danger and had come to her rescue. He'd taken several practical steps to keep her and Evan safe and to prevent any further damage to her kitchen and apartment. And he'd done it all without grabbing her, threatening her or talking down to her like she was an idiot who wouldn't understand.

Although Corie doubted she'd ever feel completely safe again after surviving her marriage to Kenny, for a few minutes last night, she hadn't been afraid. She'd been worried that Evan could have seriously injured himself, and that she'd have to dig into her meager savings to come up with the money to replace the oven if the super and building owner blamed her for negligence and didn't feel like replacing it. She'd even been unsettled by her suspicions that the fire hadn't been an accident.

But she'd felt safe with Matt Taylor in her apartment, taking up a lot of space, taking care of them, smelling like a man and saying unexpectedly silly things that made her want to laugh. She'd felt safe right up until the familiar survival instincts that had kept her alive for more than eight years had taken hold, and even the temptation of touching hard muscle and the warm skin of that tattoo peeking from beneath the sleeve of Matt's T-shirt had faded beneath her need to protect Evan and herself at all costs.

She couldn't indulge these rusty sensations of sexual awareness that had awakened inside her. But those few minutes of feeling safe, of feeling like a woman, of picking up the subtle signs of a man being interested in her, had been worth at least a slice of cherry pie.

Reaching Evan's room, she knocked softly on the doorjamb and stepped inside. He was already in his pajamas and building on his fortress. Surveying the whirlwind that was her son determined to have fun without disobeying her, Corie shook her head. She picked up his backpack from where it had hit the floor and set it in the desk chair before gathering up his discarded clothes and dropping them into the clothes basket inside his closet. She folded the sweater he'd been wearing and hugged it to her chest, hating to interrupt the bad guys attacking the ramparts of the castle and the dragon lord, or whatever that winged creature was he'd created, raising the towers ever higher in the battle of Evan's desk. But she needed to settle her fears. She opened the drawer of his dresser and set the sweater inside. "Hey, sweetie. You haven't opened a new soap or sprayed some of my perfume in the apartment, have you?"

The dragon swooped down and knocked over several tiny block warriors as he answered. "Ew, no. I don't like any of that girly stuff."

"Did you spill anything in the kitchen this morning?"

Evan pushed to his feet, his saving-the-world game momentarily forgotten as his sweet face aged with a frown.

"Mom, is something wrong? I know the rules. I wouldn't break them. I know we have to stay safe now that Dad's out of prison. I haven't even told any of my friends my real name."

Oh my. Corie's heart hurt at the maturity she heard in Evan's voice.

"Evan McGuire *is* your real name now. Remember? The judge in St. Louis said so." Her mistakes and fears had forced her little boy to grow up way too soon. She crossed the room to wrap him up in a hug, cradling his head against her breasts and stroking her fingers through his shaggy brown hair. "It's okay, sweetie. I'm okay. I'm sorry if I worried you. Mr. Stinson removed the oven from the kitchen, and it's kind of throwing me off."

He let her hug him for about as long as an eight-year-old who thought he needed to be the man of the house could stand. He pushed away, tilting his wise green eyes up to hers. "I know you don't like changes in your routine. But I didn't do anything." He crossed his finger over his heart. "I swear." He glanced over at his sprawling stronghold. "I dragon swear."

Truly, the strongest vow that Evan McGuire could give. To his way of thinking, nothing could get past the dragon protecting them. If only reality could be as assuring as what this medieval fantasy world had become for her son.

"I'm not blaming you. I just wanted to check." She spared a couple of minutes to admire his dragon beast and the newest turret on his castle before catching a glimpse of the time. "You finish getting ready for bed. Remember to set the timer when you brush your teeth. I'm going to run downstairs and talk to Mr. Stinson for a minute. When I get back, we can read another chapter of that fantasy book together, okay?"

"Okay!"

With her son excited like the little boy he should be, darting off to the bathroom to do her bidding, Corie grabbed her keys from her bag. She locked Evan in and took the elevator downstairs. When her knock on the superintendent's door produced no response, she followed the sound of men's voices out the back door of the building.

A cold wind whipped through the alley, wrapping Corie's polyester dress around her thighs and cutting through to her skin. Shivering as she stepped around the corner of the row of dumpsters, she found Matt Taylor crouched in front of what had once been her oven, with the building super leaning over his shoulder, shining a flashlight inside the appliance. Corie overlapped the front of her cardigan, clutching it together at her neck. "Mr. Stinson?" Matt instantly pushed to his feet and the superintendent stepped back, momentarily blinding her with his light before he pointed it toward the snow blowing across the asphalt. Corie tried to see what they'd been in such rapt conversation about, but she mostly saw a charred black hole. "Can't it be repaired?"

If she wasn't mistaken, Matt shifted his position to block the bulk of the wind. Not that she would warm up anytime soon, but at least she wouldn't get any colder. It was a thoughtful gesture. "Did you get a hot dinner?" he asked, forgoing any sort of greeting and *not* answering her question.

Corie nodded. She was more interested in what the two men had been discussing than the temperature of the nighttime air or the condition of her stomach. "Evan and I ate at the diner. Does this mean the oven can't be fixed?" She dropped her gaze from Matt's steady dark gaze to Mr. Stinson's disconcerting frown. "Do I have to pay for a new one?"

While she was calculating how many extra shifts she'd

have to pick up to pay for a new appliance, Mr. Stinson cleared his throat. That didn't bode well. He rubbed his hand over the top of his balding head, then stepped back to gesture to the space between the dumpster and recycling bin. "Does your son like to play with matches?"

"Excuse me?" Obeying the unspoken summons, Corie scooted around Matt and peeked into the hidden nook.

In a circle of scorched asphalt where the snow had melted away sat what she assumed was her discarded iron skillet. A black stain of soot climbed the brick wall above it and surrounded the milk carton that had melted into a flat plank and sat in a pile of ash in the pan. More surviving bits of charred debris lay scattered around it, stretching out into the surrounding snow like bony fingers, as if someone had kicked snow onto the flames to put them out. She'd like to think this was a homeless person's fire that had gotten out of hand. But the fearful suspicion crawling up her spine told her that was just wishful thinking.

Corie hugged herself impossibly tighter, automatically defending her son—automatically throwing up every defensive barrier she possessed against the nightmares of her past. Another fire. Two in two days. Her voice came out brittle and sharp. "What are you implying?"

Matt adjusted his knit cap over his ears as if he was making conversation about the weather. "I found a chemical residue coating both of the heating elements in the oven. I found the same gelatinous residue inside the lip of the milk carton."

"Why are you...?" Matt still wore his KCFD uniform and insulated jacket. He must have just come from work. Or maybe he was still on the clock. Corie backed away into the deeper snow across the alley, keeping both men in view. "Are you investigating me?"

Wally raised his gloved hands in a placating gesture. "Has your son been alone in the apartment today?"

Even worse.

"You're investigating Evan?" She shook her head, all her mama bear defensiveness welling inside her and making her shout. "He was at school or with me. All day long—until we got home a few minutes ago. I saw my oven was missing and came down to ask you about it. He's upstairs right now, getting ready for bed. But you're not going to interrogate him. He's a child. An innocent child."

Matt's tone remained calm, his stance annoyingly unaffected by her losing it like this. "I'm not accusing Evan of setting these fires with any malicious intent."

Semantics. An accusation was an accusation.

She glared at the building super. "*He* is."

Chapter Four

Katie Norwell remembered the flames shooting up into the night sky as Kenny torched their first home. A wailing toddler squirmed in her arms and tears streamed from her eyes to mingle with the blood at the corner of her mouth while her monster of a husband pinned her in front of him, her upper arms almost numb with the pinch of his grip.

As he forced her to watch his handiwork, Katie felt her entire future going up in flames. Kenny, on the other hand, seemed to be getting off on the destruction of the small house she had worked so hard to decorate and turn into a family home. "Insurance will pay for a bigger, brand-new home, more befitting my new position with the Corboni family."

She didn't bother arguing that she preferred history and character over modern ostentation. She didn't bother threatening to report his crime—unless she had a death wish. She was trapped, and he knew it. He smacked his lips as he whispered against her ear. "You're lucky I let you bring the boy out."

He didn't mean he'd done her a favor by letting her save their son. Danny would always be Kenny's prized possession. He meant she was lucky that he'd let her live.

"Corie?"

She snapped out of the memory at the firm, low-pitched call of her name.

Not Katie. She was Corie now.

That flash of memory belonged to the past. The wall of Matt Taylor standing in front of her, his dark eyes creased with concern, belonged to the present.

She rapidly blinked her surroundings into focus and gathered her thoughts. The remnants of two fires. Snow. Cold. She needed her coat. Kansas City. No Kenny. Bald man. Big man.

Corie tilted her gaze up to Matt's angular, darkly stubbled face.

He thought Evan had set these two small fires.

He didn't know what a real arsonist could do.

The hardness around his eyes softened when he sensed she recognized him and could be reasoned with again. "I don't mean Evan any harm. And I won't jump to any conclusions. I promise," Matt stated, making Mr. Stinson grumble about being accused of something himself and turning away. "I want the facts first."

"The facts are my son didn't set these fires." There was something about Matt's stoic demeanor that calmed her enough to speak rationally again. "Why would you think that?"

"Several things about them make me suspicious," Matt explained. Although she was certain he was wondering why she'd blown up like that, he was too polite to mention it. Or maybe her reaction made it look like she was hiding something. The hell of it was she was hiding a lot. "I asked Mr. Stinson if I could examine them. The signatures are too similar for me to think they were set by two different perps. The residue is what dripped into the pan and set your son's pizza on fire. The whole oven was primed to burn. If the detector hadn't gone off—if I hadn't smelled the smoke…"

She'd had nothing to put it out with beyond depriving the flames of oxygen. And she'd opened a window. This could have been a disaster. But surely not… There was no way this could be anything but a horrid coincidence, right? A chemical? The unfamiliar smell in her kitchen? A different sort of panic threatened to sink its talons into her. She stepped around Matt to confront the older man. "Mr. Stinson, was anyone besides you in my apartment today?"

"Just to move the oven out," he groused, clearly feeling underappreciated and defensive now that he was no longer the one asking questions. "I fixed the outlet, and Jeff helped me move the oven out on a dolly."

"Jeff? Who's Jeff?" She tried to picture the retired gentleman who'd fixed her garbage disposal last Thanksgiving when Wally had visited his daughter in Ohio. "I thought Phil somebody helped you."

"Phil remarried and moved to Arizona with his new wife. You probably don't know that because you're not around much," he added, as though working two jobs and spending her free time with her son were crimes instead of choices. "Jeff moved in about a month ago. Gets reduced rent as my new part-timer. He lives in the apartment right under yours—612. We were in and out of your place in half an hour."

Shouldn't that make her feel better, knowing no one had been in her apartment who couldn't be accounted for? Of course, she'd feel a lot better if she actually knew who this Jeff person was and could put a face to the name. There had to be another explanation for the fires, beyond the one that scared her more than anything else. She and

Evan were safe. She had no proof that her past had caught up with them.

So, why did she feel like someone *had* violated her sanctuary?

Her shiver had nothing to do with the cold.

Matt was still calmly explaining his concerns in that deep, resonant voice. "According to my fire captain, it's a homemade fire starter usually used in vandalism. Spray or brush the flammable substance over the heating elements and crank the temperature until it ignites. Or drop a match into a milk jug filled with the incendiary compound."

She knew what he was implying. But he was wrong. Evan had been too young to know anything about his father's line of work—an arsonist for hire. All he remembered about Kenny Norwell was the yelling and the fist that had shattered her cheekbone when she picked up her toddler and drove away with nothing but the clothes on their backs. There were no tender memories—nothing but the fires and the hospital and the running and hiding until the rest of Kenny's crimes finally caught up with him. Once she'd given her testimony and the trial and sentencing were over, Katie Norwell had secured full custody of her son, cleared out her savings and sold her car, and gone to the judge to start a new life as Corie McGuire.

Logically, she knew that Matt had no idea about her past or Kenny's expertise—he wasn't making that connection. And she knew genetics didn't make Evan a firebug like his father had been. This had to be a sick joke. Yes, her son was obsessed with dragons. But that was a coping mechanism—to his child's brain, dragons were the strongest, most unbeatable creatures ever devised. A dragon would protect him against the monsters. A dragon controlled the flames—he wasn't consumed by them. Evan could not be fascinated by fire—she couldn't go through that kind of terror again. "You think Evan is responsible? He's eight years old. He doesn't know about flammable compounds, and he would never do anything risky like that to put himself in danger." She knew kids could be curious, but she also knew her son. In some ways, he was all sweet little child—but in one way, he was mature and protective beyond his years. "Evan would never do anything to put *me* in danger."

"I'm not accusing your son of anything malicious," Mr. Stinson insisted. "But part of my job is to make sure the tenants of this building stay safe. I know boys will be boys. And you can find out about anything on the internet these days."

"No." She was as emphatic as the chill in the air. "Evan did not set these fires."

Clearly both men believed they'd been deliberately set. Clearly, both men blamed her son. Both men were wrong.

Matt took a step toward her, and Corie flinched away. She glared up at him, and he retreated a step. His voice dropped to a husky timbre, probably meant to ease the import of whatever he was about to say. "Sometimes kids experiment with things that get out of hand and are more dangerous than they thought they would be. I've done some counseling with other kids who've pulled the fire alarm at school, for example. The fire department will go in and sit with the student and explain the importance of respecting their own safety and the safety of others—how answering false alarms could take us away from someone who truly needs our help."

She shoved a lock of loose hair behind her ear and held it there, creating another barrier between her and the world that wanted to attack the person she held most dear. "I'm familiar with that program. We've had firefighters come to our school and give that same talk." She glanced at the ruined oven and charred bricks. "But you're accusing my son of arson, not pulling a fire alarm on a dare or on a lark. Evan might have put a pizza in the oven, but he did not do this."

Matt glanced over at Mr. Stinson. The older man shrugged, as though he was biting his tongue on another possibility.

Corie saved him the trouble. "*I* didn't start that fire, either." She tipped her chin up to Matt, wondering if his concern was professional or personal, and wondering why the answer mattered to her. "My son doesn't need counseling. If these are arson fires, then someone else is responsible." She included the super in her warning. "You've had a break-in in this building, and you need to step up security."

Wally Stinson clutched his coat in a dramatic gesture. "You think someone broke into this building and I don't know about it?"

Someone who'd washed his hands at her kitchen sink and wore a citrusy cologne.

Someone who shouldn't even know that Corie and Evan McGuire existed.

Suddenly, the wintry chill poured into her veins, chilling her from the inside out. "I have to go." She backed toward the door to the building. She needed to see her son. Now. "I'll pay for the stupid oven and clean up that mess myself."

"Mrs. McGuire, that's not what I'm saying," Mr. Stinson started. "You'll still get a new oven. I just wanted to make sure nothing else is gonna get damaged…"

Corie swiped her key and opened the door, hearing no more.

She hurried to the elevator. The doors opened the moment she pushed the call button. She had her finger on the seventh-floor button, and the doors were closing, when a big hand grabbed the door and pushed it open again.

Corie yelped and darted to the back of the elevator as Matt Taylor filled the opening. "I'm sorry."

"Sorry." She echoed his apology, hating that she'd screamed at her neighbor, who'd been nothing but kind to her and Evan. Until tonight. And even then, he'd been cautious in explaining his suspicions about her son playing with fire.

He stepped inside, sliding to the far corner of the elevator as the doors closed. As if a few feet of distance could make him any less imposing, or the scent of the cold, fresh air wafting off his uniform and jacket were any less enticing.

"I'm sorry," he apologized again. He pulled his stocking cap from his head and worked it between his hands before flattening his back against the side wall and adding a few extra inches of space between them. His gaze dropped to the death grip she held on the railing before those coffee-brown eyes settled on her wary, wide-eyed stare. "I know I'm a big, scary guy. I just wanted you to stop for a second and talk to me. Help me understand why you're upset—why you needed to run away."

They passed the second floor before she realized he was doing his damnedest to make himself as nonthreatening as possible. Knowing he didn't deserve to be judged by Kenny Norwell's standards, Corie made a conscious effort to loosen her grip on the railing. She blinked, trying not to look so much like prey being eyed by a predator. "First, you are a big guy, yes. But you're not scary, Matt. You're gentle and kind, from what I can tell. You startled me, that's all. I'm...more skittish than the average woman. I own that."

"Why?"

His question surprised her. Most people politely kept their distance or dismissed her entirely when she went into escape mode. "There are no gray areas for you, are there? You have a question, you ask it. You see a thing that needs to be done, you do it." He waited. The elevator slowed as she hugged her arms around herself and gave him the briefest explanation possible. "My marriage to Evan's father was not a good one. I'm overly cautious around men as a result."

"He hurt you?"

"Kenny Norwell hurt a lot of people." The elevator doors opened, and Corie hurried down the hallway, aware that Matt was following her—and equally aware that he'd shortened his stride to maintain his distance. She appreciated his thoughtfulness, hated that she projected the air of a woman who needed that kind of kid-glove treatment and was rattled enough by the conversation in the alley that she unlocked her door and headed inside without looking back. "Excuse me. I need to see with my own eyes that Evan is okay."

"Why wouldn't he be—?" She closed the door on his question and quickly threw the dead bolt behind her. Her breath rushed out on a sigh full of regret as much as relief.

She didn't want to hurt Matt, but she was more used to guarding herself than being open, more used to being afraid than trusting. Corie listened for the sound of his key in his door before she fixed a smile on her face and headed back to Evan's room.

Peeking inside the doorway, she found him busy building his fortress again. "Hey, little man. Did you brush your teeth?"

Evan glanced up from his work to roll his eyes with the exhausted look of the downtrodden masses that only a small boy who'd lost precious playtime could manage. "For two whole minutes. It took forever."

Corie smiled, relieved to see he was fine, happy to hear

his dramatic personality hadn't dimmed one iota and embarrassed to admit she owed the man across the hall an apology. "Get your book and climb under the covers. I need to talk to Mr. Taylor for a couple of minutes. I'll be right back."

"Okay. Tell Matt I said hi. And ask if he needs me to use his watch again. Maybe I could borrow it for school when we talk about technology." She arched an eyebrow and gave him the mom look. "Okay. Don't ask. I don't need a watch."

Oh, the drama. "To bed, mister."

"Yes, ma'am."

Once Evan was in bed and thumbing through the pages of his book, Corie slipped across the hall and knocked softly on Matt's door.

She curled her toes inside her sensible shoes, bracing herself for the door to swing open and the big man to suddenly fill the opening again. But he must have seen her through the peephole, because the door opened slowly and Matt leaned a shoulder against the door frame, trying and failing to look less imposing, and pleasing her all the more for making the effort.

He'd taken off his jacket and cap, rolled up the sleeves of his black uniform shirt and loosened a couple of buttons that gave her a tantalizing glimpse of another one of those T-shirts that hugged his muscular body so well. "Evan okay?"

"Yeah." Corie fiddled with the buttons of her own sweater, feeling an unfamiliar stab of heat. She buried her hands in the pockets of her cardigan, hoping she hadn't looked like she was imagining undoing the rest of those buttons on his shirt. "Are you certain someone deliberately sabotaged my oven?"

Not the way she'd meant to start that apology.

But Matt didn't seem to mind. He nodded, one curt, certain nod that made her shiver again. "The fire in the alley was also deliberately set."

Just rip off the bandage and tell him.

"My ex-husband… He went to prison for arson—insurance fraud and witness intimidation. Sneaking into my apartment to destroy an appliance or tamper with a plug is the kind of thing he would have done…to harass me. To frighten me. He couldn't grasp that I wanted to end the marriage and sue for full custody of Evan." Matt's dark eyes never wavered from hers. He knew there was more to her story, but he didn't push her to spit it out. He waited patiently until she took in a deep breath and could say it. "My marriage was a lifetime ago. Kenny has spent most of the last six years in prison. He doesn't know where we live. He doesn't know his son. He doesn't know me. Not anymore."

She hugged her arms around her waist again, the momentary heat she'd felt fading as the past swept in. "I legally changed our names. Cut all ties to where we used to live. There's no way he could find me. He can't be responsible for this." She paused to take in the scope of his broad, inviting chest, wondering what he'd do if she threw herself against him. Wondering why the arms of a man—of Matt Taylor—seemed like refuge to her tonight. She hugged her sweater more tightly around herself instead, feeling it was a poor substitute for the heat and strength she could see in him. "Those two fires make me think the impossible. They make me worry." Corie pressed her fingers to her forehead, rubbing at the tension headache twisting there. "I want there to be another explanation besides Kenny tormenting us."

"If there is, I'll find it." Matt straightened to his full

height but drifted back a step into his apartment. "Do I remind you of him?"

"Of Kenny?" Honestly, the only similarity that popped into her head was that they were both men. And Kenny hadn't even been very good at that. "No." She'd just confessed to making the stellar choice of marrying an abusive loser who set fires for a living and not being the woman Matt thought she was—and he was worried about scaring her? "You're half a foot taller than he is." And though they were both well-built men with dark hair, there was a difference about their brown eyes she wasn't sure she could explain. "His eyes are like a cold, empty void, and yours are…warm. Like a steaming cup of coffee." She allowed herself a few seconds to appreciate the heat shining from his eyes before shrugging off that fanciful notion. "Most importantly, your personalities are different. Kenny would never care that I was afraid of him. He wouldn't give me a chance to explain or defend myself. And he certainly would never apologize for startling me like you did."

Matt released a slow breath and nodded. "I can be pretty quiet. It's spooky when I don't say much."

"Spooky? Who told you that?"

"My brother Alex. And a woman I once dated."

"Well, Alex and what's-her-face are wrong. I think you just wait until you have the right thing to say." Although she could easily imagine Matt being a big, brooding presence if he ever got ticked off, he'd never shown her that side of him. "I bet there's a lot of thinking and decision making going on inside that head before you ever say a word. Maybe you're a little shy. And if that's so, I think it's sweet." She quickly put up her hand in apology. "And before you argue with me, *sweet* is a good thing."

"That's what my grandma says. If a woman calls one of us sweet, not to complain."

"I like your grandmother."

"She's one of a kind." The line of his mouth softened in what she hoped was his version of a smile.

The tension inside her skull eased a little. She liked being on good terms with Matt. She should end this conversation while she was ahead. She thumbed over her shoulder across the hall. "I'd better get inside. I promised Evan a bedtime story. We both have school in the morning, so…"

"Good night."

"Good night, Matt."

"Corie." She'd unlocked her door and pushed it partway open, but somehow he managed to stop her without touching her, without startling her. Corie turned as he braced one hand on the door frame beside her head, reversing their positions from a moment ago. "If I ever do anything that reminds you of your ex, you'll tell me, right? You won't just put up with it because you're a nice lady or you're worried about hurting my feelings or you think the truth will trigger my temper. It won't. I promise. You'll tell me to back off if I scare you?"

Kenny had rarely given her the option of pointing out when he was hurting or frightening her. If anything, he enjoyed it when she'd voiced her fears. It only made him want to torment her more, it seemed. Kenny had always needed to prove his strength, his power—and when the outside world hadn't let him be everything he wanted, he exerted that dominance over her. But Matt Taylor was a different sort of man than her ex had been. He knew he was strong, but he worked hard to play down his physicality instead of shoving it in her face. He was a little awkward, a little gruff—but he seemed like such a good man. A good neighbor. Maybe even a good friend. If she'd let him be.

Corie considered the earnestness of his request, then surprised herself almost as much as it must have surprised

Matt when she reached for his hand down at his side and squeezed his fingers. "I will."

His hand was callused and warm and infinitely gentle as he folded his fingers around hers and squeezed back. "And I'll tell you the next time I investigate anything suspicious that relates to you or Evan."

She offered him an apologetic smile. "I'm super protective of my son. I overreacted."

"No. I overstepped my authority. Thought I recognized someone acting out the way I once did."

"You acted out?"

He rubbed the pad of his thumb across her knuckles in a gentle caress, but which of them he was soothing, she couldn't be sure, because the seriousness of his expression didn't change. "I started fires when I was a little boy. Younger than Evan, but still…" His grip pulsed lightly around hers. "Had some catastrophic consequences," he added without hinting at what that tragedy might have been. "I thought if Evan was dealing with something like that, I could help. Speak to him from experience."

"You played with fire?" That was an irony she understood far too well. "And yet you became a firefighter."

He nodded. "Atonement."

Atonement. That single raw word spoke volumes yet told her little. This gentle giant was a curious one. His honesty spoke to something deep inside her. His confession, whatever it might mean, lessened the embarrassment and caution she'd felt in revealing some of her own past. Her instinct was to comfort him. Her desire was to know him better. But instinct and desire hadn't served her very well in the past. Her brain told her to run far and fast from this connection she felt with Matt. But her heart was asking for something very different.

He pulled his hand from the door frame and brushed the back of his knuckles across her cheek. Her breath caught at the tender caress. But it wasn't fear of his touch that made her lips part as her skin suffused with heat. "I want you and Evan to be safe."

Corie realized they'd been holding hands this whole time. Their eyes had been locked together, and she hadn't once felt the need to bolt. But maybe she'd be smart to at least walk away. She reached up to pull his fingers from her face and grasped each of his hands between them. "Thank you for caring, Matt. But I got this."

He nodded. "Remember what I said. Be honest with me. And if anything—anyone—makes you afraid again—"

"I'll call 9-1-1 and ask for the firefighter next door."

"You could just call my number. Here." He was the one who was finally strong enough to release their hold on each other to pull his billfold from his back pocket. He handed her a KCFD business card with his name and both his cell and the firehouse numbers on it.

"Lieutenant Taylor. Impressive." She hugged the information to her chest. "Thank you. Good night, Matt."

"Good night, Corie. Tell Evan good-night, too. I'll wait 'til you lock the dead bolt behind you."

Once she'd locked her door, Corie leaned back against it. She smiled when she heard his door close and lock across the hall. Was he always this true to his word? Did Matt show this kind of caring to everyone?

They'd held hands longer than a simple thank-you called for. Corie raised her hand in front of her face and marveled at the sensations of warmth and caring still prickling in her fingers from where Matt's big, callused hand had folded so gently around hers. Then she brushed her fingers across her cheek. She hadn't cared about a man's touch in years. But tonight, she'd actually enjoyed that simple, caring contact. She drew her fingertips across her lips, wondering if his mouth would be equally gentle pressed against hers. Or would his kiss be more demanding, as befitted his size and strength? Her pulse beat with intensified interest, and her body flushed with a long-forgotten warmth. Did she even have it in her to respond to real, raw passion like that anymore? If the memory of Matt's touch still lingered on her skin, what would it feel like if her whole body was wrapped up against his?

The heat she felt deepened and spread through her body, triggering a deliciously female response to sensations she could only imagine. Her womanly responses to men had lain dormant for so long. Once, she'd shut them down to protect at least a part of herself from Kenny, and she'd never felt compelled to resurrect that sweet tingling of normal desire in her breasts and womb. She'd never been brave enough to indulge that silky heaviness that warmed her from the inside out. Matt Taylor wasn't classically handsome, and he had no smooth charm that she could detect. But there was no denying his utter masculinity, or her basic feminine response to all that maleness. He was an unexpected temptation to her rusty hormones. He was interesting. A little mysterious and seriously hot. She was tempted to get to know him better—to do much more than simply hold his hand and share a hushed conversation at her apartment door.

"Mo-om!"

Perfect timing. Evan drew out her name on two syllables, pulling her back to reality and quashing any momentary fantasy she had about Matt. She tucked his card into the pocket of her sweater and pushed away from the door. If she wasn't careful, she was going to develop a crush on the firefighter next door. Maybe she already had.

But she had a family to support, a college degree to earn, and an eight-year-old son who needed story time and some cuddling before he'd go to sleep.

Corie didn't have time to indulge in whatever her hormones or heart were trying to tell her about Matt Taylor.

Chapter Five

After the second rapid knock on his door, Matt pulled his jeans down over his work boots and hurried out of the bedroom, tucking in his insulated undershirt and shrugging on a flannel shirt as he strode through his apartment. "Coming!" he barked.

He peered through the peephole to see which of his brothers had stopped by to tell him to hustle his butt over to Grandma Martha's old condo, where they were converging tonight to continue the remodeling and repair work needed before putting it on the market in the spring or summer. But there was no annoying brother out there. His nostrils flared as he dragged in a steadying breath to tamp down the mix of concern and anticipation surging inside him before he quietly opened the door to the blonde and her young son standing in the hallway.

"What's wrong?" he asked, reading the harried expression on Corie McGuire's face.

She hugged Evan back against her stomach and retreated half a step, possibly rethinking knocking on the Big Bad Wolf's door. "Is this a bad time?"

"For what?" He buttoned his shirt and straightened the collar, waiting for an explanation.

Corie nodded, deciding the reason for being here was more important than whatever second-guessing was playing through her head right now. "I have a big favor to ask you. I don't know if I have the right…" Not an emergency. The wariness in him eased a fraction, and he rolled up his sleeves while Corie spewed out a stream of disconnected sentences. "I got called in to work this evening. One of the girls went home sick. It's a chance to pick up a few extra hours. But it means working until closing, and it's a school night for Evan." She paused for breath. Nope. He still didn't understand what she needed from him. "I know it's impossibly short notice, but I heard you come home from work a few minutes ago, and… I'm not giving you much time to relax, but would you be able to watch Evan for me this evening?"

He needed clarity. Was she in a panic caused by time constraints? Or was he missing something more serious here? He glanced down at Evan and the green, purple and yellow plastic dragon he carried. "Babysit?"

Evan's lips buzzed with a groany sigh as he pushed away from his mother. "I'm not a baby."

The boy was put out, not in distress. This didn't sound too serious. Maybe Corie was uncomfortable asking for a favor. Maybe she was uncomfortable asking *him* for a favor. Maybe she felt like she was out of options and he was the last resort. The poor choice he'd made watching his little brother, Mark, twenty-six years ago had never been repeated. He might not be the fun uncle, but in the years since, he'd been trusted with younger cousins and nieces and nephews, and they'd all survived. In his experience, you kept the kid busy, fed him and put him to bed on time, and he'd never had an issue. If she needed a sitter, he was her man. How could he make this easier for her?

Maybe she wasn't the one he needed to make friends with.

Matt leaned against the door frame and hunched his

posture a tad, turning his focus down to the green-eyed boy and trying to sound like...not the Big Bad Wolf. "Poor choice of words, Ev. My apologies. You and your dragon buddy want to hang out for a while?" He was still looking down when he raised his gaze to Corie's. "His regular sitter isn't available?"

Color blossomed in her cheeks. "Regular? Um... I don't have anyone on speed dial—"

"Usually I go with Mom to the diner," Evan volunteered, innocently unaware of his mother's embarrassment as he matter-of-factly explained their predicament. "But that's when she works the afternoon shift after school. I can only go on Fridays and Saturdays when she closes. She calls me a growly butt in the morning if I stay up too late. And staying up until the diner closes means *too late*."

Understanding dawned. Corie didn't have a regular sitter. They went to school together in the morning, and he went to campus with her when she had classes and to Pearl's Diner when she had to work. And she'd just mentioned the need to pick up extra hours, so paying for an emergency sitter might not be an option for her.

He was trained to handle emergencies—large or about the size of a small eight-year-old boy. Matt dropped his gaze to Evan again. "Can you handle a hammer?"

Evan screwed his lightly freckled face up in a suspicious frown. "I don't know."

Matt held up a finger, warning mother and son not to leave as he dashed into the spare bedroom to pull his toolbox from the closet and retrieve a hammer. He came back to the door and found both mother and son peeking into his apartment, with Corie clinging to Evan's shoulders to keep him from following Matt inside. He wouldn't have minded the boy traipsing along behind him. "Let me show you." Matt knelt in front of Evan, trading the hammer for the dragon, letting the boy feel the weight of the tool and watching how he grabbed it with both hands in the middle. Matt moved Evan's hand to the proper position and demonstrated an easy swing. "Did anybody ever teach you to hold the handle near the end, and not up by the peen?"

"Peen?" Evan giggled, no doubt thinking that was the past tense of another word. Matt had been a boy once, too. "That's not a real word."

"The peen is the heavy metal part of the hammer that you hit the nail with."

"It is? I thought you were talking about..." His mouth rounded with an O of excitement before tilting his face up to Corie. "Mom, can I try? I want to hammer a nail."

Corie frowned. "Are you working on a project? I don't want him to get in your way."

"He won't." Matt stood, firmly grasping the hammer to stop Evan from swinging it. He had a feeling it wouldn't be too hard to keep this kid entertained. "Is it all right if I take him to my grandmother's old apartment a few blocks from here? I planned to meet my brothers to work on renovations. I'll make sure Evan's buckled into the back seat of my truck. I'm a safe driver. I drive the fire engine. Never had an accident."

"You drive the fire engine?" Evan's eager response told her that was about the coolest thing he'd ever heard. Way cooler than even the chance to hammer on something. No way was Corie going to be able to say no without disappointing her son. Or Matt. Besides, there was no need for her to. Everyone else would be showing up at his grandma's apartment with a spouse or fiancée, children and probably a dog. Matt liked the idea of bringing his own sidekick to the party. "Can I drive it?"

"You're a little young for that, bud." Matt eased his no by ruffling his fingers through Evan's soft, staticky hair.

It was funny how some of the longer strands stuck straight out or up. Evan McGuire might be a curious, sheltered kid, but he was all boy. "I'll show you my Lucky 13 truck sometime. You can climb inside, sit behind the wheel. But that's another outing. And we're not going anywhere tonight unless your mom says it's okay."

"Mom, pleee-a-ssse! He drives the fire engine and I can hammer." He hoped the kid went into music, because he could draw a word out across several different notes.

Corie shook her head, looking like she'd already lost the battle. "You're sure he won't be in your way?"

"Positive."

Corie's blond ponytail bobbed across her shoulders as she shook her head, surrendering to the boy jumping up and down between them. "You'll have him home by bedtime?"

"He'll be snoring when you get home from work."

Evan finally stopped his bouncing. "Hey, I don't snore. But, can I, Mom? Please? I want to learn about peens." He beamed a gap-toothed grin, as though saying the word out loud made him want to laugh again. "And fire engines." Evan tugged on Matt's sleeve. "Will you tell me about your fire engine?"

"You bet." Matt tucked the hammer through his belt and rested a hand on Evan's shoulder before he started that bouncing thing again.

Corie tilted her soft green eyes up at Matt, and he couldn't look away. "You'll keep him away from any power tools?"

"Mo-om!"

"My brother Mark is a registered EMT, and my first aid training is current. If he gets hurt, we'll fix him."

"If he gets hurt—?"

"He won't get hurt."

Her soft green eyes rolled heavenward, and he thought he detected the hint of a laugh. "Sometimes I can't tell when you're joking. I have to get used to that dry sense of humor." Matt felt his mouth relaxing into an answering smile. *Getting used to* would require spending more time together. He liked that idea. "Okay. To all of it." She combed her fingers through Evan's hair, trying to neaten it up a tad before she cupped his face in her hands. "Homework done?"

"Yep."

She arched a suspicious eyebrow, and Evan groaned again.

"I still have multiplication tables."

"Run and get your coat and backpack. You'll finish the math before you help Matt and his brothers, okay?"

"Okay." Evan was darting across the hall and tearing through their apartment before Corie finished her question.

Unlike her son's flyaway hair, Corie's hung thick and straight. She brushed a loose strand of it off her cheek and tucked it behind her ear. Matt's fingers tingled with the urge to do the job for her. And linger. And maybe free that ponytail to see how long her hair was when it fell loose and straight. "I hope you know what you're getting into."

Matt curled his hands into his fists and tore his thoughts away from sifting her thick, shiny hair though his fingers. "I think I can handle second grade math."

"Yes, but can you handle a second grader?"

Although he suspected she was teasing him as much as giving fair warning, Matt felt compelled to reassure her. "I'll have help. My grandmother and sisters-in-law are bringing food. There'll be plenty for him to eat. My brother Pike will bring his son. Gideon Jr. is close to Evan's age. He'll be fine."

"Okay. Thank you." Corie seemed pleased with his explanation, if a little overwhelmed by the loving, crowded scene he'd described. "I'll owe you a whole pie for helping me out tonight."

"You'll owe me nothing."

She smiled—a huge, beautiful, bright curve that gave him a glimpse of straight, white teeth and softened the tension around her lips. Didn't she understand that smile was payment enough?

"I'll bring the pie, anyway." When she reached out to squeeze his hand, Matt squeezed back. He loved the feel of her hand in his. Small and soft compared to his big workingman's hands, but strong. With sensible, unadorned nails and the faded stripe of a scar between her thumb and forefinger. Her fingers tightened around his before she released him and backed across the hallway into her apartment. "I'd better get changed. And I won't forget the pie!"

Chapter Six

Three hours later, Matt raised his hands in triumph as he busted through the kitchen wall they were taking down with their fire axes a split second before his younger brother, Mark, broke through the drywall in his section. His older brothers, Alex and Pike, slapped him on the shoulder and congratulated him before razzing Mark.

"That's how you swing an ax." Pike smacked Matt on the shoulder.

Alex agreed. "Told you he'd win."

"Not fair," Mark protested, always ready to prove himself against any of his three older brothers. "Matt's arms are a good two inches longer than mine."

"Why do you think I didn't take that bet?" Alex, the oldest and shortest of the four, teased.

Pike Taylor, the only brother with blond hair, picked up a couple of pieces of Sheetrock and carried them to the trash can in the dining room that was now open to the kitchen, save for the two-by-four framework that was coming down next. "If you don't want to give Matt credit, think of it this way—Alex and I are the real winners because we didn't have to do any of the teardown work." He glanced down at Alex, who was picking up the debris Matt and Mark had created. "Right, Shrimp?"

"Really? Shrimp?" Alex tossed his load in after Pike's. "I always thought it was you and me against the wonder twins."

"Un-uh," Mark reminded him, poking Matt in the chest. "He's two years older than I am. I'm the beloved baby boy. Grandma said so. It's every man for himself in this family."

"Matt!" Evan shot around the corner and skidded to a halt when he saw the four men laughing and ribbing each other. The dragon he carried had sprouted a second set of yellow wings, telling Matt how Evan and his nephew Gideon were staying busy. The boy's wide-eyed gaze settled on the long-handled ax cradled across Matt's shoulders. "Where's your hammer? Are you okay? Did you cut yourself?"

Matt questioned the pale tinge beneath Evan's brown freckles. "I'm fine, bud."

"Do you dragon swear?"

Um, yeah?

"What are you boys arguing about now?" Meghan Taylor, the brothers' adoptive mother, showed nary a wrinkle on her youthful features, except for the amusement crinkling beside her honey-brown eyes, when she appeared behind Evan. She carried a toddler wearing pink, fuzzy pajamas in one arm, and rested her free hand on Evan's shoulder as they peeked around the corner from the bedrooms, where she and their father, Gideon Sr., were corralling Evan, Pike's son, Gideon Jr., and Pike's little girl, Dorie. "Seriously? You two used your regulation axes to take down that wall? It's a good thing that no one lives above or below Martha's apartment with the fuss you four are making."

Matt's gaze zeroed in on Evan's pale features as the boy shrank back against Matt's mother. Had the kid been startled by the pounding and crashing? Did the potential weapon he wielded make the boy think he and Mark had attacked more than the wall? "It's a noisy job, Ev," he explained, lowering the ax to cradle it securely between both hands. "We're all good here." He wasn't sure of the protocol, but he drew a cross over his heart. "I dragon swear."

Mark set his ax in a safe corner and threw up his hands. "Speak for yourself, big guy. Mom, you know these three bullied me into turning this into a race."

"Un-uh." Their mother had heard—and dismissed—that excuse many times over the years. "The axes were probably your idea."

"I told them breaking through the wall like that could be dangerous and wanted no part of it." Pike was the next to offer up an explanation, as he swooped in to pluck Dorie from their mother's arms and blow a raspberry onto his daughter's cheek, making the tiny blonde giggle with delight. Evan tilted his chin up, looking more curious than alarmed by the farting sound and resulting laughter. "Can I help it if they won't listen to reason?"

Matt was pleased to see his mother switch both hands to Evan's shoulders, perhaps sensing the boy's nervousness at being surrounded by all this noise and activity. "How hard did you try?" Meghan asked Pike with a deadpan tone of doubt.

"Not as hard as I did," Alex insisted, tossing more debris into the trash. "That's what sledgehammers are for, I said. But have these three yahoos ever listened to me?"

Their mother shook her head, then turned her soft brown eyes up to Matt. "You're my last hope for a straight answer, son. Why would you all risk someone getting hurt and making all this racket by chopping through walls?"

"The job needed to be done." Matt might have learned that deadpan delivery from his mom. "Since it's an exercise we practice time and again in our firefighter training, I knew we could do it safely."

"And we have a winner." Meghan Taylor bent down and whispered a reassurance against Evan's ear. "I told you they were fine. Matt just beat all his brothers in the wall-chopping competition."

As their mother beamed him a smile, Matt was instantly struck by the reminder of how good it felt to be the one who could make someone he cared about light up like that. Maybe that's why Corie's smile was such a turn-on. It was rare and hard-won. And though he was probably a fool for thinking it, her smile felt like it was a special gift just for him.

While the quiet moment passed between mother and son, there was laughter and a round of applause from their grandmother, Pike's wife, Hope, Alex's wife, Audrey, and Mark's fiancée, Amy, as they joined them. The younger women were supposed to be painting the walls and trim in the living room. But the "Yay, Matt!" from Evan was the only voice of approval he needed to hear. Whatever concerns the boy had had when he'd run out to the main room disappeared with Meghan's explanation. When Matt caught Evan's gaze across the room and winked at him, the boy flashed his gap-toothed grin and dashed back into the bedroom to play.

Yep. Making someone smile felt pretty damn special.

As he had many times throughout his life, Matt thanked the fates that had landed him in this family. The competition was real, and occasionally intense, but always full of love. And the ringleader of them all—a shrinking, widowed, eighty-four-year-old woman—quieted the room by simply raising a plastic tub filled with cookies she'd baked to go with the dinner they'd all eaten earlier. Martha Taylor swatted aside Pike's hand as he reached for a cookie.

She wrapped her arthritic fingers around Matt's forearm and held on to him for balance as she stepped around the debris.

"The first snickerdoodle is for our winner," she announced, handing Matt one of her delicious cookies. He promptly stuffed it whole into his mouth while she hugged him around the waist. He dropped a kiss to the top of her snow-white hair before she pulled away and handed an equally delicious cookie to Mark. "And a consolation prize for second place."

"We always try harder." Mark held his cookie up and did a misplaced victory dance before kissing Martha's weathered cheek and hugging her, too. "Thanks, Grandma."

"What about the rest of us?" Alex pouted, drawing his red-haired wife, Audrey, to his side. "I'm starving."

Audrey poked him in the flank. "You had seconds at dinner."

"Yeah, but they weren't cookies."

"Oh, all right," Martha relented, as they'd all known she would. "Time for us all to take a break. Everybody dig in." She wrapped a stack of cookies in a paper napkin and handed them to Pike's shy wife, Hope, who'd been rubbing noses with Dorie and brushing crumbs from Pike's chin. "Take some for Evan and the Gideons."

"I'd be happy to."

"I'll help," Pike offered.

Before they headed down the hallway, Hope swiped her fingers across Pike's lips, even though the crumbs on his face were long gone. When they lingered there a second and Pike's blue eyes heated at the contact, Matt felt a spike of envy. Not because he lusted after his sister-in-law or begrudged his brother his well-earned happiness, but because he wanted that, too—that connection with a

woman who had eyes only for him. He wanted that connection with Corie McGuire.

Only, he wasn't quite sure how to make that happen. Or
if Corie was even interested in him trying.

He was thirty years old and had never been in a serious
relationship. He'd dated. He'd had sex. But nothing had
ever worked out for him. Probably something to do with
being six foot five and what that one blind date his brothers had set him up with had described as *spooky quiet*.
He didn't always have a lot to say and got stuck in his
head sometimes while he thought things through before
he did speak. He lacked Mark's glib sense of humor and
Alex's outgoing personality. Even Pike had a goofy sort
of nerd charm going for him. Matt was just... Matt. Physical. Direct. He'd been a troubled kid who didn't speak for
months after his birth parents' deaths—not until Meghan
and Gideon Taylor had done their patient, loving child-
whisperer thing with him and gotten him to open up about
the tragedy he felt responsible for. And though he'd worked
through his demons, it was still hard for him not to be that
guarded, excessively observant survivor he'd once been.

Yep. A relationship with him probably wasn't for the
faint of heart.

The man who had saved Matt's life when he'd been that
silent little boy, Gideon Taylor Sr., strode into the main
room, sliding his arm around Meghan's waist, unknow-
ingly completing the image that everyone in this family
had a partner except for Matt...and his widowed grandmother. But she'd been blessed to have been married to
their grandfather Sid for more than sixty years, until his
death this past summer. "None of the cookies made it past
those two boys and Pike." His dad pointed to each of his
three remaining sons around the room. "Talk about déjà
vu." But he was grinning. "Ma, you got any more?"

Martha held out the tub for him to help himself to a snickerdoodle. "I'm so fortunate that you're all helping me with this remodeling project. I love how you've opened the kitchen up to the rest of the apartment. Makes me sorry that I had to move." She put up a hand before Gideon could remind her of her health issues and the flight of stairs leading to the front door, which was no longer safe for her to negotiate on her own. "I know it's for the best, and I admit I'm having fun finding the perfect place to put everything in my new home. But do you know how many years I was stuck back in that kitchen cooking, missing out on all the activity out here?"

"We were all in the kitchen with you, Ma." Gideon dropped an arm around her shoulders. "You never missed a thing." She leaned into the kiss he pressed to her temple. "Come on. Let's get back to my grandkids and your great-grands and stay out of harm's way while the boys finish tearing down in here." It wasn't hard for him to reach around Martha and pluck a second cookie to munch on. "And bring these with you so the big boys don't eat them all."

Martha might be in her eighties, but she was quick. She ducked from beneath her son's arm and faced the middle generation of young men who had torn up her kitchen. "But I want to hear about Matthew's young woman."

"Oh?" Gideon and Meghan stopped and turned, both looking at Matt with hope and curiosity. Great. Now his parents would be part of the inquisition, too. "You're seeing someone?" his dad asked.

Matt carried his ax to his toolbox and slipped the protective cover over the sharp blade. Then he picked up a broom and dustpan to attack the powdery drywall dust on the floor, hoping the personal question would just go away.

"Evan's mother," Martha offered when Matt didn't immediately respond.

"We're not *seeing* each other," Matt clarified for his father. "Corie and I are friends."

His brothers and sisters-in-law filled the room with teasing catcalls. His father slowly munched his cookie, his narrowed eyes assessing the full disclosure or lack thereof in Matt's response. Gideon Taylor had earned the silvered hair at his temples after raising the four of them. He knew how to wait out his sons until he got the answer he wanted.

And though Matt had gone back to work, his younger brother, Mark, ignored the shushing from his fiancée and poked the bull. "Tell us what she looks like, Matt."

Matt focused on the muscles in his arms and hands as he worked, trying to ignore his well-meaning family. Sweep. Dump. Sweep some more. But it seemed everyone was waiting for his answer now. "Prettier than you."

"Impossible." Amy swatted Mark's shoulder at that joking remark, but his baby bro wouldn't let the subject drop. Instead, Mark pulled the trash can closer, and he and Alex helped Matt with the cleanup job. "Just trying to get a sense of who's rockin' your world, big brother. Does Evan take after her?"

Although he knew everybody in the room was hanging on the details he wasn't sure he should share, Matt couldn't help but picture his pretty neighbor. "Same mossy-green eyes." He mentally compared her image to Evan—a cautious, curious boy who didn't know whether to be the man of the house or Corie's baby boy. "Corie doesn't have freckles like Evan. Her hair's the color of a ripe wheat field."

Alex paused with the remains of a shattered two-by-four in each hand. "A ripe wheat field? When did you become a poet?"

As Alex stuffed the boards into the trash, Mark continued the interrogation. "Is she the reason you were asking Captain Redding about old-school fire starters?"

Alex pulled out his phone. "That reminds me. I did a rundown on that name you asked me about—Kenneth Norwell. Career criminal with a long rap sheet." As much as he knew mentioning the word *criminal* while talking about Corie and Evan would only make his family more curious to learn about them, Matt mentally logged the information Alex was reading off his phone. "His current address is Jefferson City. Apparently, he didn't move too far from the penitentiary once he got out. He hasn't missed a check-in with his parole officer there—met with him last week. There's no indication of him living or working here in KC."

It was no surprise that their father was going to let mention of a paroled prisoner slide. "Why do you have KCPD checking the status of a paroled prisoner?" Gideon asked. "And why are you talking to Kyle Redding about incendiaries?"

Matt supposed if he had more of a social life, his interest in helping Corie and Evan wouldn't be such big news with his family tonight. "There was an oven fire at Corie's place. I made sure it was out. Another fire the next night in the alley behind the building. Something about them seemed hinky, so I was following up on my hunch."

"Arson?" his father asked. As chief arson investigator for the KCFD, Gideon Taylor Sr. certainly knew his way around a fire—probably better than any of them, except their mother, who was captain at another firehouse.

Matt nodded. "Corie insists that Evan wouldn't mess with anything like that and that he knows all about fire safety. But if it wasn't either of them, then somebody was in their apartment. Coated the heating elements with a flammable substance. Used it again in the alley fire."

Gideon's dark eyes narrowed with suspicion. "I don't like the sound of that."

Amy hugged her arms around her waist and shivered. "Arson fires are about the scariest thing I've ever had to deal with." She looked across the room to Mark, who was already crossing toward her. They'd both barely survived the work of an arsonist this past summer. "I'd still have a home, and Gran and I wouldn't be living with this guy."

Mark hugged her close. "You *like* living with this guy."

"I do." Amy nestled her forehead at the juncture of Mark's neck and shoulder. "And marrying him."

"And marrying him." She reached up to touch his face, and the unbreakable bond the two of them shared gave her the courage to smile before turning to face the rest of them. "So, big, bad Matt rescued Corie from a fire in her kitchen. Is that what all you Taylor boys do? Rescue the women you love?"

Love? Um...

Mark rubbed his hands up and down her arms, still soothing away the nightmare they'd survived. "Red, you said you don't like to be rescued."

"Well, I don't always like it because I'm a stubbornly independent woman, and I believe I can take care of myself," she teased. "But it *is* hot."

She looked to Audrey, who linked her arm with Alex's and nodded. "Super hot. It means the world to know someone's got your back and you can trust him without reservation. It allows us to be as strong as we need to be."

Alex turned and pressed a kiss to her forehead. "That little girl we're adopting will be lucky to have you for her mama."

Why couldn't his family discuss the weather or how much they missed Royals baseball like other, normal Kansas Citians?

Matt loved Amy like a sister and believed Mark had found a treasure, but the woman had no trouble speaking her mind. "Matt's hot. I bet Corie's hot, too."

Mark's cheeks turned a pale shade of pink that matched the embarrassment Matt felt at her compliment. "Could we stop saying hot? Unless you're referring to me?"

"Oh, you know how I like to refer to you, Fire Man."

Although he was grinning, Gideon shook his head as the subtext between the newly engaged couple's banter. "Hello, you two—you have an audience—and children in the next room. Save it for after the wedding."

"Did I miss something? Who's hot?" Meghan reentered the room to stand beside her husband. "Matthew's girl-friend?"

"Mom, no. I don't have a girl… Corie is a friend. I'm just watching Evan while she's at work tonight."

"And investigating some mysterious circumstances sur-rounding her," Gideon added, his tone laced with concern. "Sounds like you're pretty involved to me, son."

"I like to know what I'm dealing with," Matt insisted. "And if Evan has anything to do with those fires, if he's trying to emulate his father or he's crying out for attention because the creep chose a life of crime over him, then—"

"You're the best man to help him." Probably better than anyone here, his mother understood just how far he had come since he'd been the troubled little boy who'd set the fire that had killed his birth parents. "Other than being a little skittish around all of us—and who wouldn't be?—I'm not seeing any indication that he's withdrawn or hid-ing something."

"Evan seems like a pretty cool kid to me," Pike added as he rejoined them. "He's making sure Junior and Dorie stay safe and share their cookies, even though Mom and Dad and Hope have been in there with them most of the evening. And that castle they're building is pretty sweet. The kid's going to be an architect one day."

Or was there something so frightening in his real life that he felt he had to keep building imaginary fortresses to feel safe?

Pike crossed the room to join them in picking up the mess they'd made. "So, we're talking about Evan's mom? Is she the one who finally woke up Matt here?"

Alex helped him move the bank of old cabinets they'd taken apart to the side of the kitchen. "She has hair like a 'ripe wheat field.' Quote, unquote."

"When did you become a poet?" Pike echoed Alex's earlier question. Apparently, Matt's factual description of Corie's hair had revealed something he hadn't intended to. "This sounds serious."

Matt realized he was surrounded on all sides and commanding way too much attention. "Don't any of you have work to do?"

Martha Taylor had an answer for him. "I don't. Certainly, nothing as interesting as this conversation."

"Grandma!"

Fortunately, his mother had always been his strongest ally. "Give it a rest, boys." From the time they'd first met in the foster home where they'd all been living, Matt, Mark, Alex and Pike had been Meghan Taylor's boys. Becoming adults hadn't changed the nickname or the bond. She reached up to cup Matt's cheek and smiled. "I know you've just been waiting for the right one to come along. I'd like to meet Corie sometime. I hope she knows what a treasure you are." Then she added, in a soft whisper for his ears alone, "I hope you know, too." As she pulled away, she added, "And remember, firefighters work as a team. If there is something dangerous around Evan and his mother, you don't take it on alone." Her look encompassed the entire room. "You have allies."

"Yes, ma'am."

Despite the dramatic sigh of disappointment from Grandma Martha, the spotlight on Matt finally faded. The younger women returned to their painting as Gideon walked his wife and mother down the hall to watch the children. Matt and his brothers got to work on the last of the cleanup and prepping the expanded kitchen for the work they were going to do this weekend.

However, Mark, in all his newly engaged happiness, wouldn't let it go. He knocked loose the remaining dangling bits of drywall and tossed the biggest piece at Matt. "They say when the big ones fall, they fall hard."

Matt caught the piece squarely against his chest and shoved it into the trash. "Give it a rest, Mark."

Evan popped in again, his mouth wrinkled with concern as he eyed the dusty residue clinging to Matt's dark flannel shirt. The kid must have some kind of danger radar. Or he was more of a worrywart than anyone his age should be. "Matt, did you fall? Are you hurt?"

As worried about Evan's paranoia as he was glad for the reprieve from Let's Pick Apart Matt's Love Life Night, Matt scooped him up in his arms and rested the boy on his hip. "I'm fine, bud. You know, in many ways, you're lucky you're an only child."

"Huh?"

Matt was already striding from the room. He'd done most of the heavy lifting tonight. Let his annoying brothers handle the rest of the cleanup. "Show me this castle you and Gid are building."

Evan's arm rested lightly on Matt's shoulder, seeming to like being able to look him straight in the eye. "Can I hammer something again?"

Matt paused at the entrance to the hallway and looked back at his brothers. "Sure. I've got a trio of numbskulls you can start with…" Matt veed two fingers toward his eyes, then pointed to Mark, Pike and Alex, indicating he'd be watching them for any more teasing…and would put a stop to it when they didn't have an audience that included an impressionable child or their delicate grandmother. Alex laughed. Pike nodded, conceding that Matt was leaving with the upper hand. Mark threw his hands up in protest, as if affronted. So much love and support. So much a pain in the—

"What's a numbskull?" Evan asked.

Matt shook his head as his brothers laughed behind him. He needed to think about how he was going to explain that one to an eight-year-old.

By the end of another hour, the kitchen was prepped for new cabinets and tile. Paint cans had been sealed, dust had been swept up, his family had given the state of his love life a temporary rest, and Matt was walking Evan down the steps to the sidewalk in front of his grandmother's condo. "This way, bud." Evan kicked up puffs of snow as he shuffled along beside Matt. "I promised your mom I'd have you in bed by nine o'clock, so we'd better hustle."

"I'm not sleepy," he protested through his wide yawn.

Matt bit back his grin. "I know. If you want to close your eyes and rest for a few minutes on the drive home, that'd be okay."

"Can I come help again? Grandma Martha said she'd bake chocolate chip cookies next time. They're my favorite. She said to call her Grandma Martha because I was a nice boy, and I was helping her, even though she's not my real grandma." Since Matt's hands were full with his ax and toolbox, Evan tugged on the sleeve of his coat to stop him. "I don't have a real grandma. Is it okay if I share yours?"

This kid worried way too much about other people's feelings and safety for someone his age. Not for the first time this evening, Matt wondered what events had shaped his young life. Corie had confessed that her ex had *hurt a lot of people*. Anger burned through Matt's blood at the idea that any of that violence might have touched Evan.

"If she said it's okay, then it's fine by me." He set his tools down on the sidewalk beside his truck and lifted Evan into the bed of the pickup so the boy could help him stow his ax and toolbox in the metal cargo box behind the cab.

Matt thought he heard the scrape of footsteps on the sidewalk. But with Evan's boots raising a muffled metallic sound in the bed of his truck, he couldn't isolate the noise. He glanced behind him to see if one of his brothers had followed them out. But the circle of illumination from the streetlamp in front of the old butcher shop was empty. A glance up the block revealed no pedestrians, either. Sometimes these tall brick and limestone buildings lining either side of the street in the City Market district captured sound and reflected it back off the hard surfaces, especially on a clear, cold night like this with little wind to dampen the echoing sounds.

Of course, there were shadows at the fringes of every streetlight and in the alleyways between buildings. And with vehicles parked along the curbs, someone hunched against the cold might not be readily visible. Matt pushed up the edges of his knit cap and trained his ears to try and pinpoint the company he couldn't see. But with Evan rattling Matt's toolbox as the boy insisted on lifting it himself, as well as his ongoing commentary about all things construction and cookie related, it was pretty impossible to hear anything else.

Probably his overtaxed sense of alertness, anyway. If he had heard the last steps of someone scurrying inside a warm building, there wasn't any real need to be concerned. This might once have been a decaying working-class neighborhood, but it had enjoyed a rebirth of tourism and an influx of professionals and young families who both lived and worked closer to the heart of the city. This wasn't a particularly dangerous neighborhood. Getting Evan out of this single-degree weather was probably a more pressing concern.

"Come on, bud." Once Evan had closed the lid and locked it, Matt helped him jump down and climb up into the back seat of his crew cab. Matt buckled him in, then ruffled the bangs that stuck out from beneath Evan's stocking cap. "Did you have fun tonight?"

"I like hammering, but can I use your ax next time?"

"Probably not the ax. It's heavy and it's dangerous. But we'll see about putting a paintbrush in your hands." There was still plenty of work to do on the condo above his late grandfather's butcher shop. Once they finished the remodel, they could sell it for a nice enough price that Grandma Martha could pay off the single-story ranch home she'd moved into that summer. The question was, would Corie be willing to trust Evan with him again? Once he mentioned axes and the fact he'd asked his brother to run a check on Evan's father, she might reconsider. "It'll be up to your mom."

"Cool." The smile Evan flashed was missing two full teeth, but it hit Matt with the same intensity that Corie's smile had.

Good grief. Maybe his family was seeing something in him that Matt hadn't fully admitted yet—he was falling for the family next door—not just the pretty mom whose smile and touch could set him off-kilter, but the little boy who seemed haunted by some of the same shadows Matt remembered from his own early childhood. The McGuires needed him. Or maybe they just needed someone—and he wanted to volunteer for the job.

Matt closed the rear door and stepped out into the street to walk around to the driver's side. But a subtle alarm tickled the back of his neck, and his fingers clutched the door handle without opening it.

He hadn't imagined footsteps. They were in a hurry now, moving away from his location. Punctuated by the slam of a vehicle door, he had to wonder if someone had been watching them. But a quick 360 didn't reveal any spies. Maybe his family's conversation about arson, and Corie's suspicion that someone had been inside her apartment while she'd been at school, were feeding his wary senses.

This wasn't a place where muggings and street crime happened much anymore—and anyone with a lick of sense would think twice about coming after him. Matt could walk the walk when it came to holding his own in a physical confrontation. His firefighter training and lifting weights weren't the only skills he'd honed over the years.

Still, the tickle at his nape was never wrong when it came to fighting fires and the safety of the men and women on his Firehouse 13 team. Something wasn't right. But what he saw as intrusive might just be a curious neighbor, wondering what was going on over the old Taylor Butcher Shop, or why the loner of the Taylor clan, who'd never even brought a date to a family gathering, now had a kid in tow.

With no obvious threat in sight, Matt climbed in and locked the doors. After he started the engine, he cranked the heat and found Evan's curious green eyes watching him in the rearview mirror. "I'm going to let the truck warm up for a few minutes before we go."

Evan pushed up against his seat belt. "Can I use your watch to count how many minutes again?"

"Sure." Matt took his utility watch off his wrist and reached over the seat to show Evan the timer feature. "Now you set it for four minutes. When the alarm goes off, I'll hear it and we'll go."

"Sweet." Evan leaned back in his seat to play with the watch that fascinated him so. "We have twenty-four minutes before I have to be in bed," he announced. "After the truck warms up, we'll have twenty minutes to drive home."

Good math skills. He'd run through his multiplication problems in a matter of minutes, and gotten every answer right, before Matt gave him the okay to go in and play with Gideon Jr. "I'll get you home in eighteen."

"We'll have to run up the stairs if we only have two minutes."

"I'll race you." As soon as the watch beeped, Matt pulled out of his parking space. There was little traffic at this hour, and he quickly passed two blocks before stopping at the red light. Matt found Evan watching him in the mirror again. "Will there be someone at the diner to walk your mom to her car when she gets off work?"

"We don't have a car."

His guileless pronouncement rekindled Matt's suspicions. "Then how does she get to school and work and then come home?"

"The way we always do. We walk. Or when it's cold like this, we'll walk to the bus stop. It's not that far."

But it was late at night, she was a woman and she was alone. "Does she ever let you walk that far by yourself?"

"Un-uh."

"Then she shouldn't, either." Movement in the street behind him shifted his attention from Evan. A nondescript van pulled out of a parking space and drove up behind

Matt's truck. The van wasn't speeding. But with its head-lights blinding him in every mirror, he couldn't get a look at the driver, either. "Hey, bud. Why don't you set the timer for fifteen minutes. You time me to see if we get home before it beeps."

Matt was glad to see Evan concentrating on the watch, telling him the boy wasn't alarmed by the vehicle behind them. But he was an eight-year-old boy—he shouldn't have to be worried about strange coincidences and sixth senses warning him of danger. That was Matt's job. On impulse, he turned right before the light changed. When the van turned the corner behind him, Matt pulled his phone from his coat pocket and punched in a familiar number.

His brother Mark picked up on the second ring. "Did you miss me?"

"Do you mind stopping by my place on your way home?"

"No." Every bit of humor left Mark's tone. "What's up?"

Matt took another random corner, and the van followed. The warning at the nape of his neck couldn't be ignored. "I'm not sure. But I'd feel better if I had some backup."

Chapter Seven

"Hey, blondie."

"Come on, sugar—you know you miss us."

Great. Now the two men at the back of the bus were blowing kisses at her.

After that "courtesy" message her attorney's office in St. Louis had left on her phone tonight, she sure as hell didn't need this.

"As a courtesy, we are notifying all our clients that Owenson, Marsden & Heath may have had a breach in security subsequent to an electrical fire in our offices, in which several computers and most of our files were destroyed. While we are making every effort to ensure confidentiality while we sort through the remains of both paper and digital records, we are still in the process of accounting for all our data. Rest assured, backup systems were in place, and we are able to continue working on all of your current or upcoming needs. We are happy to report that Mr. Heath is at home now, recovering from injuries sustained in the fire. Our temporary offices will be housed at..."

She hadn't listened to the rest of the voice mail. Current and upcoming needs had nothing to do with her. Her only legal concerns were in the past. But a breach in security? Missing records? Her attorney injured in a fire?

To Corie, that meant only one thing. Kenny.

Was he responsible for that fire? Had he gotten access to her new identity and other personal records Mr. Heath had arranged for her? Had he burned the place down to cover up evidence that he had been in St. Louis? If he could track down her attorney, could he also find her here in Kansas City?

"Whatchya thinkin' about, sugar? Which one of us you'd like to get to know better first?"

Corie hugged her backpack tightly to her chest and stared at her hunkered reflection in the bus window and at the city lights that seemed to float past as she made her way home after closing the diner. Normally she found the ride home relaxing, and she enjoyed seeing parts of the city still decorated for Christmas or New Year's, especially when the lights reflected off the snow. But tonight, the world outside was a blur. Her pulse thundered in her ears, drowning out any fun or peaceful thoughts. And she was shivering, despite her coat and gloves and the bus's heater blowing across her feet.

She fought to keep Kenny's verbal abuse from playing in her head. *"What the hell's a study group? You're not going anywhere. You're good for only two things. If you weren't so damn frigid, it'd be three. You make me look good and you take care of my baby. Understand?"* The words might be different, but the tone was the same. Her reaction was, too.

This is not Kenny, Corie told herself, forcing herself to take deep, calming breaths. *There is no proof that he set that fire in St. Louis and found out about your new life. Your world isn't burning down around you.* The two men hassling her tonight weren't Kenny. Even at his worst, Kenny had been all about appearances—the right look, the right woman, associating with people of money and power. *Those two losers are just a couple of drunks who hap-*

pened to get on your bus. You have value, Corie. You are strong. Think of the positives. Evan is safe. You are safe.

She repeated the mantra again and again, just like her therapist had advised her. *Evan is safe. You are safe.*

Her feet throbbed with the length of her day at school and the long night at the diner. But tips had been good, she'd timed it just right so that she didn't have to wait outside in the cold for the bus to arrive and she'd had enough time on her last break to get on her laptop and track down the last source for the paper she was writing for her English language learners class. Except for that phone call and those two yahoos in the back, nights like this were all worth it, right?

She'd made the mistake of making eye contact with Jordan and Harve when they'd first stumbled onto the bus at the stop after hers. Apparently, a brief glance had been invitation enough for the two drunks to slide into the seats next to and across the aisle from her, introduce themselves and start hitting on her. At first, she'd thought they might try to rob her when Jordan had put his hands on the backpack in her lap and leaned into her. But then Harve had grabbed his crotch and run his tongue around his chapped lips, and she realized they weren't after money or her computer.

"Mr. Lee?" She'd wasted no time calling out to the fatherly Black man driving the bus. He'd ordered the two booze-scented men—one with scraggly red peach fuzz on his jaw that blended into the tattoos on his neck, and the other sporting a chest-length beard that had a broken pretzel stuck in it—to move, or he'd call the police and drop them off at the next stop.

With much vocal protest and a stumble onto a seat with a startled young man whose earbuds had tuned them out up to that intrusion, they'd made their way to the back of the bus, where they continued to be a nuisance to anyone with a pair of boobs between the ages of eighteen and fifty. And since Corie was currently the only passenger left who fit that description tonight, she was bearing the brunt of their lewd noises and whispered innuendoes.

"Just one drink, sugar?" That would be Harve, with the snack stuck in his facial hair. "We could have a nightcap at your place."

Once upon a time, when she was young and naive and believed every man could be a hero, she would have turned to Kenny to make them stop. And no doubt, with his resources and criminal connections, he would have. But that was before she realized he'd be protecting his property—not her feelings of fear or discomfort. Kenny would have made a threat or punched one of those rummies or tracked them down and torched their car to make the point that nobody embarrassed him by putting a move on the woman—or anything else—he considered his.

Tonight, she had to deal with this kind of crap on her own.

Or find an ally she could actually trust to have her best interests at heart.

Corie met the driver's gaze in his rearview mirror and silently pleaded for his help. "Knock it off!" he ordered, quieting the pair temporarily. "Sorry about that, Ms. Corie."

"Corie? Your name's Corie?"

"Corie what, sugar?"

The driver grumbled a curse and shook his head, realizing too late that he'd just given those two losers more information about her. Although she offered him a reassuring smile, she hoped Mr. Lee didn't repeat his threat about putting them off at the next stop because the next stop was hers. At least, here on the bus, she had the relative safety of the other passengers and driver to protect her—or at least bear witness to the harassment if anything should happen to her. Corie still had a cold walk back to her apartment once she stepped off this bus. She didn't relish being alone at night for the block and a half it would take her to get safely inside the locked foyer of her building if those men decided to follow her.

As the bus turned onto Wyandotte and drove up the hill toward her stop, Corie peeled off her gloves and stuffed them into her coat pockets. Potential frostbite would take a back seat to security tonight. Then she dug into her bag and pulled out her cell phone and pepper spray, squeezing one in each hand. She might not be able to outmuscle or outrun Jordan and Harve if they should decide to follow her and prolong this torture, but she could outthink them. She could plan ahead and give herself options for escape. Then she shrugged her backpack onto her shoulders and prepared to book it as fast as she could to her building. If there was one thing she'd learned from her years with Kenny, it was to be prepared for any-and everything.

And to do whatever was necessary to keep herself and Evan safe.

Moving quickly, she slid out of her seat and hurried down the aisle to sit in the very first seat beside the stairs. She intended to be down the steps and out the door just as soon as it opened.

"Whoa. Slow down, sugar. We'll walk you home." Jordan lurched to his feet, with Harve shuffling after him.

"Sit down," Carl Lee ordered when he saw them coming down the aisle behind her. "This isn't your stop." He glanced across the aisle and whispered to Corie, "You hustle on out of here the moment I stop. I'll try to keep them inside."

Harve snickered and plopped down in the spot behind

Corie, dangling his arm over the top of her seat. "Maybe we need some fresh air, old man." She jerked away when his fingers brushed against her ponytail. "Besides, we wouldn't want our little woman walking home by herself so late now, would we?"

Corie practically threw herself against the partition in front of her seat and whirled around to tell the creep to back off. "I am *not* your little woman, and I *don't* need you to walk me home."

Mistake! She'd engaged them. Now they saw her response as a personal invitation to increase their taunts. "Ooh, she's feistier than I thought she was going to be." Jordan grinned from ear to ear.

"I like 'em feisty." Harve rose to his feet, and his long beard fell over the top of her seat. How she'd dearly love to yank it as hard as she could. Maybe he'd bite his tongue when his chin hit the seat, and that would shut him up.

Both men laughed. Mr. Lee muttered something under his breath and pulled his radio from the dash. Was he going to report these two? Call the police?

She turned her back to the men as the brakes hissed and the bus began to slow. She tapped 9-1-1 into her own phone and prepared to push the call button if she had to.

Then she peered through the glass and saw the tall man standing beneath the shell of the bus stop. Silhouetted against the fluorescent lights, his height and bulk were emphasized by the insulated winter coat he wore. Like a beacon in the midst of a stormy sea, Matt Taylor's broad shoulders and immovable presence showed her the way to the safe harbor she needed.

Relief, gratitude beyond measure and maybe even anticipation surged through her veins and she shot to her feet. Bless his big, bad self for showing up and being the friend she needed right now.

"Matt!" Corie was down the stairs and out the door the moment it opened.

Without any hesitation or warning, she launched herself at him. She shoved her phone and pepper spray into her pockets and grabbed the collar of his coat with both fists, pulling him toward her as she stretched up on tiptoe and pushed her lips against his. His startled breath didn't surprise her—she hadn't given him much of a heads-up. But she didn't expect his firm mouth to slide over hers in answer to her desperate ploy. She didn't expect the rasp of his late-night beard stubble to tease her skin with its own subtle caress. She didn't expect the frisson of heat that tingled across her lips and shocked much-needed warmth into her blood when his mouth settled over hers in a brief, potent kiss.

The kiss was longer than she intended, shorter than she wanted, and left the ground shaking beneath her feet as she dropped to her heels. Matt's lips chased after hers as gravity broke the contact between them. And Corie was far too tempted to palm the back of the black stocking cap he wore and guide his mouth right back to where she wanted it.

But the bus driver's warning to the men behind her reminded her that throwing herself at Matt was a survival tactic, not a mutual routine she had any right to pursue. She swallowed her shock and forced herself to continue the charade, although she could only manage a breathless whisper. "Hi, sweetheart."

"Sweetheart?" He rubbed his hands up and down her arms and his face hovered above hers, frowning in confusion until he heard Harve and Jordan's harassment.

"Hey, sugar, wait for us." The bearded man scrambled to the stairs behind her. "Don't you close these doors, old man."

"You said we'd have smooth sailin' with her, Harve. If I have to mess with that guy, then I want extra—"

"Shut up, Jordy."

Corie didn't need to explain her overly friendly greeting.

Matt's expression was cold, fierce and eerily silent as he lifted his gaze and looked over the top of her head to meet Jordan and Harve. He pried Corie's hands from the front of his coat and moved around her. Straightening to his towering height, he didn't have to say a word to stop the two men in their tracks.

Jordan toppled onto the curb in his haste to back away from the imposing welcome. Harve grabbed the sleeve of Jordan's coat and tugged him to his feet and up the stairs. "Get on back here, Jordy. This isn't our stop, after all." His dark eyes rounded like shiny black beetles as he nodded to Corie. "We'll be seeing you, Ms. Corie."

Jordan puckered his lips. "Bye-bye, sugar."

Just as Corie flinched back half a step at that final unwanted gesture, Matt strode forward. He boarded the bus, each step a purposeful stride. He stopped beside the driver and watched Harve and Jordan beat a hasty retreat down the aisle, all the way to their seats at the back. Then Matt lifted his coat to pull out his billfold and hand a business card to Mr. Lee. "You see those two hassling Corie again, you call me."

"Kansas City's Bravest." Carl took the card and nodded his ready agreement. "Yes, sir. You all be safe now."

"Good night, Mr. Lee," Corie called up to him as Matt rejoined her. "Thank you."

"Good night, Ms. Corie. Mr. Taylor." The Black man nodded and closed the door. With the hum of the motor grinding into gear, the bus pulled away.

A chill from the damp, wintry air seeped through the

wool of her coat and Corie hugged her arms around her waist. But the cold temperature wasn't the only thing that made her shiver. Harve and Jordan pressed their faces to the back windows, their eyes only leaving her when the two high-fived each other over the top of the seat.

She startled at Matt's touch and the sudden infusion of heat as he draped his arm around her shoulders and tucked her to his side. Playing his part of half a couple even better than she was playing hers, he was also watching the two men until the lights from the bus stop and streetlamp could no longer pierce the windows and her tormenters were swallowed up into the shadows.

Corie stood there, leaning into Matt's warmth long enough for her to realize that she hadn't put her gloves back on. Though stiff with cold, her fingers were fisted into the padded nylon of his black insulated jacket, clinging to him as though she had every right to attach herself to him for comfort or use him as a human heating pad. Shaking off those survival instincts that seemed to have her continually reaching for him, Corie released her grip and stepped away. She dug her gloves out of her pockets and slipped them back on. "I'm sorry about that kiss. I just…" She glanced down the street where the bus had merged into late-night traffic, then tilted her face to Matt's. "I needed them to stop. I suspected if they thought I was *with* you… It worked. Thank you."

He didn't seem to hear her apology. Or care that she'd taken advantage of his willingness to help her.

He didn't have anyone with him, either.

Where was Evan? Kenny had found them!

Corie tamped down the flare of panic that grabbed hold whenever she didn't know Evan's exact location. *Too soon to worry. Too soon*.

"Do you know those two?" Matt asked.

She shook her head, looking around. No, she hadn't seen them before tonight. Oh, damn. The panic was winning. They were all alone at this bus stop. There was no child here with them. Her apartment was a block and a half away. Was Evan at home all by himself again? She didn't see Matt's truck. There was a small group of patrons outside the bar down the street, huddling up to smoke their cigarettes—but no one anywhere close to Evan's age. Where was her son? She'd trusted Matt with one job. Okay, maybe two now that Jordan and Harve had inserted themselves into her life tonight—but she'd trusted Matt with the one thing more important than anything else in the world—her son.

"They seemed to know you," Matt went on matter-of-factly. "Why would they think you'd be an easy mark for them? 'Smooth sailing'?"

Corie even made the ridiculous move of peeking behind Matt's broad back, looking for her freckle-faced angel. "Where's Evan?"

Matt turned so they were facing each other again. His deep, patiently modulated voice barely changed its timbre, even though he hunched his shoulders a fraction to bring his gaze closer to hers and demand she focus on what he was saying. "Sound asleep on my sofa. My brother and his fiancée are with him. Ev is fine. Tell me about those two men."

Matt's eyes captured her attention. Unlike Harve's cold, creepy beetle eyes, their warm brown intensity moved through her like the potent drink they resembled. His coffee-colored eyes calmed her panic and chased away the chill of remembered fears. Evan was safe. Matt was a stand-up, trustworthy man who wouldn't do anything to endanger her son. *He's not Kenny.*

And as rational thought returned, the point Matt was

making registered. Was it her imagination, or had Harve sounded remarkably articulate for a drunk who'd been slurring every word a few minutes earlier? "He's asleep at your place? Evan's okay?"

"Yes. Are you?" Matt slowly straightened, his gaze never wavering from hers. His gloved hands fisted down at his sides, relaxed, then fisted again, as though he wanted to reach for her, but was holding himself back from making contact.

She wouldn't have minded. After the past six years of avoiding men—at first because she'd assumed they were all like Kenny and his thuggish cohorts, and later because work, school and being a hypervigilant single mom didn't allow time for relationships—she wouldn't have minded if Matt Taylor reached for her, at all.

Corie's lips relaxed into a wry smile and she nodded. "I'm fine. Thanks to you." Whether Matt was being exceedingly patient or endearingly shy, Corie wanted that connection he was too polite to initiate. She'd once been a confident young woman who'd gone after what her mother had told her she wanted—what she naively thought she'd wanted, too—until a kidnapping and death threats and Kenny's violent, obsessive world had scared that brave young woman into submission. It was nice to feel a little of her confidence returning with this man. She slipped her arm through Matt's and stepped toward the curb. "Could we head home now?"

"As long as you talk to me." He rested a leather-gloved hand over hers where she clung to his forearm, revealing that he liked sharing that friendly link with her, too, and didn't want her pulling away. The man was warm, and he made her feel safe. And his kiss had awakened something dormant and too-long ignored inside her. She wasn't going anywhere.

Falling into step beside him, Corie shared the bare bones of her bus ride home. "They got on at the stop just after the diner. You know—too much to drink and not enough action at whatever bar they'd come out of. I tried to keep my head down, but they spotted me, decided I was their chosen target. Mr. Lee told them to move—and they did. But that didn't shut them up. Then they became a nuisance to everyone on the bus. Only now I wonder if it was all an act. Harve seemed to sober up pretty quickly once you showed up."

"I have that effect on people."

Whether he meant to be funny or not, Corie smiled and pressed her cheek against his shoulder. The material of his jacket was cold against her skin, but she savored the supple hardness and promised warmth of the muscle she felt underneath. They crossed the street and walked a whole block like that, with Corie hugging herself around Matt's arm and his hand covering hers. Matt's bulk blocked the worst of the wind, and his ever-watchful eyes that scanned their surroundings and occasionally settled on her made her feel protected. Simply walking down the street arm in arm with Matt felt normal. Intimate. And far more romantic than any grand gesture Kenny had ever used to try to charm her. "It's just weird. Weird things are happening around me lately," she admitted. "First the fires, and I think someone's been in my apartment. That stupid phone call. Now those two idiots giving me grief."

"What phone call?"

Corie's breath clouded on a puff of frustration. Had she actually said that out loud? She tried to explain in a way that didn't make her sound like the completely paranoid woman she was. "A voice mail from my attorney's assistant in St. Louis. There was a fire in their office."

"Was anyone hurt?"

"My attorney sustained minor injuries, but he's doing fine now. I guess they lost several documents in the fire."

"Were any of the destroyed documents yours?"

She shrugged. She had immediately imagined the worst, but she truly didn't know. "It was just an FYI call."

Matt's fingers tightened briefly on hers before he slid his hands into the pockets of his coat. She might have imagined him hugging his elbows to his torso, keeping their arms linked together, encouraging her to remain at his side. But as he glanced over her head to track the line of cars and trucks coming through the intersection behind them as the lights changed, she sensed something about his posture had changed, grown wary. He wanted his hands free to…to what? "You didn't see a white van following the bus, did you?"

"No. It's hard to see much besides the lights through the windows at night." She studied the vehicles that rolled past them. Not a van of any kind in sight. The thrill she'd just admitted to herself at having Matt meet her at the bus stop to walk her home vanished. Had he seen something she had missed? "Why?"

"I saw an unfamiliar vehicle in the neighborhood earlier. It followed us from Grandma's place."

"Followed?" Corie stopped, yanking her arm from his. Futile thrills and chivalry and logical explanations be damned. There *was* something wrong. "Why didn't you say something?"

Matt turned. He cupped her elbows and ran his hands up and down her arms. "My brothers who are cops are looking into it. The van didn't come to our building or parking garage. I lost it by taking the scenic route home."

She didn't want reassurances. She wanted facts. She knew better than to dismiss the suspicion in his words and posture. "The van was following you? You're certain? Did you see the driver? Is Evan okay? Was he scared?" The last time she'd felt like the world was falling apart around her, it had been. She didn't intend to dismiss the things that struck her as odd and be caught off guard and forced into doing something she regretted again. "I need to see Evan. Right now."

This time, Matt draped his arm around her shoulders and tucked her to his side. His stride seemed to be longer now, forcing her to hurry her pace. "As far as I could tell, he spent the whole time playing with my watch on the drive home. I doubt he noticed the van."

Corie shook her head, feeling equally doubtful. "He notices everything."

"He does. I crashed through a wall tonight, made a lot of noise. He came running to make sure I was okay." She paused and glanced up at him. "I was," he answered her unspoken question, pulling her back into a quick step beside him. "Evan is, too. My brother Mark is with him. My brothers Pike and Alex are working on tracking down the van, although I only got a partial plate. Chances are the guy was scoping out my truck to see if he could steal it. I was more worried about you being out here by yourself."

"I'm fine. I'm going to be fine," she amended. "I've handled worse than a couple of drunks on the bus. Evan is my only concern."

Matt's arm tightened around her, partially lifting her to keep pace with his stride as they climbed the granite steps to their building. He swiped his key card and led her inside. Even being in the lobby, cut off from the cold, windy night, she felt chilled. Seven years ago, when the trouble began with Kenny—the worst year of her life—the terror had all started with someone following her and her son.

Matt punched the elevator call button. "You won't do him any good if something happens to you."

Corie hurried inside and pressed the button for the seventh floor. "I'm a grown-up. I can take care of myself. He just turned eight. He's trusting and curious and all I have that's worth anything." She was clearly rattled by the incident or she wouldn't still be clinging to Matt. Once she realized her fingers were clutched in the side of his coat, she tried to release him. But her grip seemed to be locked in place, and, damn it, her eyes were stinging with tears.

"Hey." As the elevator doors closed, Matt framed her jaw between his big hands, tilting her face up to his. "Next time you work late, let me know. I will pick you up. And if I'm on shift, I'll send one of my brothers or my dad."

She shook her head between his hands. "We've been riding the bus for months. We're not your responsibility. I can't ask you to—"

"You're not coming home on your own after dark again." He emphasized his resolute pronouncement by tightening his fingers against her hair and the sides of her neck, gently preventing another shake of her head. A soft huff that could be a wry laugh stirred the bangs on her forehead. "It's bad for my blood pressure."

"*Your* blood pressure?" She reached up to wind her fingers around his wrists. "*I'm* the one who's freaking out."

He stroked his thumb across her cheek. His leather glove was cool against her skin, but his firm touch and deep voice swept aside the world long enough for her to take a deep breath. "Let me do this small thing. Please."

She needed to think, not react. She needed to use her brain, not her emotions. And most importantly, she needed to get her mental stuff together so she wouldn't frighten Evan. Matt's patience and no-nonsense caring gave her enough of a break from her maternal panic to dial it back a notch. She believed him when he said Evan was safe. For that, she was grateful. But she didn't intend to become a burden to him. Besides, if these odd events did have anything to do with Kenny Norwell, anyone who got involved with her would be in danger. "We're already an imposition. It shouldn't be your problem."

He didn't try to lie and say she and the recent events surrounding her and Evan weren't an upheaval in his life. He didn't tell her not to worry. He didn't wheel and deal and promise to take care of her problems for her in exchange for her silence or a roll in the hay or custody of her son the way Kenny would have.

Instead, Matt planted himself in front of her like the unbending oak he was and held out his hand. "Give me your phone." He tugged his gloves off with his teeth and held them there while he typed his number into her phone and handed it back to her. "This is faster than pulling my card out of your bag." The boyish move and garbled sentence were as endearing as that unexpected response to her kiss had been intoxicating. She plucked his gloves from between his lips and held them for him while he pulled out his cell and typed in her number. Now that he could talk clearly, he added, "If you prefer the bus, one of us will ride with you. Offering you a lift doesn't mean you owe me anything. Just promise you'll call."

When he was done, she tucked each glove into the appropriate pocket of his jacket, just as she did with Evan almost every day when they got home from school. But instead of sending him on to his room to play, as she would a child, Corie wound her arms around Matt's waist and hugged him tightly, taking note of every hard plane and solid muscle pressed against her. Even though she was of average height, she scarcely reached his shoulders. Still, it felt like a perfect fit when his arms folded around her and he lowered his head to rest his chin against the crown of her hair. Corie nestled in, oddly sad that the elevator was slowing to a stop. "You're a better friend than I deserve, Matt. But you may not want to get involved with me."

"Maybe I do. Maybe I already am." The elevator doors opened, and he released her to walk side by side down the hallway together. "Have a little faith in me, okay?"

Corie reached for his hand and laced their fingers together. "Trusting you is the easy part."

Chapter Eight

Corie pushed open the door the moment Matt unlocked it, anxious to see Evan after hearing Matt's suspicion about the white van.

As he ushered her inside the shadowed living room, they were greeted by a slightly shorter, equally broad version of Matt. Although his eyes were blue to Matt's warm brown color, there was no mistaking that this was his brother. Mark Taylor pressed a finger against his lips, urging them to whisper as he nodded toward the couch where Evan was fast asleep with his arm thrown around his dragon and Matt's watch strapped to his wrist. A statuesque redhead in a paint-stained sweatshirt entered from the kitchen, drying her hands on a towel. She smiled a greeting to Corie and Matt without saying a word.

"My brother Mark," Matt whispered behind her. "His fiancée, Amy Hall. This is Corie, Evan's mom."

Although her eyes barely left her sleeping child, and the relief flooding through her made it difficult to speak, Corie managed to thank the couple before hurrying across the room. She peeled off her gloves and knelt beside the couch to peer into Evan's sweetly innocent face as he snored softly atop a throw pillow. She brushed a lock of shaggy brown hair off his freckled cheek and cupped the back of his head. He was perfectly fine—exhausted from what had no doubt been an exciting evening for him, but fine. Kenny hadn't found them. Kenny hadn't taken her son from her again. Exhaling a sigh of relief that echoed through the room, she pushed to her feet, adjusted the afghan covering him and kissed his cheek.

"Better?" Matt asked. He must have followed right behind her.

She looked up at him and nodded. "You were right. He's okay. It's just…a mother has to know." She turned Matt's watch on Evan's slender wrist to unbuckle it. "You'd better take this now or you may never see it again."

Matt stopped her fingers and slipped it back down Evan's slender wrist. "Let him keep it for tonight. I think it makes him feel safe, like he can cope with anything that stresses him."

She wasn't sure it was the watch so much as whom the watch represented. There were a lot of things about this man that made a person feel safe. Corie squeezed her hand around Matt's forearm, thanking him for the consideration. "I'll make sure we return it in the morning."

Corie felt a tug from the opposite side as Amy linked arms with her and pulled her toward the bright lights of the kitchen. "Come with me. Let's go where we don't have to whisper. I made some hot chocolate to warm us all up. And I want to show you the drawing Evan made." Her voice grew louder and more exuberant as they left Evan snoozing in the living room. "I'm going to turn it into one of my garden aliens, a miniature one he can keep in his room. If that's okay. He said he had a spot for it."

Amy handed Corie the colored pencil drawing sitting on the table and hurried to the stove to fill a couple of mugs with hot chocolate. "Garden aliens?"

"Unbutton your coat and sit for a few minutes." Clearly, Amy felt at home here in Matt's apartment, as she gestured to a chair at the rustic wood farm table. With Matt's penchant for working with his hands, she wondered if he had restored, or even built it himself. She didn't get time to ask as Amy pointed out the whorls of purple, red and yellow on Evan's drawing. "I see dragon overtones, which will be fun to incorporate. Evan is certainly bold with his color choices. I find that inspiring."

Should she be worried about the ever-expanding army of dragons guarding Evan's room?

Mark strolled into the kitchen, picking up a half-empty mug from the table and carrying it to his fiancée for seconds as she tore open pouches of instant cocoa and poured hot water from the kettle into each mug. "Amy's an artist. She works mostly in metals. She's set up shop in my garage."

"Only because mine burned down this past summer." She handed Corie and Matt each a steaming mug of cocoa before sitting in the chair next to Corie's. She thrust out her left hand. "Here's an example of my handiwork. My engagement ring."

Corie was left with little choice but to examine the twisted filigree work around the diamond solitaire. It was certainly one of a kind...as she suspected Amy was, too. "What a unique, beautiful ring."

Mark squeezed his hands around Amy's shoulders, and she leaned back into him, holding her hand up to admire the jewelry. "Mark gave me the diamond on a plain white-gold band when he proposed, with his blessing to turn it into whatever I wanted. I melted it down and created the two hearts knotted together around the diamond. The wedding bands I'm making will be plainer because of Mark's work."

Corie cradled the steaming mug in her hands and

shrugged. "Wow. You're making your own wedding jewelry, and I don't even have a hobby."

Matt stood at the counter next to the stove, stirring his hot chocolate. "Because you're working or studying all the time. Or doing stuff with Evan. Not everybody could handle all that on their plate as well as you do."

She smiled at him across the room, silently thanking him for the shout-out of praise. And, if she wasn't mistaken, that slight tilt at the corner of his firm mouth meant he was smiling back.

Finally feeling herself warming up, Corie shed her coat while Matt and Mark joined them at the table. She'd had every intention of walking Evan across the hall and getting out of Matt's hair so that they wouldn't be any more of an imposition on their evening. But the Taylor brothers and Amy were making her feel like a welcome guest. No, they were making her feel like a friend. Corie couldn't recall the last time she'd sat down with people her own age and talked about things not related to teaching, classes, work or legal matters. They chatted for another thirty minutes or so while they sipped their cocoa. She got the gist of the wedding Mark and Amy were planning for the summer on the grounds of her grandmother's farm. She heard a couple of stories about the Lucky 13 crew at the firehouse where the brothers both worked. Matt didn't add much more than a shrug to Mark's assertion that Matt had pulled him not once, but twice, from a fire. Even though Mark and Amy dominated the conversation, there was no mistaking the way they included both her and Matt with teasing gibes, complimentary observations about Evan and interesting questions that helped them get to know Corie while she got to know them.

She imagined the conversation would have gone on a good deal longer until the moment she failed to mask a yawn. She quickly pressed her hand over her mouth. "Sorry about that. It's not the company, I promise."

Mark pushed his chair away from the table as Amy squeezed Corie's hand and offered her a rueful smile. "My bad. I ramble whenever I start talking about marrying this guy. Matt's learned to put up with me." She glanced across the table and winked at the man beside Corie. "I think he might even like me."

"He does," Matt replied. "I said I'd be in the wedding, didn't I?"

Amy rose from the table and circled around to hug Matt from behind. "You did."

"Come on, Red." Mark tugged on Amy's hand. "Let's let these guys get some sleep. Corie put in a long day, and I've got a long one tomorrow." Matt pulled out Corie's chair in a sweetly old-fashioned gesture, and they all went into the living room, automatically dropping their voices as they got closer to Evan. After helping Amy into her coat, Mark shook hands with Matt and the two men bumped shoulders in a manly hug. "See you at work, bro."

"Thanks for helping out tonight."

"Like you haven't done the same for me."

Amy hugged Matt and then reached for Corie, her hug turning into a secretive whisper. "Matt's a good guy. The best there is. A bit of an odd duck—"

"Red?" Mark chided, pulling his fiancée away from Corie. "What did we say about matchmaking?"

Amy's conspiratorial whisper included Mark now. "That he's slow as molasses and might need a little nudge?"

"And on that note, we'll be going." Mark opened the door and ushered his fiancée into the hallway ahead of him. "Nice to meet you, Corie." But apparently, he wasn't immune to the matchmaking bug, either. He looked beyond her to Matt and winked. "Good night, Molasses."

Matt palmed his brother's face and shoved him out the door. Mark laughed, reached for Amy's hand, and the engaged couple headed for the elevator as Matt closed the door behind them. When he faced her, she thought she detected the faintest tinge of a blush peeking through his shadow of beard stubble. "Sorry about that. Those two can be…aggressively friendly."

Corie turned to hide the blush she was certain was staining her own cheeks and hurried back to the kitchen, where she carried the mugs to the sink and rinsed them out. "It's obvious they love you very much. It must be nice to have family you can depend on, even on short notice like this."

Moving with surprising stealth for a man his size, Matt appeared at the counter beside her and opened the dishwasher to place the mugs she handed him inside. "You don't have family? I suspected not here in Kansas City because you and Ev are always alone. You never have any company. But no family anywhere? You mentioned St. Louis earlier."

"That's where I grew up. Only child. I have a mother and a stepdad. He was pretty decent. But Mom and I severed ties. I miss the idea of having a mom and a grandmother for Evan, but I don't miss her." She could read the unspoken *why?* in his eyes. Corie shrugged and wet the dishcloth to wipe down the stove and countertop. It wasn't hard to talk about anymore. She'd made her peace with her choices when she'd changed her name and left St. Louis. "I told you my ex hurt a lot of people. But he also had a lot of money. Most of it made illegally, I discovered, doing jobs for other criminals. But Mom was willing to overlook that little detail as long as he showered her with gifts and kept me in a beautiful house that was way too big for the three of us."

"*Kept* you?"

Corie met a wall of Matt Taylor demanding answers and returned to the sink without meeting his probing gaze. He seemed to intuit that the irony of her word choices was more literal that most people might suspect. "He kidnapped Evan when I separated from him. The police didn't call it kidnapping since he was still a custodial parent. But if I wanted to be with my son, I had to be with Kenny."

"You could have divorced him, sued for full custody."

Corie shook her head. She'd been a young, vulnerable mess, isolated from any support system and afraid for her life. "The woman I was back then couldn't have."

"But you got stronger. Norwell's no longer in your life. You do have full custody, right?"

Corie nodded. "I legally changed our names and moved away from that nightmare. Started life over on my terms."

"Is that why the call from your attorney's office upset you? Do you think your mother or your ex was trying to locate who and where you are now?"

"My attorney does have that information. But Heath's office isn't even sure if anything is missing. They were calling all of his clients to tell us about the break-in, just to cover themselves legally, I suppose." She'd been so careful for so long, as had her attorney. As far as the world knew, Katie Norwell and her son, Danny, had disappeared from the face of the earth. "Kenny stayed in Jefferson City after he was released from prison. And my mother wouldn't know the first thing about break-ins and fires."

Matt started the dishwasher, perhaps giving her a few moments to tamp down her emotions. "It takes an unusually strong character to start over without any family or friends to help you."

His compliment warmed her. "When Kenny got arrested for arson and eventually sent to prison, I thought my mother would finally see him for the monster he was, we'd mend old wounds and become a family again." By the time she'd hung up the dishcloth and dried her hands, she'd found the composure to tilt her eyes to Matt's. "My mother encouraged me to marry Kenny in the first place— and she criticized me for divorcing him and taking his son from him, said that was a mistake I couldn't come back from. After all, arson is a victimless crime, she said."

If Matt was a more effusive man, he would have scoffed right then. "Tell that to the people who've lost everything they own. Who've lost the security of a roof over their heads—or worse, a pet or family member. Whether anyone dies or not, there are victims."

A fist of some long-buried grief over all she'd lost squeezed around her heart. Some parts of her past *were* hard to talk about, after all. Leaving the kitchen, Corie went to her sleeping son, sprawled on the couch, looking innocent and secure in a way she could never be. She reached down to feather her fingers through his hair and smooth the wispy spikes off his forehead. "You'd think a parent would do anything to protect their child. I would. I have. My mother's last words to me were, 'Go to him and beg his forgiveness.'" Corie shivered as though the air-conditioning had kicked on and pulled the front of her cardigan tightly around her polyester uniform. "He hurt people for a living. He put me in the hospital and kidnapped Evan so I'd go back to him. It took Kenny going to prison for us to get away from him—and she wanted me to beg his forgiveness?"

Without any warning, Matt pulled her into his arms and hugged her. Even with her crossed arms wedged between them, she felt his heat and unyielding strength. For several endless moments, she collapsed a little into the shielding bliss of his embrace. Just as she'd caressed Evan's hair a minute earlier, Matt tunneled his fingers into the hair beneath her ponytail, lifting its weight from her scalp and massaging the tension there. She didn't need any words— she could feel his empathy. But he offered her words, anyway. "Not everyone makes a good parent. My birth parents were drunk or high a lot. Mark and I barely had any supervision. I was literally playing with fire the night our house burned down, and they died. They were passed out in the living room. I managed to get Mark out. But I couldn't get them to wake up. If they'd been better parents…"

"Oh, Matt." She pulled her arms free to wind them around his waist and hugged him tight. "How old were you?"

"It doesn't matter."

"How old?" she insisted, tugging on a fistful of the flannel shirt he wore. "You said you were younger than Evan when you…acted out."

"Four."

"Only four?" She found the strong beat of his heart beneath her ear and nestled her cheek there. Her own heart was crying for the child he'd once been. "How frightened you must have been."

"I'm not trying to compare my pain to yours—or make any less of it. I just want you to know that I understand what it means to not have someone be there when you need them."

Corie rubbed her nose into the soft nap of Matt's flannel shirt, inhaling his honest, hardworking masculine scent. Kenny had never simply held her. He'd wanted her on his arm to show her off to his friends and employers, or in his bed for what she'd naively thought was unsatisfying sex simply because she was inexperienced. She'd eventually learned that the sex had never been about her at all, certainly not after she'd given him the baby boy he'd wanted. Holding Matt, being held by him, was a new experience, an incredibly addictive one that she didn't seem to have any willpower to move away from. Standing in Matt's arms, his body flush and warm and strong against hers, was like a soothing tonic and a sensual awakening all rolled into one.

"I only wanted them to notice me," Matt went on, his fingers hypnotically stroking the back of her neck above her collar. "Mark was the baby. He was cute. I was the… extra. Even at four, I knew we weren't a normal, *Leave It to Beaver* family." Her arms tightened as she imagined him as a lonely, neglected little boy. "I wanted them to feel something—fear, panic, maybe a little worry about Mark and me. *I* wanted to feel something."

"Like you were safe. Like someone cared enough to stop you from doing something dangerous. You probably blamed yourself for their deaths. They were the adults. They should have taken care of you."

Some of her hair caught in the stubble of his beard as he nodded. "I thank God every day that the Taylors adopted Mark and me. Alex and Pike, too. We were all in the same foster home. Not everyone is lucky enough to have a family like ours."

Matt's lips grazed her hair and Corie wanted to sink into him—hold him like this through the entire night. There was a joke in there somewhere about them both being the offspring of selfish, clueless parents. But a betrayal like that might still be too painful for him to joke about. Wanting to ease his pain—or find solace for her own—wasn't what their relationship was about.

Or was it? Had fate led her to the apartment across the hall from Matt because he was the rare man who understood what she'd been through? Was she drawn to him because she felt the pull of pain and secrets that resembled

her own? Was his reserved, quiet intensity meant to resurrect the confident, outgoing woman she'd once been?

Despite these few minutes of happiness and normalcy
and an unexpected desire to take this embrace to the next
level, another yawn reminded her of the reality of her life.
A wry chuckle shook through her, and she loosened her
grip on the back of Matt's shirt. Feelings for Matt were just
a foolish wish at this late hour. "Again, it's not the company." She was a little disappointed at how easily Matt let
her pull away. But the man was nothing if not imminently
practical. She should be glad that at least one of them could
show a little sense. "It's late. I'd better get Evan into his
own bed or I'll never get him up for school in the morning."

"I'll carry him."

Corie retrieved her coat and gathered up Evan's belong-
ings while Matt picked up the sleeping boy and carried
him to his bed across the hall. Something primal and utterly female stirred in Corie's womb at the strong paternal
image of Matt gently placing her son in his bed. He took
equal care setting Evan's protective dragon on the head-
board shelf and hanging Evan's coat on the back of his
chair while she tucked him in. After turning on the night-
light, she followed Matt to the front door.

The hot firefighter next door would make a wonderful father. She had a feeling Matt would be good at a lot
of things, because he was patient and observant and supportive and caring. Protecting others seemed to be hard-
wired into his DNA, and that chest, those arms, that butt
in a pair of jeans and…oh, hell. She might come with some
extra responsibility and emotional baggage, but she was a
healthy, needy, grown woman whose hormones had gotten a hold of her.

Matt turned in the hallway. "I'll wait until you lock
the dead—"

"Thank you for everything tonight." Corie might just be making the biggest mistake of her new life when she braced one hand against his chest, slid the other behind his neck and stretched up on tiptoe to capture his mouth in a kiss. She darted her tongue out to taste the firm line of his bottom lip, then felt it soften when she tugged it between her lips.

And then she realized he wasn't touching her. Her fingers were clutching the straight line of short, ticklish hair at the back of his head and his hands were fisted at his sides. Although she'd elicited a brief response when she'd suckled his lower lip, he wasn't kissing her. And she didn't think that husky huff from his chest was a groan of ecstasy.

Corie quickly released him and retreated half a step as the heat of embarrassment crept up her neck. "I'm sorry."

His fingers pulsed against his palms. "I said you didn't have to do anything you're not comfortable with. Just because my brother and Amy can't keep their hands to themselves doesn't mean I expect you to—"

"No, you said I needed to *tell* you when I wasn't comfortable with something." Her embarrassment gave way to a burst of anger, then settled into confusion. "It's a thank-you kiss, Matt. I didn't suck up my courage and *pretend* to kiss you. I wanted to do that." Nope. Here came the embarrassment again. "Unless you aren't okay with that? I mean, I know I'm out of practice, but when I kissed you at the bus stop, you sort of kissed me back. And the way you held me in your apartment, I thought..." She raked all ten fingers through hair, pulling out most of her ponytail. "Was I taking advantage—?"

"No. You can kiss me or touch me any time, any way you like." He almost sounded angry as he dipped his head toward hers and ground the words through his teeth. He snapped up straight, as though the vehemence of his response surprised him. He glanced away for a moment, gathering his thoughts before he looked back to her. "That didn't come out right." His hand batted the air and she could see him warring with whatever words he was having trouble expressing. He batted the air again, and then he feathered his fingers into the hair she'd pulled loose and the internal debate seemed to resolve itself when she didn't pull away from his touch. He smoothed the hair behind her ear and settled his hand against the side of her neck, easing her own uncertainty. "I would like to kiss you again sometime." His tone had quieted to that sexy, deliberate timbre that told her he was saying exactly what he was thinking. "For real. Not for show. Not for any reason other than… I want to kiss you."

Well, as declarations of desire went, that was hot. And it was really good for her ego to know they were on the same wavelength, after all. She smiled and reached up to touch his handsome mouth. "I'll keep that in mind." He just wanted her to know that she could move this budding relationship along at whatever pace she needed to—but that he was interested in pursuing it. She hoped he understood that she was interested, too, and that he didn't need to be shy about voicing his feelings with her. Maybe he'd also learn that giving in to his impulses didn't mean he'd frighten her the way Kenny had. Corie drew her hand down his chest before pulling back to the door. "Good night, Matt."

He touched the corner of her mouth and traced her smile with the tip of his finger, sparking an electric current that curled through her all the way down to her toes. "Good night."

When he nodded and pulled away without a kiss, she tried not to be disappointed. As she closed the door and leaned back against it, she reminded herself that she wasn't the only one who might be cautious about putting themselves out there. Matt had held her and touched her and listened and shared and awakened her heart. She closed her eyes and smiled. Good grief, she was falling hard for that one. She was feeling hopeful that she could have a normal life one day. Maybe she could even have that loving husband and big family she'd always dreamed about.

"Mom?" She opened her eyes to the shadowy darkness to find Evan stumbling into the living room.

"Hey, little man." Corie hurried to meet him and gently turn him back toward his bedroom. "What are you doing up?"

"I wanted to make sure you were home, and you were okay."

Corie nearly stumbled over the threshold as her heart seized up with his concern for her. Maybe *normal* was never really going to be an option for them. Not as long as Kenny Norwell had this influence over their lives.

"Yes, sweetie, I'm okay. Matt said you are, too." Now that he was partially awake, she helped him pull off his jeans and slip into his pajamas. "Come on. Let's get you back to bed."

He reached up to touch his dragon before climbing into bed again. "I really like Matt, Mom."

She pulled up the covers. "I like him, too."

"His grandma bakes cookies, and I made a new friend. Gideon doesn't go to my school, but we built a castle together. Can he come over and play sometime?" The big yawns she'd had over at Matt's were contagious. Evan seemed determined to get all his words out before he drifted off to sleep again. "Mark's funny. He calls Amy Red because of her red hair, and Pike calls Alex Shrimp because he's short..." Another yawn indicated this conversation wouldn't last long. "Oh, and Matt won the ax-chopping contest."

"The what?" Alarm flared but quickly went away because Evan was out, no doubt finally relaxing and dreaming happy thoughts judging by the smile on his face. Corie leaned over to give him another kiss. "Good night, little man. I love you."

She turned out the bedside lamp and left the door slightly ajar. It sounded like he'd had a grand adventure with Matt and his family tonight. There was definitely a little idolizing going on there. But she couldn't blame him. She seemed to have a thing for the firefighter next door, too.

As she headed down the hallway to her own bedroom, she heard one of the neighborhood cats who prowled the fire escapes looking for handouts or a warm spot to curl up scratching at her window. At Evan's insistence, she'd stuffed some old towels inside a box and set it on the fire escape to give them a bit of shelter from the cold. Sometimes, she had leftovers from the diner she set out for them. It was the closest thing to a pet the landlord allowed them to have.

"No leftovers tonight, sweetie." Corie folded up her work sweater and set it on the quilt beside her while she untied her shoes and toed them off her feet. Even through the blackout drapes that covered her window, she could hear how agitated the cat was, meowing and hissing and bumping into the discarded chair she'd set out there to anchor the box and keep it from blowing away. "What in the world are you so fired up about?"

Corie padded across the room in her stockinged feet. But before she reached the window, she heard another sound from out in the living room. A soft knocking at her door. Three taps, a pause, three more.

She glanced at the late hour on her alarm clock and tensed when she heard three more knocks. Hurrying straight to her coat on the rack where she'd hung it beside the door, she once more reached for her pepper spray.

Knock, knock, knock.

"Corie?"

Her breath rushed out in a gust of relief at Matt's deep-pitched whisper. She slipped the spray back into the pocket and swung open the door.

"You didn't lock your dead bolt. I was waiting—"

Corie threw her arms around Matt's neck. "Thank you. For so many things, thank you." Her toes left the floor as Matt wound his arms behind her waist and straightened, completing the hug. Her toes were still dangling in the air as she leaned back against his arms and grinned. "Ax-chopping contest? Seriously?"

"Oh. That." Her feet hit the floor and she was no longer cinched against him as he tried to apologize. "My brother and I were taking down a wall. Ev wasn't in the room at the time—"

"It sounds like a manly man thing that humans with testosterone enjoy more than they should. But I know he was safe. I feel safe with you, too—emotionally, physically." She shrugged, not coming up with enough words to explain everything she was feeling. "Firewise. Otherwise." She felt giddy, partially with relief that there was no intruder at her door, probably with fatigue, possibly because of all the new emotions swirling inside her. "I like you, Matt. I know my timing isn't great and inexplicable things are happening around us, but I do. Will I see you tomorrow?" she asked, wanting these weird, wonderful feelings she'd discovered tonight to continue.

He propped his hands at his waist and gave her the matter-of-fact answer she was getting used to. "I work the late shift. Won't get home until eight or nine."

The giddiness fled, and she felt deflated. "I'll be at work by then. Well, thank you again for watching Evan tonight. I promise I won't bug you every time I—"

His big hands framed her jaw, and his lips covered hers, silencing her apology with a kiss. He'd cut her off midsentence, and she was surprised to realize she was okay with that. Her gasp of surprise was swallowed up by the pressure of his mouth gliding over hers. Matt's tongue slipped between her lips, but she was already opening for him, already answering him. She was already grasping fistfuls of his shirt and T-shirt and the hard muscle underneath and pulling herself into his kiss.

Matt sifted his fingers into her hair and cupped her head, tilting it back to ravish her mouth. He moved forward, backing her against the wall beside the door until she could feel the pressure of his thighs against parts of her body that hadn't felt anything remotely thrilling like this for far too long. The heat of his body trapped her there, consuming her the way his mouth was consuming hers.

Although it had been a teasing joke earlier that night, Corie thought of molasses in the very best of ways. Matt's kiss was slow and smooth, addictively sweet and very much worth the wait for him to take the initiative in expressing his desire for her. Every taste, every exploration was as deliberate as his every thought.

But with a groan of regret that matched her own, Matt lifted his head, ending the kiss. They were both breathing erratically, the proud tips of her sensitized breasts brushing against his chest with every exhale. She was vaguely aware of his arousal pushing at the front of his jeans, just as she was aware of the heavy, weepy center of her wishing this had been more than a kiss. She had been too long without a man. She had been forever without the right man. Oh, how this man made her feel—physically, emotionally—every scary, delicious way she'd long forgotten she had the right to feel.

His dark eyes replaced the intensity of his kiss as he studied her face, keeping them linked together with his gaze. He watched her hair as he brushed his fingers through it, trying to smooth it back into place until he finally pulled the band from what was left of her ponytail and let her hair fall over her shoulders.

His voice was a husky whisper as he gently pried her hands from his shirt and slipped the rubber band into her palm. "I'll see you tomorrow night." She nodded at his promise because she couldn't quite find the breath to speak. "How late is the diner open?"

"On Fridays and Saturdays, we close at midnight."

"Evan?"

"He'll be with me. There's a cot in the back room if he's not at one of the tables, drawing or playing or chatting with the regular customers."

With a nod, he released her entirely and backed away with his hands raised, making her feel like pure temptation despite her baby-blue polyester dress and messy hair. "I'll meet you guys there when my shift ends. You still owe me a pie."

She laughed out loud at that and clapped her hand over her mouth as the sound seemed to echo down the hallway. Matt smiled—just a small curve at one corner of his mouth transformed him into a handsome man. And those dark, coffee-colored eyes about swallowed her up. She reached up to rest her hand against the stubble on his jaw. "Good night, Matt."

"Good night, Corie." She drifted into her apartment and

closed the door, leaning back against it. From the hallway, she heard him exhale and whisper, "Dead bolt."

Why did that reminder sound like some kind of endearment?

Corie quickly turned and threw the bolt, alleviating his concern. She splayed her hand against the door, imagining that his hand was there on the other side, protecting her, connecting them. Corie caught her abraded, swollen lip between her teeth and savored the taste of him that lingered there.

She had never in her life been kissed like that. She'd never before understood how a man could make every part of her tingle with such a sharp need with just a kiss. She'd never understood how freeing trust could be, never understood how hope and laughter could make falling in love so exciting.

Falling in love. Was that what was happening here? Was it foolish of her to want like this? To believe she was getting a second chance to be happy? To hope that Matt was feeling this way, too?

After a moment, she heard Matt's door open and close. It had been six long years since her divorce from Kenny, and this was the first time in all those years that she was looking forward to seeing a man again. She was looking forward to seeing Matt.

She heard the cat scrabbling down the fire escape steps as she pushed away from the door and headed through the apartment to get ready for bed herself and idly wondered what was making the feline so restless. Pulling the curtain aside, she peered out into the night. It was too dark to see much beyond the glass. The box beneath the chair had been knocked askew, and the snow around it had been disturbed enough that the paw prints were indistinct. Maybe there'd been one occupant too many trying to share the box tonight. Seeing no critter outside for her to worry about, Corie made sure the window was locked and pulled the drape back into place.

Kenny hadn't found them. She'd freaked out for nothing.

Besides, she had more pleasant things to think about.

Like kissing Matt Taylor again.

Many, many times.

Chapter Nine

Matt pulled the steering wheel and hung a sharp left at just the right distance to avoid the cars parked against the curb, guiding the big fire engine onto the skinny side street beside the dubiously named KC's Best automotive repair shop off McGee Street. Talk about a dead man district. This was their third job of the day, and each fire had been bigger than the last. Counting the five medical calls to back up their EMTs, the cat that was stuck in a drainpipe and the two false alarms, Firehouse 13 was way above its daily call average.

After the engine hissed and squealed to a stop, Matt set the brakes and killed the siren. The red and blue flashing lights bounced off nearby shop windows and windshields but seemed to be absorbed by the swirling orange and yellow flames shooting out of the repair shop's garage doors. Inky smoke billowed skyward, staining the snow on the branches of the ancient oaks that lined the sidewalk and bringing an early night to the evening sky.

"Nice driving, Taylor." Captain Redding put on his white scene commander's helmet. "Mark, Jackson—priority one is to make sure we don't have gas tanks, oxy-acetylene canisters or other flammables on site that haven't already gone up. Remove them if we can. Clear a perimeter if we can't."

"Yes, sir," they answered, fastening up their gear and securing their air tanks in the back seat.

Redding glanced across the cab to Matt. "You coordinate with the utility crew to make sure we've got all the gas lines cut off. I'll track down the owner and talk to whoever reported it." He studied the fully engulfed building. "This was burning awhile before anyone called it in. As far as I know, Friday's still a workday. Why didn't anyone call sooner?"

"You think we've got casualties?" Matt asked.

"I'm thinking I don't want to send any more men in there than I have to. Something's off with this one." Redding made a quick scan of the police cars blocking traffic and the local residents hanging out at a relatively safe distance from the fire scene. "Where are all the mechanics?" There was one nondescript guy with muscles and an aversion to holding his head up huddled inside his grimy insulated coveralls, talking with an older man in a suit and tie and long dress coat. "He's the only one in this crowd wearing a uniform of any kind."

Twenty-plus years of service gave Kyle Redding almost a sixth sense about fires. Hell. Matt hadn't been with KCFD for half that long, and he had a feeling there was nothing accidental about this blaze. Matt nodded toward the line of tow trucks and trailers on the far side of the building holding expensive cars and souped-up trucks in various states of repair. "Looks like they got most of their vehicles out."

"The ones worth some real money." Redding nodded. "Which is what I would do if I was going to torch my own place."

Matt followed up on Kyle's suspicion. "I'll give my dad a call and alert the arson team."

"Do that."

While the captain led Mark, Ray and the rest of the team off the truck to meet with the men and women on the second and third trucks and move them into position, Matt turned off the engine and called in their twenty to dispatch. "Lucky 13 on scene, 819 McGee Street. Captain Redding has the command. Taylor 13 Alpha out."

Then he swapped out his ball cap for his own helmet and tuned in to the chatter coming over his body radio as he climbed down to assess the scene more closely. The heat from the blaze was intense enough for him to feel it as he approached. Although hoses were out and the team was laying down a defensive perimeter to keep the fire from spreading, there was probably little they could do.

Matt adjusted his mask over his face, radioed his position to the crew and moved inside, clinging to the walls to keep his bearings as he tried to pinpoint the source of the blaze. Steam from the water gushing through the garage bay doors was as thick as the smoke, making visibility almost nil. After signaling Mark and Ray that he understood their all-clear on the ground floor, he made his way past the charred shell of a pickup up on lifts in one of the bays. A quick exploration confirmed that no one was trapped inside or beneath the vehicle. He made it to a set of metal stairs leading up to the second floor. But he was forced to reverse course as flames curled in a sinuous dance across the ceiling above him and cut off access to the top of the stairs. One by one, ceiling tiles melted and fell away, and the wood support beams holding up the second floor began to sag and crack as fire, water and heat weakened them. The thick stone walls and iron window frames would probably survive anything short of a massive explosion, but the interior of the two-story 1920s-era shop was fully involved and about to collapse.

"Taylor 13 Alpha," he called over his radio. "Everybody clear out. The top floor's about to rain down on us. Immediate source of ignition not evident. Cannot access second floor from interior. I repeat, everybody clear out."

Mark and Ray were already outside, waiting for the ladder truck to move into position to access the roof when Matt emerged. His mask fogged up as he met the wintry air and he pulled it down beneath his chin.

"Incendiaries down here are contained," Mark shouted. "The ignition point has to be upstairs."

He gave them a thumbs-up, showing his understanding. "Did you see the way the interior supports were burning? It's like somebody doused the top floor with an accelerant. This baby is going to end up a total gut. All we can do now is put it out." Matt tapped his radio, indicating to the crew that this had become strictly a containment mission. "Lucky 13, let's go to work. Watch yourselves up on that roof."

Matt was heading across the driveway to report to Captain Redding when a window exploded over his head. He jerked at the sound and instinctively raised his arm as glass rained down around him. But that was what the helmet and bunker gear were for, since falling debris and collapsing buildings were a firefighter's most common threat. Unharmed, he moved his mask up to shield his face, and looked up to see if the pressure that had blown out that window was the first in a chain reaction, and he needed to move his men back to a safe distance. Flashover would certainly occur now that fresh oxygen was flooding the confined space.

"Son of a..." What Matt saw was even worse. "Stop!"

A dark-haired man in grimy coveralls was leaning over the window ledge, engulfed by the black smoke billowing out around him. Coughing racked his body, and when he drew in a breath, Matt could hear the shallow wheeze of lungs that wouldn't fill. His face was smudged with soot and red smears he'd guess were blood, making his expression unreadable. But there was no mistaking his intention as the chair he'd smashed the window with came flying toward Matt.

Matt ran forward, dodging the chair that splintered around him, shouting to be heard over the roar of the fire and thunder of the hoses. A leg came over the edge of the windowsill. "Wait up! We'll get a ladder to you. Stop! Take a deep breath and stay put. We're coming." He waved the man back inside, pointed to the fire escape at the end of the building. "Can you reach—?" Matt turned to his radio. "Ladder! Northeast side, second floor. I've got a jumper—"

The man teetered over the edge into the smoke, leaping, falling, hurling himself away from the flames. Matt dived in one Hail Mary effort to break his fall. But he was too late. The victim hit the pavement before him with a sickening thud.

On his hands and knees, Matt scrambled forward. "Medic! I need a board now!"

Matt tugged off his mask and placed it over the man's face, giving him the oxygen he must have been starving for. He peeled off his gloves to check for a pulse. But as the EMTs swarmed in and pushed him aside, he already knew the diagnosis. Whether it was a broken neck or a broken skull, the man was dead.

Matt rocked back on his heels as Redding rushed over. Although the paramedics rolled the mechanic onto a back board to stabilize him and intubated him to push oxygen directly into his lungs, it was too late. After giving Matt's shoulder a supportive squeeze, the captain knelt beside the paramedics. "I think I understand now why someone started this fire."

Matt scrambled over to join him, needing to know why this man had died, needing to understand why he hadn't been able to save him. Faulty fire suppression system? Not passing any fire inspection period? What the hell kind of business left a man behind without making any effort to rescue him, or alerting the KCFD to attempt a rescue? "Did you find out anything from the owner?"

"That he's an entitled ass full of hot air. But take a look at this." After a sad shake of his head from one of the EMTs working on the victim, Redding picked up the man's wrist and pushed back the cuff of his coveralls. The man's fingers and knuckles were bruised and bloodied, like he'd been in a fight. Matt might have thought the fight had been with the heavy iron and leaded glass of that window upstairs, but that didn't account for the shred of duct tape clinging to his wrist.

Before the medics covered him up, Matt glimpsed the dark-haired man's bruised and swollen face. He'd clearly been in a fight. "Those wounds are hours old. They didn't happen when he impacted the concrete." Matt picked up the other wrist and discovered the skin was raw from where he'd pulled or gnawed his way free. "He didn't bind himself up like this."

"Crime scene cover-up." Redding placed the victim's hand back under the blanket and nodded for the EMTs to lift him onto the gurney and move him to the ambulance, keeping him out of sight from curious onlookers and the press photographers who were showing up to take pictures or capture some footage for the evening news. "Somebody left this man for dead in there."

"Hold up a sec." Matt asked the medics to wait while he took another look at the man's damaged wrist.

The captain leaned in beside him. "What is that? A homemade tattoo?"

Matt studied the markings that looked like they'd been scratched into the skin by the same instrument the man had used to free himself. Suspicion prickled the back of Matt's neck, and he wiped the soot away from the patch sewn above the man's chest pocket to read his name. "Maldonado." The man whose car had been remotely set on fire a few days ago. The confidential informant who was allegedly ratting out the next generation of the Meade crime family. "My uncle Cole needs to see this."

Redding ordered the medics to stay with the body and protect it. "I'll call KCPD."

Two hours later, night had fallen, and with the fire out, the temperature had dropped to a chilly twenty-three degrees. And while the Lucky 13 crew was combing the building to check for remaining hot spots and overhaul the debris, KCPD had arrived on the scene in the form of Matt's uncle Cole, along with his NCIS partner, Amos Rand.

Matt was running on fumes, taking a break and sitting on the running board of his fire truck while he downed a bottle of water. Other than removing his helmet and breathing apparatus, he still wore his bunker gear for the warmth the layers provided. He stood when his uncle and his partner walked up, extending his hand to greet them. "Uncle Cole. Agent Rand."

"Matt." Cole held on to his nephew's hand for an extra moment, his eyes narrowed in familial concern. "You look like you've been rode hard and put up wet. You okay?"

"Long day."

Cole nodded his understanding. Sometimes, first responders saw some wicked things that stuck with you—like a man desperate enough to choose one kind of death over another. "I'll need your statement when you're ready."

"Let's get it done." Matt crushed the empty water bottle

and tossed it inside the truck. He told them what he'd witnessed with Enrique Maldonado's death and his suspicion about the cause of the fire. There was only one worker on site besides the dead man, and he hadn't seen that first mechanic since he'd had time to walk away from the fire and scan the crowd again. Finally, someone had managed to save all the expensive vehicles they had on site—but not their last employee?

"Sounds like potential insurance fraud to me," Cole suggested.

Amos agreed. "Maybe Meade needed an influx of cash and decided to torch his own place."

"Or he was destroying evidence." Matt nodded toward the forensics team from the crime lab who'd been talking to Cole and Amos. "Has your crime scene team found anything?"

Amos pulled his wool cap more securely over his buzz cut of hair and hunched against the damp chill in the air. "They can't get into what's left of the offices upstairs yet, but they found a sticky substance on the arm of the chair Maldonado used to break out the window. They'll have to match it in the lab, but it looks like remnants of duct tape. He was secured to the chair and worked over before the fire started. Trapped and unable to evacuate. Maybe he was unconscious—maybe they thought he was dead. Nobody tried to save that guy."

Somebody had. But it had been too little, too late. Matt heard the sound of the victim hitting the pavement again and again in his head. "If I could have just gotten to him sooner. If I had known he was up there—"

"This isn't on you, Matt," Cole insisted. Captain Redding had said the same thing, ordered him to take tomorrow off and to check in with one of the KCFD counselors, if necessary. "Whether as a result of another crime like arson or assault, or deliberately planned to play out like this, we've got ourselves a homicide. One we should be able to tie to the owner of this place, Chad Meade."

Amos turned his back to the graying, slightly heavyset man in the suit and tie being escorted by a uniformed officer across the driveway to join them. "Speak of the devil."

Although Matt had spotted him in the crowd with the missing mechanic when the Lucky 13 crew had first arrived on the scene, he hadn't realized this well-to-do man who wore polished patent-leather oxfords instead of sensible snow boots was the business owner. He didn't strike Matt as an auto repair sort of guy. But then, he didn't look like Matt's image of a man who'd spent several years in prison, either. But this was Chad Meade, wannabe crime boss and the object of Cole and Amos's investigation.

"If it isn't Mr. Taylor and his enigmatic partner," Meade said in a friendly enough tone, although Matt got the distinct impression there was nothing friendly between him and the police. "We meet again. I was told you wanted to speak to me and, of course, I was eager to help find out who is responsible for this monstrous tragedy. Thought I could spare you a few minutes between phone calls and press interviews." He held up the cell phone he carried. "I've been talking back and forth with my insurance gal. I'm guessing this will be a total write-off." He glanced up at Matt and gave a practiced laugh. "These old buildings from the '20s are built like bomb shelters on the outside. But KCFD couldn't save much on the inside, could they?"

Cole made no pretensions of this being a civil conversation. "How much of a profit is this *write-off* worth to you, Chad? Aren't you on parole?"

He turned the collar of his coat up against the cold. "That's why I'm running a legitimate business here, Officer."

"It's Detective."

Amos removed the toothpick that he'd been chewing from the side of his mouth and tapped his chest. "And Special Agent. *You* need to try harder if you want us to believe you've gone legit."

Meade pointed to the smoking wreckage of the garage. "Can I help it if the competition doesn't want me to succeed?"

"You're claiming this was a setup?" Cole challenged.

"I have enemies, Detective. My uncle Jericho was an influential man—not everyone agreed with the way he ran his business. I've learned from the mistakes he made and I'm doing well for myself. But some people can hold a grudge for a long time." He pulled back the edge of his leather glove to check the time, as if he was calculating how much longer he'd allow this conversation to last. "You, perhaps. How is your lovely wife, by the way?"

"I'm here to do my job, Meade." Cole clearly had no intention of letting Chad Meade bait him into an argument about the last time Cole and his wife, Tori, had investigated the Meade crime family. "You've got a casualty here. One of your employees, Enrique Maldonado. He was trapped in the fire. He didn't make it."

"I heard. That's too bad."

Matt's hand balled into a fist at the lack of sympathy, or even empathy, for the life that had been lost.

Cole nodded. "Yeah, it's too bad he had his hands taped together and was probably unconscious when the fire started and had no chance of surviving."

Chad Meade met Cole's hard, unblinking blue eyes and finally smiled before looking away. Since members of Chad's family had once tried to kill Cole's wife, there was certainly no love lost between them. "I know nothing about that, Detective Taylor. But I assure you, the company takes care of its employees and their families. Now, if you'll excuse me, I need to talk to my insurance people and do a little PR spin with the press." He gestured to the burned-out shell of the garage. "Historic landmark destroyed. It breaks the locals' hearts."

Cole shoved his hands into his leather jacket, probably hiding the fists he'd made, too. "We'll be investigating this fire for arson. Maybe you think we can't get you for murder, but even a case of insurance fraud will put you back in prison."

"I'm just the investor who owns the property. An entrepreneur. What would I know about setting a fire like this?" He wiggled his gloved fingers in the air. "I don't even smoke anymore." He turned and waved to a brunette reporter who waved back and invited him to speak on camera. "Gentlemen. If you'll excuse me, I have to go."

Amos followed a few steps behind him. "We have more questions for you, Meade."

"I'm certain you do." Despite his perfect, capped-tooth smile, Meade's tone was laced with a threat now. "I'm not in the business anymore, gentlemen. And your investigation borders on harassment."

Cole was one cool customer, throwing Meade's excuse right back at him. "If you're not in the business, then you've got nothing to hide."

Chad Meade smoothed his tie inside his suit jacket before reaching into the chest pocket of his coat. "But I *do* have work to do, calls to make. A family to express my condolences to." He held out a business card. "If you want to speak to me again, contact my lawyer."

Amos snagged the card and stuffed it into the back pocket of his jeans as Meade strolled away. "That man is one smug SOB. He does know we've built a paper trail on him, doesn't he? That we can track his import and export shipment schedules to match up with trafficking in and out of KCI and the river port? What we need is witness corroboration. Several witnesses would be better."

Cole shook his head. "Now that Maldonado's gone, we'll be starting from scratch again, trying to convince someone to turn on Meade." His expression was grim as he looked to the blackened shell of the Art Deco building. "But if this is the result of turning on him…"

Matt listened to their case against Chad Meade, and a few inexplicable observations about this fire began to make sense. "Can I show you something?" The three men went to the body lying in the back of the ME's van. Cole and Amos flashed the badges hanging around their necks and vouched for Matt as a witness. With permission from the medical examiner, Niall Watson, who remained to observe their interactions with the body, the three men climbed in beside the gurney. Dr. Watson issued them all sterile gloves and proceeded to unzip the body bag.

"Can you identify the victim?" Dr. Watson asked, adjusting his glasses on the bridge of his nose. "I found no ID on him. No wallet, no phone."

"It's Enrique Maldonado," Amos confirmed. "May I?" Amos pulled a knife from the sheath on his belt and slid it beneath the top of the victim's boot. Once he'd pried it far enough from the victim's leg, he reached inside and pulled out a set of dog tags on a thin chain. He dropped the tags into a bag the ME held open before sealing and labeling it. "Perps don't usually check the boot for anything but hidden weapons. Those will confirm his ID. Maldonado was working undercover for me out of NCIS. We believe Meade has his hand in moving illegal arms in and out of the country by hiding them in those expensive cars he imports and exports. Enrique was our inside man who followed the trail here to Kansas City." Amos's light-colored eyes narrowed as he looked down at the body. "He was a good man. He wasn't even a field agent, but we gave him the job because he's so good with engines and cars. No one would question his expertise."

Cole rested a hand on Amos's shoulder. "Sorry about your man, Amos."

"He was a good Marine." The dark-haired agent closed his eyes completely for a moment, inhaled a deep breath, then opened his eyes, ready to work again. "He's been feeding us intel for months now. We still don't know if Meade is running this operation, or if he's a middleman and we still have to identify who he's reporting to."

Cole studied the victim's battered face for a moment before looking away. "Burning his car wasn't persuasion enough to keep Maldonado from meeting with us. Was his cover blown and Meade found out he was a cop? Or is this the going payback for anyone talking to the police now?"

Matt had an idea about that. "If Maldonado was working for you, that could explain what I found." He lifted the stiff left arm from the gurney and pulled back the stained, torn sleeve. "I thought you might want to see this." Dr. Watson snapped a photograph of Maldonado's forearm, and the letters and number that had literally been scratched into his skin.

N4 Jeff C FB

Cole pulled out his phone and took a picture of the code. "You think he did this? Or was it done to him?"

Matt laid the arm down and picked up the victim's right hand to show them the bloody nails. "With everything on fire around him, and nothing to write with, he carved this himself." Cole and the ME both snapped pictures of the hand, as well. "I think he jumped because he wanted to make sure you got his message. I can't be certain what it means, but it looks like he was trying to preserve the writing in case his clothes caught on fire and the body burned."

"N4. Enforcer," Amos translated. "Jeff C? Jefferson City? Meade's hired himself a new enforcer from Jefferson City. Probably an ex-con who just got out of prison there."

Ex-con? Like Corie's ex?

"Is that why the call from your attorney's office upset you?"

"My ex hurt a lot of people."

The back of Matt's neck prickled with awareness. He glanced outside the ME's van at his crewmates finishing their cleanup and joking with each other now that the danger at this scene had passed. He stepped to the edge of the van to look at the gathering of reporters and cameras closing in around Chad Meade. But he wasn't sure what his instincts were trying to tell him.

"What's the FB?" Cole asked.

Matt glanced back to see Amos scraping some goo off the bottom of the dead man's boot. "Looks like petroleum jelly." He showed it to the ME, who opened a jar for him to scrape the substance into.

What details was Matt missing here? "May I?"

He brought the jar to his nose to sniff the contents. Oh no. Hell no.

"You ever seen anything like that?" Cole asked.

Matt had. His blood sped through his veins like a freight train.

Corie said her ex started fires.

"Kenny stayed in Jefferson City after he was released from prison."

That's why the hairs on the back of his neck were standing out straight. He handed the jar back to the ME, who capped it as evidence. "Get another sample of that to my dad, chief arson investigator at KCFD." Matt jumped from the back of the van to the ground. "You need me for any-thing else, Cole? There's a phone call I need to make." The sooner the crew cleared the scene and he wrote up his preliminary report, the sooner he could get to Pearl's Diner and to Corie and Evan. But all that would wait if he couldn't hear her voice and know that she was okay.

"Go." His uncle shooed him on his way. "I'll contact Gideon about the potential arson. Thanks for your help tonight. I'll keep you in the loop if we find out anything about the fire itself."

Matt was backing away, even as he was unbuckling his turnout coat and reaching inside his BDUs to pull out his cell phone. He nodded toward the victim Niall Wat-son was zipping back inside the body bag. "FB. Firebug. Check out the name Kenny Norwell. Find out if he's got any connection to Chad Meade. And send me Norwell's picture if you can get it."

"Done." Cole called after him, "Who's Norwell?"

"Someone I hope is still in Jefferson City."

Chapter Ten

"Answer your phone!" Matt growled the order at the cell phone he'd anchored to his dashboard.

When Corie's voice mail started up again with its pleasant but impersonal greeting, he punched the disconnect button. He'd already left three messages, apologizing for running late, asking her to call him, telling her he had some information he wanted to share in person, trying not to sound completely desperate to know that she was okay.

He'd had to settle for a single text.

Hey, Matt. We're slammed tonight. Call you back when things lighten up.

At least if she was super busy, she wasn't alone. And he couldn't imagine any universe where she didn't make sure Evan was safe, as well. They were probably fine, and he was too exhausted by the day and his anticipation at seeing her beautiful smile again to be able to filter out the negative thoughts.

He forced himself to take a deep breath and slow to a stop for the red light at the next intersection.

He had no proof that her ex-husband was in Kansas City, breaking into her apartment, setting small fires around their building and killing undercover agents. Uncle Cole had texted him a copy of Kenneth Norwell's mugshot. A man could change his looks a lot in six years—grow a beard, shave his head or dye his hair or let it grow long. Still, Matt had memorized the image and had wearied his brain trying to recall if he'd seen anyone like that around Corie and Evan. If he'd seen anyone like that in the crowds of lookie-loos at any of the area's recent suspicious fires. But he'd been focused on doing his job—putting out the flames, not spotting the man who may have started them.

Cole had also shared that Norwell's residence was in Jefferson City. His parole officer confirmed that Norwell had been at every check-in since his release. Still, Jeff City was only a two-and-a-half-hour drive from KC. Close enough to get to Kansas City to set a fire and get back in time for his required daily meetings. But did that put him in the city long enough to play games with Corie's sense of security? Did that give him time to drive to St. Louis to torch an attorney's office to find her new name and address in the first place?

Someone was conducting a harassment campaign against Corie and her son. Someone wanted her to be unsettled and afraid, possibly to distract her enough to drop her guard so she wouldn't see the big threat coming— and maybe just because some sicko got off on gaslighting her and seeing her afraid. And there was no denying that someone had started those fires at their building with a flammable goo that bore a remarkable resemblance to the accelerant used to burn down Chad Meade's pricey automotive repair place.

It could all be a tragic coincidence. Or it could be that Corie's violent past had come back to haunt her in the worst of ways.

Matt drummed his fingers against the steering wheel, counting down the seconds until the light turned green and the car ahead of him pulled out. He had a portable siren and flashing lights in his truck he could turn on to cut through traffic faster, but the only justifiable emergency was the worst-case scenario playing through his head and twisting at his heart. And as far as he knew, that hadn't happened yet.

Plus, Corie and Evan weren't the only citizens he was responsible for here. An arsonist in Kansas City? An uptick in the number of fire calls KCFD had answered in the past month—everything from the woman this morning who had accidentally ignited a pile of laundry when she tried to light her water heater to the gut job at Meade's automotive shop this evening—were cause for concern that no one should be ignoring. Not every fire was arson, but every fire was dangerous—and a potential killer, even if you hadn't been bound up and left for dead in the middle of one.

Unfortunately, it was a single-digit Friday night during the long haul of January, and the bars and eateries around the City Market were open and doing a booming business. There were dozens of patrons hurrying along the sidewalks, getting in and out of cars and buses and cabs, and hundreds more were already inside, staying warm while they flirted and partied and filled their bellies with food and drink. Every one of them could be at risk if Kenny Norwell was in town, setting fires for whoever paid him the right price.

Matt tapped on the accelerator as the light changed. "Don't project the worst."

But the tension cording the back of his neck warned him that the worst was yet to happen.

He turned the corner and spotted the familiar neon sign and bright light from the interior spilling through the big glass windows of Pearl's Diner at the far end of the block.

But he was too far away to see inside, to spot Corie's bouncing ponytail or Evan's shaggy brown hair. Parking was going to be a bear around here, and he vowed then and there to pull into the first available parking space he came across that would fit his big truck, and then he'd run the rest of the way to the diner. He'd told Corie he'd get off by eight or nine, and it was half past ten. In the past, he hadn't minded the responsibilities he enjoyed as a lieutenant at Firehouse 13. But tonight, every frozen hose, every incident report that needed at least a preliminary summary, every offer of support and camaraderie from his crewmates over that last rough call had taken precious time away from getting to Corie and Evan. Even the twenty minutes he'd stopped to shower the smells of soot and death off him and change into jeans and a sweater had taken too long.

Now he was circling the block for a second time, seriously rethinking turning on his flashing lights and double parking outside the diner's front door, all because he wasn't good at putting his thoughts into words. He wasn't sure he could express his fears about Norwell finding a way to track down Corie and Evan's new names and showing up on their doorstep again without Matt sounding like he was barking out orders and scaring her.

Especially if this turned out to be nothing. Maybe the fires were accidents. Maybe Chad Meade had killed Agent Rand's man himself. And maybe this gut-deep edginess had less to do with arson fires and more to do with the feelings he had for Corie that were bottled up inside him.

His phone rang on the dash. When he saw the name on the screen, it didn't ring a second time.

Matt pushed the button to answer the call. "Corie."

Not Corie. He heard noises in the background, some garbled talking, the clink of dishes and silverware, a couple of raised voices, but nothing he could make out.

"Matt?" Evan's voice sounded small and nasally. Was he crying? "Is it okay if I call you?"

"Sure, bud." Matt's heart lurched in his chest. Was something wrong? Was that why Corie hadn't called him back? He ratcheted down the tension that threatened to leak into his voice. "Are you okay? What are you doing on your mom's phone?"

"Mom needs help."

"What's wrong?"

He heard a big sniffle, and then Evan's voice grew stronger. "The customers are being mean to her." Customers. Plural. So probably not Norwell. Surely Evan would recognize his own father. But then, he would only have been one or two when Norwell went to prison. Corie would know him, though. Would she let on to Evan that it was his father? Maybe her ex wasn't even in town, and the fires at their building were just a coincidence that overlapped Uncle Cole's investigation into Chad Meade's resurgence in organized crime and arms smuggling, and whatever was going on at the diner had nothing to do with the information he'd learned this evening.

Maybe someone had been rude about their service or had stiffed Corie on her tip. Maybe the kid took umbrage with that. Matt knew he would. But he kept his tone even and reassuring. "Not everybody is nice, Ev."

"They broke my dragon."

The night turned red behind Matt's eyes, and he bit down on the urge to curse where Evan could hear him. That plastic dragon was just a toy. But that toy clearly had emotional value to Evan. Heck, the kid literally swore by that dragon. Breaking it would damage more than the toy. It was a security blanket for Corie's son who'd grown up without a father. And damn it, it was Evan's.

"Some bullies aren't nice at all."

"The man with the beard said he was going to eat some of my bricks, but I think he hid them in his gross beard or his mashed potatoes. You can't eat plastic bricks. Mom's trying to make him give them back."

Hence the raised voices. "Is he hurting your mom?"

"I don't think so. But they're loud."

Finally. Another pickup was pulling out of a parking space across the street about half a block up from the diner. About damn time. "How many mean customers are there?"

"Two."

Gross beard? "There's the guy with the beard. What does the other man look like?"

"He has red hair and more freckles than I do."

Those jackasses from the bus. He remembered their names—Harve and Jordy. It took a lot to trigger Matt's temper. But with Maldonado's death, one too many arson fires, the possibility of Corie's ex working with Chad Meade and some stupid, drunk hicks hitting on Corie and breaking Evan's dragon, there just wasn't enough calm left in him to control his rage. "Did either of those men touch her?"

"Um…" Hell. They had. They'd put their hands on her.

Matt slammed on his brakes and angled his truck across the lane of traffic, staking claim to the parking space the moment the young couple climbing in left. "Is she okay? Are you?"

"Uh-huh."

"Do you dragon swear?"

He could almost hear the energy flowing into Evan's tone, and the confidence puffing up his chest. "Yes. I'm okay. Mom said to call you to see when you were coming before she called the police. When are you coming?"

"I'm parking my truck now."

"The red-haired guy asked Mom if her boyfriend was

going to save her this time." The sound of fear in Evan's voice eased a little as curiosity kicked in. "What does that mean? Are you her boyfriend?"

"Damn straight I am." Matt whipped into the parking space. "Hang up the phone and tell your mom I'm coming."

"Mo-om!"

Then there was no more call. Matt grabbed his cell off the dash, pocketed his keys, put a hand up to stop the car bearing down on him and jogged across the street. Thanks to the diner's booth-to-ceiling windows, Matt had a clear view of what was happening before he ever reached the front door at the corner.

Harve and Jordy were easy to spot at their table in the middle of the restaurant with their mountain-man hygiene and penchant for making a scene. Neither one could be mistaken for the man in the mugshot of Kenny Norwell.

That didn't make the scene any easier to dismiss. Matt saw a wingless plastic dragon and brightly colored blocks scattered across the table and plate in front of Harve. Despite Evan's red-rimmed eyes, he sassed something to the bearded man and grabbed his dragon. When Harve shoved Evan away from the table, Corie dropped her empty tray and scooted Evan behind her, lambasting the bearded man. Matt lengthened his stride when he hit the sidewalk in front of Pearl's, running the last few yards.

A pregnant woman in a business suit stood at the front register, on her cell, reporting everything she was seeing, hopefully on the phone to 9-1-1. One older gentleman stood up at his table in the booth opposite Harve and Jordy and the McGuires, pointing a finger at the two men and rebuking them. That earned him Jordy jumping up and shouting "Boo" or some other startling word that sent him tumbling back into his seat beside a white-haired woman. The rest of the customers watched the scene with wide-eyed shock or buried their gazes in their menus and plates, trying desperately not to get involved.

Involved was the call of every Taylor. Step up when someone needs help. Matt might not be a Taylor by blood. But he was a Taylor down to his very bones.

He swung the door open.

"It's one thing to get handsy with the waitstaff or harass a nice gentleman like Mr. Wallace," he heard Corie chide. "But you touch my son…"

The tinkling bell that jingled overhead sounded inordinately loud and somehow menacing in the sudden silence from every table. Matt made no effort to hunch his shoulders or tone down his anger. He knew how to make his presence known. Big dude at the front door. Black stocking cap, black jeans, black coat. Spooky quiet. Barely breathing hard despite a run through the cold night air. Dark eyes lasered in on the freckled hand clamped around Corie's forearm. Long, purposeful strides took him right up to the table where Harve Gross Beard and Jordy Freckle Face were harassing Corie and Evan.

"Well, if it ain't the boyfriend." Jordy announced Matt's arrival like a rehearsed line. "The boy said you'd show up tonight." But he glanced nervously across the table at Harve, unsure how to proceed.

Matt could help with that. "Let her go."

Although the younger man's grip instantly popped open, Harve chuckled, urging his friend not to panic. "This is all a misunderstanding. The waitress just brought us our pie. We're gonna sit and enjoy dessert."

"No." Simple. Succinct.

Harve fisted his hands against his thighs and Jordy shifted to the edge of his seat. Both were dead giveaways to the two men's intentions.

Matt Taylor had a brother who was a highly trained

SWAT cop. Another was a street patrolman who handled a K-9 partner. Hell, he'd grown up with three brothers. He knew what to do in a fight.

Not that this would be much of one.

When Harve shoved his chair back from the table, Matt toed the edge of the hard plastic tray on the floor, tipped it up into his hand and whacked the bearded man across the face, knocking him back onto his seat. Without wasting any movement, he jerked Harve's coat down his arms, twisting the sleeves and cinching them together behind the back of his chair. Jordy jumped to his feet and cocked his arm back to take a swing at Matt.

He heard Corie's shriek of a warning, raised his arm to deflect the blow and twisted to plant his fist in the middle of the red-haired man's solar plexus, stunning him. Before Jordy could catch his breath or yell uncle, Matt had pinned his arm behind his back and shoved his face down into his roast beef sandwich. When Harve tried to wriggle his chair back to kick out at him, Matt stomped his big boot down on his foot. The man yelped in pain and shouted for someone to call the cops, that he and his buddy were being assaulted by some bigfoot wild man. Matt was peripherally aware of a few customers snapping pictures of the altercation with their phones, but no one was calling anybody to help these two.

While Harve moaned in pain, Matt leaned over the man he had pinned to the table. "You two need to pick on somebody your own size. Not a little boy."

"We were just havin' some fun," Jordy argued. "He knows we were playin'." He turned toward Evan. "Right, kid?"

Corie hugged Evan closer to her side as the brave little man answered. "You're a bully! Bullies get sent to the office."

Matt twisted Jordy's arm a little harder, his eyes telling Harve he would do the same to him if he tried anything else. "Return everything you took from this boy. Now." With a nod to Corie, she loosened Harve's coat sleeves so he could free his hands before she backed away to hug Evan to her side again. Harve emptied his shirt pocket and dumped the plastic bricks on the tabletop. "All of them," Matt ordered.

Muttering a curse under his breath, Mr. Gross Beard dipped his fingers into the mashed potatoes on his plate and dug out three more pieces. When Matt raised an eyebrow, he dropped the pieces into his glass of water and swished them around to get most of the food off them. Then he fished them out with his spoon and put all of them in a napkin he handed to Corie. "Sorry, ma'am."

Corie took the napkin and guided Evan back to the last booth where the body of his dragon now sat. She settled her son into his seat and urged him to start rebuilding his toy.

"Mister," Jordy whined. "You gotta let me up. You're killin' me here."

No. He'd seen killing today. This was just a friendly conversation among three men who were about to reach an understanding. "Are you going to touch this woman again?"

"C'mon. She's pretty. I just wanted her attention. She smiled at everybody but us—" Matt applied the slightest of pressure to his wrist. "No. No, sir."

"Are you going to harass her or anyone else in this restaurant?"

There were no excuses this time. "No, sir."

Matt released his grip and stepped back, making sure Corie and Evan were behind him, and there was a clear aisle to the front door. "Get out."

Jordy eagerly grabbed his coat and booked it to the

front door. Harve was slower to rise to his feet and adjust his jacket onto his shoulders with a firm snap of the material. His eye contact seemed to say that this *conversation* wasn't over. "You don't know who you're messin' with, *Boyfriend*."

Matt didn't take kindly to a threat like that. "Neither do you."

Eventually, Harve, too, backed away from Matt and headed for the door.

The entire diner seemed to be holding its collective breath as the bearded man stopped at the hostess stand and pulled out a wad of cash in his money clip.

"I don't want your money." The dark-haired woman cradled one hand protectively over her swollen belly and held her cell phone up and snapped a picture. "You two aren't welcome here anymore. If you come in again, I'll call one of my close connections at KCPD—like my husband." She put the phone back to her ear. "I'm texting you the second man's picture now, hon. Uh-huh." She held out the phone again. "Detective Kincaid would like to speak to you."

"Harve, come on." Jordy waited in the open door, letting the cold air rush in and chill the air. "One of them dates Bigfoot? And the other's married to a cop? I don't care how good the money is, we're out of our league—"

"Shut up."

"I know you said we owe—"

"Move!" Harve shoved Jordy outside. The bell above the door dinged as the door finally closed behind them.

How good the money is? Was somebody paying those two to harass Corie?

He had a sick idea of who that might be.

Before they reached the curb, Harve was on his phone texting someone. Matt stood at the window and watched, waiting for them to leave, not just the diner, but the whole neighborhood. After Harve put away his phone, he glanced back at Matt and offered him a mocking salute. Then the light changed, and Jordy pulled his seething partner along with the group of people crossing the street. A dark muscle car with tinted windows screeched to a stop at the far curb and the two men climbed inside. Harve must have texted for the ride to pick them up. But that was no car service to arrive this fast. That had to be a buddy of theirs, waiting close by. Maybe close enough to have watched the confrontation through the diner windows.

Matt glanced down at the license plate and committed it to memory. But he made no effort to call it in until he was certain that the yahoo twins and their unseen chauffeur had driven away. Then he quickly texted the plate number to Cole and asked him to ID the vehicle owner and possibly find out Harve and Jordan's last names.

Finally exhaling a sigh of relief that the incident was over, Matt exchanged a nod with the woman at the hostess stand, now fully engaged in a conversation with her husband, who was no doubt feeling just as worried and far away from where he needed to be as Matt had felt a few minutes earlier. Only then did he turn to Corie. "Are you two…?" Corie launched herself at Matt, throwing her arms around him while Evan latched onto his waist in between them. Funny how much better he felt now, too. "Okay."

The elderly gentleman who'd tried to help led the applause. Matt wound one arm around Corie and kissed the crown of her hair, inhaling the homey, enticing scent of baked goods, hard work and fruity shampoo that was hers alone. He palmed the back of Evan's head and held them both close, strengthened by the needy, welcoming grasp of their hands, loving the sense of completeness he felt at holding mother and son in his arms.

After introducing himself and making sure the older

gentleman was okay, Matt thanked him for attempting to intervene. Mr. Wallace sat down, and he and the other patrons returned to their meals and conversations. Corie fisted a hand in Matt's coat and stretched up on tiptoe to press a kiss to the edge of Matt's jaw. "Thank you. I know I keep saying that but, thank you."

Every nerve ending in Matt's body zinged to the imprint where her soft lips had grazed his skin. The adrenaline that had spurred him into the diner was pulsing erratically through his system now, his hyperalertness to all things McGuire now warring with the bone-deep weariness from the day. He needed to keep it together for a while longer, trade some information, ensure they were safe—or there'd be no rest sufficient to help him recover from losing them. "Did they hurt you or Evan?"

"No."

He tipped Evan's head up to his and winked. "You dragon swear you're okay?" Evan grinned at Matt's under-standing of the boy's highest code of honor. Evan crossed his finger over his heart and nodded before running back to his booth like the happy child he should be to start building again.

With Evan gone, Corie moved her arms to Matt's waist and snuggled closer. "I dragon swear, too," she teased. "But I'm not too proud to admit that I've never been hap-pier to see anyone in my whole life. I knew when those two walked in and asked to be seated in my section that there was going to be trouble." With an angry huff, she pulled away, but only to move to his side and hug herself around his arm, turning toward the last booth by the win-dows where Evan was playing. "What kind of man gets rough with a child like that? Steals from him like it's some kind of joke?"

"No kind of *man*." Matt leaned over and kissed the

crown of her hair. "I figured Evan would be safe with you here. But I was scared at how far you might go to protect him."

She shook her head. "I got another waitress to cover the table for me, thinking if I wasn't there to entertain them, they'd eat fast and leave. But when they approached Evan, I had to step in." She rubbed her cheek against Matt's coat sleeve. "Of course, I know they only did it to get me to react. But it was nice to know I had backup before I charged in to do battle."

He covered both her hands with his. "I will always be here if you need me. I'm glad you called."

The pregnant boss lady had circled around the middle tables and met them near the back booth. She extended her hand to Matt. "I'm Melissa Kincaid. I run Pearl's Diner. Your meal is on the house."

"Matt Taylor. I appreciate you calling the police." Although he shook her hand, he shrugged off her offer. "I just want coffee and a slice of pie."

"Still on the house." She held up her phone before tucking into the pocket of her jacket. "And don't worry about Corie's safety when she's here. After the story I just told my husband, Sawyer, I imagine half of KCPD will be eating their meals here the rest of the weekend. Those two won't be bothering any of us again."

Corie released Matt's arm to exchange a hug with the dark-haired woman. "Thanks, Melissa."

"Thank your boyfriend here. By the way, my husband wants to meet you." Melissa smiled at Matt before nodding toward the booth beside her where Evan had spread out his toys, drawings and plastic building bricks. "Corie, take ten. I'll get your orders out for you."

Corie slid into the vinyl seat beside Evan while Matt pulled off his stocking cap and unzipped his coat. Although Corie spared a few moments to ruffle Evan's hair and inquire about the state of repairs on his dragon, when Matt settled onto the seat across from them, he felt her feet sliding between his under the table. He might have thought it was an accident until a few seconds later when her fingertips brushed against his knee. Although some surprisingly naughty thoughts leaped to mind at what they could be doing under the table, Matt chilled his brain and captured her hand in his, linking them together away from prying eyes.

"Sorry about the *boyfriend* thing," she apologized, capturing her bottom lip between her teeth in a frown. "Evan shouted it out to the restaurant as a warning to Harve and Jordy. I'm afraid the appellation stuck."

Man, how he wanted to kiss that bottom lip, ease her discomfort, ease his own. "I'm okay with that."

That sweet mouth blossomed into a smile. "I am, too."

Not for the first time, Matt noted how much he enjoyed holding this woman. How much he loved watching the nuances of her expression. How much he looked forward to hushed, intimate conversations like this one.

Sure, he'd spent part of the last few nights fantasizing about what it would be like to have Corie in his bed. As much as she seemed to like touching him, it wasn't a stretch to imagine undressing those decadent curves and tasting those soft lips and lying with her skin to skin, burying himself inside her, bringing them as close as two people could physically be. Although he knew her to be cautious, he also knew the woman who tugged him down for an impulsive kiss, who reached for him when he was being too careful for her, who stroked his lips and caressed his face and hugged herself around him in a way that was slightly possessive and made her smile that sexy, heart-robbing smile.

Yeah, even now, his body was aching to be closer to hers. But there was something just as soothing, just as satisfying about sharing a connection as simple as holding hands with Corie. With Evan babbling on with a play-by-play of how every brick fit together to rebuild his dragon, another waitress taking their order for coffees and cherry pie, his own thoughts racing as he tried to make sense of everything he was learning about the potential threat surrounding this family, holding hands with Corie under the table felt like a lot more. It was a secret bond for just the two of them to share.

It felt like something deeper, something stronger. Something permanent.

Matt was losing himself in the gentle green of Corie's eyes when his phone dinged with a text. Not wanting to release her hand, he set his phone on the tabletop and pulled up the message as soon as he saw it was from Cole.

Car registered to a Jeff Caldwell.
No record. Get this. His address is the same building as yours. You don't know him?

Matt frowned. He knew several of the people in his building. But he worked long hours. Kept to himself unless he had a family event. Or he was worried about Corie and Evan. The only Jeff he could think of was Wally Stinson's part-time super. And that was just a name to him. He'd never actually met the guy.

But he hated the idea that this guy had a link to Corie. What were the odds of another one of their neighbors showing up at the place where she worked? Of that same guy knowing Harve and Jordan? Of that man living in the apartment directly below hers?

"Ow."

For one fuzzy moment, Matt wondered at the change he saw in Corie's eyes. They were darker. Her pale brows were arched with a question.

Too late, he realized how much his grip had tightened and quickly released her hand. "Sorry."

"You didn't hurt me," she assured him. "But you went away somewhere. I'd say 'penny for your thoughts,' although I'm worried they're not good ones. Is this the spooky quiet side of you that you mentioned?"

His phone dinged with another text from Cole.

Without last names, it will take longer to ID Harve and Jordan. A buddy of mine, Sawyer Kincaid, just walked over from his desk and asked if I knew you. Said you got rid of the riffraff at his wife's restaurant. You're not thinking of switching sides and becoming a cop, are you? :)
I've attached Caldwell's license photo.
If you need anything else, let me know.
Stay safe.

He thanked his uncle and pulled up the photo. Although the man looked vaguely familiar, Matt couldn't place Jeff Caldwell as anyone he'd seen at their apartment building.

And though brown hair and brown eyes like his own were a fairly unremarkable look, he knew he'd seen this guy. But where? Matt splayed his thumb and forefinger across the screen, enlarging the picture to look for anything uniquely discernible, like a scar or crooked teeth. Beyond a spatter of brown freckles across his cheeks, he saw nothing to make this guy stand out in a crowd.

"Matt?" Now Corie's hands were both on top of the table, scooting aside their coffee mugs and reaching across to grasp his. "What's wrong? You're scaring me a little."

Right. This was the part where he usually lost the

woman he was interested in—when he got locked up inside his head and failed to communicate.

But as he struggled to find the right words to say what was necessary without alarming her, Corie picked up his phone and flipped it over, hiding the screen. Her skin blanched as she sneaked a panicked glance at Evan. As soon as she saw her son was distracted, she leaned across the table, dropping her voice to a whisper. "Why do you have a picture of Kenny?" she whispered.

"Your ex?"

And just like that, all the niggling bits of information swimming through his brain made sense. It took every ounce of strength Matt possessed not to leap across the table and pull Corie and Evan into his arms.

He picked up his phone, turning the image away from Evan and texting the information to his uncle. "His driver's license says Jeff Caldwell. This man is Kenny Norwell?"

"Yes. He's gained some weight and his hairline's receding a little, but that's him. Now answer *my* question. Why do you have that picture?" He followed the muscles contracting down her long, pale throat as she swallowed hard. "Spooky quiet isn't going to cut it tonight, Matt Taylor. I've worked hard to erase that man from my life. You need to talk to me."

Matt's gaze swiveled around the restaurant and landed on the reflections of the three of them in the window. He silently cursed that he couldn't see much beyond the glass besides traffic lights and streetlamps. How was he supposed to protect this family from a threat he couldn't see? "Have you seen him around any of the places you frequent? Here? Home? School?"

"No. Have you?"

He glanced across the table at Evan. "Maybe we shouldn't discuss this here."

She pulled her hands up inside the cuffs of her sweater and hugged her arms around her waist. Painfully aware of not wanting to alarm her son, Corie turned slightly in her seat. Although little more than a whisper, her tone was precise. "Ten words or less, Taylor. Tell me something before I get scared completely out of my mind."

He heard the sound of breaking glass in the distance and wondered if that was his hopes for a relationship with Corie crashing and burning.

"He owns the car Harve and Jordy drove off in."

For a moment, he thought she was going to pass out, there was so little color on her face. Matt reached clear across the table to cup her alarmingly cool cheek.

"Breathe, sweetheart. I'm not sure what's going on yet. But I will not let him hurt you."

Corie started to shake her head, her disbelief in his vow or his ability to make good on it evident in her hopeless expression. But then Evan suddenly rocketed to his feet, standing on the seat beside her, and her indomitable maternal instinct kicked in. "Whoa, sweetie. What are you doing?"

Ignoring her hands at his waist, Evan pressed his face to the glass, peering into the night. "Matt? Is that your truck?"

And then Matt realized he'd heard it, too. The breaking glass hadn't been in the restaurant or his imagination.

He spotted the flames shooting up from the windshield of his truck. Someone nearby was screaming. Others ran, both toward and away from the fire. He heard the squeal of tires spinning on the icy pavement, speeding in place until they found traction.

"Call 9-1-1." Matt grabbed his coat and rushed out the front door and into the street to deal with the blaze. "KCFD!" he shouted more than once, ordering pedestrians and vehicles out of harm's way as they slowed or stopped completely to watch the glowing liquid and the flames it carried with it spread across the hood and plop onto the pavement like a lava flow. He caught a glimpse of a white van racing away in the opposite direction as he vaulted into the back of his truck and pulled the fire extinguisher from the steel storage box there.

From his higher vantage point, he quickly assessed the potential hazards of the situation. The broken whiskey bottle and charred rag on the ground indicated someone had tossed an old-fashioned Molotov cocktail at his truck. Possibly the driver of the white van. Or Jeff Caldwell/ Kenny Norwell or whatever he wanted to call himself. But he didn't see any dark muscle car racing away from the scene. Maybe Harve and Jordan had come back to exact revenge for the public humiliation of being bested in a one-sided fight.

And maybe he needed to be the firefighter he was and think about preventing personal injury or property damage. The vehicles were parked tightly together here. And traffic was becoming a slow bumper-to-bumper parade as concerts at bars or games on TV ended, and the patrons who'd been enjoying them left for home or their next entertainment destination. A lot of gas tanks in a confined space was a chain reaction fire waiting to happen. And if that flammable, tar-like substance got on anyone's clothes or skin, the slow-burning gelatin would be difficult to wash away, leaving horrible, painful wounds.

"Feel free to call 9-1-1," Matt yelled to the group of young twentysomethings circling closer, filming the fire. "Stay back!"

Traffic was backing up into the next intersection now, as drivers were too curious or frightened to pay attention to where they were going. If he didn't get control of this situation fast, he'd have a traffic accident to deal with, too.

Matt jumped down from the bed of his truck, shielded his face from the worst of the slowly expanding flames and laid down a layer of foam over his windshield and hood. While the driver parked in front of him thankfully arrived and moved his car out of harm's way, Matt continued to spray the extinguisher. But he was running out of juice fast because the viscous goop that was clearly the arsonist's weapon of choice was spreading faster than he could contain it.

Then he felt a hand at the small of his back. "Where should I spray this?"

What the hell? Matt whirled around on Corie. "Get back inside!" Instinctively, he circled an arm around her waist and walked her back toward the diner. Then he snatched her off her feet and spun her out of harm's way as a car swerved around them. She hadn't even stopped to put on a coat or gloves. "What are you doing here?"

She twisted out of his grasp and held up the small fire extinguisher she'd brought from the diner. "Enough atonement. You need help."

"You think this is about me needing to be a hero?" Her cheeks were chapped with the cold, and the only thing she had on over her polyester uniform was that navy-blue cardigan. "You'll freeze out here."

She completely ignored his arguments. "I called 9-1-1. They said they'd be here in a matter of minutes."

Shouts and honking from vehicles down the road who couldn't see what was happening this far up the road forced them to raise their voices. "What about Evan?"

"Melissa is with him. At least let me divert traffic."

"It's dangerous out here. And I'm not just talking about the fire."

"You can't face Kenny alone," she warned him, her gaze boldly searching his for understanding.

So, she thought her ex was responsible for this fire, too. She wasn't running or hiding. She was here to fight.

He shouldn't be turned on by that.

Matt tunneled his fingers into the silky hair at the base of her ponytail and dipped his head to capture her mouth in a quick kiss. Gratitude and understanding and something far more primal burned between them in the short seconds of that kiss. Then he peeled off his coat and draped it around her shoulders, taking the second extinguisher from her while she slid her arms into the sleeves.

"I'll handle traffic." He was tall enough to be seen over several vehicles down the road. He pointed to the flames dripping beside his front tire and pooling against the curb. "Lay down some foam along the edge of the sidewalk. We can't let this spread beyond my truck. Stay where I can see you. The guy who started this fire could still be part of this crowd somewhere. Evan needs you."

"And I need you." With a nod, Corie went to work. "Be careful."

She was soon joined by two men who'd brought fire extinguishers from one of the local businesses. Matt heard her repeating his orders, directing the other volunteers as he stepped into traffic and warned the next vehicle to slow down and give the burning truck a wide berth. He directed the oncoming cars into a single lane and urged the east-bound vehicles to cross the yellow line and keep moving.

As soon as he saw the B shift crew from Firehouse 13 turn the corner, Matt exhaled a sigh of relief. Once the police arrived and took over traffic duty, he jogged forward to meet the team and give them a sit-rep. One of them threw a bunker coat around his shoulders, identifying him as the firefighter he was. He shooed away the medic who wanted to check him for injuries and directed her to the civilian volunteers who'd helped them fight the fire. The threat to his truck had been neutralized, but he was more concerned about the puddles of incendiary goo still burning inside the perimeter Corie and the two volunteers had laid down before running out of suppressant foam. They'd need a hazmat unit to clean up whatever chemical had been inside the bottle. And they'd need to secure a sample to send to the crime lab to compare to the samples from the other fires.

As a police officer approached him to take his statement, Matt turned to watch Corie huddling inside his coat, watching his crewmates go to work. There was little more than that wheat-colored ponytail showing above the collar. Every cell in his body wanted to go to her, but he needed to make a full report before the perp or perps went to ground and couldn't be located until the next fire or something worse.

It was that *something worse* that was turning him inside out with a sense of impending doom. This fire had been personal. A message to him—the clock was ticking, Corie belonged to another man, he'd never be able to protect her. Or something as crudely prophetic as the fire that had destroyed Enrique Maldonado's car—stop talking to the cops...or die.

The problem with an arsonist working as an enforcer and sending graphic messages like this one was that there was a huge risk for collateral damage. Jobs stolen. People injured. Lives lost.

Matt wanted an APB out on Kenny Norwell, Harve and Jordy, and that muscle car, along with the white van.

He wanted Corie and Evan in his arms now. Brave, beautiful Corie who wasn't afraid of hard work or of him, and her brave, smart son who missed no detail and cared so much about others. Matt needed to know they were safe. He needed to see Corie's smile again. Every day of his life.

He needed to admit that he was long past falling in love with the family who lived across the hall. The family who needed him.

The family who made him need things that no bullying wiseacres, ex-hubby arsonist or killer was going to take from him.

Chapter Eleven

"I want to stop on the sixth floor." Corie had her keys out as she and Matt waited for the elevator. "Knock on that bastard's door and look him right in the eye."

Matt cradled Evan's sleeping weight against his chest. "It's after one in the morning, Corie. What if it isn't him?"

"Then I will apologize profusely and come upstairs to live the rest of my life in shame and paranoia."

He didn't even try to hide that hint of a grin that creased the chocolatey-cinnamon stubble of his late-night beard. But the grin vanished as suddenly as it had appeared by the time they stepped onto the elevator. "What if it is your ex-husband? Do you have a plan for what you'll say or do when you see him? Do you really want him to see Evan?"

"I'm sure he already has!" she snapped, then immediately dropped her voice back to a whisper. "Evan is the only thing he ever wanted from me. If he's stalking me and you, then he's seen Evan with one or both of us. If Jeff and Kenny really are the same person, I want to know it. He was in my apartment, Matt. He sabotaged my kitchen to start a fire. He could challenge me for custody of Evan if a judge heard about that."

"He's a felon with a criminal record. No one is going to take your son from you legally. You're too good a mother for that. And I won't let them do it any other way." He loosed one arm from around Evan to hug her to his side and dropped a quick kiss to her lips. "All right. I'll go knock on his door. You get Evan to bed."

"No. I'm coming with you. Either I'd be alone with Evan upstairs or I'd be alone down here. I don't want to be alone if Kenny has found us."

His shoulders lifted with a stalwart sigh. "I don't want that, either. But you'll take Evan, and I'll take point so he has to get through me first. If he's there, you take Ev and run. Call 9-1-1. Ask for Cole Taylor. Ask for any Taylor. Help will come."

"What will you be doing while we're running?"

"Having a conversation. Your ex ever have a penchant for guns or knives I should worry about?"

She shook her head. "But he knows how to set fires in a dozen different ways."

"I know how to put out fires in a dozen different ways."

No doubt. "He's strong, Matt. He knows how to fight."

Matt glanced down the straight line of his nose and over the jut of his broad shoulder at her. Right. Matt was strong and knew how to fight, too. He'd made short work of Harve and Jordy tonight. And though she knew Kenny would be more skilled and aware than either of those numb nuts had been, she had a feeling Matt could hold his own in any situation.

She leaned into him, hoping she wasn't asking too much of this good man. "I just want to live a normal life. Raise a healthy, happy son who isn't always worried about the monster coming and him losing me. I want friends and more children. I want to teach and love and live the life that Kenny and my mother cheated me out of. I don't want to be afraid anymore."

"Evan's a smart kid. Stronger than you think. You're

stronger than you think. Besides, you've got that cool plastic dragon to protect you."

She giggled, patting the backpack that held Evan's creation, but her laugh was a wry sound that revealed more despair than humor. "You're our real protection dragon, Matt. You're big and strong and can harness the fire."

"I thought dragons were the bad guys until I met you two." His big yawn seemed to startle him. But Matt shook off his fatigue and stood up straighter, reaching across the elevator to push the number six button. "All right. We'll knock on our neighbor's door. If he was near the diner when we were and threw that Molotov cocktail, he won't be asleep, anyway."

A minute later, Corie was hefting her sleeping boy into her arms, along with his backpack and hers looped over either shoulder. Although he was slenderly built, Evan was a growing boy. She knew what a treat it was to have Matt literally shoulder some of the parenting burden from her. "I've got him," she assured him, reaching around Matt to knock on the door and start this meeting that was making the nerves roil in her stomach.

No answer.

Matt knocked. "Mr. Caldwell? It's Matt Taylor from the fire department." He put his ear to the door and knocked again, each time a little louder. "I don't think he's home."

A door opened across the hallway behind them and a woman in her pajamas and robe and a hot-pink scarf wrapped around her head peered through the gap between the door and jamb. "I know it's Friday night, folks. But do you know how late it is?"

Matt tipped the brim of the KCFD ball cap to her. "Yes, ma'am, I do."

She huffed at that answer and pulled her flowery robe

more securely around her. "Well, some of us have to work on the weekend. Keep it down out here."

Corie stepped in when Matt's straight-to-the-point communication technique failed. She pointed to number 612. "Do you know Mr. Caldwell? Mr. Stinson's part-time super? I'm Corie McGuire, your neighbor from upstairs."

"Jeff keeps to himself. I like that about him." Not-so-subtle hint noted. The woman tipped her gaze up to Matt and frowned. Then she looked from Corie to her son dozing on her shoulder and frowned again. "He's up a little late, isn't he?"

Since they clearly weren't going to charm any information from this woman at this hour, Corie jumped on the first plausible lie that sprang to mind. "Yes, he is. That's why we're looking for Jeff. I've locked myself out of our apartment. He has keys."

The woman dropped her gaze to the keys dangling from Corie's fingers before arching the sternest eyebrow she'd ever seen. "I'm calling Mr. Stinson. He'll deal with you."

The door closed on Corie's thank-you.

"You're a terrible liar," Matt teased, easing Evan from her arms until the building super arrived.

"Yeah. But I'm getting us into the apartment, aren't I?"

Well, technically, Wally Stinson was getting them into Jeff Caldwell's apartment.

Mr. Stinson looked less than thrilled when he stepped off the elevator in a pair of slacks and a wool robe hastily pulled on over his pajamas. His ring of master keys jingled as he shuffled along, smoothing his comb-over into some semblance of coverage on top of his head. "This isn't your place, Mrs. McGuire. Yours either, Mr. Taylor." He glanced over at the door to 613. "Miss Alice wasn't too happy that your noise in the hallway woke her up."

Corie didn't point out that his noisy key ring jangled

more loudly than their knocking had. "It's vital that we speak to Mr. Caldwell. I think he broke into my apartment."

Wally frowned, debating whether or not her claim had any merit. "You said that before, that you think he jiggered with your oven."

"That's right."

"Any proof?"

Corie touched the door. "I think it's in here. I want to talk to him about it, but he isn't answering."

Mr. Stinson pushed his glasses up on the bridge of his nose. "That's because he works most nights at a distribution center. He only helps me during the day. Now y'all go on about your business and let the good people in this building get some sleep."

"That's even better." Corie darted in front of him to stop his retreat. "We could go in there without him knowing, see if any of my stuff is in there."

"I haven't gotten any complaints about other tenants being robbed." First this man had accused her son of setting fires, and now, like the woman in 613, he seemed to be calling her a liar. "Why would you think this man is stealing from you and messing with your things?"

She glanced over his head to Matt's steely expression. And when he nodded, Corie confessed what she suspected was true. "He's my ex-husband."

Wally's posture withered for a moment. "Ah, hell. I had no idea. We went through something like this with my daughter. Her no-account ex cleaned out every television and computer in the house when they were getting divorced. He pawned most of it." Wally gave her a pitying look and patted her shoulder as he changed direction and pulled out the key to unlock Jeff Caldwell's door. "If that's the case here, if he's taking or breaking your stuff,

I'll fire him on the spot. But like I said, he usually isn't here nights."

"Then this is the perfect time to look, right? Thank you, Mr. Stinson."

Mr. Stinson opened the door to a dark apartment. He turned on the light, and the place didn't look that much more welcoming, with a card table and chairs set up in the living room, and an old recliner facing a state-of-the-art television. There wasn't a single decoration or personal item anywhere.

Matt placed Evan back in her arms and led the way inside, his gaze constantly moving to take in every detail. "Doesn't look like he stays here much at all."

"Do you see what he took from you?" Mr. Stinson asked.

"What?" The super startled her from her inspection of a stack of porn magazines beside the recliner. He'd bought them retail. There was no subscription name or address on them. "There's hardly anything here."

"What did he take?"

Her sanity, peace of mind and well-being. But, of course, Mr. Stinson assumed a much more monetary reason for Kenny, er, Jeff, to be in her apartment. "Do you mind if we look around?"

"Your boyfriend already is."

Boyfriend. She really was getting used to having others link her and Matt together as a couple. She wondered if he minded.

She didn't. She didn't mind being linked to Matt Taylor at all.

"Corie." Matt's quiet tone filled her with more dread than a shouted warning would have. Hugging Evan tighter to her chest, she followed him to the kitchen. He put out his arm to keep her from moving any closer than the archway.

It didn't stop the sheer terror from reaching her, though. The place was a science lab and an engineering station all rolled into one. There were stained measuring cups and hot plates on the counters. Jars filled with that clear, yellowish sludge that had coated the hood of Matt's truck and bubbled the paint up and melted his windshield wipers as it had burned. The same goo they'd found in the alley fire and inside her oven. There was an open toolbox with pliers and screwdrivers and a tinier metal box that looked like it was filled with delicate dental tools. On the floor was a box of wires and technical equipment—packaged disposable cell phones, computer chips, something that looked like bundles of firecrackers. On the opposite counter, there was a stash of three whiskey bottles whose labels matched the one that had shattered against Matt's truck. There were diagrams stuck to the refrigerator with magnets. There was a picture mounted there, too.

A well-worn, often-touched, picture of Evan when he'd turned one. They'd gone to the photography studio that day after Kenny had made her redress their son in a suit and Velcro tie instead of the cute baby blue overalls she'd put him in. There was a big *D* in the picture behind the posed shot—a *D* for Danny Norwell.

Even though he was sound asleep, she cupped the back of her son's head and turned him from the disturbing sight. The tears that stung her eyes were angry, fierce. This was her old life, the one she thought she'd escaped from. "This is Kenny. He used to have a setup like this in our garage back in St. Louis."

"Who's Kenny?" Mr. Stinson asked.

"Jeff, of course," she hastily corrected herself. "I guess he goes by Jeff now."

Matt had his cell phone out, snapping pictures. "I'm calling Uncle Cole. He and Agent Rand will definitely want to see this." He turned her toward the living room. "Stay here. I want to check out the rest of the place. Mr. Stinson, you'll stay here and watch her."

Although issued as an order, not a request, the older man nodded.

"We'll be fine," Corie assured him. "Just be careful."

Once Matt headed down the hall to the other rooms, Mr. Stinson pulled out one of the folding chairs for her, but she was too keyed up to relax. Not here. Not with evidence that pointed to the arson fires Matt had been forced to deal with. "Is this a meth lab?" the older man asked, nodding toward the kitchen.

"Something like." One thing Kenny had never whipped up in the garage was drugs. He'd always said he needed a clear head to work with the compounds he did create for clients who wanted a job done a certain way. "Some of those chemicals are combustible and flammable."

"What would he need those for?" Wally asked.

"Starting fires."

"Not in my building. He… I never knew any of this was here." Mr. Stinson ran his fingers through what was left of his thinning hair. "He knew his way around electricity, carpentry, plumbing—all of it. I played poker with him and a couple of his buddies one night."

"A couple of his buddies?" Corie almost sank in the chair as her knees wobbled beneath the weight of her suspicion. But she had Evan in her arms. She needed to be strong. Smart. Smarter than Kenny. "Does one of them have a dark, almost black beard? The other is tatted up. He's a redhead with freckles."

Wally nodded. "Yeah. Harve and—"

"Jordy."

He seemed surprised that she knew the men's names. Hell, she was surprised to know such things. Corie didn't know whether to be angry or feel foolish that she'd been in the dark about the danger creeping into the corners of her life for so long. "Do you know their last names?"

Wally scratched his head again, sorting through memories. "Jeff Caldwell, of course. Jordan Cox—we made a few jokes about his name. And Harve..." He snapped his fingers as the name fell into place. "Harve Mohrman. He told me he met Jeff in—"

"Jefferson City?" Prison. Harve and Jordy were prison buddies of Kenny's. Even Kenny's alias was a nod to his stay in the pen. Jeff Caldwell? Jeff City? Jeff C?

"Yeah. How did you know?"

Matt reappeared from the hallway, a dangerous purpose to his stride. "We need to go."

"Why? What did you see?"

He scooped Evan from her arms to hurry her along. "We may be disturbing a crime scene."

Something was wrong. Something was very wrong.

"What is it? A dead body?" Something worse than that? Something about her? Evan?

"Corie..."

She evaded his outstretched hand and hurried down the hallway, peeking into the first bedroom, the bathroom, ending up in the bedroom that was located where hers would be on the floor above them. As she entered the room, a sudden shock of cold seeped through her coat and clothes and chilled her skin.

But there was no window open. In the middle of January, there was no air-conditioning running.

It was the room itself, filled with hate and vengeance and the kind of obsession found only in horror and serial killer movies.

The smell got to her first. Something burned and pungent, like incense or a hundred scented candles. There was no furniture in the room besides a table and chair and a cardboard box that looked suspiciously like the one she'd set outside on her fire escape for the neighborhood cats.

Three of the four walls were a sick shrine to her. Pictures from her wedding to Kenny. Pictures from her childhood. Pictures of her waiting at the bus stop near Pearl's Diner, sitting on a bench on campus talking to a professor, monitoring recess duty at her school. There were pictures and newspaper clippings of fires, the shells of burned-out buildings, fiery car crashes and the charred remains of bodies. The images papered the walls and were decorated with bits of yarn pinned to the walls. Burned matches and broken lighters, even a perfume-size bottle of that flammable goo, hung from different strings. Spray painted over the collage of pictures were words and phrases like *child-stealer, kill the witch* and worse.

The fourth wall was tainted simply by being in the room with all the angry, vile images. It held pictures of Evan. Formal ones from when he was very young to candid shots of him on the playground at school here in Kansas City and one of him standing in the bed of Matt's truck, illuminated only by a streetlamp. If the kitchen had been the workspace of an arsonist, then this was his place of worship.

Corie couldn't move. She couldn't think, couldn't feel.

She could only startle when Matt walked into the room behind her, thankfully, having left Evan resting someplace where he couldn't see this. "Looks like he's been using the fire escape to go up to your apartment. That's possibly how he got in and out of your place."

It hadn't been a noisy alley cat pacing on her balcony. Kenny had been there, right outside her bedroom window, and she'd never even suspected.

There was so much hate, so much obsession in this

room. She didn't know whether to scream or cry or simply surrender to the inevitable.

"Come on, sweetheart. Nobody needs to see this except the police." Matt turned her into his arms and walked her out of the room.

She leaned into him, grateful for his strength and support. "I never had a chance of living a normal life when I left Kenny, did I."

Chapter Twelve

Another two hours had passed by the time Detective Cole Taylor and NCIS agent Rand had finished their interviews and left Corie's apartment to go back down to apartment 612, where a team from the crime lab was processing the evidence in the elusive Jeff Caldwell's apartment and members of the KCFD were safely packaging and removing the flammable chemicals and fire-starting devices her ex-husband had kept there.

They were as certain Jeff Caldwell was Kenny Norwell as she was, although no one could find him. And they were certain he was the man a mobster named Chad Meade had hired to do some jobs for him, including torching a car and a building and covering up the scene of a murder. Cole Taylor and his NCIS partner had left discussing the possibility of Kenny turning state's evidence against Meade.

If they could capture him.

If he didn't find another way to hide himself in plain sight and never be found again.

Matt's uncle had also promised a round-the-clock watch on their building while his parents, brothers, sisters-in-law and extended family members she'd lost track of stopped by to bring food, offer a place to stay and trade hugs, handshakes and promises of support that extended to Corie and her son...because Matt said they were important to him.

Corie had never seen such an outpouring of love before. Certainly, the Taylors were nothing like life with her family or Kenny had been. She'd met so many Taylors, she couldn't remember all their names, much less put faces to which branch of the family belonged with whom. But each and every one of them had made her feel as welcome as Mark and Amy had the other night. Like she was a part of something bigger than herself. Part of that family she'd always wanted. An extended family where she could let her son visit a grandparent and know he would be safe and nurtured and loved in a way Kenny and her mother never could.

While the outpouring of love and support had gone a long way to help her bury the images from Kenny's *kill the witch* room, she had no doubt Kenny was targeting her now, tormenting her for his own pleasure or because he wanted her off her guard, giving him an opportunity to steal back the son he'd accused her of taking and punishing her for daring to want something better, safer, more loving than the world that Kenny and his crime buddies offered.

Somewhere along the way, Corie had gotten her second wind. Anything she could do to help the police helped Evan, and she'd do anything for her son. She'd brewed several pots of coffee and served up multiple snacks brought by each of her guests. With all the comings and goings, no matter how quiet they'd tried to be, Evan had awakened at two thirty. He'd eagerly talked to Pike Taylor, petted his K-9 partner, Hans, and arranged a tentative play date with Pike's son, Gideon. He'd carried his plastic dragon with him the entire time he'd joked with Mark and Amy and played host to their indulgent guests.

She would carry the fear, the sense of impending doom for them both. Seeing her son so happy tonight was worth anything she'd gone through in her life—and anything that was yet to come.

But now that all the Taylors were gone, save for one tall, overbuilt firefighter who she feared would give his life to protect her and Evan, she had a different problem on her hands.

Matt was exhausted. He'd hinted at having a rough day on the job, and she suspected that was the reason he'd been so late getting to the diner in the first place. As he hugged his mother and father and locked the door behind them, Matt leaned back against the door and exhaled a deep breath. He looked haggard and tired—always incredibly strong—but now suddenly vulnerable somehow. He'd done so much for her, so much for Evan. Maybe now he'd let her do something for him.

Corie crossed the room. She watched him breathe in deeply and open his eyes to give her one of those almost-there smiles before she reached up to gently cup his stubbled jaw. "You smell good," he murmured in a husky voice.

"And you look exhausted. Come with me." She linked her arm through his and walked him over to her sofa. "You've been this big presence hovering around the room all night, keeping watch. Now it's your turn to relax and regain some of your strength. Sit. I'm taking watch over this apartment tonight."

He folded his long legs and sat back against the cushions, although his dark, hungry gaze never left her. "Corie—"

"No." She placed a finger over his firm lips, silencing whatever protest he was about to make. "I don't remember which brother it was, but they promised that someone would be watching the building all night. I'm in charge inside these walls. You can drop your guard for a little while and rest."

"I *am* beat," he admitted, his lips brushing like a caress against her fingertip. "But I can't shake the feeling that there's something more I could be doing to stop this maniac and protect you."

"Atonement?" She nudged his knees apart and moved between them to sit on his lap. It put her in the rare position of being eye level with him, and she made the most of it by leaning forward to press a lingering kiss against his lips. His hands tightened on her thigh and hip as he sighed against her mouth and then deepened the kiss. Although his deliciously languid possession of her mouth kindled the good kind of fire deep inside her belly and made her breasts feel heavy with anticipation, she also suspected his leisurely response spoke to his fatigue. The man had a physical job. He'd had a physical night putting Harve and Jordy in their place and dealing with his truck. Then there was the emotional roller coaster of discovering Kenny's dangerous workspace and heinous obsession room. Plus, for a man who leaned to the introverted, quieter side of things, dealing with all the police and family and firefighters who'd been in the building these past two hours had probably taken a toll on him. She wondered if *exhaustion* was a strong enough word for what he was feeling right now.

And so, because this was about what Matt needed, and not the deliciously sinful and cherished way his mouth and hands made her feel, she broke off the kiss and tipped his head to gently press her lips to the shadows beneath each handsome eye. Then she hugged him close and whispered against her ear. "You don't owe me anything. You don't owe anyone another piece of your heart and soul and protection and dedication. You've repaid the price for that fire you set as a child a hundred times over. Set your crusade aside for a few minutes and let someone take care of you for a change."

His hands rubbed big circles up and down her back. "Corie, sweetheart, you don't have to do anything."

She pulled away, hating that he saw their relationship in such one-sided terms. Yes, he was incredibly strong and smart and just and wonderful, but he needed to understand that she intended to be an equal partner in this neighbors–turned–friends–turned something infinitely more precious that had grown between them. Kenny had kept her—like a trophy, like breeding stock. But he hadn't loved her, and he'd destroyed any effort to love him.

Matt Taylor was too good a man to feel like he still owed the world a debt. "I don't *have* to do anything. But I want to." She scooted off his lap and pushed him back into the cushions when he tried to stand with her. "Now. What do you need?" She didn't have a lot to offer, but she would grant him whatever he asked. "Something to eat? Drink? I've got cold milk or apple juice. Or I can make more coffee. Sorry, I don't have anything stronger. Do you need a quiet place to sleep for a while?"

He grabbed her hand, stopping her from going into the kitchen. His gaze raked over her from head to toe, stopping with particular interest on her mouth and breasts, telling her one thing he wanted. One thing she would willingly give him.

But then Evan dashed into the living room, reminding them both they weren't alone. "Are you going to bed, Matt?" Evan asked, jumping onto the sofa beside his favorite hero. "Mom said it's *way* past my bedtime. Is it past yours?"

"Yeah, bud. Your mom was just telling me that I need to get some shut-eye."

Evan looked crestfallen. "Oh. You're going back to your apartment now? You're leaving?"

Matt glanced up at Corie, and she answered the question he hadn't even asked. "He's staying with us tonight, sweetie."

"Yay!" Evan's cheer was cut off by a yawn that Matt quickly echoed.

Corie squeezed her son's shoulders. "Come on. Let's get you into bed so Matt can get the sleep he needs, too."

"Okay. 'Night, Matt." Evan fell forward across Matt's chest, winding his arms around his neck.

Matt's long arms gently completed the hug. "Good night."

Evan sat back, his eyes narrowed in an earnest frown. "Do you want my dragon to keep the bad things away for a while? I put his wings back on him and fixed his face."

Matt squeezed Evan to his chest again and brushed a kiss against his soft brown hair. "Nah. You keep him with you tonight. But thanks for havin' my back. Love you."

"Love you, too." And then Evan bounced off the couch and ran to his room, heedless of the two wide-eyed adults staring after him.

After the door to Evan's room closed, Matt glanced up to Corie. "Is that okay? He really does mean a lot to me. He…feels like family."

Corie smiled as the lingering warmth from Matt's kiss expanded to bathe her heart in sunshine. "I'm very okay with that. After all, if you're going to be in a relationship with me, you're going to be in a relationship with my son. And I can't think of a finer role model for him."

Although she sensed that he wanted to ask what she meant by *relationship*, Corie focused on the offer she'd made. "Close your eyes and rest, Matt. It'll take me ten minutes to get Evan back to sleep. Then I'll come back and slice you another piece of that pie if you want."

His dark lashes were already brushing his cheeks as she chastely kissed the top of his head and hurried after Evan. "Don't you worry about us—or anything else—for ten minutes. That's an order."

By the time Evan had dozed off and she'd changed into her pajamas and brushed her teeth, Matt was sound asleep on the couch. His long frame was spread out with his feet hanging off one end of the couch and his head angled up on the armrest at the other. His staunch expression that was more serious than handsome while he was awake had relaxed in slumber, easing the harsh line of his mouth. This rare glimpse of boyish abandon invited her to run her fingers across the crisp dark hair at his temple and press a kiss there.

She was glad she could do this little thing for him, giving him a quiet sanctuary free from worry and guilt, even if just for a few minutes. Because she was certain there was plenty to worry about in their future, judging by Kenny's vindictive behavior and the promise of his own personal retribution plastered across the bedroom walls below hers.

Even though this was a different apartment, and her door and windows here had been checked multiple times by Matt and at least three brothers and an uncle, the last place she wanted to go was her own room. Not alone, at any rate. Not by the fire escape window, where they suspected Kenny had lurked on at least one occasion. Corie feared that if she went into her bedroom and closed her eyes, all she would see were the vile, violent things on the walls right below hers.

Shaking off that unpleasant thought, she checked the front door to make sure it was secure. She needed sleep, too. Her bedroom might feel off-limits, but there was a cushy chair out here where she often fell asleep reading a book. After turning off the lamp, Corie retrieved a couple of throws from the hall closet. She came back to untie Matt's boots and tug them off as quietly as she could without waking him. Then she spread one of the throws over his sleeping body.

He'd earned his rest. He'd earned her gratitude and admiration. He'd earned her trust and compassion. She tucked a pillow beneath his head and kissed his grizzled cheek. Even though she smelled the soap from his shower, she still detected a whiff of the smoke from the fires he'd fought today and tonight. It felt so right, having him here. It was reassuring to know he was safe, too. For a little while, at least. She thought of him as the embodiment of security. But tonight, she would be the one to give him shelter. She would be what he needed tonight. Something tight and guarded unfurled in her chest as she gazed down at the man whose face was softened by the shadows.

She really had fallen for this good man.

Maybe she hadn't been as careful with the boots as she'd thought. Maybe this alert, wary man had simply sensed her presence. Or maybe she'd projected her wish into his head.

Before she turned away, Matt grabbed her hand and pulled her onto the couch with him. "I guess I needed a little more than ten minutes. Is this okay?" he asked, snaking his arm around her waist and pulling her back against his chest, spooning behind her. "I'll go back to my own apartment if you want."

"You're not going anywhere," she said as he pulled the blanket over them both. The heat of his body snugged so closely to hers quickly made her drowsy. This was bliss, to feel so important, so warm and wanted by a man. This was the dream she'd always had about finding the right man, and she drifted slowly, contentedly toward that dream.

But then Matt suddenly tensed behind her, his breath a sharp huff against the nape of her neck. "Dead bolt?"

Corie laughed and turned in his arms. "Already taken care of."

There wasn't much room to maneuver on the couch, but she ended up flat on her back, smiling up at his confused expression. "What did I say?"

"*Dead bolt.* I think it's becoming my code word that means you care. You say it to me every night when you leave."

He feathered his fingers through her loose hair, smiling down at her. "So, I don't have to come up with flowery words or recite any poetry to impress you?"

She grinned at the joke. "I don't think that's your style. It's not mine, either. I like honest and straightforward."

His eyes were dark, pools of midnight in the shadows above her. "I saw a man die in front of me tonight. Plunged to his death and there wasn't a damn thing I could do to save him." His fingers tightened briefly against her scalp and then he was rolling back against the cushions, his arm thrown over his eyes. Tears pricked her own eyes at the pain in his voice. "A little too honest and straightforward, hmm? Sorry about that."

Corie turned into him, hugging him tightly. "Oh, Matt, I'm so sorry. Why didn't you say anything?"

"I was a little preoccupied tonight."

"Taking care of my troubles when you had your own." She pressed a kiss to the warm skin above his collar, stretched against him to tickle her lips against his stubbled neck and sup on the strong beat of his pulse there. "What do you need? How can I help?"

She nibbled on the point of his chin before batting his arm away from his face and crawling right on top of him to reach his mouth and offer him the gentle absolution of her kiss. Her legs parted and tangled with his, sliding between his muscular thighs, already discovering the responsive hardness behind the zipper of his jeans. The nap of her flannel bottoms caught against the denim and muscle underneath, creating pockets of vivid awareness where the material caught and pulled against her skin.

His lips chased after hers as she moved to explore the hard line of his jaw and the surprisingly supple spot beneath his ear that seemed to be packed with a bundle of nerves that made him gasp for breath. She rode the rise and fall of his chest as Matt sucked in several deep breaths to control his responses to her bold exploration. "I'm not good at explaining what I feel. What I need."

"Then show me."

At last, his arms settled around her again. He branded her butt with the palm of his hand and pulled her fully on top of him, dragging her most sensitive places against the hard friction of his body. Giving him the freedom to express himself without words seemed to unleash something powerful and hungry inside him.

With a ragged breath that sounded like her own needy moan, he palmed the back of her head and held her mouth against his, feasting on her lips, demanding she open for him before his tongue swept inside to claim hers. With her body draped over his like a blanket, they didn't need the throw she'd brought from the closet. They were already generating all the heat either of them could need. The throw quickly landed on the floor beside them, and the knit pajama top she wore followed right behind it.

Matt's hands were firebrands against her bare skin, urging her toward a euphoric release she'd never experienced before. She found the hem of his sweater and T-shirt and tugged them up his torso. Her hands were equally greedy as they slid inside to explore his strong, wide chest. She felt a quiver of muscle here, the tickle of crisp curls of hair there. The turgid male nub poking to attention beneath the stroke of her fingers.

Her world rocked in a dizzying circle as Matt suddenly sat up, spilling Corie into his lap. She helped him peel off his shirt and sweater, and then she slipped back in his arms, the heat of skin against skin making her feverish with desire. Making love with Kenny had never lasted this long, much less driven her into this frenzy of need, the eagerness to pleasure, this pure delight in being pleasured.

He lifted her slightly and dipped his head to pull the tip of her breast into his mouth. "Matt," she gasped, unfamiliar with the fiery arrows zinging from her sensitive nipples down to the weepy heaviness between her legs. "Is this…? Are we…?"

"I want you." She clawed her fingers into his hair, holding his wicked mouth against her straining breast as he worked the pebbled nipple between his tongue and lips and teeth and squeezed the other breast in his hand. "I want you," he repeated on a husky moan against her skin.

She had no problem understanding what he needed from her. Corie hoped she was being equally clear. "I'm yours."

To hell with atonement. This brave, good man needed healing, not penance. He needed to believe that whatever he'd done as a child did not make him the man he was today. He needed to know that he was perfect and loved. In her arms, he was most assuredly loved.

"Floor okay?" he breathed against her mouth before reclaiming her lips. "Need…more space."

Corie's answer was to lean back over the edge of the couch and pull Matt with her. They toppled onto the floor together, her landing eased by the rug and blanket and the support of Matt's arm. Then there was a fumble of hands, both eager and out of practice, as they shed the remainder of their clothes and pulled a condom from Matt's wallet. But every touch was a heady arousal, every bump was a perfect caress.

Then Matt was on top of her, sliding into her. Corie closed her eyes to savor her body's pure, primal response to his weight making the pressure building inside her almost unbearable. But he was holding himself back, balancing himself on his arms when she wanted to feel all of him against her.

Her eyes fluttered open and she caught him grimacing at the struggle being so patient with her was costing him. "Matt." She framed his face between her hands, ran them over his shoulders. She linked her heels around his hips. "Let go, Matt. Don't hold back. You're safe with me." She arched her body up into his. Her head fell back as he sank deeper inside her and began to move. As he took her to the peak and they crashed over together, Corie hugged him tight with her arms and her legs. "And I'm safe with you."

Sometime later, after redressing in a layer of clothes in case Evan should awaken early and find them together, Corie and Matt were spooning again on the couch, cocooned by the warmth of the blankets and each other's bodies. The weight of Matt's arm was a possessive band around her waist, but she didn't feel trapped. The tension that had consumed him earlier had eased, leaving her feeling cherished and necessary, not used the way sex with Kenny had been.

This was how it was supposed to be between a man and a woman.

Matt's body was a furnace at her back as he brushed her hair off her neck and whispered against her ear. "Dead bolt."

And as sleep rose to claim her, she smiled and closed her eyes. "I love you, too."

SMOKE.

Matt blinked his eyes open to the darkness of early dawn, unsure if the haze in his vision was due to the hangover of sleep deprivation or if something more was going on here. When he had slept, he'd slept deeply, contentedly. But two hours wasn't nearly long enough. Corie's couch was half a foot too short for his long body, as the stiffness in his neck would attest to.

But Corie herself was a dream. The woman liked to snuggle in close as she slept in his arms, either teasing him with the pillowed mounds of her lush breasts flattened against his chest, or rubbing that sweet, round bottom against his groin. The weight of her in his arms had given him a subconscious sense of reassurance that she was safe—and an arousal that had led to a second, more leisurely, yet no less incendiary round of lovemaking following that cathartic, healing tumble onto the rug where she'd encouraged him to be his big, bad self with her and let his fears and guilt and haunting memories of a boy who had never been enough be consumed by their mutual passion.

He loved Corie McGuire. He hadn't said those exact words, but he'd felt them. He'd shown her.

Did she understand?

And then the reality of the moment slammed through him like shots from a gun and he sat up, wide-awake.

He was alone. Her apartment was filled with smoke.

His nose never lied. Where was the fire?

"Corie?" Matt tossed the blanket aside and stepped into his boots. He'd lace them up later. Right now, he needed to understand what was going on here, and he needed to find her. He grabbed his wrinkled sweater and slipped it on over his T-shirt and jeans. "Corie!"

"In here." A true mother, she'd run into Evan's room first and woken him. Rubbing the sleep from his eyes, the boy was groggy, hopefully from being unexpectedly roused from bed and not from smoke inhalation.

Matt knelt in front of him, checking for any signs of pulmonary distress. "Take a deep breath for me, bud." No coughing fit. He squeezed Evan's shoulder as he stood, telling him everything would be all right. Then he reached over to cup the side of Corie's neck and jaw, sifting his fingers into the heavy silk of her hair. "You?"

"I'm fine." She pointed toward the kitchen. "Why didn't the smoke alarm go off?"

He wanted the answer to that question, too. But whys were for later. "Shoes, jeans on both of you now. We're evacuating until I know what's going on."

Corie steered Evan back into his room. "Winter coats?"

He nodded.

While they dressed, Matt called it in and made a quick tour of her apartment. In the kitchen he found that the smoke detector had no battery in it. It didn't take any stretch of the imagination to believe Kenny Norwell had entered the apartment again at some point to sabotage Corie's safety protocols. But if he was so hell-bent on getting his son back, why would he endanger Evan like this?

There was a bigger game being played here, and Matt worried he was already a step behind whatever Norwell had planned.

Protecting Corie and Evan was still job one. The police and his father's arson team could work on taking down Chad Meade and his firebug for hire—Matt's focus was much closer to home.

But he couldn't find an ignition point from any of the usual suspects—appliances, electrical outlets, improperly stored chemicals. The floor in Corie's bedroom felt spongy as he jogged across it to check the fire escape. Flames and smoke were pouring out of the window right below Corie's, blocking their descent. He didn't need a degree in fire science to understand what was happening.

He closed the door behind him and ran to the living room, gathering Corie and Evan and leading them straight to the door, where they all put on their coats. Corie looped her bag over her shoulder, and Evan had grabbed his most prized possession—his dragon.

"The apartment below yours is on fire," he said, helping Evan zip up that too-tight coat of his.

Corie pulled a stocking cap over Evan's head. "Mr. Caldwell's… Kenny set his own place on fire?"

Matt checked the door to make sure it was safe to open, then ushered them both into the hallway. The smoke wasn't as thick here, but the haze hanging in the air told him it was seeping upward through every available vent, crack or open window. The flames would follow soon enough.

"We need to evacuate this floor and everything above us."

Corie nodded and jogged to the fire alarm on the wall. But when she pulled it, nothing happened. "This isn't working, either."

Matt ran to the far end of the hall and tried that alarm. Silence. Corie's ex had been very thorough.

He pounded on each door he passed, "Fire! KCFD, you need to evacuate. Fire!" A few doors opened immediately, and Matt repeated his orders. "Make sure your neighbors get out."

He rejoined Corie and Evan and guided them toward the stairwell, doing his best to ignore the twin sets of green eyes that were so wide with fear. "You need to get out of here, too. Stay off the elevator. Take the emergency stairs."

Corie grabbed a fistful of his coat. "What about you?"

"I'm a firefighter, sweetheart. I need to do my job. And I need to know you two are safe so I can do that job right."

Her grip tightened on his coat and she pulled him down to exchange a quick, hard kiss. "Do it well. We need you."

He walked them down to the sixth-floor landing, intending to part ways. He wanted to check out Norwell's apartment and get the other residents on the floor evacuated.

But a determined eight-year-old blocked his path. "I want to stay with you." Evan hugged his dinosaur in his arms. "I'm not afraid."

Matt went down on one knee in front of Evan and hunkered lower to look him in the eye. "You're the bravest boy I know, bud. But you need to respect the fire. Get your mom outside and the two of you stay together until I can reach you. Can you do that for me?" A familiar inspiration hit him, and he unbuckled his watch and strapped it onto Evan's wrist. "Here. Set the timer for ten minutes. I'll be down to join you by then."

"Ten minutes? Dragon swear?"

Matt crossed his heart. "Now go."

Hand in protective hand, the two most cherished people in the world to him walked away. Matt hurried onto the sixth floor, relieved to hear the blare of sirens in the distance. He knocked on doors and scooted the startled residents out to the emergency exits. He stopped when he reached the bowed door of apartment 612. The crime scene tape crisscrossing the door had been sliced through. He heard the rumble of something on the other side, like the whooshing ebb and flow of the tide rising along the beach. He knew that sound—heat, pressure, flames filling the confined space. This whole area was about to blow.

The snooty lady across hall was only too happy to have him knocking on doors now. As he turned her to follow her neighbors to the exit stairs, Matt tried to reason out why Norwell would torch his own apartment. KCPD and the crime lab had already been in there to gather evidence against him. The fire endangered his son. An explosion could destabilize the building's structure, bringing it down on all of them, killing anyone who couldn't get out.

The evacuation.

Matt swore. This was all about getting Evan and Corie out in the open. It was about hiding in a crowd distracted by noise and fear.

It was about kidnapping his son. Again.

Matt pulled out his phone to call Corie to warn her.

And that's when he heard the man screaming for help. From apartment 612.

"Help me! Somebody, help!"

Matt's heart sank. He had no choice. People before property. And he wasn't going to have another Enrique Maldonado flinging himself off a balcony because he couldn't escape the flames and smoke.

Matt texted his brother Mark, told him his location and what he was about to do. Then he steeled himself with a deep breath, prepared himself for the blast of heat, and kicked in the door. Fire literally poured out into the hallway as the man's screams turned to gratitude. "Hey, it's the boyfriend. Help me. Please."

In between hacking coughs, he recognized the man's voice. Jordan Cox. For half a second, Matt thought about turning around and running downstairs to Corie instead of rescuing this worthless piece of trash. But he'd already notified his team that he was going in, and they'd risk their lives looking for *him* if he didn't show up where he said he'd be.

He hoped his boots were thick enough to protect him from this walk through hell. "Shut up and do what I tell you this time," he commanded, racing into the searing heat and toxic fumes. "You take in more smoke if you talk."

The damn fool wouldn't listen. While Matt pulled out

his pocketknife and cut Jordy free of the duct tape he'd been bound with, the redheaded bully prattled on. "He said he didn't need my help anymore, that I was a liability. He said he could kill two birds with one stone. Please don't let me die."

Despite a blow to the head, probably to subdue him long enough to bind him to the chair, Jordan seemed aware and ambulatory. Still, he'd never make it through this fiery sludge in those tennis shoes. Since time was of the essence, there was no debate. Matt put his shoulder to Jordy's midsection, secured his arms and legs and lifted him up in a fireman's carry.

With flames melting the carpet and igniting the wood subfloor in the hallway now, Matt carried the smaller man to the exit stairs. There he set him down, but clamped a hand around Jordy's arm, partly to keep the man standing and moving through every cough, and partly because he intended to hand him over to the first police officer they met once they got outside.

On the third floor, he asked, "Did Norwell hire you to harass Corie?"

"Yes, sir."

"Why?"

"'Cause he's pissed at her for taking his son. He wanted us to rough her up, scare her a little. He said he was too busy to do all the work himself." On the second floor, Jordy tried to apologize. "He doesn't like that you're in the picture. He said he had to change his plans once you got involved."

"Do you know his plans now?"

Jordy shied away, knowing Matt wouldn't like his answer. "Keep the kid. Kill your girlfriend."

"Move."

The air was cold when they made it outside, but it was

also clean. Matt sucked two deep breaths of reviving air into his lungs. Most of the cops out here were managing traffic and crowd control, but he got rid of Jordy and started his search to find the McGuires.

He found the building super first. "Stinson! You got a list of tenants we can go through to confirm that everyone has evacuated?"

The older man pulled it up on his phone and started checking people off.

Where was the woman with hair the color of a ripe wheat field and whose smile lit up his heart? And that spunky little boy who was everything Matt could want in a child of his own?

He skimmed the crowd again, his training not allowing the man in him to panic. He even glanced at the passersby pausing their morning walks and commutes to work to ogle the drama of lights and fire engines and flames and dark smoke pouring out the sixth-floor window. They should have made it down and out through the exit stairs ahead of him. The tension in his neck corded up with the very worst of warnings and he ran back to Stinson. "Where are Corie and Evan?"

"They aren't with you?"

"I sent them down ten minutes ago."

The balding man scrolled through the list on his phone. There were no checks beside the tenants of apartment 712. "I haven't seen them."

When he spotted a familiar white van parked against the curb halfway down the block, Matt ran to it. "Corie! Ev!"

Inside, he found a remote arson lab with nearly all the same ingredients and equipment Norwell had kept in his apartment. He also found Harve Mohrman unconscious and bleeding from a head wound. Was he supposed to suffer the same fate as his buddy Jordy? Had Norwell's attempt to kidnap Evan from the crowd outside their burning building failed? If so, where were Corie and Evan now? Or was leaving the van unlocked and in the open like this an impromptu attempt to frame Mr. Gross Beard for all the arson fires?

Matt stepped out of the van and made three calls, summoning a medic to treat Mohrman, a cop to arrest him, and Corie's cell.

It went straight to voice mail. Again.

And then he saw the black muscle car, already three blocks down, darting through the growing crowd of rush-hour traffic, speeding away. The damn van was one more misdirection giving Norwell more time to get away with his prize.

Not this time. Matt wasn't sure what to do next. He couldn't afford getting caught by another diversion. He'd lose all trace of Norwell before he got down to his truck in the parking garage. If Norwell had Corie, she was as good as dead. If he had Evan, the boy was as good as gone.

No. No way. He'd lost one family in a fire. He wouldn't lose another.

He spotted Kyle Redding's white scene commander helmet and ran. "Captain!" Then he saw the engine parked farthest from the scene and changed direction. When he saw the Lucky 13 logo on the side, he kissed it with his hand and climbed inside behind the wheel. He hadn't understood all of the changes that had happened in his life this past week, but he knew one thing very, very well.

He turned the key over in the ignition, and the engine's powerful motor roared to life.

But Redding had chased after him, grabbing the door before Matt could close it. "Taylor! What are you doing with my engine? You're supposed to be off the clock today."

"Take it out of my paycheck, boss." The car was still in

sight but getting farther away. If it turned a corner or crested a hill… "Ignition point is apartment 612. Flames are in the hallway encroaching on the apartment above it." Corie's apartment. "I've got a secondary emergency, sir. Let me go."

His brother Mark was there, too, opening the passenger side and climbing in. "Come on, bro. Talk to us. What's wrong?"

"He took them."

"Corie's ex? He took the kid, too?"

Matt turned on the lights and siren. He'd clear a path through traffic and get to them quicker this way. "Call Cole and Rand. Tell them I've got a bead on Norwell. Give them the GPS on my engine and follow me."

"I'll handle the tracking," Redding insisted, climbing down and calling dispatch. "You're on my orders, Taylor," Redding said, giving Matt the backup he needed to keep his job. Stealing a fire engine for a personal mission tended to get one fired. And jailed. "Go find this guy who's burning up my city and give him hell."

"Captain?"

"I had a woman I loved once, too." He tapped the door of the truck, signaling Matt he was clear to move out before striding away. "Go! I want that arsonist behind bars."

Instead of jumping down, Mark put a helmet on Matt's head and tossed a coat around his shoulders. "You don't have to do this, Mark."

His baby brother grinned. "Hell yeah, I do. We're a team, remember? We have been since the day I was born." He smacked Matt's shoulder the same way Captain Redding had tapped the truck. "Lucky 13 rolling."

Chapter Thirteen

Corie woke up to throbbing headache and the coppery taste of blood in her mouth.

A pungent chemical smell hung in the air, stinging her sinuses, and making her eyes water. But when she reached up to wipe the tears from her cheeks, a sharp pain tore at her wrists, pulling out some of the hair and bruising her skin. What the…?

Crystal clarity returned with a vengeance and she sat up straight. She was strapped to a rolling office chair, her wrists and ankles bound by duct tape. That same yellow-ish goo Matt had showed her from her oven fire had been painted in a large circle around her chair. Her clothes were damp with it, too.

Now she remembered the figure she'd seen in the smoke when she and Evan had been evacuating their apartment building. She'd assumed it was another resident following them down the stairs. But then he'd run up on her.

She'd known one frightening moment of recognition as the man's face cleared the smoke. Dark hair. Thick chest. Cold eyes. She'd instinctively pushed Evan behind her as Kenny's fist connected with her cheek, splitting it open and emptying out a bucket of ball bearings that swirled inside her skull. She fell to her knees as Evan screamed and reached out for her.

But Kenny got between them first, cupping his hand beneath the boy's chin. "Remember me, son?"

Evan backed into the corner of the stairwell landing, avoiding his father's touch. Since sentimentality hadn't worked to instantly win him over, Kenny went back to the tactics he knew best. He jerked Corie to her feet, the sudden movement doing nothing to help the concussion he'd probably given her. "Kenny, don't do this," she pleaded as the world spun in circles around her. "He doesn't know you. All you're doing is scaring him."

"Good. Then he'll understand." Kenny's grip tightened painfully on her arm, keeping her upright when she would have stumbled. "You do exactly as I say, Danny, or I will hit her again. Now come with me. And act like we're all just going for a nice little stroll."

Corie had barely made it to his fancy black car when the dizziness made her puke. She'd passed out in the back seat without knowing if her son was safe. Now, minutes? Hours? Sometime later, the very chemical that was supposed to kill her had acted like smelling salts and roused her to awareness.

She quickly took in her surroundings. Judging by the large louvered windows running the length of the walls, it looked like she was on an upper floor of a converted warehouse. She seemed to be smack-dab in the center in an open commons area. But on either side of her were cubicle walls, desks, papers. It was Saturday and these offices were closed. So, there were no employees she could call on for help.

She spotted Evan at one of the windows, kneeling on a stack of office chairs and looking out at something through the window that had been propped open. Under normal circumstances, she'd have been frightened to see him leaning so close to an open second-story window. But these circumstances were far from normal, and right now she was helpless to keep either of them safe. At least he had his dragon with him to give himself comfort. He hugged it to his chest and rocked back and forth.

Corie frowned as her vision cleared. No. He was picking the dragon apart, piece by piece, glancing over his shoulder to the cubicles on her right and then dropping the colorful plastic bricks one or two at a time out the window.

They both turned their heads to the sound of raised voices as two men argued behind one of the dividing cubicle walls.

"I said no moonlighting."

"I've done every job you've hired me to. The results have been satisfactory, yes?" She recognized Kenny's voice immediately.

"Yes. But I'm not paying you to screw with your ex-wife. You're drawing too much attention to my operation."

"You said you wanted this building burned to the ground. You don't get to say how I do it."

"I pay you good money to take care of my enemies."

"And I will. These boys will be in bankruptcy long before they think of horning in on your territory again. This job takes care of two problems—yours and mine." Corie heard footsteps and knew the men were on the move. "Now give it a rest, Meade."

Corie sat up as straight as her bindings allowed, trying to get a glimpse of whom Kenny was arguing with. Maybe she could convince that man to help her. Maybe he'd at least take Evan with him and drop him off at police station or firehouse. Maybe she had a chance to at least keep her son safe.

Her movement caught Evan's attention, and he saw that she was awake. "Mom!"

He jumped down from the stack of chairs and ran toward her.

"Evan, stop!" She eyed the puddle of goopy gel and knew Kenny had rigged this whole place to go up in flames along with her. "Stay back! Don't get any of this stuff on you. It'll burn, sweetie."

A hard arm in steel-gray coveralls caught Evan by the shoulder and pulled him several feet away from the flammable gel. "Your mom's right, Danny."

"I'm not Danny!" Her boy twisted away and kicked Kenny square in the shin. "The dragon beats the monster every time!"

"What does that even mean?" Kenny was still rubbing his injured leg and cursing. "What kind of garbage you teaching my son, Katie?" He turned his curses on Evan and Corie nearly ripped her arms from their sockets trying to break free and get to him to protect him. "You need to man up, kid. No son of mine is going to believe in all this pansy fairy-tale stuff." He snatched the dragon from Evan's hands. "What is this supposed to be, anyway?" He tossed the dragon at Corie. She ducked, but the toy hit the floor hard and broke into several pieces.

"No!" Evan shouted, lunging after his longtime version of a security blanket.

"Evan, stop!" she shouted, not wanting him any closer to this death trap. "Do as he says. Please."

"Stop calling him Evan. His name is Danny, after my dad."

Evan swung his small fists at the monster who'd sired him. "It is not! Matt's my dad now. He's Mom's boyfriend and he loves me. Matt said so."

Kenny backhanded him across the mouth. "Shut up—"

Corie came unglued, sliding forward in her chair and crashing to the floor. "Don't you touch him! Evan!"

"There ain't no other man who's your daddy but me."

The man Kenny had addressed as Meade stepped out from behind the cubicle wall. He had graying hair, and though he wore a pricey tailored wool dress coat over his suit, she could tell he wasn't a classy guy. He walked right past Evan, who sat on the floor, holding his cheek and sobbing. He didn't offer a handkerchief or a smile or ask if Ev was okay. That man was no ally to her. "I'm leaving. I was never here. I've had my fill of domestic squabbles years ago. You're fired."

"I've got what I want," Kenny shot back, clearly uncowed by the man's intended threat. "I've got plenty of money in my bank account and I've got my boy."

The older man turned and pointed a finger at Kenny. "If I hear that you've stayed in the country…"

"You'll hire another enforcer to come after me?" Kenny laughed. "Let 'em try. I have a reputation as the best in the business for a reason. Your secrets are safe with me, Meade." He waved off the man who had employed him. "Now get out of here and let me work."

Kenny picked up a bag she assumed was full of tools or money or both and started packing the items he'd used to imprison her and prep the building for the fire. But he had no pity for her son, either.

Corie managed to push herself up onto one elbow, putting her at Evan's level. "Hey, son. Look at me." Her poor baby had a mark on his face, and his eyes were puffy and red. But he was her brave little soldier. He sniffed hard and swiped away his tears. That's when the saw the black watch that was far too big for him dangling from his wrist. She wasn't giving up hope until her very last breath. She wasn't letting her son give up, either. "Look at your watch and practice telling time. Start counting how many minutes it takes for Matt to get here."

Kenny laughed at what he thought was a ridiculous challenge. "Your boyfriend isn't coming to save you, Katie. I left him with plenty to do. He'll never find you. Not until this place has burned to the ground and Danny and I are on a plane to a tropical beach in the Caribbean."

Corie didn't intimidate the way she used to. She wasn't isolated and vulnerable to the likes of Kenny Norwell or her mother anymore. She had friends. She had the makings of a new family. She had a future.

She had her very own fire-eating dragon.

"You don't know Matt Taylor."

MATT DROVE THE fire engine up and down the skinny throughways and parking areas in the warehouse district north of City Market. He'd killed the lights and siren, creating as much stealth as a diesel truck this size could manage. He'd wasted too many minutes getting stuck behind a line of vehicles merging into one lane around a construction site. If he'd been thinking, he'd have had dispatch clear a construction-free route for him.

But he hadn't been thinking. He'd only been feeling. Fear. Love. Loss. Anger. He needed Corie to get inside his head and help him make sense of it all. He needed her beautiful smile to keep the shadows of the past at bay. He needed her boy to make him laugh and get him excited about being a father. He needed her. Period.

Mark's sharp eyes had kept the black Charger in sight until it had turned off into this maze of old manufacturing plants and shipping warehouses that had been converted into office buildings, condos and modern businesses.

"Where's the car, Mark? Where did he take them?"

Ironically, Mark, the comic of the family, was the one who kept a cool head. "It's only been a couple of minutes since we lost them. He probably drove into one of these warehouses and pulled down the door to hide. He's still here. This complex is locked down for the weekend. We'd have heard him driving away."

Matt glanced across the cab of the truck, wanting to believe. But searching every warehouse, garage door, even just on this single block was a daunting task. "We need backup. Call it in. Call everybody in. Alex. Pike. Mom and Dad."

Mark pulled out his cell phone and picked up the radio off the dashboard. "I'll get on the horn with them and any personnel from the nearest station who can give us a hand."

"I can't lose them, Mark. It's the first time it's ever felt right for me. I can talk to her and…she says I'm funny and…"

Matt's gaze zeroed in on the small dots of primary colors and purple and green sprinkled across the pavement in front of the shipping door off to his left. "Hold on."

While Mark chatted with dispatch, Matt climbed down from the truck to figure out what he was looking at. His mood lightened with every step. He picked one, and then another, cradling the tiny plastic building blocks in hand. He glanced up at the second-story window that had been propped open and knew these were a deliberate clue. "Evan McGuire, if you're not careful, I'm going to adopt you."

Tucking the bricks into his pocket, Matt searched for a ladder or fire escape that would give him the access he needed to see inside the warehouse. A dumpster and the drainpipe above it did the trick, too. Although Matt couldn't see into the open window from his vantage point, he could see in.

He nearly lost his grip and plummeted to the ground at the sight of Corie strapped to a chair and lying in a puddle of Kenny Norwell's home-brewed fire-starter kit. The setup was just like the fire that killed Enrique Maldonado.

After a quick descent, he climbed back into the fire engine and shifted it into gear. "That place is rigged to burn and Corie's trapped in the middle of it. She won't be able to get herself out."

"Backup's en route. Did you get eyes on Evan?"

"No. But Norwell's there, so the kid has to be around someplace." He knew a lot of different ways to prevent fires, to put out fires, to rescue someone trapped in a fire. But a locked door stood between him and getting the job done. "We get one shot at this, Mark. Once Norwell knows we're onto him, Corie will be at his mercy."

"You know I'll follow your lead. What do we do?"

And then he knew. A moment of clarity washed over Matt like one of Corie's smiles. He shifted the engine into reverse, backed into an alley, then straightened the big machine to meet the shipping bay door at a ninety-degree angle. "Hold on to something."

"You're not gonna…?" Mark buckled himself in and grabbed the hand bars as Matt shifted gears and stomped on the gas. "Whoa, baby! Who said you were the shy one?"

MEADE AND KENNY were arguing again.

Kenny never had played well with others. "When we made the agreement to work together on the outside, I said yes because the money is good. But I am my own boss. Understand?"

On the outside? Kenny and this Meade had been in prison together?

She wasn't sure how that was helpful, other than with the two roosters going at each other, each trying to assert his superiority over the other, they weren't paying any attention to her. Kenny probably believed he'd put her in an inescapable trap, and Meade didn't care.

Since she was already covered in the accelerant, it didn't

make any difference if she got more on her. So Corie was tapping every last bit of her strength to crawl her way to one of the desks. She wasn't sure how she was going to lever herself up high enough, but one of those drawers or pencil caddies had to have a pair of scissors or a box cutter she could use to free herself.

Evan was back on his stack of chairs beneath the windows, thankfully engrossed in watching the dials on Matt's watch and, without realizing it, believing in a miracle.

Corie had her teeth hooked onto the edge of a drawer and, millimeter by millimeter was tugging it open when she heard the loud roar of an engine outside. Both men turn to look toward the window. "What the hell is that?"

The entire building shook, and Corie fell to the floor as something big and powerful crashed through the garage door below them.

Evan tumbled off his perch but quickly climbed back up to peer out the window. "It's Matt! It's his fire engine!" He swung around to share the news with Corie. "He's here!"

"Evan, run!" He hesitated for a moment, no doubt concerned for her. "Run!"

He took off, leaving her sight as he raced for the far door as fast as his little legs could take him. She heard voices shouting down below, running footsteps, someone calling her name. There were sirens outside now, too. She could barely hear herself think.

But Corie could see the look of pure hatred on Kenny's face.

"You'll never take my son from me again." He flicked a match between his thumb and finger and dropped it into the puddle of chemicals that covered the floor. The goo burst into flame like a burning pool of oil and raced across the room toward her. "Die, witch."

He took off after Evan. "No!"

The next several things happened so quickly that Corie wondered if her concussed brain was hallucinating.

The nearer door burst open and two firefighters rushed in with a hose.

"Corie!"

Matt? "I'm over here."

Two police officers rushed in behind them, guns drawn. A rangy German shepherd led another officer inside ahead of a shorter man armed with some kind of assault rifle. Matt used hand signals to send them all off in different directions. "The boy is our number one priority."

He left the other firefighter to open up the nozzle and spray a gushing waterfall that wiped Mr. Meade off his feet. Then he turned the hose, catching the edge of the fire trap with a powerful stream of water.

"That's all the length we've got, Matt!" Mark Taylor. "I can't reach her."

"I can."

Matt ran straight toward her, his thick boots and bunker gear the only deterrent he needed to race through the flames and kneel beside her. "Matt! Don't!"

He pulled a knife from deep inside his coat and flipped it open to slice away the tape that bound her right wrist. He trailed a gloved finger over her bruised, swollen cheek. "Oh God, sweetheart, you're hurt."

"Should I tell you I've had worse?"

"No." He moved to her right leg.

Even though she couldn't feel her fingers, she still reached to rest her hand against his stubbled cheek. "I love you."

"I love you." He looked up from freeing her left wrist. "Wow. That was easy to say."

"You're a strange one, Matt Taylor. But I think you're the right one for me."

"Yeah?"

"Yeah. That's why you have to go. This isn't safe. I need someone who loves Evan to be with him now."

"*You* love him. *You'll* be with him." He never glanced over his shoulder while he cut the last of her restraints. But Corie had a clear, eye-level view of the fire dancing across the pool of accelerant, following the path that led straight to her. "You have to go. I'm about to go up in flames."

"Then it's a good thing I'm a firefighter." He shrugged out of his bunker coat and wrapped her inside it. Corie felt rather than saw the heat of the flames reach for her as he carried her through the fire. Seconds later, he set her on her feet and tossed the coat aside. They were near the windows now, several yards beyond the perimeter of the fire. "Get these clothes off."

She fumbled with the buttons on her sweater and blouse while he unsnapped her jeans and peeled them down her legs. "You have to go after Evan. He went out the other way."

"He's got a lot of people I trust looking out for him."

"But—"

"You've raised a smart kid. His trail of breadcrumbs is how I found you." He tossed the last piece of tape aside. "Clothes, woman. I don't want any accidental spark to trigger a reaction. I don't intend to lose you."

"My hands are numb. The circulation's been cut off."

"Understood." He took over and stripped her down to her bra and panties and gathered her into his arms. For a split second, she looked up into warm brown eyes and knew she would be safe. She knew she could trust his word that her son would be safe, too. "Hold your breath. This is going to hurt."

Corie filled her lungs with air and buried her face against Matt's chest. He clutched her tightly against him as Mark hit them with the full blast of the fire hose. By the time Matt signaled his brother to cut off the hose, several other firefighters were streaming in with longer hoses that allowed them to reach the spread of the chemicals and douse the flames.

She felt Matt's lips at the crown of her hair. "I don't smell it on you anymore. I think it's safe to move you outside now. I want you checked out by a medic."

She felt like she'd been hit by a freight train, and she was already starting to shiver after being drenched to the skin. But there was still only one thing on her mind. "I'm not doing anything else until I see my son."

"How about you put on some dry, chemical-free clothes? Blanket!" Matt gave the order, and seconds later Corie had two blankets, one wrapped around her like a sarong, and the other draped over her shoulders. "Evan's okay, sweetheart. He's with my mom and dad in an ambulance, getting checked over by medics. Norwell and Meade have been arrested by my uncle Cole. Jordy turned himself in, and Harve is on his way to the hospital. I'm guessing he's got jail time in his future, too."

Corie stared up at Matt, dumbfounded. "How? How do you know all that? How can you be so certain?"

He pulled the earbud out of his ear and showed her that he'd been listening in to official radio chatter this entire time. "A little birdie told me."

Corie didn't know if she wanted to swat him or hug him. "Why didn't you tell me?"

He smoothed her wet hair away from the wound on her cheek and tucked it behind her ear. "You were the one in imminent danger. That's where my focus needed to be."

"Atonement?"

"No. Love." Then he gently laced his fingers together with hers. "Let's go get our boy."

* * * * *

COMING SOON!

We really hope you enjoyed reading this book.
If you're looking for more romance
be sure to head to the shops when
new books are available on

Thursday 24th April

MILLS & BOON

THE HEART OF ROMANCE

A ROMANCE FOR EVERY READER

MODERN

Prepare to be swept off your feet by sophisticated, sexy and seductive heroes, in some of the world's most glamourous and romantic locations, where power and passion collide.

HISTORICAL

Escape with historical heroes from time gone by. Whether your passion is for wicked Regency Rakes, muscled Vikings or rugged Highlanders, awaken the romance of the past.

MEDICAL

Set your pulse racing with dedicated, delectable doctors in the high-pressure world of medicine, where emotions run high and passion, comfort and love are the best medicine.

True Love

Celebrate true love with tender stories of heartfelt romance, from the rush of falling in love to the joy a new baby can bring, and a focus on the emotional heart of a relationship.

HEROES

The excitement of a gripping thriller, with intense romance at its heart. Resourceful, true-to-life women and strong, fearless men face danger and desire - a killer combination!

From showing up to glowing up, these characters are on the path to leading their best lives and finding romance along the way – with plenty of sizzling spice!

To see which titles are coming soon, please visit

millsandboon.co.uk/nextmonth

LET'S TALK

Romance

For exclusive extracts, competitions
and special offers, find us online:

⬤ MillsandBoon

𝕏 @MillsandBoon

⬤ @MillsandBoonUK

♪ @MillsandBoonUK

Get in touch on 01413 063 232

For all the latest titles coming soon, visit
millsandboon.co.uk/nextmonth

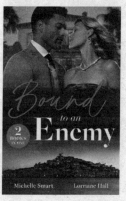
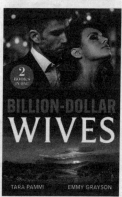

afterglow BOOKS

Afterglow Books is a trend-led, trope-filled list of books with diverse, authentic and relatable characters, a wide array of voices and representations, plus real world trials and tribulations. Featuring all the tropes you could possibly want (think small-town settings, fake relationships, grumpy vs sunshine, enemies to lovers) and all with a generous dose of spice in every story.

♪ @millsandboonuk
📷 @millsandboonuk
afterglowbooks.co.uk
#AfterglowBooks

For all the latest book news, exclusive content and giveaways scan the QR code below to sign up to the Afterglow newsletter:

SCAN ME